FIREBALL

ISBN: 979-8-9852653-1-6 (Paperback)

Library of Congress Control Number: 2021923294

To Mom for listening and smiling at my stories for as long as I can remember. To Sarah, Molly, Tom, Tim, and Michael for encouraging me to write this book, although it was only to get me to stop telling Fireball stories at family functions. Nice try! To Nancy without whom nothing would be possible for me. And to my Dad for giving me the best inheritance any son could ask for.

Author's Note

I wrote the first draft of this novel in less than a month. The task was made easy by me wanting to push the stress of the COVID pandemic out of my mind, having already done more than twenty years of research, and the odd sensation that Fireball was with me as I wrote. The editing process took a wee bit more than a month. A special thank you to my family and friends who tolerated and helped me during that process.

In writing the story, I tried to stay as close to the historical facts as possible. That too was made easy. For that, I thank the archivists, librarians, and historians who helped me with my research. Where there were gaps or conflicts in the historical record, or the natural flow of the narrative required it, I looked to my own life experiences and those around me for inspiration. Together, the historical facts and inspiration of life and those sharing it with me made the story whole.

I conveyed most of the dialogue in modern English for readability purposes and because my skill in historical linguistics is seriously lacking. In the places where 19th-century accents and phrases are employed, I am confident that it is how the characters would have spoken or at least have been familiar with. Some of the phraseology is pejorative but I felt it needed for insight into how characters thought and to offer a reminder of the historical context.

In closing, as much as I enjoyed writing *Fireball*, I enjoy the idea of sharing it with you more. Stories are nothing if they are not shared. In my mind, you will laugh at the parts where I laughed, cry at the parts where I cried, and wax philosophical where I did the same. To those of you with whom I share that magical bond, I wish you the very best.

Prologue

Queens, New York
February 1992

My father was dying. He was feeble with cancer ravaging his sixty-year-old body but he could still secure our full attention in an instant, usually with a stern stare or a barked "listen up." He used that phrase so often I felt as if my brothers and I must have been in a constant state of obliviousness otherwise. The "old man," as we called him, clearly had something profound to say and my brothers and I were there to listen.

"Our last name is not Rowland," he declared. A significant statement considering that was the only surname the lot of us had ever used. A series of last names our ancestors had willingly abandoned ran through my mind, *the Hitlers, the Crappers, the Dickmen.*

"I don't know what the real name is," my father advised, "but I want you to find out." He articulated the request looking directly at me, so my brothers were off the hook. The quest was to be mine and mine alone. I am sure my father would give my brothers other tasks, maybe as tailored as this one was to me. I was a history buff, had a degree in the topic, and was working as an investigator at the time. In theory then, if someone was to discover the true family name, I was the man for the job.

Why my father had not searched out the true name on his own is unclear. But there on his death bed, it seemed important for him to know. His family ties had been attenuated. His mother died when he was a toddler and his father faded from his life shortly after due to grief and alcoholism. It could be that he feared being abandoned yet again. As if heaven had a reception area where you checked in to have your ancestors claim you. He did not know who to ask for.

Unfortunately, my father died before I was able to relay to him what the true name had been. In fact, it took me years to utter it myself with any degree of certainty. The story of how and why the name changed turned out to be a fascinating one and I share it with you here. It was such an adventure to discover it that I wonder if my father made the request more for my sake than his. The process allowed me to learn about a period in history and people I had known little about. The story of those times and people offered me some valuable life lessons that I like to think have made me a better, more compassionate person. I hope you draw some lessons from it yourself, my Dad's gift to you.

Chapter One
The Departure

Limerick, Ireland
September 4, 1851

The *Hopewell* was a majestic looking three-mast sailing vessel and it lay moored peacefully along the quay on the River Shannon. While its passengers were waiting to board, more than one prayed the ship's name would prove prophetic. For if hope was ever needed, it was then and there.

Ann McNamara and her 17-year-old son, Francis, stood away from the rest of the crowd. Ann had an old trunk beside her and in it the last of her belongings. Francis had a canvas bag flung over his shoulder containing a change of clothes, a few dried fish, smoked vegetables, and a book his mother had just given him.

While most of those on the quay were focused on the *Hopewell* and the activities of its crew preparing for departure, Ann's attention was on her son. She studied his face, knowing it would be the last time she would ever see it. Francis was still just a child in her mind, although he had matured and grown so much in the past year.

How tall would he have grown, she thought to herself, had food been plentiful? Normally, Ann could avoid that kind of pointless speculation but not on this day. She and her family had suffered terribly during the famine. Wishing or making believe it did not happen was more than unproductive, it was dangerous. She had to conserve her energies to keep herself and her family alive.

So, Ann focused on what was in front of her and trying to improve things moving forward. Unfortunately, the future orientation had its own drawbacks and there on the quay they were blatantly obvious.

Ann lamented that she would never know Francis in his adulthood. Nor would Ann meet the person Francis would marry or know her own grandchildren. The realization broke Ann's already heavily scarred heart.

As for Francis, he was desperately trying to take in every sight, smell, and sound around him. He furrowed his brow in deep concentration, trying to memorize it all. Francis did not want the place of his birth to become foreign to him. He feared that each new experience in America would displace a memory of Ireland until, eventually, Ireland would be out of him altogether. Taking with it his lineage, his understanding of the world, and his identity. It was then Francis turned to his mother and saw the painful anguish on her face. He felt ashamed at selfishly entertaining his own fears and anxieties while ignoring those of his heartbroken mother.

Francis spoke to his mother in the Hibernian English common in the west of Ireland at the time. The speed in which he spoke, his fluctuating intonation, and the stress he placed on some consonants and deemphasis of others had their roots in the ancient Irish language and shaped his delivery of English words. He spoke as if softly singing a song and posing everything in the form of a question.

"Don't worry, Ma. Once I find work in America I'll send everything I can along to you." He went on to remind her,

"Once you get to Longford, check in with the post office. I'll send my letters and banknotes there. With a little luck, I'll earn enough to return to this very spot in no time at all with Mathew and Jamie under each arm," Francis added, referring to his older brothers already in America. "It will be like old times except we will have you living in a fine house with not a worry in the world."

Francis was offering false hope and both he and Ann knew it. No one returned to Ireland once they left. But Francis felt false hope was better than no hope at all, and Ann loved that her son at least tried.

The last boarding call caught Francis and Ann by surprise. There was too much to say and too little time to say it. Ann grabbed Francis and hugged him tightly. Gently, Francis freed himself and kissed his mother on the forehead for he was now head and shoulders taller than she was.

With that, he was out of her reach forever. She watched him walking toward the ship, at first with his posture defeated, his head hung and his shoulder slumped. With each step, however, he consciously straightened himself to look more confident and purposeful. Whatever fate awaited him, Francis would face it standing tall. His father would have been proud.

Part of Francis was excited to board the *Hopewell*. He had seen it and other ships like it from a distance during his time along the Shannon Estuary. Francis was more familiar, close up at least, with the smaller and often crudely made boats used for river and coastal fishing.

The *Hopewell*, in contrast, was made by craftsmen and designed for the mighty ocean; at least that is what Francis was staking his life on as he approached the gangway.

Craning his head up, Francis marveled at the height of the masts which constituted at that moment the tallest things in Limerick. Even with the sails tightly furled up to the yardarms, the rigging and associated equipment conveyed sophistication and speed. Francis had admired the ship's streamlined silhouette, which fueled images of the vessel gracefully gliding over the ocean and cutting through the fiercest of waves.

The awe Francis felt soon gave way, unfortunately, once he was on board. The weathering from repeated trans-Atlantic crossings left the black paint of the hull chipped. The ship's decking had deep cracks that housed small puddles of saltwater. Dry rot blemished the ship's rail and the smell of mold emanated from deep within the ship's innards.

The owners of the vessel had just relented to the captain's pleas for a complete overhaul at the end of this voyage, as even the ship's steering was becoming sluggish with wear. "The ship will be worthless to you if we run aground in some God forsaken place," was the cornerstone of the captain's argument.

More disconcerting than the appearance of the ship, now that Francis was aboard, was its mass. It was much smaller than he imagined. He walked the full length of the ship, bow to stern, in less than sixty paces. And covering the beam, the widest part of the deck, took less than half that. What had appeared so large from the safety of the quay, now looked as if it could be swallowed up by a single ocean swell. But there was no time for second thoughts for Francis or anyone else on board, the gangway had been drawn up and the ropes pulled back from the cleats of the quay.

Ann's eyes began to fill with tears, she had witnessed her son take his last steps on Ireland's shores. The line of a thousand generations had just been broken. She stared at Francis's somber face as the ship slowly began to drift away from the quay, the Union Jack unfurling at the back of the ship hinting at the breeze that would eventually, coupled with the outgoing tide, propel the ship to sea.

Desperate to give her son some kind of assurance, Ann shouted: "You'll never be alone Francis. I will pray for you constantly and God will protect you!" Francis was already too far away to hear.

In the harbor, the ship moved dreadfully slow, as if to taunt Ann. Her son close enough to see but too far away to hear or hug. She wished they had talked more during their last hour together in their ancient gandelow, a small fishing vessel whose seaworthiness was even more questionable than the *Hopewell*. They had rowed the gandelow down the River Fergus to the Shannon and then onto Limerick from their home in the Village of Clare, or Clarecastle as some would call it. Ann was too heartbroken to talk much while Francis was distracted, constantly staring downriver as if he were pursued by a ghost.

Ann knew that things would be difficult for Francis in the United States but his chances of survival were better there than they were in Ireland. The letters home from her older boys, Mathew and Jamie, indicated they were eating regularly and able to get by but not much more than that.

They apologized for the meager sums they were sending home, and even that was often more than they could afford.

"Life's trials and tribulations," her son Jamie explained, "did not stop on Ireland's shores. Instead, just the accent of the person kicking your ass changed." No tales of streets of gold. But at the same time, Ann saw hints of hope in her older boys' letters. And hope could not be found anymore in Ireland so Francis would have more by leaving.

Francis did not have to be told life was and would continue to be harsh. His entire existence had been nothing but, and even the difficulties of his voyage to the New World were clear to him. The price of his ticket included a daily ration of dried bread, called seabisket, and rain-barrel water. Luxuries of broth and salted meats would require more cash, cash he did not have. So, once the food for a day or so that he carried with him was gone, Francis would have to do without or improvise. Scarcity skills, Francis assured himself, he had mastered well in recent years.

Once there was enough propulsion, the *Hopewell* turned completely away from the quay leaving only the back of the ship for Ann to see—her son's face now out of sight forevermore.

She continued to eye the back of the ship as her thoughts began to shift from anxieties about her son's fate to her own. She glanced back to the street corner just outside the harbor area, looking for the donkey-drawn cart that would take her along roughhewn roads to the very center of Ireland, County Longford. For the first time in her life, Ann would be leaving her home along the west coast of Ireland. She had arranged to take up residence with her daughter, Patricia—who everyone called Patsy, and Patsy's husband, a Protestant young man by the name of Albert Cummings.

Albert worked a few years in Limerick at his relatives' import and export business. It was a mystery to the McNamaras what type of goods the Cummings dealt in. Last fall, Albert inherited a barley farm, a large one Ann was told, in northwest Longford. Albert asked for Patsy's hand so she could accompany him. He assured Ann that her daughter would be provided for as would the anticipated grandchildren. They would never know want the way Ann and her children did. *Was that a slight at my husband?* Ann thought, but she checked herself. Albert seemed like a good man.

Albert added he would never raise a hand to Patsy, knowing Patsy would just as quickly detach said hand and hang it on the mantel. Ann knew it to be true as Patsy could be fierce— a trait she came by honestly. All the children had one trait or another from her husband, traits that had the capacity to be a blessing or a curse, depending on the circumstances.

Once the *Hopewell* was completely out of sight, Ann sat down for the first time since arriving at the quay earlier that morning. Perching herself on her battered trunk, she began steadily monitoring the street corner where she was to meet the cart, owned by a family friend, going to Longford.

She feared she would be treated like an intruder in Albert and Patsy's home or, even worse, as a burden. That fear stemmed, ironically, not from rejection by her son-in-law but her own daughter.

While all of Ann's children could be harsh at times, understandable with the life they had known, Patsy could be the harshest of them all. Perhaps because she was actually the most sensitive of the lot, Patsy found it necessary to take on the toughest façade. Ann understood why her daughter acted so. When Patsy felt she was safe and no threats were about, her true nature would show. Patsy could be funny and kind, but more often than not in her life, Patsy needed to be on guard. They all did. Because Patsy was a pretty young woman she was judged more harshly for it.

The oldest and only daughter to survive infancy, Patsy grew up in a house full of extraordinarily rambunctious boys. She compensated by taking charge and ordering her brothers around. She could not dominate the boys physically but she could cut them to the quick with her calculated words. Patsy's ferocity stood in stark contrast to her sweet and diminutive appearance. Her father loved that contradiction and she was, by far, his favorite. The boys could not strike back at their oppressive sister physically fearing their father's wrath. They could, however, speak their own minds as words were always permissible in the McNamara house as long as they were witty. Not as biting in their rhetoric as Patsy, the boys took their shots, referring to their sister as the "tyrant" and "she-devil."

Of all the things they could have complained about in regard to their sister's reign, they focused most on Patsy's intimidating nature keeping the neighboring girls away—girls that the boys had an interest in.

"Please," Patsy would counter, "it's the heinous, ugly mugs of yours that drive the Colleens away!"

It was those kinds of statements from Patsy that required Ann to do damage control for her boys. Ann would take pains to assure each boy separately of their handsomeness and future value to womenkind. A man without a reasonable degree of confidence was a menace, Ann knew. Without confidence, men may strike inward or outward, but they would strike somewhere. Ann did not want that for her sons. In her conversations with the boys, Ann also urged them to be more sympathetic and inclusive of their only sister, but that was wasted breath. What was not wasted on any of them, sibling rivalries aside, was that their status as a family trumped all else. Patsy would defend her brothers—tooth and nail—against anyone other than herself. In turn, the boys would respond to any threat that endangered their sister.

Surely, she was a tyrant—but she was *their* tyrant.

As Ann continued to wait on the quay for the cart that would take her to Longford, she thought back to years past when she would pray for an end to her children's bickering. Now that she got her wish, she regretted it deeply. The quiet on the quay as she waited, and the loneliness it represented, was more of a torture than the sibling ruckus had ever been.

Thinking back, Ann realized that children fighting is simply part of life, a byproduct of energy and striving. She also knew that the fighting would later help the children learn how to resolve disputes and navigate relationships outside the home. The sibling tension and dynamics also, at times, brought humor.

On one occasion, when the children were little, Ann asked Patsy to mind her younger brothers while Ann attended to the outhouse. Ann reminded Patsy she needed to remain vigilant as the boys were prone to wander off and sometimes "didn't have the sense that God gave them." Patsy took her charge seriously and with a rope tied the boys together through loops in their pants that were otherwise used for twine belts and suspenders. She then tied the rope to the halter of the family's aging and slow-moving cow.

Proud of her ingenious solution, Patsy took Ann to see it only to find the cow meandering in the pasture dragging three pairs of empty pants behind. The bottomless boys were in the distance, laughing and running as fast as their little legs would take them. The thought of it could still make Ann laugh years later.

With still no sign of her ride in sight, Ann tried to get more comfortable sitting on her trunk there on the quay and decided to briefly rest her eyes. In doing so, she instinctively followed her nighttime ritual of three Hail Mary's, three Our Father's, and a listing of each of her family members for God to watch over—as if he needed reminders. Ann ended the ritual with a brief discussion with her husband. She found it easier to talk to him now that he was dead. Gone over a year, she advised him of Francis's departure and asked her husband to "protect all your boys, they still need you." Ann figured she would soon be able to watch over Patsy herself so her husband could concentrate on the boys.

If her husband were to do what was asked, he would have to spread his attention far and wide. Their oldest boy, Mathew, was in Philadelphia. The stable and logical one, Mathew had been Ann's rock. Then there was James, whom everyone called Jamie. He was in New York City. The devilish prankster, Jamie served the family by distracting them from their woes.

The two older boys had left Ireland together a few years before but, to their parent's chagrin, parted ways in the New World. Their thinking, more specifically Mathew's thinking, was that they would double their odds of finding good fortune if they separated. Their father, upon hearing the news, thought both boys boneheaded—never divide already limited resources. Had he not taught them that? Ann's reaction was one of dread. The family was splintered enough—why would they add to it? She hated the thought that she herself would never see the boys again, but them not seeing each other as well broke her heart.

The truth was that even if the boys doubled their odds of success by separating, their chances of good fortune remained abysmally small. Mathew and Jamie were young and inexperienced. They had no money, no particularly marketable skills, and there was no one looking out for them. But the United States represented hope and that was more than Ireland could afford them. While Ann had at one time planned to keep the rest of the family intact in Ireland, the death of her youngest child—her baby—Patrick, and that of her husband showed her otherwise.

Even if it cost her everything she owned, and it would, Ann decided that it would be better for Francis, her only remaining son, to try his luck outside of Ireland. She surrendered the lease on the small farm in County Clare that had been the family home for a generation, sold all the fishing equipment the family had subsisted on since the famine, and auctioned off the last of her home furnishings that included a cradle made by her father. In the process, she gave up her very own independence, something at one time she valued more than anything else, just to give her son a chance.

There was one thing, however, Ann refused to sell—
although she was not entirely sure why. It was her husband's
favorite book, a book on Irish history and that mentioned the
McNamara clan by name. The book, she decided, should go
with Francis. It would be his sole physical connection to
Ireland, aside from his own flesh and blood.

At first, Francis thought the gift impractical and wished the
memento had been a clover, a pebble, or something else
easier to transport. But on the long, lonely nights of his
voyage to the New World, and times alone afterward,
Francis found solace in the book and read it over and over.
Ann was a wise and intuitive woman.

With her wait on the quay for the wagon entering its second
hour, Ann's drowsy thoughts moved on to her own youth,
her courtship with her husband and the excitement of being
a young mother. She had not thought about her own
appearance in a long time. Ann had to remind herself that
she was once a beautiful young lady. She had flowing raven
colored hair, sparkling green eyes, and alabaster skin. Now,
in such desperate times, Ann thought such things were vain
and shallow. But there had been a time when they were not.

Since grey had overtaken her hair, sadness dulled her eyes,
and worry ruddied her skin, Ann was glad her mirror was
one of the first things to sell for Francis's trip. She would
only groan whenever she passed it anyway. To console
herself, Ann rationalized that she gave up her beauty so her
children could have it, and indeed they all got the attractive
gene.

More importantly, what the children got from Ann was unconditional love, support, and a model on how to deal with adversity. Ann was intelligent, compassionate, and even tempered. Those traits did not diminish over time. They grew in proportion to her husband's inner decline and loss of resiliency.

Stephen Francis McNamara had been Ann's one and only love. But the thought of him as she sat on the quay evoked mixed feelings. The early years had been wonderful. He was handsome and charming, and that smile could melt her heart no matter how angry she was at him. But that smile was seen less and less often, and even when it did appear in later years, it would vanish just as quickly as it would form.

He went by the nickname of "Seas," with most assuming it was a play on his middle name in Gaelic—*Proinséas*. Instead, the moniker came from an event in his childhood. Barely more than a toddler, he fashioned a makeshift raft and, while his mother was distracted, took to the Shannon— imagining himself a sailor like his father. He quickly was caught up in the current and pushed toward the open sea.

Frantic, his mother summoned the entire village for the rescue effort and the villagers managed to return the unfazed youngster home safely. To ensure he would never live the incident down, however, the villagers took to calling him Seas, and the name stuck.

As an adult, Seas was taller than most, having three inches or so over the average five-foot, five-inch Irishman of the time. He had a confident air about him, although that confidence in himself and the world around him would eventually erode. When Ann first laid eyes on him in his early teenage years, Seas was a towhead. As he matured, his wavy hair turned ash. He had bright blue eyes and rosy cheeks.

Over the course of their marriage, Ann had noticed that Seas went from discussing his fears and problems with her in an effort to find solutions, to just ranting about his frustrations. He seemed caught in an echo chamber, his articulation magnified his woes and drowned out thoughts on how to cope. Life could be unfair and arbitrary, that was true, but fighting against that fact was pushing Seas toward near madness. His once mighty clan had fallen on tough times and Seas was left on the outside looking in on financial and political dealings in his home county of Clare.

Ann was sympathetic, things were difficult for Seas and it was hard to look at the bright side when you were poor and uninfluential. But Ann could not understand why Seas, like many others of his generation, compounded their problems by retreating to the bottle. He drank Poteen or the Devil's Spittle, as it was called, to numb himself. And he was successful in that regard, but he deadened himself to his pain as much as his blessings. Chief among those blessings was his family.

But whatever woes Seas and any other Irishman thought they had would soon pale in comparison. The "Lumper potato" was introduced to Ireland in the early 19th century. As the name implies, it was not much to look at and it tasted like soap. What distinguished it was its nutritional and economic profile.

The potato supplied all the required vitamins and minerals and could be grown cheaply and in copious amounts. Manna from heaven for Ireland's growing underclass. Seas and Ann grew it on the small farm they leased to supplement the fish and eels Seas caught in the nearby River Fergus.

The Lumper potato's attributes were so great that in some places it was grown at the exclusion of all other crops. It became the staple for a sizable part of the population. But as quickly as the potato would prove itself as a source of life in Ireland, it brought death.

In 1845, a microscopic pathogen, likely from Central or South America, reached Ireland. Spreading quickly, the pathogen tainted both potatoes in the fields and in the storehouses. People who ate the contaminated tubers contracted deadly cholera and typhus.

While there had been crop failures in Ireland before, this time was different. The blight was more widespread, lasted multiple years, and sparked a severe panic. Most people in Ireland, being so poor, barely got by when the fields were plentiful. Now, with the potato failure and the export of other foodstuffs to England by the landed aristocracy, little was left, and people died in inconceivable numbers.

Between starvation, related disease, and forced emigration, the Irish population declined by forty percent in just a few years. The country's Irish Catholics bore most of that loss. They were the overwhelming majority of the populace overall, but nearly all of them were relegated to the lower rung of society. Systematic oppression from, and mismanagement by, British overlords and the Catholics own self-inflicted wounds of overpopulation and alcoholism trapped them in poverty.

Seemingly oblivious to the plight of the poor in Ireland, British and landed interests in the country operated as if the famine did not exist. Hundreds of thousands of families were evicted because they were unable to pay their biannual gale, or rent, during the famine. Some fought back against the evictions, often through secret societies. County Clare had the Terry Alts and the Ribbonmen, while other counties had the Molly Maguires.

The Ribbonmen would be resurrected decades later in New York City to fight against discrimination targeting Irish Catholics. The Molly Maguires, said to be named after a woman who froze to death along with her young children after being evicted in the famine, remerged in Pennsylvania to protect exploited Irish coal miners. The violent resistance of both groups in the United States proved just as futile as it did in Ireland.

The famine led to masses of starving, homeless people roaming the cities and countryside alike. Their numbers and desperation overwhelmed and destabilized everything they met. American abolitionist and former slave Frederick Douglas was in Ireland at the time as part of a European tour. He wrote that: "[t]he limits of a single letter are insufficient to allow anything like a faithful description of those painful exhibitions of human misery, which meet the eye of a stranger almost at every step. I spent nearly six weeks in Dublin, and the scenes I there witnessed were such as to make me blush and hang my head to think myself a man." Inflation on whatever foodstuffs were not affected by the famine grew unchecked. Rivers became overfished and wild game hunted out. Seas feared he could no longer keep the family alive with his fishing. He and Ann began discussing whether it would be better to go to a workhouse or to risk emigrating to another country.

The workhouse had little appeal. Disease and abuses were known to be rampant there. Besides, the family members would be separated by gender and they would all eventually be thrown out as destitute as they went in. At the same time, they didn't have the money for the whole family to leave Ireland. The consensus Seas and Ann reached was that the older boys, Mathew and Jamie, emigrate to the United States. That would reduce the number of hungry mouths to feed, and hopefully, the boys could send money back once they established themselves in their new home. Seas would have to keep the rest of them going by drinking less and fishing more. To make the fishing successful, he would have to risk coastal and ocean excursions in his small boat designed only for calmer, river waters.

At first, Seas took to his enhanced obligations with vigor. But he soon found himself physically and mentally exhausted. In that weakened state, he returned to alcohol use. After his first relapse, Seas was embarrassed. After the second, he became angry with himself. On the third, he began blaming Ann and the family for depending on him. With the fourth, it was the world to blame.

What had been episodic anger and occasional violent outbursts for Seas, became a steady state. Then, at some point, without a word, he just left.

Francis, although still a young teenager, picked up on his own where his father had failed. He fished and lay ell traps day and night, he went out in all weather conditions, often out in the ocean, along the coastline, putting himself in great jeopardy. But one day Seas returned, sober and looking apologetic although no verbal apology was offered.

Ann was cold to him and essentially ignored him other than to shout that Francis was risking his very life while Seas was nowhere to be found. Seas stormed out of the house upon hearing it but stayed in front of the family's cottage. He waited there for hours until Francis came home looking exhausted.

Shocked to see Seas, whom he had feared was dead, Francis stood dumbfounded. Seas said nothing, just put his arm around Francis and gave him an approving nod. Francis walked inside but Seas did not follow him. Instead, Seas slept outside, as he had been doing for weeks in fields all around the surrounding area. Sometimes drunk, more often not. The next morning Francis walked outside groggy to prepare for the day's fishing.

Seas asked Francis, "Can I help you with the fishing today?" Ann watched and listened quietly from the cottage's only window. It was the first time Seas had asked Francis's permission to do anything. It was an acknowledgment of Francis as a provider and responsible person.

"Sure," Francis replied, "but don't get your hopes up too much, it seems like everything else in Ireland, the fish are all dead or emigrated."

Seas laughed and assured, "Today will be a big haul, you'll see."

"If the gandelow doesn't sink beneath us, it is old as the hills and has as many holes in it as my pants," said Francis, making Seas laugh yet again, this time like he used to in the old days Ann thought to herself—still watching from the window.

"No worries," Seas reassured his son. "Your grandfather was one of the most famous fishermen in all of Ireland. People say he would just wave his hand and the fish would jump right into the boat with smiles on their faces."

Francis groaned, "I know, I have heard that story a time or two, but that ability to attract fish must not be hereditary. My gift is more in the area of repelling fish and, when I do corner them, I have to club them into submission—there are no smiles."

"You know, I used to think Jamie was the funny one," Seas said laughing again, "but I am starting to think he can't hold a candle to you." The laughter would be the last thing Ann would ever hear from her husband as he and Francis headed away toward the river and Ann continued to watch from the window.

****

Father and son arrived at the storage area off the water's edge where they kept fishing gear and moored their small boat. They were startled to see members of the Toobin family from upstream stealing the McNamara netting and other equipment.

There had been rumors for some time that the Toobins were poaching other people's traps, stealing livestock, and taking tools that families depended on for survival. Francis had noticed the theft of some of his family's belongings but didn't expect something as brazen as this—taking complete fishing sets, in the light of day and very near the McNamara home.

The Toobins and their ilk would not have dreamt of it, Seas thought, if all his boys were home. Nor would they have done it in days past when the McNamaras were a powerful force in the county. But things change and now no one checked the Toobins' temerity and it emboldened them.

Seas directed his son, calmly but sternly, to get help from the neighbors, the O'Connors and the Keohanes.

"But Da!" Francis started to say but Seas stopped him and growled, "Do it now!" There was no question Seas was back in charge and no deference offered to the 16-year-old Francis in light of the physical threat posed by the Toobins. Francis ran off as directed to get help.

Seas then stood between the Toobins and his son. Positioning himself on an incline in the path between two rising hills, Seas was trying to counter the Toobins' superior numbers. Seas then looked to engage the Toobins in an argument to buy time. Since he knew the given names of some of those now aggressively approaching him, he shouted them out instinctively trying to humanize the encounter.

Unfortunately for Seas, the confrontation would be all too human. The Toobins exploited their advantage in numbers and set upon the sole McNamara from multiple directions. In his mid-forties and weakened by drink and hard luck, Seas did not have the physical strength he once had.

What he did have, however, was an endless store of rage that for too long he took out on himself and those he loved. Now he would focus the rage on just one of the Toobins, its patriarch who went by the name Maurice. Seas could not fight them all but he could fight one of them. That strategy too would be for naught.

Seas was left on the path with knife wounds in his back and stomach. His face was severely beaten and stomped. Maurice Toobin would have a black right eye and swollen nose. Otherwise, the Toobins got away with murder.

But that was a year ago, a lifetime in a famine-ravaged country. Now Francis, thinking of his father, was on the deck of the *Hopewell* sailing along the River Shannon nearing the Atlantic. As they approached the junction where the Fergus River fed into the Shannon, Francis strained to see if there was still any smoke rising from the shore of the Fergus. Smoke from the Toobins' homes, boats and other belongings that Francis had set aflame just a few hours before leaving for Limerick with his mother.

Chapter Two
The Voyage

The Atlantic Ocean
September-October 1851

The *Hopewell's* crew directed the passengers to go to the hold and settle in, warning that they would soon be in the rough waters of the Atlantic. It was not uncommon, the crew advised, for people unfamiliar with life at sea to be swept overboard and drowned.

In the hold, a large open space in the middle of the ship with one set of stairs providing access to the deck, Francis sat on stacked bags of wheat. Next to him was another young man who, like Francis, had dark hair and blue eyes.

His name was Michael Scanlon. Only slightly older than Francis, Michael had recently surrendered the lease on his small, failing County Kerry farm. In return for leaving, Michael's landlord had given him the funds needed for passage to the United States.

Returning a family favor, Michael agreed to help Mary Rowland who was on the ship with her two young children. Mary, in her early thirties, was going home to the United States. She and her husband had been doing Protestant missionary work and helped many Irish, including Michael's older brother and sister, Thomas and Ellen, immigrate to the United States as Protestant converts.

Mary's husband died six months previously from dysentery, a martyr to his missionary work. If it were not for Michael

Scanlon, she would be traveling alone with two young sons, five-year-old Mitchel and an infant John.

After arriving in New York City, Michael would accompany Mary and her children to Norfolk, Virginia. His sister, Ellen, now lived in the same city with her husband, Martin Moriarty, and Michael would start his American life there. Mary would take up with her in-laws, Mr. and Mrs. George Rowland, in Norfolk.

Francis's plans were not as concrete. He would be greeted in New York by his older brother Jamie. Beyond that was a mystery. Francis, having no money, was hoping his brother had prospects for him.

Another possibility for Francis was going to Philadelphia where his oldest brother Mathew resided. The challenge again would be paying for the trip between New York and Philadelphia—which could be on opposite ends of the North American continent as far as Francis knew.

The hold of the *Hopewell* was overcrowded and there were too few wooden berths for people to sleep on. Tensions rose as people tried to find adequate room on the floor for their belongings and to sleep. A large man in his late twenties spread himself out and pushed both Francis and Michael's belongings out of the way in the process. Michael said nothing but Francis spoke up at once.

"Are we kicking each other's bags, is that what we are doing?" Francis asked sarcastically.

The heavily bearded man stood up, in part to show his size advantage. "What are you going to do about it?" The man growled.

"It's not me but you who will be deciding," Francis said calmly, "this voyage will be tough enough, do you really want to add fighting to it—today with me, tomorrow with him," pointing to another man nearby who responded with a surprised look on his face. Francis went on, "and keep fighting so everyone comes out worse for wear? Or do you just want to stop kicking my belongings?"

The bearded man grumbled and then returned to his spot, but noticeably left room for Francis and his things. Later, Michael asked Francis, "What would you have done if that ruckus ended in a fight?"

Francis grinned, "I would have been anointed for sure," using the slang for a beating. "But if I didn't challenge that fella he likely would have made this a very long trip."

"Smart," Michael said impressed, "you figured saying something was your best option."

"Hell no," responded Francis. "I didn't think at all. It just happened," Francis said with the word *think* sounding more like *tink* with his brogue.

Michael liked Francis's irreverent sense of humor. He also respected the spark and fight Francis had in him; the famine had beaten that out of most people. Yet, Michael also sensed Francis could be a bit of a wild card and could create problems, problems that could implicate Michael by association. It was a risk Michael was willing to take as he thought he had found a friend in Francis, and indeed he had.

When there was sufficient light in the hold, Francis would pull out the book on Irish history his mother had given him.

It led Michael to ask, "You can read?"

"No," Francis replied, "I use the book to shield my eyes when your ugly face gets to be too much."

Michael laughed and quipped back: "The book works both ways Francis and, on behalf of all our fellow passengers, thank you for bringing it."

"Yes, the less we see of you the better," chimed in the bearded man who Francis had confronted at the very beginning of the voyage.

"You are all very charming, the lot of you," responded Francis with feigned hurt.

It was indeed impressive that Francis was literate. He came of age when schools and other institutions collapsed in Ireland. The famine brought with it disease, economic instability, and social upheaval. The mechanisms of a civilized time could not withstand the pressure, and things like literacy became luxuries inaccessible to many.

Drawing on the lessons of his own father, Seas had tried to prepare his children—including Francis—for the world they would face, not necessarily the world they wanted. Being harsh and letting them fend for themselves was part of it, but so was formal education.

At great financial sacrifice not fully appreciated by the children at the time, they were taught English and Gaelic and were fluent and literate in both. Seas had his limitations as a father, but he tried his best with what he had. With his wife Ann's support, he gave the children powerful tools: literacy in the prevailing language as well as the language that could link them to their past.

When Francis told Michael his full name shortly after the two boarded, Michael remarked, "A McNamara, I am honored to be in the company of royalty."

"Yes," Francis replied, "and I had the wisdom to join the clan at the pinnacle of its wealth and influence, which is why I am on this wreck of a ship with you."

****

The truth was the McNamaras were once of high standing. They could be traced back to the time of Irish kings and were said to have been given huge tracks of land in County Clare by Brian Boru himself. The family had holdings in the fishing industries and other enterprises. For hundreds of years, the family was prosperous—but that changed.

British control of Ireland, unsuccessful revolts, and discrimination against Roman Catholics depleted much of what the McNamaras had and held for generations. Irish Catholics, at various times, were denied by their English conquerors the right to vote, to hold public office, and denied property rights.

The family had been particularly devastated by the seizures of land in the late 17th century by British Protector Oliver Cromwell. Cromwell had just suppressed a rebellion in Ireland that he blamed on Roman Catholics, including the McNamaras. The little land the McNamara's were able to retain was subject to stiff taxes dictated by the Parliament in London, and to support the Anglican rather than Roman Catholic Church.

Among the labyrinth of English laws that burdened Irish Catholics was the Popery Act. The law required the property of Irish Catholics, upon death, to be divided equally among all the landowner's sons. With large families common at the time, the law broke up farms to the point that they were no longer economically viable and could not be capitalized to support Irish industrialization or other endeavors.

A particularly divisive provision in the law allowed the oldest son in Irish Catholic families to keep all the property if the son renounced Catholicism and converted to the Church of England.

By 1845, at the outbreak of the potato famine, nearly all the property in Ireland was owned by Protestants and absentee landlords in England. Any wealth the McNamaras were able to retain up until that point was through political maneuvering, their aggressive nature, and leveraging a degree of celebrity they enjoyed.

The McNamara family had members who were well-known academics, poets, and authors, as well as mercenaries. James McNamara, born in the same village as Francis albeit sixty years earlier, had a distinguished career in the British Navy.

He rose to the rank of Rear Admiral and earned recognition as a hero during the Napoleonic Wars.

The fighting inclination of the McNamara's beyond James was well-known. One of the earliest descriptions of a McNamara chieftain said that he was the "Supporter of his adherents and friends, and exterminator and destroyer of his enemies." A historical document from the 1600s detailed that, at the time, the McNamaras were fighting amongst themselves, with the O'Briens—another prominent family in western Ireland—and with the English, all simultaneously.

Records also show that members of the family were involved in an inordinate number of duels. The very same Admiral James McNamara, hero of the British Navy, was tried for shooting and killing General James Montgomery in 1803.

By characterizing the matter as a duel of honor, rather than what it was—a dispute over where the combatants' dogs could relieve themselves—the Admiral was acquitted. That disposition was aided by the Admiral calling high ranking individuals to be character witnesses, including the Viscount Alexander Hood, Lord Admiral Horacio Nelson, and one of the ancestors of Winston Churchill. So, at least some of the McNamaras had connections when it mattered.

The Admiral's exploits, however, pale in comparison to those of Francis's great-uncle John "Fireball" McNamara. Fireball was the son of Colonel Frank McNamara, a Member of the Irish Parliament before it was disbanded and the standing Clare County Grand Jury. The last of the clan to hold government office.

The nickname "Fireball" came from John McNamara's boast that a fireball would be the last thing anyone would see who dared him to a duel. That confidence did not deter challengers, as some accounts suggest he was involved in fifty duels in all. Fireball had a sharp eye, a steady hand, and a bag full of psychological tricks to allow him to survive the contests. He sought to intimidate and rattle his rivals by taunting them right before the duel began, winking at them, and calling out loudly to his pistols—one he named: "Death without a priest."

Fireball could also be witty and charming and was celebrated for his personality at courts across Europe where he worked as a mercenary. Things began to decline for Fireball after he was wounded at the Battle of Vinegar Hill, the high-water mark for Irish independence prior to the 20th century. Rumors of his vices soon outpaced anything flattering and some accounts had him hanged as a highwayman or simply dying as a pauper two years after Francis was born. Fireball was buried less than six miles from Francis's boyhood home.

Fireball's decline coincided with the final and most precipitous step down for the clan. By the time of Seas McNamara, Francis's father, the family had been relegated to leasing—not owning—a subsistence farm in County Clare. Although at five acres the farm was larger than that worked by most Irish Catholics in the area. The farm also came with a cottage with stone walls, a broad window, and solid timbers—reclaimed from nearby shipwrecks—that supported a thatched roof. This stood in contrast to other, more desperate Catholics who lived on small lots and in mud hovels that they shared with their livestock.

The most valuable aspect of the farm leased by Seas McNamara was that it was situated only a few hundred paces from the River Fergus. That allowed Seas, and his wife Ann, to feed the family from both land and sea—at least until the famine.

****

For seven weeks, the *Hopewell* was Francis and Michael Scanlon's home. They got to know each other well as they faced the vagaries and dangers of their voyage together.

The first storm they encountered in the Atlantic was terrifying. The thunder echoed in their chests and left their ears ringing. There was a distinct charge of electricity in the air as each thunderclap was preceded by a lightning flash. The storm was right above them and seemed fixed on staying there. As the waves grew more violent, the hold was plummeted into complete darkness. The crew sealed the hatch leading to the deck in effort to prevent flooding, but not before ordering the passengers to extinguish all the lanterns. Just one candle falling over, the crew shouted to the passengers, could leave the ship and everything in it burned to the waterline.

The darkness magnified the nauseating effect of the ship rolling about and the disconcerting sounds of the vessel's frame creaking and groaning against the assault from wind and wave. Adding to the horrible din of the storm was the sound of passengers desperately praying for mercy in Latin, Gaelic, and English. And most upsetting of all was the distinctive cries of children frightened to their marrow, children that included the two young Rowland boys.

Francis found himself instinctively trying to distract the children. He told them, in a voice he forcibly kept calm, a story. The story of when his father, just a child himself, went out to sea alone on nothing but a little raft. The dolphins and other sea creatures protected him, Francis explained, because they love children. Francis articulated the story with such conviction that it was as if he was relaying undeniable facts. He explained, with equal confidence, that the children on the *Hopewell* were safe as the marine life would ensure no harm would come to them.

When the story was done, to lighten things up further, Francis told the children he was going up on deck right then and there to complain to the ocean. Its rolling waves were ruining his sleep. Francis made noises in the dark as if he were falling all over the place trying to make his way to the stairs. The mere sound of the pratfalls and Francis's expletives was enough to make the children, and the adults, laugh.

Recognizing what was done for the children, the bearded man—who only days before almost came to blows with Francis, whispered in the dark to the younger Irishman, "Now I am glad I didn't kill you."

Francis responded, "Me too."

Michael offered a compliment as well, "That was nice what you did there."

To which Francis replied, "The kids were an easier audience once they realized I was the only show in town not trying to kill them."

The truth was that Francis was terrified himself during the storm but his compassion for the children overrode his inclination to crawl into a ball. He thought of his baby brother Patrick. The two were very close. It was beyond upsetting when Patrick contracted the fever, the same fever that had killed neighbors, cousins, and countless others across Ireland. What made it worse was that Francis's parents forbade Francis from going anywhere near Patrick when the younger boy took ill. They were afraid the fever would kill Francis too.

For days, Francis—from a distance—would call out to Patrick, read to him, tell him stories, and sing songs that Patrick liked. In the beginning, Patrick would cry out in turn for Francis. With each passing day, however, Patrick's voice weakened until there was nothing.

Francis begged his mother and the parish priest for something he could do to help his brother. Francis read the Bible and he prayed harder than he ever had before. In the end, it did not matter—Patrick died anyway. Francis could not understand why his innocent brother, at 11 years old, had to suffer and die. From that point on, faith would not be much of a resource for Francis.

While Francis's compassion toward children had its roots in his relationship with Patrick, the source of his loathing of authority figures is a little more complex. Francis's open hostility toward the captain and the crew of the *Hopewell*, particularly after the storm, made that loathing clear. Sure, his father—his initial authority figure—was arbitrary, even physically abusive at times, but Francis held no animus toward him.

Instead, Francis's anger focused more on the societal and cosmic forces that made he and his family miserable. As a child, Francis would befriend the animals on the family farm only to see them slaughtered. To live, Francis was told by those around him, he would have to take life in one form or another. Misery and pain were unavoidable parts of the process. Who would be so cruel to design such an existence Francis pondered? Surely not a loving God or a caring society he concluded.

The closest manifestation of a societal power on the *Hopewell* was the captain, Abraham Dixon. Francis would often refer to Dixon as "the jackass" in conversations with Michael. In contrast, Michael found himself sympathetic to Dixon but would never tell Francis that, fearing Francis would remove Michael's pancreas or another organ of import.

Michael tried to imagine from the Captain's perspective the pressure of navigating the rough seas of the Atlantic and carrying the fate of 150 desperate souls. Michael also noticed, when no one else did, that Dixon welled up at the funeral services aboard ship for two passengers. The passengers, weakened and ill when they boarded, died just hours apart and midway through the voyage to America. Michael suspected that these were not the first nor the last funeral services over which Captain Dixon would have to preside.

Not weighed down with such sympathies, Francis had a list of complaints against Captain Dixon, which he frequently enumerated for Michael. Francis argued the "ass head captain" gave the deceased passengers "a Protestant funeral" when they were Roman Catholic. Considering himself a sailor, although he had never been more than a few miles from the coast in his small fishing vessel, Francis also criticized the captain's navigational skills. "Is he actually aiming for storms?" Francis would mutter when they hit rough seas.

The antagonism began when the Captain publicly chastised Francis for trying to leave the hold and get on deck. Citing safety concerns, the Captain ordered Francis, and the rest of the passengers, to stay in the ship's hold until directed. It took all Francis had not to charge and headbutt the Captain because of Dixon's condescending tone.

He thought better of it when Michael pulled him aside. Michael reminded Francis, "They can put you in chains and throw you overboard, then alter the ship's manifest as if you never existed."

Francis's reaction to the Captain was excessive, but Michael understood it. Everyone their generation in Ireland had simply seen too much. They watched family and strangers alike starve, become ill, and die in the gutter. They all knew too well the sight of desperation and smell of decomposing bodies.

Michael had a recurring nightmare of skeletons chasing him in rags, begging for help—help that Michael could not give. The dream would end with Michael falling into a pit filled with people, not people begging, but people beyond help. It left Michael with terrible bouts of depression, anxiety, survivor's guilt, and Post-Traumatic Stress Disorder, although all those terms would be foreign to him.

Francis, Michael knew, was having his own nightmares. While Michael pushed the pain of his experiences inward, Francis pushed them out. It was not a question of whether Michael's or Francis's approach was better, the pain was going to exact its toll one way or another. Now adding to it all was the anxiety of starting life all over again in a new country, with little money, and even less standing.

The reality for Francis, and one that stuck in his craw, was that he was at the complete mercy of the Captain and crew of the *Hopewell*. He was always at the mercy of someone, someone arbitrary and indifferent to his suffering.

Below deck, Francis could not contain himself. "Captain Dixon is concerned with our safety, is he?" Francis grumbled, but only within earshot of the passengers he trusted. "Staying in this dark, dank hold will be the death of us all. Shouldn't we be able to pick our own poison? If we want to take the risk of going above deck, we should be able to," argued Francis.

Most of the passengers surrounding him agreed. Many of them would even sneak up to the deck with Francis. Other passengers warned Francis not to do so, but the glare they received in response was Francis's way of telling them to keep their mouths shut. He desperately needed air, to see the sun and the moon, and he would do so one way or another.

Francis had figured out when the Captain would be sleeping and when more sympathetic crew were on watch to go topside. The fresh air that he obtained during these brief intervals felt like a stolen luxury. It gave Francis strength, whether it was from the energy of rebelling or from the physical benefit of outdoor exposure. The hold was indeed a miserable place and becoming worse each day.

The smell was overwhelming. The hold had the vile mix of body odor, poor sanitation, and the endless vomit that flowed from sea and countless other sicknesses befalling the downtrodden passengers. Smells including the desperation of passengers from earlier voyages as well. Adding to the misery was the fact that the hold was not originally designed for transporting people. It was made for hauling timber and other goods. The sole retrofit of hard wooden berths did little in terms of making passengers comfortable. With the ship overcrowded, there were not enough berths anyway. The hard planked floor was the bed for many.

The open design of the hold proved particularly problematic during rough seas. If passengers tried to stand it was not uncommon for them to be tossed about. They would inevitably kick and stomp on those around them. It got to the point that if anyone rustled too loudly at night as if they were going to stand, everyone curled up defensively and covered their vitals.

Onboard things like privacy, sunlight, and clean air were scarce if existent at all. The meager, colorless food they were offered, Francis speculated to Michael, was designed to make them yearn for more famine.

"Hell itself will look like the land of milk and honey after this voyage," Francis joked.

There was an edge to what Francis said and Michael knew that was because Francis did not have money and had to get by with the minimum ration of bread and water. Mary

Rowland, with a greenish hue to her complexion since leaving port, would often give Michael her food as the smell of it made her sick. Michael, in turn, would share what he received with Francis. It was a generosity Francis would never forget.

During one of the more difficult nights of the crossing, one of the other passengers remarked that vessels like the *Hopewell* were known as "coffin ships" due to the high death rate among passengers. Some ships had more than half their passengers die in transit, and overall, one in every ten leaving Ireland on a ship for North America never made it.

"Coffin ship please," replied Francis sarcastically, "they only cover you with oiled canvas as long as it takes to mumble an Orange prayer and then dump you into the sea with your pockets emptied and a ballast rock stuffed up your ass. Coffins are for rich people."

"Wow, that is quite a visual Francis," said Michael, "with that kind of eloquence, will you speak at my funeral?"

"I am sure to become a very popular public speaker in America, so Michael you'll have to give the date well in advance and I'll see what I can do," countered Francis with a smirk.

There was no disputing that the transit aboard the *Hopewell* was unpleasant, even dangerous. But others had it worse. There had been slaves and prisoners chained to the boats that carried them, pondering if it would be better to go down with the ship rather than face the fate awaiting them ashore. Earlier pioneers sailed in smaller ships and with less information to guide them. Others hazarded the seas during times of war and rampant piracy. One constant threat to them all, however, was the turbulent weather of the Atlantic.

Not too long before Francis started his voyage, a ship called the *Hannah* left port in Northern Ireland with two hundred famine emigrants aboard. On a dark night midway through its journey to Canada, the *Hannah* encountered a severe windstorm. The passengers, if they were able to sleep through the rough seas, were woken by icy water seeping through the hull, pierced by a rogue iceberg. The captain, recognizing the extent of the damage, escaped with his first and second officers aboard the ship's only lifeboat. The rest of the crew and the passengers were left aboard the ill-fated ship. Tragically, a month later, a nearly identical set of facts would play out with another ship, the *Maria*, this time with a death toll of 109.

More than one hundred ships under British registry would be lost around the world to storms, fires, and running aground in the weeks Francis was aboard the *Hopewell*. All of that considered, Captain Dixon was not doing such a bad job although Francis would not see it that way.

Chapter Three
The Arrival

Cities of New York and Brooklyn
October 21-22, 1851

The weather bode well for their American arrival that Tuesday morning. The passengers' lined the deck, their bluegreen eyes matching the clear skies above them and harbor water beneath. The *Hopewell* was anchored in the Verrazano Narrows between Staten Island and Brooklyn. A small boat was disappearing in the distance toward the visibly more developed Manhattan Island.

The captain had given copies of the manifest, passenger list, and other documents to a man wearing an official-looking hat. The man had arrived in that small boat and was now racing ahead to notify Customs officials in lower Manhattan that the *Hopewell* was cleared and prepared to arrive in port.

"Make sure your belongings are all ready to go, we'll be pulling ashore in an hour. Take five more minutes on deck and then go back to your quarters," instructed the captain, dispassionately. Francis bristled at being directed once again by the captain and being further rationed life necessities like air and sunlight.

Below deck, Francis complained to Michael, as he did frequently, about the Captain. This time, however, Francis detailed a plan to confront Dixon once they docked. On solid ground, they would be on equal footing and that is all Francis felt he needed.

"You going to take on the crew too?" Michael asked, hoping the introduction of that obstacle would dissuade Francis. It did not. Francis suggested Michael handle one or two of the crew, and Francis's brother, Jamie, who was scheduled to meet them at the pier in New York, would take care of the rest.

"Alright," said Michael, "but I get the small ones, Jamie has to tackle the real brawlers."

Still too angry to laugh, Francis allowed his impractical thinking to continue. It was driven in part by his anxiety upon arriving in the new world without knowing what would await him, aside from his brother. Francis's assumption that Jamie could help in the assault on the Captain and crew reflected how immature Francis still was in some ways. He retained an exaggerated, childish view of his brother's strength, deeming it superhuman. Francis was only thirteen years old when Jamie left for America and recalled his older brother being the one who kept the teenage bullies in Clarecastle in check. Also, Jamie was the only one who could handle the family patriarch when the old man was drunk. That did not translate to the ability to combat several rough and ready sailors, but Francis's anxiety and anger had him bypassing logic. Anger not just at the Captain but at being torn away from his home, being made a stranger in a strange land and doing it all while impoverished.

The Captain, a man of his word—which may explain why he did not talk much—had the *Hopewell* pulling dockside within the promised hour. The dock's ramp led up into Battery Park, the largest open field left in downtown Manhattan. The park served, at one point, as part of the defensive works for Castle Garden—a stone fort that had been built in the lead up to the War of 1812. The Castle had since been converted into an opera house and the park a reception area for newly arrived immigrants.

When the last passenger stumbled off the *Hopewell*, struggling with his oversized bags, the gangway of the ship was drawn up and the ship returned to the crowded harbor, taking captain, crew and Francis's plan of confrontation with it.

Francis, Michael at his side, watched as the *Hopewell* disappeared among the chaos of other vessels crisscrossing the waters between Long Island, New Jersey, and Manhattan. Michael was relieved Francis would not be able to act on his lunatic plan and could save face, assuming Francis would have abandoned his overly aggressive plan at the last minute anyway.

Michael tried to distract Francis, "Will you look at all those ships?"

There were indeed a vast number of vessels of every shape and size. The bridges and tunnels that would one day connect the metropolis did not exist yet, so virtually everything and everyone around the city had to be transported by ship. Francis said nothing, prompting another question from Michael.

"Francis, what do you make of those ships belching black clouds?"

"Steamships," Francis advised. "I saw one last year when I was fishing off the coast."

The two friends then took turns pointing out the different variety of steamships among the armada in the harbor. Some of the steamers had been converted from sailing ships, with engineers replacing the masts with huge churning sidewheels. There were also hybrids, keeping their sails to supplement the steam if the wind was right. The ships that amazed Francis and Michael the most were the ones that had no means of propulsion visible at all. With their props below the waterline and smokestacks appearing designed only to choke the air, the ships glided as if by magic.

"What other miracles do you think this place has in store for us?" Mary Rowland chimed in, approaching Francis and Michael now that she and the children were ready to leave. As the two Irishmen began helping Mary with her bags up the ramp there was a bone-chilling crash from the harbor.

Those on the dock turned to see the *Hopewell* elevated out of the water atop a smaller vessel, the North Carolina bound, *Sarah Ann Fowler*. The *Fowler* had abruptly changed course to avoid running aground on Bedlow's Island, where the Statue of Liberty would stand thirty-five years later. The *Hopewell,* with its sluggish steering mechanisms that the Captain complained about in Ireland, could not get out of the way.

The *Fowler* sank in minutes; its crew jumping into the chilly water of the harbor, saving nothing but the clothes on their backs. The *Hopewell* looked as if it were going to sink too, listing heavily starboard. To the credit of Captain Dixon and his crew, they scurried about and improvised fixes that kept the *Hopewell* afloat.

"Look at that Michael," Francis said, sarcastically, "There is a God."

Michael did not laugh, and Francis felt bad having said it. His guilt softened when other ships came to rescue the *Fowler's* crew and to stabilize the *Hopewell*. Francis's attention would then be drawn elsewhere.

There was a large crowd in Battery Park awaiting the new arrivals. Francis, Michael, Mary, and the children grew anxious at the noise and chaos. The area was known throughout the city as the *Bandit's Bazaar*. In the waiting crowd, there were criminals of every description seeking to exploit the exhausted, overwhelmed newcomers. Some conmen posed as government officials, others money changers, others still as transportation coordinators or placement agents for housing and employment. Not to mention the traditional pickpockets, baggage snatchers, and muggers who were about.

The threat of the Bandit's Bazaar would quickly dissipate for Francis and his friends.

"Fireball, hey Fireball!" A man called in a nice but misfitting suit and wearing a black fiddler's cap carefully set at an angle.

Francis looked at Michael Scanlon and said, "Give me a minute" and ran to intercept the man who was shoving his way through the crowd toward them.

Michael stayed with Mary Rowland and her children just a few yards into Manhattan, Mary trying to shake the seasickness she still felt. With growing concern, Michael and

Mary discussed how they would get from New York to Norfolk. They hoped to find a ship going directly to Norfolk harbor or, alternatively, to Richmond, Virginia but figuring that out in the chaos of the park seemed impossible.

Francis returned and introduced everyone to his brother, Jamie, who took off his fiddler's hat and bowed in an exaggerated fashion. Their similar, although not identical, appearance revealed that they were brothers before Francis had said a word. Jamie was slightly shorter, stockier, and seemed to be quicker to smile and, based on how he shoved his way through the crowd, even more willing to throw a punch than Francis.

Jamie, an easy conversationalist, asked if everyone was all right after their long journey and if they needed anything. Mary mentioned having to make arrangements for a ship to Norfolk.

"No problem," Jamie advised and motioned for everyone to follow him. His confidence and burly appearance allowed him to cut through the crowd while the others in the group behind him struggled.

Jamie stopped at a makeshift table with a sign in English and German: "Train, Ship and Ferry Tickets." Jamie whispered into the man's ear; the man shook his head in understanding.

Jamie returned and asked, "How many tickets do we need?" Francis responded, "Two adults, two young children."

Mary looked at Francis and asked him, "Are you sure that you won't come with us to Virginia, Francis?" Mary had grown fond of Francis, although she thought him rough around the edges. He was kind to her during her seasickness aboard the *Hopewell* and protective of the children. Also, Mary felt she was making headway toward converting Francis to Protestantism.

In hearing Mary out, however, Francis was just being polite. Mary was a kind, compassionate woman, and a caring mother. Francis liked her not because of her religious zeal, but despite it. Francis also knew Mary had misinterpreted the whole conversion business in Ireland. Sure, people converted from Catholicism when she offered them help, but they would convert to some other denomination the next day if that allowed them to stay alive. Francis surmised that if the devil offered a warm oatmeal breakfast, the country would be Pagan by noon.

"No, I have to stay here in New York to keep tabs on my brother," Francis said, producing a smile from Jamie. The real reason was cost. Francis had no money and the fare to Norfolk, even at the discounted rate Jamie negotiated, was $12. And that was on a packet ship, which carried mail, so its cost was subsidized by the government already.

As Francis was secretly determined to go to Norfolk with his friends, he held out hope. As soon as they were alone, Francis planned on asking Jamie for the fare. Francis knew America could not have changed his brother that much. If Jamie had the money it was as good as in Francis's pocket.

Jamie marched back from the ticket desk with an extremely excited five-year-old Mitchel Rowland on his shoulders. Mitchel, coached by Jamie, announced they had four tickets and a reserved cabin on the steamer named—ironically—the *City of Norfolk*.

Not much of an imagination in naming the ship, Francis thought, but he marveled at the news nonetheless for the benefit of Mitchel. Francis advised Mitchel not "to let Uncle Michael Scanlon too close to the steamer's smokestacks. The coal soot will make him fart and no one wants that!" The young boy laughed.

Michael rolled his eyes and Mary wondered how she would clean up her son's language and humor after seven weeks with Francis McNamara. At the same time, she knew he was kind to the boy and would protect her and the children with his life if needed. Mary was just as happy to be with him and his brother now as she was overwhelmed by the city and had to bide time till their next departure in the morning. Michael also appreciated having familiar company, as he saw more people surrounding them in Battery Park than he had seen in his lifetime in Ireland.

Michael asked Jamie, "You called Francis 'Fireball,' is that some kind of nickname?"

Francis begged Jamie not to tell the story, which made Jamie want to tell it even more. When they were children, Francis's older brothers teased him incessantly. Francis would lose his temper and futilely attempt to strike back at his siblings, prompting the older boys to laugh at him and mockingly say "Look out, here comes Fireball," referring to their infamous and reckless great uncle.

"Happy?" Francis inquired of Jamie and Michael. They both simultaneously responded, "Yes, Fireball" and laughed.

By that point, the group had stood still too long. Hawkish panhandlers, pickpockets, and others looking to roll people, started to surround the McNamaras, Michael Scanlon, and the Rowlands.

"No business here," Jamie shouted nicely but sternly to the crowd. He then guided his group out of the park and toward uptown.

"What are your plans while in the city?" Jamie asked.

Mary responded that they had lodging with family friends in Greenwich Village. "We will hire a livery to take us," said Mary.

"You can, but you won't," replied Jamie. "A friend of mine will be here shortly and he'll take us all where we need to go."

As if on cue, a livery pulled up with a horse looking as worn as its driver, Edward Fitzpatrick.

"A thousand welcomes to you, the entourage of Mr. James McNamara. My faithful steed and I are at your service, to resolve all bets, debts, and favors." Fitzpatrick announced melodramatically.

"As you should, Edward," responded Jamie—feeling the last part was an unnecessary disclosure by a sore loser.

"Have you ever had German food?" Jamie asked Mary and Michael. Francis, being the little brother, had no say. "If you think there are too many Irish here," Jamie began his city tour lecture, "start counting the Germans but I'll tell you their beer gardens are portals to heaven itself."

Having no idea what a beer garden was, but by the name and the company she was keeping, Mary asked "What about the children?"

"Germans love kids, especially with sauerkraut," Jamie said tussling the children's hair. "You and the children are in the company of fine gentleman, have no fear," Jamic assured Mary.

Edward rolled his eyes from his driving seat and asked, "Where to?"

Between Edward and Jamie, it was a royal tour. The most majestic churches and their spiers, Wall Street, the beautiful brownstone homes, and the theater district were all pointed out. The recent arrivals marveled at the fancy clothes worn by the men and women uptown. Mary took particular interest in the fashion, although she had always dressed plainly herself.

In Ireland, everyone had grown accustomed to people in rags, grimy shawls, and going barefoot. In New York, people with means wore colorful stripes, checks, and plaids. Wool, linen, and cotton all seemed to be in style, with silk used for accents. Men and women often wore matching stovepipe hats, women's being slightly smaller in height and decorated with a veil or flowers. Women's skirts were hooped and blouses had wide, puffy sleeves. Men wore vests, tailored overcoats cut tight to the waist, and colorful neckerchiefs. Both men and women wore leather boots and shoes, many coming to a narrow tip at the toes.

Having now seen the fashionable men in New York, Francis looked at his brother Jamie and shook his head. Jamie's outfit reflected effort, but his execution left much to be desired. His suit looked as if he stole it off a corpse, someone well to do, but a corpse nonetheless.

Much of the commentary Edward and Jamie offered during the tour was complete nonsense. They made up church names, suggested any building worth looking at was designed and built by an Irishman they knew and criticized plays in the theatre district without ever having seen them. Even with their imaginative exposition, the true majesty and immenseness of the city came through.

"Where do you live?" asked Mary's son Mitchel.

"My primary estate is under renovation, so I rent in the downtown area," replied Jamie with a fake pompous air. Jamie's plan, already arranged with Edward, was to keep the guests as far away as possible from where he really lived, the Five Points. Francis suspected something was wrong in the living arrangements response, but he trusted Jamie and let it go.

On upper Mott Street, there was a mix of ethnicities. The Italians would eventually make the area home and that block would become the center of "Little Italy." However, that was still a few years away. As Jamie had Edward pull the carriage to the curb, the Germans seemed the most numerous in the area. The Irish were a close second and others of every race and ethnicity made up the rest. Native New Yorkers did not seem to frequent that block at all. Jamie led the group on foot, Edward in tow, through the labyrinth of what had been an old theater.

Mary was the first to notice what Jamie would explain was *oom-pah* music. They had arrived at one of the most popular beer gardens in the city. The group approached a large German-looking man serving as the maître d'. The novelty of the man's huge circular mustache and porkchop sideburns made young Mitchel giggle. Jamie did not wait for any feedback on the child's snicker. He just asked in a matter-offact fashion to speak to Will Mandelbaum.

The maître d' stiffly asked the group to step aside, which they did. A few minutes later, Will Mandelbaum arrived and hugged Jamie.

"Let me get you all set up," Mandelbaum said disappearing into the bustling crowd of patrons.

When he returned, Mandelbaum led Jamie, Edward, Francis, Michael, Mary, and the children to their table. Not any table but a private one with a commanding view of the dance floor and orchestra.

Will, winking at Jamie, told the group if they needed anything at all to just let him know. Then, as if they had been waiting on the group to be seated, German folk dancers took to the broad wooden dance floor. The men were in traditionally embroidered *lederhosen* and the woman in white blouses with puffed sleeves, laced bodices, and colorful skirts and aprons.

Mitchel mimicked the dancers from tableside, as much as his five-year-old body would let him. The dancers twirled, stomped, and leg slapped in rhythm to the Bavarian music.

"Wonderful," Mary remarked loudly, having never seen anything like it.

"Well then," Jamie said standing up from the table as the dance floor transitioned from the folk dancers back to waltzing patrons. "May I have the honor," Jamie asked, offering his hand to Mary.

"Absolutely not!" protested Mary, "I have not danced in years and will be a total embarrassment."

"Nonsense," Jamie assured, "follow my lead and if all else fails, just do what Mitchel did. Twirl in a circle and slap yourself as if you have ants in your pants. They will mistake you for one of the Bavarian professionals."

Mary relented with a laugh, and she was glad she did. She had a huge smile on her face the entire time she was on the dance floor with Jamie. When she returned to the table, her cheeks were flushed and she was out of breath. She excused herself to get air outside and asked Michael to mind the children.

Not remembering Jamie ever dancing in Ireland, Francis was impressed how his brother gracefully led Mary during the waltz. "Where did you learn to dance like that?" Francis asked.

"New York makes you worldly among other things, little brother." Jamie's response was just vague enough to make Francis worry.

Jamie then dropped his voice to a whisper, "Things must still be horrid in the old sod," referring to Ireland. "Your poor friend Mary is the worst sort of *skinnymalink*," Jamie noticing Mary's incredibly thin frame while dancing with her.

"She is a good person and has been through a lot," Francis said in a defensive tone. "She and her family came over to Ireland to help people for no reason other than maybe make her path to heaven a little straighter." Francis went on, "Her husband died of the scoots for his trouble," using a euphemism for dysentery—considered one of the worst ways to die in Ireland.

"God love her then," Jamie replied, looking at Mary's children with sadness. "But," chided Jamie after a moment, "don't be thinking all the people in the states are like Mary. Sure, some Americans are good and the majority keep themselves ambivalent about most things. There are an increasing number, however, developing a strong dislike for us Irish. They argue there are too many of us, and we bring in too much desperation, and I agree with them. But I won't be apologizing for being alive or being given a rotten start."

The charming smile Jamie had most of the night had vanished but he had to force it back as Mary, his guest, was returning to the table. He pulled her chair out in gentlemanly fashion and engaged her in conversation as if the concerns he conveyed to Francis had never been uttered. Mary had been followed by a trio of waiters bringing more food and drink to the table.

Francis, Michael, and Mary looked at each other in shock. They had assumed the thinly sliced bread, gherkins, and cheeses already on the table were the complete meal. Now platters of more food and pitchers of beer were being added atop the thick white tablecloth.

Bill Mandelbaum then reappeared as if from nowhere to explain how he had personally selected the newly arrived course from among his favorites and those of his family in Germany. There were meatballs in a creamy white sauce, sauerbraten, sausages of every description, asparagus, potatoes, radishes, and mushrooms. Mandelbaum suggested his guests sample the lagers and wheat beers to choose what they preferred with their meal.

Francis and Michael's eyes grew wide, both starving teenagers, they looked as if they just met the meal that would finally satiate them. Also, this would be their first experience with copious amounts of beer.

Mary, upon seeing their faces, took a motherly role and warned Francis and Michael that their stomachs may not be ready for so much rich food and drink. Francis, respecting Mary so, listened and only sampled what had been offered. Michael, reminding himself that there was no guarantee of a next meal, gorged himself as he tried to keep pace with Jamie and Edward in clearing the plates and pitchers. Michael would be terribly sick that night, and it would be Mary caring for him in her typical nonjudgmental way.

Mary hardly ate anything at all. Instead, she busied herself ensuring the children had enough and did not make too much of a mess, or too loud a ruckus, although that would not be a problem as the racket Jamie and Edward generated with their boisterous storytelling could not be rivaled.

The two told funny stories at each other's expense. They clearly liked and trusted each other, and it showed. Francis was glad to see his brother had made such a good friend and, based on the expense of the dinner, was doing well. It bode well for Jamie being able to help Francis finance his way to Norfolk with Michael and Mary.

Even with all their wit, a mutual trait they honed at pubs in New York they frequented, Jamie and Edward—and the rest of the table—would fall silent at any mention of Ireland. It was as if they were having an enjoyable time at an Irish wake, and then someone mentioned how much they were going to miss the deceased. To break the longest of those silences, Edward stood up—wobbling a bit as his drinking was catching up with him. He announced he would tell a story so profound and close to his heart that he had never told it before, not even to Jamie.

As if fighting back tears, Edward started: "When I was back in Ireland, I had a plow horse that was unquestionably the smartest animal God ever put on this green earth. He understood every word I said and he could communicate with me in his own way. When times grew hard and money scarce, I had to do something desperate. 'If you win a race against the landlord's prized thoroughbred,' I told the plow horse, 'you could save us both. But, if you lose, you're off to the highest bidder and I will have to leave our beloved Ireland poor and broken-hearted.' Let me tell you, as sure as I am standing here, that horse looked me in the eye with such confidence that I knew he would win."

Unexpectedly, Edward stopped talking. Some assumed he just lost his train of thought, or that he had drunk so much he was struck mute. Instead, Edward was ensuring he still had his audience's attention for the big ending.

Michael asked, "What happened, did he win the race?" That was the sign Edward was looking for and continued.

"I will tell you," Edward said, "there on the starting line my old plow horse stood in the shadow of the behemoth thoroughbred. He looked at me again as confident as could be. When the starting bell sounded, the thoroughbred took off in a flash. My horse, however, laid down on the ground and went to sleep. I shouted at him, 'Why the hell are you sleeping?' The horse responded 'I have to get up early if I am to see you off on that boat to America. I conveyed to you quite clearly I could not beat that thoroughbred, but you heard what you wanted to hear didn't you.' That I did, that I did." Edward then looked up to heaven and then at his audience, closing with: "The smartest animal in the world, indeed."

Mary laughed, and then even more so when Jamie quipped, "He tells that one better sober."

Wiping a tear from her eye from laughing so hard, Mary declared, "A tear of laughter can undo a dozen from sadness." She so needed this day. Her work had been difficult in Ireland, she worried always about the welfare of her children, and she was still broken-hearted at the loss of her husband. She had feared her troubles were such that she would never smile again. Thanks to this time with Jamie and Edward, she knew her fears had been unwarranted.

Jamie took his turn standing up, "Here is to old friends," raising his glass toward Edward, "new friends," nodding at

Mary and Michael," and to "wee friends" crouching down to Mitchel and his sleeping infant brother, John. "And, of course, to my little brother, Francis 'Fireball' McNamara!"

"Hear, hear," said the table, "hear, hear," said Edward, conspicuously out of sync with the others.

"Well," Jamie announced sadly, "Mary, Michael, we need to get you to your lodging. Edward, or more specifically his smarter and better-looking horse, will take you there forthwith."

As they left the beer garden, Mary said to Jamie, "How much do we owe?"

"It is us who owe you my lady, your beauty, charm, and wit, have enriched us all beyond measure."

"Please," Mary said earnestly, "I need to pay our share."

"When Francis and I visit Norfolk, the debt will be repaid then," said Jamie.

"It's a deal," responded Mary. A deal that would never come to fruition.

Michael was then about to ask what he owed but Jamie turned to him and said, "And for noble services in the form of tolerating my intolerable brother, please accept today as a gift of appreciation."

Michael laughed, "It was quite a chore." He said, looking at Francis.

They walked the short distance to the livery and horse. Mitchel began to cry when told that, for the first time in weeks, he would be without Francis. "It's ok, Francis promised to visit," Mary said to her sobbing son and Francis alike. "And won't he be surprised by how much you have grown and how much you will have learned from your schooling," she told her son.

Mitchel called out, holding back more tears, "Do you promise, Francis?"

"I do," Francis said, "I promise to be surprised by how much you have grown and how much you have learned."
Francis slowly turned toward Michael and at first gestured for a handshake. Thinking the better of it, Francis hugged his friend instead.

"You made the trip interesting," Michael said.

"You made it survivable," Francis responded.

On the *Hopewell*, Michael, despite pains of hunger in his own stomach, shared food with Francis and did so in a way that allowed Francis to save face. Francis trusted Michael and felt their personalities and approach to life complimented each other. They were better together than they were alone. Those kinds of friendships do not happen often, if at all, in a lifetime, Francis thought to himself.

Jamie slapped Francis on the back, "Come on brother, it's time for your first job in America."

****

The brothers walked southeast from the beer garden on Mott Street. Along the way, Jamie confessed—apologetically—that things had not been easy for him in the United States. While Jamie advised he had been getting by, it was only barely and by doing things he hated. If he could avoid Francis from having to follow the same path, Jamie assuredly would have done it. But, he could not. The path, should they want to survive, was going to be the same for both of them.

Jamie had no legitimate job prospects for Francis nor any store of cash his younger brother could draw from. Any substantive paydays Jamie had found, were followed by periods of no income at all. To the degree Jamie had formed connections, they were only to the city's vile underbelly. "Real jobs, the good-paying ones that make you welcome at church on Sundays, are hard to come by for an Irishman, particularly a Catholic one," Jamie advised glumly.

"Do you at least have enough to get me to Norfolk with Mary and Michael?" Francis asked. "Sounds like Mary may be able to get me a job there."

Embarrassed, Jamie disclosed that he was not in a position to lend Francis money.

"But soon enough. A break here and there is all we need," Jamie offered in an attempt to restore his brother's sagging spirits. "This is not Ireland. Something will eventually break for us here; we just need to stay strong. Crawl if we have to, do what it takes, so we are there the day the break comes."

Reeling from the disappointment that Jamie could not help him financially, Francis asked, incredulously: "Then what was with all the butter upon the bacon tonight," referring to Jamie's extravagance. "The coach and driver, the dinner at the beer garden, turning down other people's money, how could you do that if you are broke?"

"I was just trying to give you a different start here than me and Mathew had." On their first day in the city, the older brothers had been robbed and watched helplessly as another new immigrant was murdered trying to resist the same gang of thieves.

Jamie admitted everything he had done since picking Francis up at Battery Park had been a facade. "I called in every marker I had and went into debt to make today happen for you and your friends. The beer garden is owned by the Mandelbaums," Jamie advised. "They have the largest fencing operation in the Five Points. Do you know what a fencing operation is?" Jamie continued before Francis could answer, "They buy and sell stolen property. I do business with them, so do you know what that means?"

"Yes, I know, I am not an idiot." Francis snarled.

"Before you make boasts about your intellect, you may want to remind yourself that you know nothing about how this place works and what it can be like. I do, and it is a heartbreak. Even this damn suit," which Jamie looked so proud of earlier in the day, "is stolen."

Jamie once more looked to humor to defuse things. "Not the hat, that I purchased straight up."

Responding in kind, Francis said, "That may just be the saddest part of the whole thing. I just assumed you were wearing that hat on a dare. So why do you wear it, blindness or to cover a heinous growth on that oversized noggin of yours?"

The brothers laughed a bit, then silently contemplated their mutually bad situations. Even their brother Mathew, who risked a second move in hope of finding a better start in Philadelphia, was languishing according to his letters. "How do you stand it?" Francis asked earnestly. "I mean this place was supposed to be better?"

"Oh, it is better than Ireland at least," Jamie said with conviction. "Maybe not as much better as we would like, but it is definitely better. Not as many people starve here, disease isn't as rampant, and some people are making inroads. Do you remember Tommy McGlynn from up the road in Clarecastle? He is a captain in the Police Department in this very city. I know because he arrested me a few months back. A captain that is big doings. So, sure there is crime and desperate people here, but that stuff is everywhere. We just have to have faith, do what we can to hang in there. Again, a break will come."

The last statement struck a bad chord with Francis and put him back in an angry state. He knew Jamie was only trying to help and Francis himself used the false hope speech with his mother before leaving Ireland, but the futility of it all was getting too much to bear.

"Hang in there, things will get better; I am tired of hearing it. I am tired of trying to convince myself of it." Francis's face reddened as he spoke. "The famine will subside next year, Da will stop drinking soon, Patrick will get better—all I need to do is pray. Well, it is all malarky and poppycock."

Francis went on: "The famine is never going away, Da stopped drinking just long enough to have a knife plunged into his back, and Patrick died a slow, miserable death no matter how much I prayed. So, forgive me if I don't fall for it anymore."

"What is the alternative?" Jamie asked poignantly as if he honestly wanted to know the answer. But he knew, as did Francis, there was no alternative. What the conversation showed was that all they had was each other and their bonds as brothers. Fighting over circumstances they could not control made little sense, other than to work off their frustrations on people they could trust.

It was Jamie who broke the contemplative silence that followed, "I met someone here," he said with a coy smile.

"Who?" Francis asked.

"It is complicated, and you'll meet her soon enough," Jamie explained. "but, right now, I need you to focus. We are getting close to the meeting place. It will be a little risky tonight, so keep your eyes open and wits about you. If all ends well, there will be some money in your pocket and, trust me, this place is much nicer once you have moolah."

Immediately adhering to his brother's request, Francis began to alert himself to his surroundings. With each step he took, those surroundings changed—and for the worse. Jamie was taking him closer to the heart of the Five Points. That heart was a dark one, literally and figuratively.

It was long after sundown yet there was still a mass of people on the street, including children. Jamie explained that absent the most extreme weather, people preferred to stay outside over the cramped, ill-maintained tenements in the neighborhood.

The people and buildings in the Five Points stood in stark contrast to those Francis had seen earlier in the day on the tour led by Jamie and Edward. Gone were the well heeled, manicured crowds along with the elegant, expressive structures.

The children of the Five Points ran with no shoes and in tattered clothes older than themselves. The adults all wore headcovers of one sort or another, hiding their matted, greasy hair. Their dingy clothes soiled to the point that the filth seemed to be holding the people upright. Francis assumed a lack of clean water and money for soap contributed to the situation. For some people, however, they preferred not to go naked while washing the only suit of clothes they owned. The buildings looked as pathetic as the people. Ramshackle tenements of three and four stories, held together by warped wood and peeling paint. As many windows broken or missing, as could be found intact.

Francis had heard about the Five Points before his arrival; all immigrants did if they were planning to stay in the city and were desperate enough. A neighbor in Clarecastle, upon hearing Francis was emigrating, lent Francis a collection of essays about New York. Most of the articles were nothing more than propaganda characterizing the city as the New Jerusalem. One essay was not as flattering. It was specifically about the Five Points and written by Charles Dickens, famed author of *Oliver Twist*.

Dickens wrote of his brief tour of the Five Points: "From every corner, as you glance about you in these dark retreats, some figure crawls half awakened, as if the judgment hour were near at hand, and every obscene grave were giving up its dead. Where dogs would howl to lie, women, and men, and boys slink off to sleep, forcing the dislodged rats to move away in quest of better lodgings."

While Francis had hoped Dickens was exaggerating, now— seeing the place firsthand—Francis deemed the author a master of understatement.

Situated on Manhattan's lower eastside, slightly above what would become the city's municipal center, the Five Points led the United States in every conceivable slum statistic. Poverty, crime, disease, child mortality, dilapidated housing, poor sanitation, population density, unemployment; the works. The Five Points was home to the recently arrived Irish, who were pushing out—sometimes hostilely—the free blacks living there since the abolition of slavery in New York decades before. And it was in the middle of the Five Points that Jamie planned to meet with his loose-knit group of thieves.

The meeting place was called, paradoxically, Paradise Square—for it was neither paradise nor a square. Originally designed as green space, the square served as a makeshift residence to the area's homeless population, most struggling with mental and physical conditions that stemmed from malnutrition, addiction, and hard luck. The square had also been repurposed as a garbage dump. Prominent among the discarded items Francis could see was a peg leg. The pirate's remains presumably lay elsewhere in the pile.

Jamie advised that when the stench of the square got bad enough, the city paid locals to clean it up. Those same people would fill it once again with refuse, "The steadiest gig in town," Jamie called it. As to the shape of the "square," it was an irregular triangle formed by the intersection of three thoroughfares: Little Water, Cross, and Anthony Streets.

Jamie and Francis were not there long when they heard a distinct whistle from two men approaching from the shadows. "That is them," Jamie advised. As the men drew closer, Francis could see they were Irishmen. Their coloring hinted at it; their accents gave it away as they spoke during their approach.

"Who is your girlfriend?" The shorter of the two men asked, referring to Francis. Jamie laughed, Francis did not.

"He is with me; he is going to help." Jamie said, conspicuously avoiding introductions. New people were constantly joining and abandoning the crew. Some left for better paying criminal enterprises, others were lost to arrest, illness, or injury. Yet others simply vanished without a trace, a phenomenon in the Points nobody seemed to care about.

The only requirement for new recruits was that they look the part, be vouched for by a pre-existing member, and help the crew make money. In Francis's case, his similar appearance to Jamie gave away that he was a relative, but that was irrelevant, the real test was whether he could help the crew make a score.

The taller of the two men handed Jamie a piece of paper, saying: "This is what they want us to snatch." He then waited a few seconds then asked, innocently, "What does it say?" Neither of the two men could read.

Jamie looked at the paper and advised, "They want a bunch of fancy carpets stored in a warehouse." Then, as if taking the time to read it twice, Jamie spat out, "Way over in Red Hook." Jamie turned the paper over back and forth as if something were missing. "We are going to need a boat, along with a horse and wagon, but they don't say what we are going to get paid for all this." Jamie said, puzzled.

The shorter man handed over another piece of paper, having memorized what the fence had told him. "These are the instructions to hand the stuff over, and how we will get our money."

Studying the new document, Jamie mumbled "forty dollars." That was what the average laborer in the city could earn in a month, working six days a week and 12 hours a day. Split among all the participants in the theft, however, it was not much—especially considering the cost of the boat, and a horse and wagon. Clearly not worth the risk the gang was taking and their expertise as thieves, but too much to refuse in their desperation. The carpets needed to be delivered to the fence no later than dawn at a back alley off Greene Street, a little north of the Five Points. So, at least they did not have to worry about storing the goods.

Pulling his younger brother aside, Jamie stated: "Well, Francis, you'll feel a real connection to the place we are going. It is in the proudly independent City of Brooklyn. The ugly, half-witted, little brother of Manhattan."

"Your humor is getting increasingly grating," Francis replied indignantly. He was getting tired.

Jamie smiled at successfully annoying his brother and then became serious. Drawing a map on a scrap of paper off the ground, Jamie provided Francis detailed instructions where to find Edward Fitzpatrick, who the brothers had just left not more than an hour before outside the beer garden.

"You can always find him at the pub on Leonard Street. Now, don't get lost," Jamie said pointing once again on the map the path to the pub. He then ran his finger along the map to a second location, "and this is where me and the other boys will be waiting for you, Edward, and Edward's wagon."

After a pause, Jamie added, "Worse comes to worst, there are directional boards with the street names at most intersections, and corner buildings have street names painted onto their sides or carved into their foundations."

Nervous, Francis followed Jamie's instructions to a tee. Even down to the suggestion that Francis try not to look like a "new armpit in the neighborhood," who could be easily robbed or tricked. Seeing the anxiety that particular point created for Francis, Jamie tried to assuage the fear by reminding Francis, "You don't have two pennies with you to rub together and you look even more broke than that, so nobody will bother you—probably."

"Probably," Francis mumbled to himself, "very reassuring."

Upon arriving at the pub, Francis looked around but did not see Edward. None of the bartenders or patrons would even acknowledge knowing Edward, at least not to Francis who was a perfect stranger. Then, from a private room in the back, Edward emerged. He recognized Francis immediately, almost with a sigh.

After listening to Jamie's message as conveyed through Francis, Edward mumbled, "Oh that poor horse of mine." He walked out saying nothing more, Francis following him.

Edward and Francis walked in silence, down ever-darkening streets—as it was nearing midnight. Upon reaching a single-story clapboard structure that served as a stall and storage shed, Edward entered. Giving no indication if Francis should follow, Francis elected to go in as he had no desire to be alone in this strange place.

While he hitched his horse to a flatbed wagon rather than the livery carriage Francis had seen earlier, Edward began to sing. "The Bard of Armagh"—an Irish rebel song that Francis knew well. Francis hummed along and Edward nodded in recognition.

"Daphne's favorite," Edward advised, referring to the horse. "She likes all things Irish, which is surprising since she has never set hoof in the place."

Once they left the stall, Edward and Francis drove the wagon toward the East River, swaying and rocking in concert with the rattling wagon over cobblestoned streets. They reached the waterfront to find Jamie and the two other men waiting a few yards offshore in a flat-bottomed barge with large, extended oars and a "sweep" in the back to steer.

Not an attractive vessel but a practical one considering the task they would be undertaking. The three men moved the barge onto a ramp to load the horse and wagon. The group, Jamie, Francis, Edward, and the two unnamed coconspirators, started the trip toward Brooklyn, a little more than a mile across the East River.

Francis pointed to the most well-lit area along the Brooklyn waterfront. "What is that?" He inquired.

No one responded at first. Then Edward advised: "It is the Fulton Street Ferry Station at the foot of Brooklyn Heights. The busiest ferry station in the world, running around the clock and transporting more than thirty thousand people and tons of goods every day. Which reminds me, we should think about knocking over that ferry one of these days, that would be a good haul."

"And draw a lot of attention," Jamie noted to kill the wild idea in the cradle. He then looked over, appearing tense and tired himself, at Francis. "If you're going to keep asking stupid questions," Jamie said in a snarky tone maybe to impress the other members of the crew, "tell me now so I can throw you overboard."

Francis became quiet and just watched the shore as he continued to help row the barge. Edward patted Francis on the shoulder and said, "There is no such thing as a stupid question just stupid older brothers." Francis smiled. Edward assumed Francis was sulking at his brother's rebuke, but Francis had only gone quiet because he was exhausted from his long day and the stress of the criminal endeavor they were about to undertake. Little did Francis know that the crime had already started, the barge he was on had been stolen by Jamie and the other two men.

The group brought the barge around Brooklyn's southern tip, which also constituted the western end of Long Island, of which Brooklyn was a part. Now aided by a square sail, the boat made good time reaching the Red Hook piers. The area was dark save for a handful of fires kept by squatters living in shanties along the marshy beach. The crew navigated the boat into the Atlantic Basin, a manmade channel in Red Hook that was home to a number of warehouses and storage yards.

It took a while to find the specific warehouse they were looking for, as it was dark and they were navigating a barge that was anything but nimble. It was one o'clock in the morning and not a soul was around, or so it appeared. The people requesting the stolen items assured in their note that the warehouse would be unguarded. Another job aided, if not hatched, from the inside, thought Jamie. The plan's organizers had bribed the warehouse's nightwatchman to take ill and leave. There was still the risk of random patrols by the Brooklyn police who were notoriously rough on their suspects. So, Jamie would have to take precautions.

When they docked, Jamie told Francis to remain with the boat while he and the others went to the warehouse. "If you see a cop, move away from the boat, shout, kick over cans do whatever you can to tip us off but leave the boat. That is the only way we can get Edward's ass and wagon out.

"Horse, God damn it, he is a horse not an ass." Edward said, listening in and feigning insult.

Turning back to Francis, Jamie added, "Tip us off, then get yourself out of here." Now talking slowly to ensure Francis took it all in, Jamie advised: "Walk away if you can, run away if you have to. Make your way over to the ferry, and I will meet you there. Either tonight or first thing in the morning. If a cop stops you, tell them it is your first day in the country, which is true, and that you got terribly lost. Tell them you took the ferry over earlier from Manhattan and were now trying to get back. You may get some sympathy if you look pathetic." Jamie then looked at Francis laughingly, "In other words just be yourself."

Jamie then wrote down an address on a piece of paper. "This is where you are living. Ask for Eileen Brady." Jamie said handing the paper to Francis.

"Who is Eileen Brady?" Francis asked.

"Jesus, Mary, and Joseph! Stop with the questions and just do what your loving brother tells you to do," Jamie said in an exasperated tone with the adrenaline of criminal work beginning to flow through his veins. With a pat on Francis's back, Jamie headed away with the other men toward the warehouse.

It seemed to Francis, from his vantage point two hundred yards away, that it took the men forever to reach the warehouse and then to get in. It was because the men were being slow and deliberate, not trying to make noise or make themselves conspicuous.

Eventually, Jamie pried open one of the bay doors to the targeted warehouse.

Edward, along with horse and wagon, pulled into the cargo bay. He shut the door after he was joined inside by the other men. All four of them were now gone from Francis's sight, and he had no idea what was going on inside.

Not more than ten minutes later, a police officer on horseback rode up to the corner right outside the warehouse. Francis had not noticed the officer earlier because the lawman's approach had been concealed by the dark of night and adjacent buildings.

The officer, a stocky mustachioed man in his late thirties, got down from the horse. Francis assumed in a panic that the officer had seen something and was going to investigate at the warehouse. Instead, the officer stood still long enough to take off his cap and his large blue overcoat. He threw them over the saddle and led the horse to a trough just outside the bay doors of the warehouse. It was unseasonably warm for October and the officer, thinking he was alone, decided to get out of uniform and give his horse a break.

Edward, from inside the warehouse, also saw the officer standing out in front. Assessing the situation best he could through the cracks in the warehouse's bay door, Edward then ran up two stories to where Jamie and the others were organizing the items for removal. Edward grabbed Jamie and whispered, "Your brother's lookout skills are seriously lacking, there is a cop standing right in front of the bay door."

"Damn it!" Jamie said, peering himself from one of the warehouse's windows on the upper floor. He saw the officer wiping down his brow and neck with a handkerchief. Jamie also could see the horse's behind, the rest of the horse and trough obstructed by the angle. Jamie moved back to update the other men while Edward continued to watch from the window.

A few minutes later, Edward laughed obviously with no concern for noise. He shouted to the others, "You have to see this!"

The other men rushed to see what Edward was talking about. By the time they reached the window, there was nothing below. No officer, no horse, just an empty street.

"Where did the cop go?" Jamie asked, confused.

"He is chasing Francis," Edward answered.

"And you think that is funny?" growled Jamie.

"I do, as Francis has a distinct advantage. The ballsy bastard stole the cop's horse. Last I saw, the sweat-soaked cop was pursuing Francis like a banshee on foot but was quickly losing ground. While I concede Francis looked nothing like a seasoned horseman, he was smart enough to be clinging to the animal for dear life. And more importantly, he drew the cop away from the warehouse and the boat. Smart, enterprising lad, if I do say."

Jamie was not as upbeat. Francis could fall from the horse, run into other mounted police and a million other things could go wrong. Jamie envisioned himself having to write his God-fearing mother. Telling her how Francis, his first day in the new country, got himself arrested for stealing a policeman's horse. The thought of the Brooklyn Penitentiary, likely to be Francis's home should he be caught, gave Jamie a shudder.

"Alright, let's load up and get out of here," said Jamie with a heavy heart. "That cop may come back any minute."

Edward ran down and pulled the horse and wagon onto the street. Using the warehouse's rope and pulley system, the rest of the gang lowered the stolen carpets onto the wagon. They were back on the boat and rowing toward Manhattan within minutes. They were professional thieves and prided themselves on such. Francis was not, and Jamie can only hope that beginner's luck would compensate for his brother's lack of experience.

****

It was close to four o'clock in the morning by the time Jamie returned to the home of Eileen Brady, which was also a house of prostitution that she managed. Jamie had given Francis Eileen's address before the robbery and hoped Francis had somehow eluded capture and made his way there.

"Jamie," Eileen said, greeting him: "Why can't you be more like your brother? He is a perfect gentleman with excellent taste, remarking on my beauty and talents as a conversationalist."

Eileen and Jamie were a couple, and Jamie was lucky as Eileen was one of the savviest people in the Five Points. It was no secret that Jamie would be dead already if Eileen had not been there to steer his criminal career. Why she had taken a liking to him, Jamie had no idea.

"I should wring your neck," growled Jamie at Francis, the younger McNamara caught off guard. Jamie entered the room just as Francis was bouncing on a large, overstuffed couch. Francis was not used to such luxurious furniture and he was still, after all, more a seventeen-year-old boy than a man. When he first arrived at the establishment managed by Eileen, Francis had tried to touch the thickly textured wallpaper, something he had never seen before.

"No, no, honey," Eileen said with a wink, "touching costs and besides, in this place, you shouldn't be touching anything at all." Francis smiled sheepishly and placed both his hands in his pockets.

Eileen then ushered Francis into the office she used to manage the brothel. "You'll be safe in here," Eileen advised although she feared the very essence of the building could be detrimental to the teenager. While he had undoubtedly seen horrible things in Ireland, Eileen knew the young man's understanding of the world could be made all the worse by seeing what went on in a brothel. She would eventually find him somewhere else to stay even if Jamie could not.

"Francis just got here, red-faced, no more than twenty minutes ago," Eileen told Jamie. Then, to give the brothers some privacy, Eileen left the office and closed the door behind her.

"Before you say anything," offered up Francis, "I was going to do exactly as you said, tip you off about the cop and then run. But I had been on that damn *Hopewell* for so long my legs were too wobbly. I was also so nervous seeing the cop that my mouth went dry. I could not get a peep out. Since I was closer to the horse than anything else, I figured…" But Jamie stopped him and hugged Francis in relief.

"You are one lucky bastard," Jamie declared, pushing his brother away. Never having been accused of being lucky before, Francis was struck by the proclamation. Jamie continued, "Adding to your luck, the boys agreed to up your share of the loot assuming you were still alive."

"That reminds me," said Francis, "I have something for you." With that, Francis tossed Jamie a police whistle. "It is the only keepsake I took aside from the change in the cop's jacket pocket," Francis advised and added that he left the horse, policeman's hat and jacket which had been draped over the saddle—along with a note of apology—outside "the ferry that Edward was so kind to point out." Francis emphasizing Edward's name to zing Jamie. "No such thing as a stupid question," Francis quipped.

Jamie handed Francis his cut from the criminal endeavor which was both exhilarating and disappointing at the same time. American money but not enough to get him to Norfolk with Michael, Mary, and the children.

Looking at Francis's face, Jamie knew what his brother was thinking. "They are good people, and I can see why it's hard to say goodbye, especially after all the goodbyes you have had of late. But a couple of more scores and you can go see them. For now, let's get a drink."

****

Although the city had limited operating hours for pubs, certain ones stayed open all night and day. Jamie knew which ones. Since they were already near the seaport, he chose one a stone's throw from the East River.

Jamie ordered a bottle and some glasses from the bartender, James Dolan, whom he knew from the Five Points. "Take care of my little brother," Jamie said shaking hands with Dolan. Dolan was an affable man, although he, like most of the men at the bar, looked as if he had been through tough times. Francis's brother then went to the rear of the pub to talk some business, again seeking to distance Francis—albeit marginally—from such affairs.

Francis took a few shots from the bottle Dolan had left for him. In doing so, Francis hoped to steady himself after what had been a remarkable day. He felt that more happened in the past twenty-four hours than his entire life up to that point. Quickly a buzz set in. He had not been old enough nor did he have the money to drink much in Ireland. Neither did he have the frame to absorb much liquor. He was still growing, and the famine had kept him lean, so a little drink went a long way.

Thinking himself hallucinating, Francis spotted Captain Abraham Dixon at the bar. Dixon was drinking by himself, lamenting—Francis assumed—the collision involving the *Hopewell* the previous day. The Captain looked despondent. Having a vessel severely damaged while under your watch was the kind of stuff that would end a seafarer's career. Dixon had spent hours in interviews with the harbormaster, giving information to insurance agents, and even more inquiries were to follow.

For the first time, Francis found himself feeling sorry for the Captain. After all, he had gotten the passengers into New York safely. The harbor was so congested, Francis did not know why more collisions did not take place.

Francis poured two shots and walked over to Dixon to offer him one. The Captain, already drunk, looked up and recognized Francis as the troublemaker on the last crossing.

"What do you want, you Irish piece of shit?" The Captain said belligerently.

The bartender, James Dolan, heard it and knew right away this was not going to end well. Francis took one step closer to the Captain, and that was it. Whether due to his upbringing or genetics, Francis had a violent streak. But he had two kinds of violence. There was the deliberative type Francis exhibited back in Ireland in his handling of the Toobins who had murdered his father.

In that case, Francis calculated for a year and worked through various scenarios. He scouted the Toobins' property several times and planted flammable materials in advance. On the day of his attack, he got himself onto the property at the darkest time of night, just hours before he would leave the country. Francis dunked himself in water beforehand to decrease the likelihood he would accidentally set himself aflame. He created a small diversionary fire that would slowly grow in a barn on the outskirts of the property, letting loose the family's farm animals in the process. All that designed to draw the Toobins out and to give him time to loop back toward the canal where most of the Toobins' possessions lay.

While the Toobin clan tried to put out the fire in the barn and to retrieve their animals, Francis lit up everything else they owned that was closer to the water's edge. He then rowed away and hours later was on his way to the United States and his mother on an eighty-mile trek to the protection of her well-to-do son-in-law. Not an eye for an eye, but close.

With Captain Dixon, the violence would be different. It was more the spontaneous variety, with a visceral outrage and disregard for the consequences. Underneath it was resentment over how Dixon had treated him and the rejection of the peace offering. But those things only served to flip the switch. Francis was now totally on automatic pilot. In that one step toward the captain, Francis's brain was subject to what some would call an emotional hijacking.

After throwing the contents of one shot glass into the Captain's face and pelting the older man in the forehead with the other glass, Francis set upon the disoriented Captain with punches, knees, and kicks.

Francis was so focused on the Captain that he did not feel other people from the bar pushing him, and the Captain, onto the street. Fighting inside the bar was frowned upon. The change in air temperature did eventually bring Francis's wits back, as did his brother trying to hold him still. Dixon lay unconscious on the ground, either from the beating, the drink, or both.

"Well Francis," Jamie assessed, "this man may have wronged you, but he is not all bad because he is allowing you to take that trip you wanted." Jamie reached down and pulled out the expensive-looking watch that was partially visible from the Captain's coat. Jamie proceeded to rifle through Dixon's pockets pulling out bills and change. "Yep, give my regards to Michael, Mary, and the kids." Jamie said as he handed everything over to Francis.

It was more than enough, and Francis tried to give some of it to Jamie.

"No, no," said Jamie walking away from Dixon's prone body. "This is your score. Stay in touch little brother and keep a low profile on the docks until you ship out. I'll ask Dolan behind the bar to council your friend here when he wakes up that it may be best that he forgets who you are."

Jamie pushed Francis toward the slips where he could reunite with his friends heading to Norfolk. But not before saying to Francis, "I'll miss you, brother." He also reminded Francis to check in with the third surviving McNamara brother, Mathew. "He must be bored mindless there in Philadelphia making hats." Jamie referring to Mathew's most recent occupation as a hat maker. "Maybe hats as ridiculous as you claim mine to be," Jamie quipped.

Francis laughed at the idea of his brothers both making and wearing awful hats, but then he turned serious. "What about," but Jamie would not let him finish.

"Don't worry about a thing Francis. I will write Ma and explain everything to her. I will tell her that I saw you off as you began a splendid tour of the coast with new friends. And I will be fine here in New York."

Francis feared that last statement would not be true.

****

Francis walked exhausted and drained toward the slips and maritime ticket area, not far from where he had departed the

Hopewell the day before. Along the way, he passed a church and doubled back to see a priest preparing for the first morning mass. Francis entered and asked the priest to return something to Captain Abraham Dixon of the *Hopewell*. He then gave the priest the watch.

The priest asked if confession should be heard in relation to the item. "No Father," Francis replied, "I am just doing the best I can. This life is not of my making." The priest countered, "I don't think that is true, every thought you have, everything you do shapes your life. Let God help you make the right decisions."

"I think God should start with others, the ones in charge first." Francis stated as he left. He patted his pockets, knowing that he had enough cash from the robberies of the warehouse and of Captain Dixon to get to Norfolk and to eat along the way. Keeping the watch would have just been greedy and serve only to kick a man, the Captain, when he was already down.

Asking around for the slip used by the *City of Norfolk,* Francis made his way to the ship with little time to spare. He almost cried in frustration when he was told he would have to buy his ticket further up the pier. Pressing his wobbly legs as much as he could, Francis ran to the ticket clerk and was able to return just as they were preparing to pull away the gang plank.

Francis walked around the steamer until he heard the shouted greeting from five-year-old Mitchel. Michael and Mary seemed earnestly happy to see Francis as well. Michael let slip he knew all along and asked, "How did you get the money for the ticket?"

"I filed a complaint about the accommodations on the *Hopewell* and they gave me a refund," Francis said with a mischievous smile. Michael instinctively knew not to ask anything else, at least not in front of Mary and the children.

Chapter Four
The New Home

Norfolk, Virginia
1851-1855

It took two days for the packet steamer *City of Norfolk* to cover the 350 nautical miles from New York to Norfolk. For Francis, Michael, and Mary's children, the ride was much more pleasant than the crossing from Ireland.

The *City of Norfolk* was not as crowded and cramped as the *Hopewell*. There was an entire deck on which passengers were free to roam. There were also cabins for passengers, allotted based on ticket type, available for privacy and sleep. A deck below was for cargo and mail and on the top of the ship, a pilot's house and two tall smokestacks. Even the food on the *City of Norfolk* was better—fresher and more diverse.

The coal exhaust from the smokestacks would flow away, into, and in front of the ship, all depending on the wind. The captain was skilled enough that, more times than not, he could keep the smoke blowing away from the passengers. Aside from the occasional acrid coal emission, the voyage was relaxing. Relaxing, that is, for everyone but Mary.

"She should have developed sea legs by now," Francis commented to Michael midway through the trip. Mary had planted herself on the deck of the *City of Norfolk* in a canvas and wooden folding chair, situated as near as possible to the rail. For a brief period in New York, Mary seemed better but once again at sea she looked pale and weak. Even more so than she did while in the hold of the *Hopewell*.

Between the nausea that plagued her and the considerable weight loss she had in Ireland, Mary looked more the part of the famine refugee than what she was, a returning aid worker who helped the desperate masses.

Mary, always finding a way to be thankful, contemplated how fortunate she was to have Michael and Francis help her with the children on the trip. She had been counting on Michael, but Francis was a surprise. Francis could be crude but *God knows what he has been through*, Mary thought to herself.

Francis and Michael returned with the children to where Mary was sitting. "Mitchel has something for you, Mary," announced Michael, mysteriously. The youngster precariously carried a tray with tea, water, and bread. Mary thought for sure he would drop it, but Michael walked beside him to prevent such a calamity. Francis held and fussed over the baby as if he were the mother.

In addition to the help with the children, Mary appreciated Michael and Francis's irreverent humor to make her feel less self-conscious. It is bad enough having gastrointestinal problems when you are alone, but in front of hundreds of other passengers it is particularly humiliating, she thought.

Francis treated Mary's bouts of vomiting and loss of bowel control as a normal occurrence not worthy of a second thought. He had seen indignities of all sorts during the famine. Those indignities, he knew, did not reflect on those arbitrarily victimized. Rather the suffering was further evidence in his mind of the harshness and randomness of fate.

"You may need this for tonight if you go inside to the cabin area," said Francis, placing a bucket next to Mary.

"Aren't you sweet?" Mary said, half-mocking but appreciating the gesture.

"Don't be deceived Mary," chirped Michael, "we have a bet over how much of that bucket you can fill. Francis is either banking on rough seas or is feeling the bug coming on himself and will be making contributions of his own to the bucket. As for me," Michael continued, "God willing, Mr. McWavy and Ms. Hurl won't get the better of me tonight." Michael referring to some of the personifications passengers on the *Hopewell* gave to the cause of their seasickness and its most common symptom. Everyone took ill at one point or another during the voyage. Miserable food, stagnant drinking water, and poor sanitation made it inevitable.

"Charming, absolutely charming," remarked Mary rolling her eyes at Michael's wager claim.

The smart money was on an easy night. Mary had already checked with the crew and they reported a clear forecast for the charted course to Norfolk. To let her rest, Michael and Francis took the children to play elsewhere on the deck. Mary pulled the bucket closer, no longer caring what others on the boat thought. She was not well.

****

The sun shone brightly on the Elizabeth River where it meets the Chesapeake Bay. The paddle wheel of the *City of Norfolk* steadily churned toward its namesake. They would be in port soon. The crew, being kind to new arrivals unfamiliar with the area, pointed out Hampton, Portsmouth, then the outskirts of Norfolk—all three cities near each other.

Francis liked the look of Norfolk. He and Michael had examined the city directory kept on the boat. The population numbers reflected in the directory were less intimidating than New York City, their only frame of reference for American living.

New York City, which did not yet include Brooklyn and Queens, was the largest city in the United States by far. Its population had nearly doubled in the preceding decade, exceeding 600,000 people. Nearly half of the residents were immigrants. Although most were from Ireland or other English-speaking countries, there were enough other immigrant groups for critics, including Francis, to refer to the city as the Tower of Babel.

Norfolk had a more manageable population of 14,000 and its growth, more than a third since 1840, was not as frenetic as New York's. One in three people in Norfolk were black, 80 percent of those enslaved. Francis had seen black people before as sailors in Limerick and other ports in Ireland. He assumed the black sailors would look or be otherwise distinguishable from the slaves but they were not.

Some of the free blacks in the city had been able to secure financial success for themselves, earned recognition as tradesmen, access to key institutions—such as courts of law—and even in isolated cases owned slaves for profit themselves—the ultimate status symbol in the South. Poor free blacks, in contrast, struggled with obstacles even beyond those of poor whites. Those obstacles would intensify with the arrival of white immigrants—like Francis and Michael Scanlon. The desperation of the immigrants effectively undercut wages, increased competition for low-end housing and other resources, and added to racial distinctions and tension.

At that point, Francis did not see himself as a financial threat to anyone. In fact, he had an underlying anxiousness about what he would find in Norfolk. In Ireland, he had been warned by well-meaning friends not to immigrate anywhere south of the Mason-Dixon line, except for the larger cities of Charleston, New Orleans, and Savanna, Georgia where Irish Catholics had established footholds. The rest of the South, with its agricultural economy, gentrified society, Protestant leanings, and reliance on slave labor, left little room for the Irish like Francis.

Yet, there did not seem much room for Francis in the North either. He, along with every other person on the *Hopewell*, knew of the growing anti-Irish violence in northern cities. Jamie, Francis's brother in New York, had reminded Francis of growing sentiment against Irish Catholics as well. Francis brief time in the Five Points drove home the quality of life he could expect in the North.

At least in Norfolk there was the possibility Mary Rowland could find Francis and Michael Scanlon work and offer support. Mary advised that her family, more specifically her husband's relatives, had several business enterprises in Norfolk. Francis and Michael had scoured the City Directory of Norfolk aboard the ship for the Rowland name. Sure enough, several Rowlands were listed including a George, Hamilton, Thomas, and William Rowland. More importantly, those same people were listed as officers in banks and insurance companies, as merchants, and commercial real estate investors. Even the town's most tenured blacksmith was a Rowland—John operating out of a location called Union House.

So, as Francis headed down the gangplank to take his first step in the Commonwealth of Virginia, he felt good enough to push his underlying anxieties aside. Feeling good, a sensation that had grown almost foreign to him in recent years.

Mary had gone down the gangplank first with the children, followed by Michael and then Francis. The men carried the few belongings they had along with bags for the Rowlands. Mary and the children traveled comparatively light and had only a few more items being carried up from the lower deck by the crew.

As they waited, Mary felt dizzy but mentioned nothing. She attributed it to being seasick for so long. However, the arduous voyage across the Atlantic was only part of what was plaguing Mary. Before she left Ireland, she had been feeling worn down. Over preceding months, she had protracted colds and other maladies.

"Nineteen North Catharine Street!" Michael yelled up to the livery driver, taking his cue from Mary.

"It will feel so good to be home again," Mary said, as if to bolster her strength for this very last leg of the trip. Then she hesitated, "I am sorry," she said, looking at both Michael and Francis.

"In time, this will be our home too," Michael offered to spare Mary's feelings.

"Yes, it will." Mary said with as big a smile as she could muster. She felt with Michael and Francis she could say nothing wrong—a sign of true friendship.

They arrived at the house and Mary instructed Mitchel to run inside to surprise his grandmother, Abagail. Mitchel looked so much like his father now, Abagail would have no problem with recognition. It would also remind Abagail of the shocking loss of her son in Ireland. A loss in God's service and his ensured admission to heaven had been all that she had to console herself until now with her grandchildren's arrival.

Based on the time of day, Mary assumed her father-in-law, George, would still be at his office a few blocks away. She was not sure where her sister-in-law, Sally, would be. Mary desperately wanted to see all the Rowlands. Not having much of a family herself, she adored her in-laws and they loved her in return.

"It's absolutely beautiful!" Remarked Francis to Michael, referring to the large, two-story residence with freshly painted white clapboard and forest green shutters. The front door, with its intricate woodwork and stained-glass top light, was particularly impressive. Francis entertained the thought that someday he could own such a fine house and then dismissed the idea as ridiculous.

Mary labored up two small sets of steps leading to the house. She took a deep breath and smiled before entering. Only moments later, as Michael and Francis were still organizing the baggage, they heard a scream. It was not Mary who screeched, but her mother-in-law, Abagail. Michael and

Francis ran into the house to find Mary, semi-conscious, on the floor.

Abagail quickly took charge. She directed the Irishmen to place Mary gently onto the large couch in the parlor. Simultaneously, she shooed Mitchel into a backroom and took John—the infant—into her arms. Abagail then directed Michael to summon Dr. Balfour, advising that his office was on the corner of Market Street and Widewater.

Abagail told Francis to get her husband from his office at 24 Roanoke Square. Neither Irishmen had any idea where those addresses were, but they would ask until they did. They were aided when Sally, Mary's sister-in-law, approached the house after a shopping errand. Sally, only a year younger than Francis, but appeared even younger than that, accompanied Michael to get the doctor once she was told of the situation. She pushed Francis in the right direction toward Roanoke Square to get her father.

"Everyone knows who he is, keep asking for George Rowland and you'll find him," Sally assured Francis. In doing so, she projected the same veil of practical, takecharge stoicism that her mother did.

The doctor arrived at the Rowland home first, with Michael and Sally on his heels. The doctor took Mary's pulse, felt her for fever, and as she came around asked her a series of questions. George Rowland, a large, middle-aged man burst into the house, out of breath, with Francis in tow. Once Francis had notified George that Mary was at home ill, George took off without asking a question. Francis was happy to follow as he had no idea how to get back on his own.

George and Abagail listened respectfully to Dr. Balfour, who speculated, deferring to Mary's explanation, that Mary was just exhausted. He directed that she get several days' rest and asked to be notified if anything changed.

Mary tried to allay her in-law's concerns, as they considered her one of their own. It was just exhaustion she confirmed for them and asked to see her children. Mary's face brightened and she smiled broadly upon seeing her boys.

George asked Abagail who the two young Irishmen were standing in the hallway. "Oh, thank God for them," Mary chimed in. "Michael!" Mary called. Michael quietly entered with Francis a step behind.

"This is Ellen Moriority's brother, Michael." George gave a nod of recognition, as he knew Ellen well. "And this is his friend, and favorite of my children, Francis McNamara," Mary said, pointing to Francis. "Seriously, Father, we wouldn't have made it across the Atlantic and through New York City without these two."

George told Francis and Michael to follow him outside. George said he very much appreciated them caring for his daughter-in-law and grandchildren. He directed them to come back tomorrow, and he would have some money for them.

"Thank you," said Michael.

Francis thought it best to push for what they really wanted. "Is there any chance of employment? We want to carry our weight," voiced Francis.

George thought for a second. "Alright, come to my office on Monday morning. You know where it is," he said pointing at Francis.

Francis had no idea where the office was and only found it originally through sheer luck in his panicked state. This time they would find it through perseverance with Francis and Michael wandering the whole city until Francis recognized the office. The effort would prove worth it.

For housing, the pair of Irishmen would look to Michael's sister, Ellen. She had been in the United States for more than three years. Ellen had made the crossing with yet another Scanlon brother, Thomas. Thomas went to the western part of Virginia to try his luck there. Ellen decided to stay in Norfolk, with help from the Rowlands, whose church facilitated Ellen's escape from the famine.

While in Norfolk, Ellen met Martin Moriority. She had been working in the dining hall of a large boarding house in which the Rowlands had an interest. Martin, as did most men, noticed Ellen's beauty. Dark hair with a fair complexion and green eyes, she was indeed striking.

Martin was a benign, nondescript man who pursued Ellen vigorously. Working as a clerk at the local courthouse, processing paperwork for civil suits, Martin could not offer much money but he could offer stability. And to Ellen, who had been in the throes of instability most of her life, stability was invaluable.

Martin and Ellen were married within six months of meeting and had two sons, Timothy and Dennis. For Ellen, life was good. While Martin could be a bit bland, he was kind and gentle and worked hard to provide for the family. The one peeve Ellen had, although she did not articulate it, even to herself, was that Martin was not a hands-on father. It was as if he was unsure what to make of his boys. That was alright, Ellen assured herself; she knew what to do with them, which was love them to pieces.

Sally Rowland, Mary's sister-in-law, offered to show Michael and Francis where the Morioritys lived. On condition, she said, flirtatiously, that one of the Irishmen—looking at Francis—escort her back home.

Michael elbowed Francis in teasing fashion, "Looks like you are in with the pre-pubescent crowd."

Sally indeed looked like a baby. Her vulnerable appearance would have compelled Francis to walk her home in any event. He had heard about, seen, and participated in so much violence—both in Ireland and New York—he assumed Norfolk was the same.

While parts of Norfolk were as tough as any other town, the residential areas where the Rowlands and Morioritys lived were relatively crime-free. But the chivalry of the time required Sally be escorted home. And she both expected and wanted it, and Francis had been raised by his mother to be nothing if not chivalrous. So, chivalry and his assuming others lacked it put Francis at Sally's side.

****

They arrived at the Moriority home, a small, older structure that just reinforced the majesty of the Rowland's house in

Francis's mind. Sally knocked on the door and a curtain moved from the window aside the door.

"Oh my God!" A woman shouted pulling open the door and diving into Michael's arms before Francis could get a look.

"Come in, come in," Michael's sister—Ellen—said. There was a short, balding man standing next to the fireplace, Martin Moriority, Ellen's husband. Two children were on the floor playing with toys. The older child, guessed Francis, could not be more than three years old. That was Timothy. The younger, Dennis, was close to a year.

Sally laughed as Ellen swooned over seeing her brother Michael again. It went on for a while. Ellen then caught Francis's eye and said, "Another handsome son of Erin I see." Michael introduced Francis as his friend from the voyage over. "Well then," Ellen said, giving Francis a long hug which she only broke to tend to one of the children.

With Ellen taking the children to bed for the night, the others moved into the kitchen and Martin Moriority lit wood in the stove for tea. Not the most social person, Martin tried his best to keep up conversation. It was not easy for him, but his wife Ellen expected him to at least try and he did because he loved her.

On this occasion, however, Martin did not have to try for long—not with 16-year-old Sally Rowland in the room. Conversation came easy to her, in fact, she spent all her days talking, little else and she directed the conversation between herself and the three men at the table, subtly keeping Francis a little more engaged than she did Michael and Martin.

Based on the nature of Sally's inquiries of Francis, Michael Scanlon smirked and kicked Francis under the table about Sally's obvious interest. As polite and witty as she could be forward, Sally detected what Michael was doing and began peppering him with questions so he did not feel left out.

Sally's focus shifted altogether once Ellen returned from taking care of her sons. Sally had grown close to Ellen since the latter had arrived from Ireland. With no sisters of her own and her sister-in-law off doing missionary work, Sally fashioned Ellen into the older sister she wanted.

Francis listened in as Sally raved over the improvement in her hair's texture following Ellen's advice. "All my girlfriends are talking about combing their hair a hundred strokes each night with a coarse brush," Sally stated, "but you are right Ellen, it is much better to just gently run your fingers through your hair instead. My hair never looked so good since I started doing it, has it Francis?"
"I imagine not," Francis responded, puzzled for he had never seen Sally Rowland before that very day.

It was not Sally's hair that Francis had been admiring. It was Ellen's. She had coiffed her dark black hair off her face and expose her ears by having a braid, as thick as rope, wrapped around from the center to the back of her head. It brought attention to her heart-shaped face and tiny seashells for ears from which Ellen proudly had the dangling earrings her husband Martin had given her. Most working class-woman did not wear earrings. Francis—seeing them on Ellen—thought they should.

Entranced by everything Ellen said and did, Francis had to forcibly try to remain engaged with the others in the room. It was as if for the first time in his life he did not think about a thousand things simultaneously, but just one. Was it because she was attractive and acted like she did not know it? Maybe it was because she was so kind and caring toward her brother, her husband, her children, and her young friend Sally Rowland. For a long time, mere survival had pushed things like romance and sex out of Francis's mind, now they were at the forefront.

The rest of the evening was a blur to Francis. As he walked Sally Rowland home, as promised, Francis fell silent. Sally would have none of it. If Francis did not at least nod in response to her constant probes, she would pinch his arm. Sally was a character and, in time, would be a beauty in her own right. On that night, however, Sally could not—in Francis's mind at least—compare to Ellen.

Francis would not dream of telling Sally how he felt toward Ellen. One reason being that Sally had an infatuation of her own, that toward Francis. Second, Sally Rowland seemed incapable of keeping a confidence. Francis figured with all of Sally's bantering, anything and everything in her head would eventually make its way out into her fountain of words, whether Sally wanted them out or not.

Francis would not be able to share his thoughts with his only friend in town, Michael Scanlon, either. Ellen was Michael's sister, married, and a mother of two no less. So, Francis would have to keep what he felt to himself.

"Your castle," Francis said to Sally, marking their arrival at the Rowland home.

"That is strange," Sally advised, "the front door is ajar. My parents never leave it open like that."

Francis, concerned, walked ahead of Sally up to the entrance of the house and looked into the front parlor through the opened door. There George and Abigail Rowland sat, without speaking a word, staring off as if in a trance. They even ignored Mary's son Mitchel who was pacing between them. The boy noticed Francis in the doorway and ran to him.

"Mommy is dead!" Mitchel exclaimed.

The boy had a better understanding of what that meant than other children his age. It had only been a year since Mitchel's father died, and Mitchel knew that he never saw or heard from him again. Mitchel desperately wanted to talk to his mother, even if just to say goodbye. But that would never happen and he knew it. Quite a burden for a five-year-old boy.

The doctor theorized, for Mary's in-laws' benefit, that Mary died of a broken heart. The loss of her husband in Ireland was just too much for her. Dr. Balfour went on to explain that death by heartbreak was common, happened all the time he assured, as if it had been documented in medical journals.

The real reason Mary died was that she contracted a virus while nursing a starving infant who had been abandoned outside their mission in Ireland. While the doctor claimed that a romantic cause of death was common, Mary died from the most uncommon cause of all, helping a perfect stranger. It would also cost the life of her infant son, John, who died just weeks after Mary from the same virus, contracted as he nursed.

Mary's death hit Francis hard. He had not met anyone as genuinely kind as Mary. She was compassionate and caring, and just a nice person to be around. Now she was gone.

Although he did not appreciate it at the time, the impression Mary left on him helped Francis with the next stage of his life before the shadows caught back up with him.

****

In the four years that followed, Francis thought of Mary from time to time. To his surprise, she had been right. Hope did exist. His life had progressively improved since arriving in Norfolk. Thanks to George Rowland, Francis worked consistently. He made himself one of the most trusted employees at the Rowland Wharf and Shipyard. He never missed a day of work, applied himself one hundred percent, avoided conflict, and made himself a student of everything at the wharf. He had been given an opportunity, a gift from Mary Rowland, and he made the most of it.

Francis lived modestly. Moving out of the Moriority home as quickly as he could because he felt awkward around Ellen, Francis found low-rent accommodations just outside the city, where other Irish congregated. He ate in a disciplined manner, mostly fruits and vegetables from local gardens and nearby farms. Most of his protein came from fish he bought from the ships docking at the wharf. Francis did not drink alcohol much, deciding it was not good for his finances nor his wits.

Eventually, Francis saved enough as to require a bank account, which he opened at the Exchange Bank of Virginia on Main Street. He started to send money home to his mother in Ireland. Through a Protestant minister trusted by the Rowlands, Francis even sent final restitution to Captain Abraham Dixon—replacing the cash he had stolen from the man in New York.

Francis had the means so he felt obligated to return the funds to Dixon. However, Francis would never apologize for the robbery and assault. He had various justifications for being so obdurate. The most compelling being that without stealing that money he would have been trapped in the Five Points as one of its thugs, one of its victims, or both. That realization made him think somberly of his brother, Jamie.

It was not all pleasant in Norfolk. There were losses too, losses beyond just Mary Rowland.

Michael Scanlon, Francis's friend during the voyage from Ireland, became a victim of wanderlust. He joined the Army on a five-year enlistment. In letters to Francis, Michael advised that he was out West and if Indians did not kill him, the heat and bugs would.

Francis also stayed in touch with his brothers by letter. He wrote them about once a month, and they responded in kind. Mathew was determined to make his way into mainstream American society by becoming a merchant in Philadelphia. Jamie did not detail what he was doing, which Francis considered troublesome.

It was through his brother Mathew that Francis learned of his mother's death. Ann McNamara, when Francis left her in

Ireland, had been worried that she would be a burden to her daughter, Patsy, and son-in-law, Albert, with whom she would be living. Ann instead proved to be a Godsend to the couple.

Albert was already showing signs of illness when Ann arrived. Ann busied herself helping Patsy in caring for him and managing the farm. When Patsy took ill as well, Ann took care of the couple and everything else that needed to be done.

The doctor eventually diagnosed Albert and Patsy with consumption, a fatal pulmonary disease later known as tuberculosis. The disease slowly suffocates its victims, death ushered in by bloody coughing fits and extreme weight loss. The condition literally consuming people before they die— hence the name.

With the disease being so contagious, the doctor told Ann she would contract it as well unless she left the farm and what remained of her family in Ireland. Ann stayed anyway caring for Patsy and Albert until she had to bury them.

Knowing what fate awaited her, Ann grew sick and then died alone and was left to rot. No one, other than a family member, would risk their own lives to help her due to the nature of consumption. And Ann's family was gone.

Mathew, the oldest son, had been notified of Ann's death himself months after the fact by the postmaster in Ireland's County Longford. Sparing Mathew the details, the postmaster indicated Ann simply died in her sleep. Mathew knew, however, that both Patsy and Albert had died of consumption. So, he knew as well that Ann likely died of the miserable disease herself, except she would have been all alone. The thought of that was too much to bear, so Mathew—the practical one—chose to believe she died peacefully in her sleep and that is what he relayed to his brothers.

Mathew advised Jamie and Francis that the postmaster would be returning the most recent letters to their mother, as they had been left unopened. Assuming the letters had banknotes intended for their mother, Mathew suggested they all use the money to get drunk, the only solace he could offer. Not taking that advice himself, Mathew redirected his own money to the parish church in their native Clarecastle, asking that prayers be said for his parents and departed siblings.
With that, their ties to Ireland were severed. There was nothing left for them there anymore other than ghosts and memories.

****

Francis decided not to get drunk with the money returned by the postmaster either. He had developed better ways to deal with grief and hardship. Francis resumed sailing and fishing, as he had done in his childhood trolling the River Fergus and the Shannon. On a handful of occasions when he was a youngster, Francis had braved the ocean off County Clare with his father. Francis noticed his father seemed more at peace on the water than anywhere else. The angst the old man had on land seemed to drift away at sea. Now that Francis was getting older, he found the sea had a soothing effect on him as well.

Upon hearing of his mother's passing, Francis spent two days in a rented fishing boat. However, he did not fish at all, nor did he sleep. He just stared lost in a trance across the vast ocean trying to picture Ireland once again in his mind. With it images of his mother, his father, sister, and brother— Patrick.

When he returned to shore, he was no longer in mourning. Instead, he was ready to act on the commitment he made to his departed family members. He would do the best he could in this new world in their honor.

****

Francis worked harder than he did ever before. His efforts paid off and he was promoted from laborer to craftsman's mate at the wharf. That meant he went from loading and offloading arriving vessels to carrying heavy tools and supplies, and doing prep and cleanup work, for the master craftsmen who maintained the wharf and repaired the crafts using it. Soon, Francis was sure, he would be made a craftsman's apprentice and eventually become a craftsman himself.

To aid in his plan, Francis began recording in a journal everything the master craftsmen did that he thought effective and even things they did that did not work at all. A middle child, Francis realized early on that he could learn vicariously from others. Collective wisdom was usually superior to individual wisdom, Francis had concluded.

With the fiscal confidence that came with his steady pay and the promise of career advancement, Francis invested in a second-hand, fifteen-foot sailboat. He refurbished it himself, getting tips from the master craftsman at the wharf. Francis used it as an advance on his training. The boat was large enough for the bay and to reach a barrier island just off the Virginia coast. It allowed him to catch enough fish for his own consumption and to sell for extra cash.

Francis became bold enough to start looking at a larger vessel he might buy for commercial use. By looking at the most successful people around him, including the Rowlands, Francis learned that owning your own business was an effective way to succeed in America. Francis even played with the idea of trading up vessels until he would own and captain his own steamer.

Francis's interest in seafaring also led to him making two new friends. Abraham Simmons was an aging, free black man who ran a bait and tackle shop near Rowland Wharf. Reverend Francis Devlin of St. Paul's Church in Portsmouth was a fishing enthusiast himself and friend of Abraham's.

When Francis was new to fishing the local waters, Abraham gave him advice on where to go, how to look for oysters, and how to open-water fish—the American way. Abraham had lived in Norfolk his whole life and knew the city, its surrounding waters, and its people like the back of his hand. Abraham found Francis funny and enjoyed the perspective of someone not yet fully indoctrinated in Norfolk and Southern life. In many ways, Francis kept a foreigner's perspective and innocent wonder about his new home.

Reverend Devlin met Francis on a rainy day in Abraham's shop. They talked about many things, but the Reverend took note when Francis mentioned that he planned to camp on the barrier island. The next day, the Reverend left a book on camping with Abraham to loan to Francis. The Reverend went on to loan other books as well. None of the books, it should be noted, dealt with religion because Francis never expressed an interest in it. The Reverend respected others.

That barrier island that Francis discovered not far off the coast became his special place. He would camp there whenever he could. It was beautiful with a broad beach, grove of trees, and the sounds of gently crashing waves and the song of birds that braved the trip over from the mainland. He enjoyed the solitude when he was there alone.

On one occasion, Francis offered to take Sally Rowland to the island but she made clear she had moved on from having any interest in Francis, romantically at least. She did offer, with a devilish smile, to put Francis on her "ever-growing waiting list."

"Very generous," Francis responded, "but McNamaras rot on the vine."

"Yes," she said, "I can see that!" Both she and Francis laughed at the quip.

On occasion, Francis would run into Ellen Scanlon around Norfolk. He initially referred to her as Mrs. Moriority, but she insisted that he call her by her given name. While his feelings for her had not changed, Francis had been maturing and he was better able to manage his mercurial inclinations. A gift, he thought, from his departed friend, Mary Rowland.

Also, Francis cared about Ellen and he did not want to put her in an awkward position by sharing his feelings. At the same time, Francis was protecting himself. It was better to be a star-crossed lover in his own mind than risk learning from Ellen that she had no romantic feelings for him at all.

So, he said and did nothing to pursue Ellen.

That was until June 6, 1855. It was a Wednesday and Francis was working on the bulkhead at the base of the wharf. He climbed up to the wharf's ledge to retrieve some tools when he noticed Ellen walking with her two boys heading toward the nearby storefronts. Francis called out and waved. Ellen smiled as the boys ran toward him, happy to see him again. They peppered him with questions, as they always did when they saw him in the past. They asked about his tools, what he was doing, and when was he going to take them fishing as he promised at one point to do.

"Well, stranger! Good to see you." Ellen said interrupting and trying to physically corral her boys so they wouldn't be too much of a nuisance to Francis.

"Good to see you too," Francis responded, trying not to stare too intensely into her eyes.

"What have you been doing with yourself these days?" Ellen inquired.

"Working mostly," Francis advised, "but I have been doing some sailing as well. I tell you that barrier island out there is a hidden gem. It is beautiful and I have it all to myself. I would go there every day if I could. I am off from work tomorrow, in fact, and heading there. The weather is looking perfect." Francis scanned the sky for effect.

Ellen smiled, "That sounds wonderful. I would love some peace and quiet in a beautiful place for a change." As she spoke, she playfully rolled her eyes in the direction of the boys, conveying that she loved them but they were a handful.

"Come along with me," Francis said, shocked at the opening Ellen had given him, if that is what it was. "I was planning on leaving from here at eight in the morning—is that too early for you?"

The offer caught Ellen by surprise, and she felt guilty at unconsciously hinting for an invite. Then, she surprised herself by responding, "Please, eight o'clock is midday for me these days." Now she felt guilty at not just hinting that she wanted to impose, but by actually imposing. Not that Francis saw it as an imposition at all. Presumably, it was the guilt and her instincts to be courteous that drove her next statement. "I'll make a picnic lunch."

"It is a date then," Francis blurted out.

Ellen's face reddened and her mouth opened in shock, she had not intended to agree to a date. She had just been trying to make conversation and admonished herself for giving Francis the wrong idea and letting things play out as they did. She was not that kind of woman, especially that kind of married woman. Yet, she could not explain why she responded as she had.

Fearing she would just make things worse by talking again, Ellen took a deep breath. Her instincts were to run away and avoid ever seeing Francis again but she needed to make things clear and proper with him.

At the sight of Ellen's cheeks reddening, happiness bolted through Francis. He interpreted it as blushing and blushing meant that she had feelings for him. Now it was Francis who was going to run, not out of embarrassment but to deprive

Ellen of the opportunity to recant on joining him on the island. He tipped his hat and quickly scrambled down to the undergirding of the wharf ostensibly to resume his work but actually to preserve his win.

Knowing she had to nip this in the bud, Ellen went to the railing and shouted down to Francis. "Hey, monkey boy!" Referring to Francis's rapid climb away from her, "Get back out here."

Francis stuck his head out from the bulkhead, holding himself horizontally via cross supports between pilings. Ellen looked down at him from the railing, *God, she is beautiful*, Francis thought as he looked up.

But rather than call the whole thing off, Ellen found herself trying to contain things. "Do I need to bring anything special for the boys for the boat ride or the island?" She asked.

Guilt flowed through her once again, using the boys as a shield—*despicable* she thought harshly to herself. Why was she handling this so awkwardly, she pondered? She did not know—consciously at least.

In his excitement, Francis had forgotten all about the kids. Not that he minded. Tomorrow he was going to have more time with Ellen than he ever had before. And, if he bombed in conversation with her, Ellen's boys would prove to be a nice distraction for them all.

"No, I'll have it all covered, no need to fuss," Francis said, tempted to waive at Ellen but that would have meant letting go of the wooden support and him plunging into the water below.

"Alright," Ellen said, "And remember, you are not really a monkey so be careful climbing around down there. We'll see you in the morning!"

****

The next morning Francis got to the dock early and prepped his small boat. He feared it would rain and ruin everything. Clouds had rolled in. His anxiety was misplaced though, rain would not be a problem, the clouds would burn off. The wind, more specifically the lack of it, would be another matter. Francis would have to row and that would take most of the day. He thought of one of the beaches along the shore of the Elizabeth River as an alternative destination.

Abraham Simmons stepped out of his shop. Always there, Francis concluded that Abraham must eat, sleep, and everything else in just that one location. You need bait at three o'clock in the morning, Abraham's place is open.

"Bring me some real eels and crabs this time, not that puny stuff you unloaded on me last week!" Abraham shouted to Francis.

"Not today, I have passengers!" Francis advised.

"Since when are you a charter vessel?" Abraham retorted.

Just then, Ellen arrived and walked down the ramp to Francis with a hand grasped on each son. Abraham saw how Francis looked at Ellen and knew Francis was smitten. However, Abraham also knew Ellen—he knew everyone in Norfolk—

and that she was married. Abraham tried to convince himself that Francis could not be that stupid.

But fortune smiled on Francis, a perfect wind picked up as soon as he and his passengers cleared the northern tip of Norfolk. When it did, he put aside the oars and put his passengers to work to employ the sails, explaining to them the mechanics of sailing and sailing terms. All of it was lost on Ellen and the boys, but Ellen smiled and looked interested so as to not insult Francis.

It would end up being a fast run to the island. Too fast for Ellen once the small boat heeled with the force of the wind caught in the sails, she feared the tiny vessel would tip over. But they were not moving fast enough for the impatient boys who laughed as one side of the boat rose and the other dipped, and they were sprinkled with droplets from the wake.

"Are you taking us to China?" Timothy, the oldest of the two, asked thinking of the furthest place on earth he had ever heard of.

"No, to do that I would have to make my way over to the Pacific and I stay away from that ocean," he advised the literal Timothy, "too many mermaids!" That remark resulted in Francis having to explain to the boy the legends surrounding the mythical sea-creatures which left Timothy thoroughly perplexed.

"So, mermaids remind us how the ocean can be both beautiful and perilous to a sailor." Francis concluded, convinced the boy now understood.

"If they are half fish, how do their privates work?" Timothy asked.

"Not sure, that is one you have to ask your mother." Francis replied.

Ellen smacked her hand to her forehead at the thought of the arduous task Francis had just assigned her. "Well, that is going to keep me busy for the next year!" She mockingly growled at Francis.

Once on the island, the boys' excitement escalated and they began to run around. Francis cornered them as quickly as he could, advising that he had to inspect the island for pirates first. That being a ruse so he could plant things for a scavenger hunt with items he had purchased the afternoon before when Ellen advised the boys were tagging along.

"Seems safe for now," Francis advised, and proceeded to tell the boys of the tale of Seas the Pirate, who used the island to hide his booty. "If you look around, you may find some of his treasure." Francis advised.

The boys were thrilled. Timothy took off like a shot. His younger brother Dennis on his tail. After covering the entire island, twice, the boys came back empty-handed and crestfallen. "No treasure," they reported sadly.

"Of course not, you don't have a treasure map." Francis advised, "You can try this one," handing Timothy a pirate map of Francis's own creation.

With Francis giving guidance as to north, south, east, and west, Timothy—with Dennis still on his heels—read and followed the map. They found where the X marks the spot. They dug down into the sand a few inches and discovered a cigar box with candy, sketchbooks, and coloring pencils.

The boys marveled over their find and ran back to their mother to show her. Ellen feigned interest in their discovery and smiled at Francis. She thought how it would be good for her husband, Martin, to play with the boys so.

Francis asked the boys to draw a picture of their mother with their new sketchbooks, a task they began excitedly, but did not finish. Timothy, before losing interest, had drawn what Francis thought was a nose. Dennis drew an abstract series of circles. *Did that kid just draw shit?* Francis thought to himself.

Ellen smiled at Francis reflecting her appreciation for him entertaining the boys, both of whom were now in the water. "Not too far out!" yelled Ellen sternly.

To allay her concerns, Francis rolled up his bell-bottomed pants, took off his shirt and went into the water with the boys. As she watched, Ellen thought about the day she first met Francis. She considered him a boy at the time. He was barely seventeen and not fully developed in mind, body, or spirit. But that was years ago and now, she had to acknowledge, he was not a boy anymore.

As evidence of Norfolk being good to Francis, he had been able to pack on more than thirty pounds of lean muscle. She noticed, while Francis had been rowing the boat, even his hands and forearms were sinewy. It is amazing, she thought, what a difference healthy food can make. Francis's work was such that it challenged him physically but he also had time to recover. Mentally, he retained his sense of humor but his edge, which Michael Scanlon had once remarked upon to his sister Ellen, was gone. The horrors of the famine were behind him too, it appeared.

Ellen laughed at the way a large curl fell onto Francis's forehead. He had a flume of dark hair and spent most of the day running his hand through his hair to push it back. Francis's eyes were complex, sensitive blue with flecks of green.

Francis worked so often outside he was more tanned than your typical Irishman. He had no tan line that Ellen could see, so he must have been swimming in the nude at the island. Ellen was snapped out of her thoughts when she heard Francis asking the boys, "Shouldn't your Mom come in?"

With the boys urging him on, Francis ran up the beach and began to chase Ellen, who laughingly warned, "Don't you dare!" Francis caught up to her, swept her up into his arms and marched triumphantly toward the splashing boys.

Knee deep in the water, Francis gently released one of his arms, letting Ellen's legs drop into the water, her upper body straightened in the process and both her hands fell upon his bare chest.

This is not right, Ellen chastised herself. She was a married woman with children and Francis was a single man. At that, she applied pressure to both her hands, shoving Francis into the water. He flailed in an exaggerated fashion making the boys laugh yet again.

A few hours later, they packed up and began the trip back to Norfolk. The boys were unconscious. Ellen said, almost in a whisper, "This has been such a nice day for the boys," consciously leaving her own enjoyment out of the reference, "thank you so much."

Looking at the boys and then directly into Ellen's eyes, Francis replied, "The pleasure was all mine."

It was then that Francis saw it, it was not a lack of desire that held Ellen back. Absolutely not, he told himself. It was obligation and fate, fate that never quite worked in his favor. He had his day with Ellen, and that would be all.

As he navigated the small sailboat around a handful of steamers and larger sailing ships moored outside of Norfolk, Francis explained to Ellen the ships were awaiting clearance from the harbormaster. One of those ships, a steamer from the Caribbean, was the *Benjamin Franklin*. What was on that ship would change everything.

Chapter Five
A Storm Arrives

Portsmouth & Norfolk, Virginia
June-August 1855

It did not take much to see that Francis was depressed. The first to notice was his friend Abraham Simmons. Francis had become uncharacteristically quiet when he entered the store and did not laugh at jokes or poke fun anymore. Having seen Francis's face that day when Ellen walked down the ramp for the boat ride, Abraham knew it was a case of heartache.

Abraham asked Francis directly about it. Trusting Abraham, Francis detailed his dilemma. Abraham was sympathetic in more ways than Francis could imagine. For most of his life, Abraham could not pursue his loves, his interests, his anything. He had been born into slavery and, for a while, believed that was the way it was supposed to be. The person who had the legal rights to his labor was an author who, on a European tour, was confronted by other writers regarding the hypocrisy of American liberty while condoning slavery. The result was that Abraham got his freedom. No compensation from the man who unjustly profited from the enslavement but freedom.

Abraham asked a fundamental and practical question of Francis: "What was Ellen saying about the situation?"

"Nothing," Francis answered, "she will not talk to me now and avoids me at all costs."

"Well then," responded Abraham, "seems you got your answer. Not the answer you want, but an answer."

Noticing that he failed to make his friend feel any better, although Abraham knew he spoke the truth, he suggested that Francis talk to their mutual friend Father Devlin.

"I don't think a priest would have the frame of reference for this type of problem," Francis grumbled.

"It's your heart and soul that hurts, right?" Abraham asked, giving Francis time to think. "Isn't that the bailiwick of church folk?" An interesting remark considering Abraham himself was an agnostic.

"You can talk to him in that babble you all speak, nobody will know what you're talking about," goaded Abraham.

"It's Gaelic," retorted Francis, "and damn you, Abraham!"

Abraham knew, by the last remark, he had struck a nerve and helped his friend. Francis would talk to the priest. Father Devlin was a smart, insightful man. Just as importantly, he was compassionate and went out of his way to help others. Attributes much needed but too rare in this troubled world of ours, thought Abraham.

Father Francis Devlin, a fellow Irishman, had been pastor of St. Paul's Roman Catholic Church in Portsmouth for eleven years. Twenty years Francis's senior, he emitted an air of wisdom and kindness. "Francis, what do I owe the honor?" the priest asked. Usually, they exchanged books through Abraham. This time, Francis returned the book on medieval history in person.

"I have a problem," said Francis.

"I am sorry to hear that my friend, what can I do to help?" Father Devlin asked while pointing for Francis to sit in one of the rectory chairs.

Francis laid out his problem, with a degree of embarrassment.

"Not an easy one Francis, I can see why you're struggling with it. God gives us all these emotions, thoughts, and feelings, but no instruction manual to deal with them, aside from the Bible, of course." Father Devlin said kindly.

Psychology as a recognized field was still years away. Yet, Father Devlin was already using what would become its principles. He incorporated aspects of church doctrine, including prayer and meditation. Along with concepts rooted in philosophy, logic, and other sciences. The priest coupled it all with compassion and respect for the sanctity of the individual, and he could point to results among his parishioners.

In some respects, the Catholic Church was progressive for its time. Popes had condemned slavery and the slave trade for hundreds of years. Pontiffs and other Church leaders directed that the sacraments and services be open to people regardless of their status as slave or freeman, or their race. The Church was also on its way to being the largest charitable organization in the world, operating clinics and hospitals, schools, and caring for the elderly and infirm. At the same time, the Church demanded it be viewed as God's one and only earthly arbiter of good and bad. It remained quick to pass judgement and damn those who did not fit or support Church dogma. Devlin's techniques, as they reflected on nontraditional ways to view the brain and soul, would have been considered unorthodox, if not heretical, by much of the Church hierarchy. Consequently, Father Devlin kept what he was doing close to the vest.

Father Devlin's work with Francis started with a discussion on the distinctions between thoughts and actions. "Envision our thoughts as being like the weather," the priest offered, "you don't have much control over them. But you do have control over how you respond. That is where your decisions and actions come in. If it is cold and snowy, you can put on a warm coat or jump into the ocean naked. I would not recommend jumping into the water but that is your choice," the priest said smiling, pleased with the thought of his witty analogy.

"So, you have feelings for this Ellen but there are many obstacles in the way. There is the matter of societal norms, your own moral code, and Ellen's view of things. It is cold and snowy Francis so what are you going to do?" Father Devlin asked.

Francis looked down to the ground and then up to the priest, "Well, normally I am a *jump in the water man* but that doesn't work out very often. So, I see your point, a coat it is." Then looking quizzically at the priest, "What exactly is a coat in this situation?"

Devlin, having anticipated the question, said, "The good news is that the options are limitless, and it's you who decides what to do. It could be just giving the situation time to see if your feelings fade. You can make that process more palatable by focusing on distractions that you are passionate about. Fishing and sailing, for example." The cleric tapping into their mutual interests. "If you are daring," the priest continued, "you can take the bold step of tackling how you think about the problem itself."

Puzzled, Francis asked, "How the hell would I do that?" His gut reaction that the priest was now talking gibberish. Then, having a knee-jerk reaction from his youth, Francis made the sign of the cross realizing he had just said "hell" in a rectory.

Having spent many years salvaging lost souls, Father Devlin had heard, and seen, much worse. Unfazed, the priest answered, "For starters, once you recognize and label a thought, you can change how you choose to treat it in your mind. Even give it physical qualities. Treat it as something big or small, colorful or bland, as something loud or soft. Ultimately, you can choose to disregard your thoughts altogether or alter them so that they are more useful to you. You steer the ship."

Francis said nothing, quietly trying to wrap his head around what the priest was saying which was much different than what he had ever heard from a priest before. Different, in fact, from what he had ever heard from a person of any sort.

"I recommend Francis, because all this warrants a lot of thought, that you pray on it." Father Devlin trying to bring the discussion to a close.

Here we go, the sales pitch, Francis thought to himself, envisioning that he had to sit for hours in a church pew.
Seeing Francis's facial expression, Father Devlin added, "If the idea of prayer is not resonating with you right now, think about maybe using a diary or journal to write down your thoughts. You may be surprised what solutions will come to

you in the process of simply writing things down." The priest sought to leverage Francis's ability to read and write, skills many of his immigrant parishioners did not have.

Francis was not buying it. Things like famine, crime, poverty, and heartache were way too real to be prayed or journaled away. Father Devlin laughed upon seeing the disbelief on Francis's expressive face. "In time, my friend, you will see how much God trusts you and how much power you have. As the poet John Milton once said, 'Our minds allow us to make heaven out of hell, and hell out of heaven,' and truer words have never been uttered."

Francis still had his doubts, to him hell was always hell—it could not be changed by humans. But Francis did agree it was possible—if not likely—people would ruin heaven. *Just my luck*, he thought, *I'll earn my way into heaven just in time for it be turned into hell by me or some other knucklehead.* But the Milton characterization was witty, and witty always counted for something with Francis. So, Francis would think about it.

The reality was that Francis did not understand much of what the priest was suggesting and disagreed with portions of what he did understand. Francis was not a "fallen-away Irish Catholic." He would describe himself as, "The rolled-away across the ocean, hiding amongst the trees, kind of faithful." So, prayer and asking for God's intervention would be out. But the young man had to agree, he felt better simply talking to the priest so there had to be something in what Father Devlin was saying.

As Francis stood to leave, thanking Father Devlin in the process, the priest made his way over to a large bookshelf.

"Here you go, Francis," Father Devlin announced, tossing Francis a book on moral philosophy—one of the priest's favorites. "It's not light reading but worthwhile and you are up to it," the priest added with confidence in his voice.

The kindness and wisdom shown by Father Devlin, for a brief time, had Francis thinking maybe he should return to the Church. He did not know it, but Francis had just reached the zenith of his time there along the Chesapeake Bay. He had stabilized himself economically, made progress in improving himself as a person, and was exploring ways to increase his resiliency in the face of problems. Francis had been surrounded by good people and opportunities. He had blossomed physically, emotionally, and even spiritually. The question was now whether all that would be enough to see him through as terrible storms were brewing.

****

Francis returned to Father Devlin's church in Portsmouth a few weeks later after finishing the book the priest had given him. With a list of questions in mind for the priest's counsel, Francis looked forward to resuming their conversation. Oddly, Father Devlin's personal effects, including a clerical collar and cassock, had been thrown about on the grass between the church and rectory building.

Trying to make sense of it, Francis thought that Father Devlin was preparing for a camping trip. A cot and halfcollapsed tent were amidst the mess. The priest came out from behind the leaning tent, looking worn and disheveled. Father Devlin was surprised and alarmed to see Francis.

"Please Francis, keep your distance!" shouted Father Devlin. "Something is wrong, very wrong," the priest advised, putting up his hand in a stop motion. He looked exhausted. "There is an illness and I have been tending to the sick and dying. It is awful."

It was yellow fever. A mosquito borne, flu-like illness that made many of its victims' jaundice and raised their body temperature, hence the name. It was particularly deadly to those who were new to warmer climates, among them the recently arrived Irish immigrants.

"It is spreading. I seem to have it and I don't want to get you sick," Father Devlin said saddened. "Francis promise me you will leave. Go to Richmond, go to New York, go anywhere but get out of here."

Francis was shocked and was reluctant to leave his friend in such desperate condition. "Do you need anything?" asked Francis.

"No," barked the priest harshly, evidence his mental focus was teetering. Father Devlin then mumbled something to himself before calling out, "Wait! Yes, Francis, I need to go back to the waterfront where the sick and dying are. I am needed there and, I am afraid, I now belong. There is a box of bibles in the church I can use, please bring them out and leave them by the gate. Don't come any closer than that."

The priest knew the fever was highly contagious but did not know at that time how it spread from person to person—no one did.

Doing what he was told, Francis carried the bibles to the gate. Bibles, the only weapons, along with his faith and good intentions, Father Devlin could bring to the fight. Francis then noticed that Father Devlin had collapsed and either fallen asleep, passed out, or died. It was hard to tell which, but Francis feared it was the latter.

Francis cried and said in Gaelic looking at the prone priest: *"Is duine cineálta uasal tú, go bhfóire neamh agus do ghrá go léir ort.* Translating loosely to: "You are a kind and noble man, may heaven and all you love greet you."

They buried Father Devlin only a few yards from where Francis last saw him. He was 42 years old. The priest had cared for others stricken by the fever until he was at death's door himself.

Francis had tears in his eyes when he left Father Devlin, making plans to leave the Norfolk area just as the priest had asked. As Francis navigated his sailboat along the coast of Portsmouth back toward Norfolk, he thought through what belongings would prove to be necessities and how he would notify others of the epidemic so they could save themselves.

As soon as he tied up his boat at Rowland Wharf, Francis ran up the ramp and entered the bait shop yelling, "Abraham there is something wrong!"

"I know," his grey-haired friend advised, "It is a fever, a bad one. It is spreading quickly and lots of people in Norfolk have taken terribly ill today. Fevers have never bothered me but folks like you are not used to them. Francis, it will kill you. You have to get out and get out now!"

Rather than respond to Abraham directly, Francis recounted what happened with Father Devlin. Francis felt he had to share the trauma of it or go mad.

Abraham and the priest had been friends for years and the news hit Abraham hard. Abraham walked over to the window in his shop overlooking the water, staring out thinking of Father Devlin and others who would soon be lost.

Trying to fight off panic, Francis began peppering Abraham with questions about what fevers in the area had done in the past. Abraham turned back from the window and looked Francis directly in the eye.

"Listen to me," Abraham grumbled and then shouted, "Francis, get out right now!" Abraham did not want to lose yet another friend. And to save Francis, Abraham would never lay eyes upon him again.

Francis ran from the shop without saying another word, trying to gather himself in the process. He would need money. He would withdraw everything he had from the bank, bypassing his apartment figuring he would be able to purchase any personal effects he would need once he was wherever it was he was going. Before he left, however, there were two other places Francis had to go. He had to ensure the Rowlands and Ellen knew about the fever and that they were safe.

The Rowlands lived closest, so Francis went there first. The Rowlands were already loading their effects onto a wagon, so they knew. Upon seeing Francis, George Rowland reprimanded the young Irishman for coming. It was too dangerous for Francis to be heading anywhere but out of town.

"It is only a matter of time before they call for the militia to seal off the roads and the port," George advised. "Once the quarantine is put in place, those left in the town will be at the mercy of the fever. And fevers have no mercy." George then urged Francis, "Get out while you still can!"

The advice was now the same from everyone Francis met that cared about him. And he planned to act on that advice as soon as he could. Right before he was about to begin his sprint toward Ellen, however, Francis saw Mary Rowland's son Mitchel, now nearly ten years old. The sole survivor of what had once been a family of four. The boy looked both confused and scared as he sat in the back of the Rowland's wagon.

"It will be all right, Mitchel. Remember you were able to best the mighty Atlantic Ocean as a mere babe. Now that you are a strapping young man, nothing can best you. Not even a blasted fever." Francis said encouragingly. "Just mind your grandparents and your Aunt Sally," nodding toward Sally Rowland who was taking her position in the wagon next to the boy. Mitchel forced a smile despite his apprehension and confusion. Sally hugged Mitchel close, and George and his wife, Abagail, settled into the front of the wagon and rode off.

With that, Francis resumed his trek. He ran toward the Moriority home and Ellen. To Francis's surprise, Martin Moriority was in front of his house painting the picket fence that separated the home from the dirt road in front of it.

"Martin, you heard about the fever, right? You are leaving?" Francis asked.

"Yes, I heard but I am not going anywhere," Martin said indignantly. "Folks around here are losing their heads; I won't lose mine. There have been plenty of illnesses that have come and gone, and this town and its good people are still here."

"What are you talking about? I saw people dying in Portsmouth and that is just across the Elizabeth River. Others are saying people are already coming down with it here in Norfolk. Sure, people are panicking but with good reason," argued Francis.

"I have invested everything I have into this house and I'll be damned if I am going to leave it," countered Martin. "Some of us don't leave our homes at the first sign of trouble." An obvious slight to Francis for having left Ireland. Martin forgetting for the moment that his own wife left Ireland as well. In fact, every American either left someplace themselves or had ancestors who had at some point.
"Where is Ellen?" Francis asked while looking around.

"Why do you care?" Martin snorted, his agitation now showing on his face.

Not seeing Ellen outside the home, Francis walked past Martin into the house shouting Ellen's name. Martin threatened to have him arrested. Ignoring the threat, Francis marched into the kitchen where Ellen was feeding her two sons.

"This fever is bad, Ellen, like famine bad. You have to get out, you have to get the boys out, and you have to get your asshead husband out of here!" Referring to Martin. Finished with what he had to say, Francis turned around and left.

Ellen was slacked-jawed; she could not get a word out until Francis was gone. She did, however, have plenty of words for Martin. To his credit, Martin heeded his wife's request and made provision for Ellen and their children to leave Norfolk and stay with friends in Mathews County, further up the Chesapeake. Martin chose to stay in Norfolk himself, thinking it necessary to protect his job and his home. A decision that would cost him dearly.

Now out of breath from his sprint that had covered half of Norfolk, Francis approached the bank. There had been a run and the bank had closed hours before with all the cash gone. Most of that money left in the hands of the bank's managers. A crowd of irate depositors demanding to be made whole was mulling outside the bank building, trapping inside the two tellers the managers had left empty-handed. The crowd forgetting for a second that the last thing they should be doing during a fever outbreak was to congregate and to be shouting at the top of their lungs. From their shouts, Francis could tell that no cash was left, and waiting around would not likely bring him any. So, he left.

As he readied himself for one last sprint to his sailboat, Francis hesitated. He just realized that he had been carrying with him the whole time the book on moral philosophy he intended to give back to Father Devlin. It reminded him that there was indeed something he had to get from his apartment. When he finished the detour and eventually set foot inside his boat, Francis had the clothes on his back and two books, the one on philosophy given him by the priest and the other on Irish history given to him by his mother. He wasn't sure why he considered the history book essential but he did. Francis was more sentimental than he let himself admit.

He set sail for the one place he knew he could clear his mind and think through his long-term options. The barrier island.

As wind started to fill the sails of Francis's small boat, he looked back to see the Norfolk that had been so good to him. In the next three months, the fever would kill three thousand people. It would represent a sizable percentage of the Norfolk and Portsmouth population sealed inside the cities during the quarantine that was imposed just as predicted by George Rowland.

Many more people who seemed to have survived the illness would have their quality of life and life expectancy diminished from residual organ damage. A parting gift from the fever which only began to break when the weather cooled and mosquito season ended.

The yellow fever had been introduced to the city by the crew and bilge of the *Benjamin Franklin*, the ship Francis and Ellen had seen moored in the harbor a few weeks before.

There would be one other residual effect of the fever outbreak, and it was working its way through Francis.

Chapter Six
The Turning Point

Chesapeake Bay, Atlantic & Philadelphia, PA.
August-September 1855

For all the times Francis had gone to the barrier island, he could count on one hand when other people were there. Francis felt he had the island so much to himself he had the right to name it, addressing the fact that the oasis was nothing more than an anonymous dot on the charter map of the area. Francis flattered his sanctuary with the name of Scattery. The eponym an isle more significant in every way at the mouth of the Shannon Estuary in Ireland.

Just when Francis needed the solitude of the island most, it would be denied him. The barrier island had been overrun by people trying to escape the fever raging in Norfolk and Portsmouth. They did not want Francis adding to the mix and several people yelled at him from the shore to stay away. One man, brandishing a pistol, shouted "I'll shoot if you get any closer!"

Francis's stomach tightened as he turned his boat away from the island, his one and only plan dashed. He desperately racked his brain as to what to do next. Mathew, his brother in Philadelphia, was his closest relative and seemed his best choice. The downside was that Philadelphia was two hundred miles away. Francis's small sailboat had no navigation equipment and he did not even have a map covering beyond the southern Chesapeake Bay.

With a decent wind, Francis figured he could make Philadelphia in a few days. Should the weather turn on him, however, it could take a week. Should the weather go from bad to worse, and it was hurricane season, he could be lost at sea forever.

The risk had him contemplating making the trek on land, but that had its own hazards. It would take several days on foot even if Francis knew what roads to take and he did not. Moreover, Francis had no money so he would have to beg for food and water along the way. That would make him reliant on the kindness of strangers, a worse risk Francis concluded than braving the seas.

To hedge his bets, Francis decided to sail north but stay extremely close to the coast. He would go ashore to rest and avoid any severe weather that arose. Once on land, he would ask for directions. As for eating, Francis figured once again he would have to tap into the fasting skills he developed during the famine.

That night, Francis pulled into an undeveloped inlet. He secured his boat and found as good a place as any on the beach to sleep. After making a small fire, Francis fell unconscious. He was both emotionally and physically exhausted. But that did not keep him from waking up in the middle of the night with a start.

Francis was drenched in sweat and recollections of his nightmares fresh in his mind. In his sleep, he had seen images of Father Devlin collapsed on the ground, Mary Rowland looking sickly aboard the steamship, and heard calls from his dying brother Patrick pleading for help. Death and misery. Everything seemed so futile to Francis now. His years of hard work and progress wiped out in an arbitrary instant. The things that gave him hope for a happy life gone.

Worse, Francis was now feeling as if he were not alone in his own mind. It was as if another entity had invaded, an entity espousing intrusive and depressing thoughts. His brain had him questioning what was real and what was an illusion; what were his thoughts versus those of the invader?

Francis had never experienced anything like it before. It was, he thought, like what his friend Michael Scanlon described as nightmares aboard the *Hopewell*. Francis desperately wanted to talk to Michael again. The pair had a way of helping settle each other.

But Francis was very much alone. Michael was a frontier soldier a thousand miles away in Texas. Mary Rowland, like Father Devlin, and Francis's parents, and brother Patrick and sister Patsy, were dead. For all that Francis knew, Abraham and Ellen were gone too. The thoughts of his isolation fed the darkness.

At dawn, Francis returned to the sea exhausted and sore. His muscles and joints were painfully stiff, even his bones ached. Francis attributed the pain to having slept, more accurately trying to sleep, on the uneven sand the night before. The discomfort was not just from that but his darkened mental state. Francis's brain was twisting his thoughts along with his body.

Fearing that he had overshot the entrance to the Delaware River leading to Philadelphia, Francis pulled ashore in a place he would learn was Lewes, Delaware. While there, he was able to get fresh water in what impressed him as an ancient port town. There Francis secured updated directions from a grey sailor who looked as old as the port itself.

The somber mariner had been sitting on the dock as if waiting for death, with his eyes constantly looking out onto the Atlantic. *It comes from the east then*, Francis thought to himself as if the sailor had some magical insight into the end.

Throughout the rest of the day, Francis struggled. He could not concentrate with negative thoughts crowding his mind. Normally, Francis would not fixate on things such as death but now it was all he could think about. The lack of concentration cost him another day on the water as he mistakenly entered canals off the Delaware that did not lead to Philadelphia.

The second night Francis slept on the floor of the boat amongst the cattails of a vast marshland. Most of the night he spent staring up at the stars and listening to the sounds of the marsh, dozing off only in short intervals.

****

Eventually, Francis made it to Philadelphia. His small, secondhand boat looking as exhausted and worn as Francis himself. By calling to people ashore, Francis learned that the Vine Street Wharf would be the closest place for him to dock in relation to where his brother Mathew worked. At the wharf, Francis docked his boat at an open slip. He did not have the money to pay the fee and did not know when he would be back. Francis resigned himself to the fact that his faithful ship would be confiscated, and he would never see it again.

The wharf and surrounding buildings looked new. This was because there had been a devastating fire a few years before and everything had to be rebuilt.

There were a lot of Irish working on the docks and in the warehouses, and a good number of free blacks as well. They worked beside each other but not *with* each other. The tension was a matter of economics. The groups competed against each other for jobs and that drove wages down and mutual desperation up—and they resented each other because of it.

The streets in Philadelphia were more organized and neatly laid out than Norfolk and New York—the only other cities Francis was familiar with. The streets were numbered and with a pattern of cross streets named after trees. So relatively quickly, Francis found his way to Sixth Street and Chestnut.

Sure enough, there was the sign for the New Hat Store where Mathew worked. The storefront and factory facility above it were huge. Since his employment was more stable than his residence, Mathew had his mail sent to the hat shop and that was Francis's only means to contact him. Mathew had not been shy about his aspirations of eventually having his own shop, a big step up the social ladder for a famine Irishman.

Francis looked a wreck and felt worse, so he planned on waiting until he saw Mathew rather than surprise him in the store among his coworkers. The plan required patience as it took hours before Mathew finally appeared, hours in which Francis nervously wondered if his brother may have used a back door or possibly an alley he could not see from the street.

But Francis's surveillance of the front door paid off. Mathew exited the building with two other men, presumably colleagues. They walked in Francis's direction.

Mathew took a double take. It had been years since he had seen his little brother. He was caught off guard by Francis's appearance, but there was no mistaking his own. Especially since, of all the siblings, Francis and Mathew looked the most alike.

Although still in the throes of a depression, Francis could not help but smile at his brother's reaction. Mathew hugged Francis and kept asking his coworkers "Can you believe it? This is my little brother," although Francis was now both taller and stockier than Mathew.

The coworkers excused themselves and Mathew asked Francis to come with him to lunch. Although Francis had not eaten in days, he was not hungry. He took Mathew's offer anyway.

Mathew led the way to his regular spot, always having lunch on Thursdays at the Cahill Martin Tavern on 5th Street. He was on friendly terms with the staff and patrons alike. The owner, Joseph Cahill, greeted Mathew with a friendly handshake and an observation.

"By the looks of him," gesturing to Francis, "he belongs to you." The reference between the physical resemblance would come up repeatedly while Francis was in Philadelphia.

"This is my little brother." Mathew said proudly, "Just in from Virginia."

The two brothers made their way to a long table, one of several in the dark establishment. The only decoration to be found was the intricate woodwork along at the base and around the mirror of the bar. Everything else reeked of plainness. Mathew ordered for them both, knowing the menu board by heart and Francis not having any preference. Well, at least he thought he had no preference until Mathew ordered kidney and liver.

"It's good for you," Mathew said to Francis as if he was replacing their mother.

The barkeep whistled for Mathew to pick up the two ales he ordered, and Mathew placed them on the table between him and Francis.

"So brother, tell me everything. We have a lot to catch up on!" Mathew implored. As if to brace himself for the report, Mathew placed his elbow on the table and his chin in his hand.

Francis offered highlights, giving Mathew more details as to the circumstances of their father's death and how Francis sought to even the score with the Toobins.

"To hell with them!" Mathew growled, referring to the Toobins. "They are lucky you did not burn down their house with them in it. You had to do something Francis, and you did the right thing." Mathew said it recognizing how hard it must have been for Francis alone, without his brothers there to help him.

Then Francis went on to describe their sister Patsy's wedding, with the McNamara attendance weaker than any other event in a millennium. Mathew wished he, and the masses, could have been there for Patsy. "God rest her soul," Mathew said, all of Patsy's childhood harassment of her brothers long since forgiven.

Francis then tearfully moved on to the last time he saw their mother on the quay in Limerick. In her shawl, looking old, sitting atop a worn-out trunk that contained what few belongings she had left. Everything else she had given for them. And she would eventually give even more caring for their sister Patsy. Both brothers fell silent at the thought of it.

Wiping away his tears and clearing his throat, Francis went on to detail his one day with their brother Jamie in New York and his time in Norfolk. Francis had conveyed as much to Mathew previously in letters, but this time he added more details and responded to Mathew's questions.

When Francis told Mathew about the fever outbreak in Norfolk and the reason for his trip to Philadelphia, Mathew asked a question Francis had not thought about, "Do you have it?"

Thinking about the strange way he had been feeling, Francis hesitated. "It makes people sick to their stomach and their skin yellow. They die pretty quick, so I don't think so."

"That is good," Mathew replied, "because I would hate to have to kick your ass in the hereafter for killing me."

Francis did not laugh, and Mathew could see he had been through a lot.

"Alright, let's get you a room so you can rest up, and get you some new clothes," said Mathew in an authoritarian tone—akin to their father's voice.

"Yeah, there is a problem, I don't have any money. I have a sailboat worth a few dollars, but that may have been confiscated already at the wharf," confessed Francis.

"It's alright, brother, I can help you. One day I am going to be mayor of this town. I am making progress. We just have to get you back on your feet and you'll be good as gold. You'll be laughing again in no time," assured Mathew in a conspicuously upbeat tone.

Francis wanted to cry. He did not share his brother's optimism. He feared he would never laugh again. Yes, he was fortunate to have his oldest brother there when he needed him most, but Francis stressed because Mathew was his one and only lifeline. Francis knew that he was close to the abyss. He was broke, depressed, and left vulnerable in a world that crushes people day in and day out. One person, he feared, would not be enough to save him.

The tavern acted as an all-purpose service center for new arrivals to the city and Mathew knew how to work it well. He quickly had leads on a room—more specifically a cheap bed. A job would take more doing but Mathew had an idea on that too. And worried about his little brother's somber state, Mathew insisted on accompanying Francis to check on the sailboat.

****

At the Vine Street Wharf, they approached the sailboat just where Francis had left it. There was an old man standing nearby eyeing the boat. "Want to buy it?" Francis queried the old man as he checked the inside of the vessel for the anchor and other items. They were still there.

"If this is your boat, you owe me a dollar for use of the slip," the old man said with attitude, "and an apology as well. You just don't use people's property without asking. Where do you think you are, Ireland?" The old man picking up on Francis's origins based on his appearance and brogue, and those origins triggering the old man's intolerant, nativist leanings.

Francis's depression lifted in a heartbeat, which would have been good news had it not been replaced by rage. The old man's nasty tone was one thing, his insult to Ireland—when Francis was worn so thin, was too much. It struck a chord with Mathew as well.

Mathew knew even more than Francis about anti-Irish bias among many in America, particularly in Philadelphia. Mathew had seen the charred remnants in the city's neighborhoods of Kensington and Southwark. Twenty people died and scores of buildings had been burnt to the ground, including two Catholic churches, in nativist riots targeting Irish Catholic immigrants.

Mathew had a greater ability to control his temper than did Francis. With Francis so emotionally agitated to start with, the gratuitous instigation made Francis's fuse even shorter than usual. Mathew recognized what was happening. He noticed the change in how Francis held himself, the sternness and determination of his expression, the reddening of his face, and the tone of his voice. Francis was going to "lose the rag," as they said in Ireland. And he was going to do it, nature and nurture arguments aside, in the same way their father did.

If Mathew did not do something to stop the encounter now, he would have to help Francis bury the old man's body later.

"I'll tell you where I think I am," Francis growled as he strode toward the old man, "In the company of a complete and arrogant fool."

Mathew grabbed Francis from behind and held on with all his might, which he feared would not be enough. *Jesus, he has grown*, Mathew thought to himself, now fully appreciating how much taller and muscular Francis had become.

The old man did not expect Francis's reaction and quickly backed away. Mathew swung around to the front of Francis pitting all his weight into his younger brother's chest but was losing ground.
"He is an old man, just an old man, you don't want to hurt an old man," Mathew whispered to Francis. Mathew succeeded in making Francis think consciously, the subconscious rage now had to take a back seat. Francis broke off the attack.

****

"Take me for a ride," Mathew said, signaling toward the sailboat but not taking his arms off Francis out of fear his brother was just feigning de-escalation, an old family trick. Within minutes of being on the water again, the rage hormones began to subside altogether within Francis, and totally disappeared when Mathew got Francis to laugh—an impressive feat all considered.

Mathew recounted when, shortly before he and his brother Jamie immigrated, all the McNamara boys decided to do something together—something they would remember. They trekked, on foot, an entire day from their home to the Cliffs of Moher. The cliffs, more than seven hundred feet high at points, overlook the Atlantic and are among the most beautiful geological features in the world.

At the time, the poverty was such that Mathew was wearing thick sack socks in lieu of shoes. While Francis and the youngest McNamara brother, Patrick, were a distance away admiring the cliffs' beauty, Mathew thought of pranking his youngest siblings and enlisted his brother Jamie to help.

Mathew took off his sack socks and handed them to Jamie, and then made his way down to a small outcropping about twenty feet below the cliff's edge. Mathew laid down as if he landed there from a fall from above. Jamie held Mathew's socks in his hand and looked desponded at Francis and Patrick when they returned.

Jamie told them, in feigned dismay, "I tried to hold onto Mathew by his feet," looking at the socks, "but he slipped out of my hands." Jamie then looked over the cliff's edge as if he were afraid what he might find. Francis and Patrick looked as well to see Mathew splayed out on the outcropping below. They shrieked in horror which made the older two brothers break out in laughter.

Francis, even years later at the retelling, had to shake his head in disbelief. "The both of you are idiots," he said, referring to Mathew and Jamie. "I remember thinking God help America with these nit-wits coming in."

"We had to make sure you wouldn't forget us," offered Mathew with a smile.

"You don't forget that kind of stupidity," noted Francis. To his credit, Mathew persisted in trying to lift his brother's spirits further, telling every funny family story he could think of and reminding Francis how they had sailed down the Fergus together as youngsters, just as they were now sailing down the Delaware.

The brothers followed the Delaware River retracing how Francis entered the city. In this direction, as they faced forward in the old sailboat, New Jersey was on their left and Pennsylvania, more specifically Philadelphia, on their right. They hugged the Philadelphia shoreline to where it meets the Schuylkill River.

They navigated the backchannel that separated Philadelphia proper from League Island, later home to the Philadelphia Navy Yard. There, they came upon what struck Francis as a technological marvel. The just completed Girard Avenue Bridge.

The bridge, which allowed foot and carriage traffic to cross the Schuylkill into the city, was impressive. One of the longest bridges of its day, it spanned more than a thousand feet and reached more than thirty feet up from the water of the river. The angled wooden supports of the bridge's threespan sections gave it an elegant appeal and the appearance of stability. The fact that people could envision, design, and construct something so grand gave Francis hope—a valuable commodity since the onset of his depressive episode.

The bridge made Francis think of his late friend Mary Rowland and her having asked, "What other wonders await us?" The bridge's symbolism of how people could work together and produce something that helped them all collectively was a triumph she would have appreciated. It was good Francis did not know then that the bridge would ultimately be condemned a few years later due to poor design and shoddy construction. But on that day, however, it stood as a testament to human possibility.

After passing underneath the bridge, Mathew suggested Francis steer the sailboat to the old ferry station. The company that operated the ferry had been bankrupted by the very bridge that Francis had been marveling at. The area now was falling into disuse. Mathew indicated the sailboat would be as safe there as anywhere else, especially if they pulled the boat out of the water and covered it with one of the discarded tarps lying about.

After concealing the boat, Francis followed Mathew up the nearby embankment onto Girard Street. They went east on Girard which was a major commercial thoroughfare. On the corner of 12th Street, Francis noticed an office and storage facility operated by the Quartermaster of the United States Army. Francis was unsure what a quartermaster was, and he had become too tired to ask.

The signs related to the Army, which included recruitment posters for the 8th Infantry and other units, made Francis think of his friend Michael Scanlon. Michael enlisted in the Army while in Norfolk and was now stationed at a fort in Texas. Francis was overdue in writing Michael, but he had nothing positive to tell him anyway. The fact that Michael was Ellen's brother, the woman Francis loved, complicated things even more in terms of correspondence.

The brothers turned south on Broad Street and trudged several more blocks until finally reaching Walnut Street and Eddie McNevin's boarding house. Mathew was acquainted enough with McNevin to make introductions and to avoid being exploited for the cost of a bed, sheets, and toiletries. Francis flopped onto the bed and Mathew instructed him to drop by the shop the next day at noon. From there they could buy Francis some clothes, as none of Mathew's clothes would fit his larger younger brother. Besides, Mathew wanted Francis to look good when he introduced him to someone special, but Francis did not hear that part as he had fallen asleep.

The sleep, more accurately a nap, only lasted a couple of hours. It was not even restful as Francis had nightmares, although this time he could not remember the details. Waking in a new place, Francis felt disoriented and he had to wait until the church bells rang to know what time it was— only ten o'clock in the evening. His first exhausting day in Philadelphia seeming to last forever.

Francis could not go back to sleep despite his exhaustion. The intrusive thoughts and overthinking worsened as the night progressed. All the negative things he had seen, done, and even contemplated in his life came back and stayed with him as if a cancerous boomerang. Francis decided at least to stay put in bed to not stress his body any further.

The moonlight struck his room in such a way that the money Mathew had left, pocket money for Francis to use, shone brightly on the bureau aside the bed. Francis was not hungry, but he did appreciate everything Mathew was doing for him.

****

The next day, Mathew demanded Francis try on clothes that were too fancy to be practical. "I don't need these," Francis complained.

"No, I do," Mathew responded, explaining that he was bringing Francis to meet his fiancé and her family that night. "You will be the only family of mine they will meet. So, please—please—be charming Francis and leave the brawler home," begged Mathew.

"Fiancé? You never mentioned that in your letters," remarked Francis.

"This is because things are moving fast. Her father is wellto-do and can set me up with my own shop. Imagine that Francis, my own shop, here in America. Just as importantly, he can help get you a job."

"Wow! That is fantastic, I am happy for you, Mathew," said Francis earnestly, "What is her name?"

"Emily, Emily Whitney and, you should probably know this," Mathew became very serious, "her father is a complete and utter jackass."

"So, it's true, a girl marries her father," quipped Francis, starting to get his sense of humor back.

"No, I am serious, like Oliver Cromwell and a Charles Trevelyan type jackass." Mathew said referring to British leaders responsible for atrocities against the Irish. "But he is a means to an end. And that end will benefit us both, so promise me you will not lose it with Mr. Whitney tonight?"

"Aren't you the cute hoor," Francis said, using the Irish phrase for one acting dumber than they are in order to shape things. And to tease Mathew further, Francis added, "Is that what you call him, Mr. Whitney, not Dad?"

"Yeah, well, I will be taking to calling you *gobshite*." Mathew responded, with both he and Francis's brogues thickening and their use of native phrases increasing the more they spoke together. But lost in the exchange, however, was that Francis never provided the requested assurance his brother had asked for in relation to not losing it with Mr. Whitney.

****

That evening, Francis and Mathew took what impressed Francis as a smart innovation, a horse-drawn streetcar that traveled on rails. The rails lessened resistance so the horses could pull more weight for longer distances with reduced effort. Francis had seen one before when his brother Jamie had given him a tour of New York City, but the one in Philadelphia was brand new—in operation only a year.

Mathew explained how his future father-in-law moved to West Philadelphia because the new transportation would eventually increase the value of homes there. "He is always thinking about money," Mathew advised, with a measure of respect.

The brothers arrived at the home—a mansion really—on Chestnut and Thirty-fourth Streets. It was almost as impressive as the Rowland house in Norfolk, although of a totally different design. It was a large, stone three-story structure, with a wraparound porch covering half of the home's large footprint. Its windows were huge and each one let in, Francis guessed, four times as much sun as he was getting in from the dirty window in his boarding house room.

The lawn surrounding the home had ivy as ground cover, and a little flower garden equipped with a bench for thought and reflection in the back. Again, Francis dismissed thoughts he could ever have such a home while, in contrast, Mathew was picturing himself feet up on the living room sofa, smoking a cigar.

Francis met Emily and thought her nice, although not the conversationalist Mathew needed as a foil. Emily had lost her mother some years before and it was just her and her father in the residence, not including the help: a cook, a maid, and a gardener/handyman—all potato famine Irish. Her father, Gordon Whitney, was heavyset, with thinning white hair, and a large set of graying porkchop sideburns.

At first, Mr. Whitney did not say much. He was too preoccupied reading the newspaper from his armchair to acknowledge anyone, let alone a newcomer like Francis. Once Mr. Whitney came to the dinner table, however, he only shut up to swallow his meal. It seemed Mr. Whitney, a successful businessman, believed that his expertise applied to all areas of human endeavor, and some of the Almighty's as well.

Mr. Whitney's broadcasted opinion on immigration was decidedly against, even though he was surrounded by Irish immigrants and their presence contributed to his business success. The desperation that drove immigration also drove down labor costs. That made the "nativists" angry and resentful but made men like Whitney rich.

The growing Whitney empire was built on textile manufacturing and retail. What Whitney would never acknowledge out loud was that it was also built on the backs of immigrants and poor nativists whom Whitney paid enough to keep alive, but in squalor.

Francis was thinking to himself that Mathew should move out of Philadelphia as soon as he got married. Otherwise, even if Mathew had the patience of Job, he would eventually strangle the pompous old windbag, Gordon Whitney.

Whitney eventually slowed down in his lecture and Mathew took it as a cue to introduce Francis. And to keep it relevant for Whitney, Mathew did so by including a business reference.

"Mr. Whitney, Francis here did interesting work operating a wharf and boatyard. A profitable line of business in Virginia." Mathew stated proudly looking at his brother.

"Be mindful of your elocution Mathew. You are starting to sound very Irish again." Whitney made the remark despite knowing Mathew had been working extremely hard to sound American.

It was true Mathew's brogue had intensified due to his exchanges with Francis whose accent was even more distinct. But Whitney's rebuke was still harsh and provocative in light of the composition of his guests.

At first, Francis bristled at both Whitney's insult and the thought that his brother was abandoning his Irishness. But not wanting to appear rattled by Whitney and to let his brother save face, Francis attempted to distract those at the table with humor.

"Actually, to my ear, Mathew is talking so slowly these days and pronouncing his Hs and Rs such that I would say he sounds more Canadian than anything else." Francis offered an imploring smile as he spoke. He assumed the comment unoffensive because he had heard that "Americans" and Canadians teased each other good-naturedly.

The attempt fell flat. Whitney just stared at Francis blankly, Emily looked puzzled, and Mathew coughed awkwardly.

While Whitney was always hard on Mathew, his future sonin-law was actually a source of pride for the businessman. A diamond Whitney deemed himself shaping out of the pile of shit that he considered the Irish. Mathew had worked his way up taking on every unenviable task in the Whitney organization.

Looking at Francis, Whitney said, "Your brother has made great progress here in Philadelphia. Not just in how he speaks but in business. He has been willing to learn and work hard," as if normally such traits were beyond an Irishman.

"And thankfully he abandoned that anathema of Papism and join our church."

As if intending to either drive a wedge between the brothers or test Francis's malleability, Whitney just stared at Francis awaiting a response.

"You're a Protestant are you now, Mathew?" Francis asked turning to his brother smiling—trying to hold his rage at his brother for completely selling out. "Very progressive and intellectually flexible of you," Francis continued with the smile painted on his face.

Whitney interrupted before Mathew could respond, posing questions himself to Francis. It was at this point that Mathew recalled Francis had not formally promised to avoid tangling with the prospective father-in-law.

In Mathew's mind, Francis—like everyone else in their family save their mother—would fight tooth and nail to combat a stupid slight. That trait was most embodied in their father who drank and fought because life was unfair. Having watched it, Mathew knew that response not only failed as a remedy but usually made things worse. And this time, should Francis choose to brawl with Whitney, the result could undo years of Mathew's hard work and compromise. Sacrifice calculated by Mathew to eventually leave him independent and no longer beholden to Whitney and those like him. Mathew just needed time and some luck to beat them at their own game.

But Mathew would soon learn Francis was not their father.

"Are you still a papist?" Mr. Whitney asked of Francis. The first part of Francis's reply was true, and the second part was pure malarky.

"No, I am not a Catholic anymore." Francis advised.

Then to take charge of the conversation, Francis said with a smile, "Mathew has told me in his letters that he has learned a lot from you. So, you may be interested to know, I have been trying to apply some of those lessons myself albeit from afar. There have been some bumps along the road but that has only given me a chance to show—what is it you call it? Perseverance."

"Splendid!" Mr. Whitney exclaimed with one large eyebrow lifted. Prompting the old man to offer something positive in a backhanded way, "Mathew tells me you are looking for work. Now I cannot show any favoritism, it is bad enough what I have done for Mathew, so I would have to start you at the very bottom."

"I wouldn't expect anything more," Francis said, continuing to smile to mask his growing animosity. "But you know, based on what both Mathew and I have learned from you and other factors, I realize that I may not be ready yet for such an opportunity. I feel that I need to do more to ready myself and also to do my part to thank this country for welcoming me in my wild state."

Francis went on talking through his smile: "I have a friend in the army at Fort Davis in Texas. He is fighting savages. He advised they desperately need men. If you trust me enough to offer me a job, I feel confident enough I can be a good soldier and do my part in the fighting. You know, so others more worthy can stay here at home." Francis glanced at Mathew.

Continuing Francis said, "Out West, I am told, it is easier to spot the savages than it is here in the East. Out there, they paint themselves red. In any event, I will return to you with the West pacified and as a better man in a better country."

Mathew was completely puzzled by what Francis just said and had no idea how Mr. Whitney would take what was clearly passive-aggressive nonsense.

"Outstanding," said Mr. Whitney gleefully. "Mathew, why didn't you tell me you were sharing my teachings with others."

Mathew just shrugged his shoulders, mystified as to who was pulling the prank on him, Francis, Mr. Whitney, or both.

"There may be some money to be made in this. A book or lecture tour," Whitney remarked, proud of himself. "I can't imagine many Irish can read or have the pluck you two have, but there may be enough to turn a profit."

****

On the way back home, Francis and Mathew walked the entire way as the streetcar had stopped service for the day. The long walk is what both needed.

"Turning down a job here for the Army, what are you thinking?" Mathew questioned.

Francis sighed and tried to be as kind as he could: "Mathew, you are my brother and I appreciate all the help you have given me. Especially now, when I needed it most, but if I had to spend any more time with that man, I would batter him!"

Mathew laughed and acknowledged that his impending father-in-law could be a handful. "He can't be all bad," Mathew noted, "Emily is as sweet as they come, and he presumably had a hand in that."

"Presumably," Francis replied, implying more doubt than certitude on the matter.

"I have to admit, you really had me going," disclosed Mathew, "I had no idea what you were going to make up next and whether Whitney would keep falling for it." Then Mathew looked down sheepishly and, referring to his religious conversion, asked if he had disappointed Francis.

"Look Mathew," Francis said grabbing his brother by the shoulders, "We were all dealt a terrible hand, me, you, and Jamie. We must survive and if that means compromising and doing things we don't want to do, then so be it. In time, if we are lucky, we may get a chance to make decisions on our own terms."

Francis continued as if for the first time he was the wiser brother: "Of the three of us, you are the furthest along in reaching that day. So, don't be so hard on yourself."

"I can only imagine what Da would say to me," posited Mathew referring to their father. "He hated the Protestants so much."

"Get over yourself," Francis responded, "You were a terrible Catholic and you'll be an even worse Protestant, Da would say the laugh is on them."

Mathew, a big smile on his face, agreed. "Can I buy an Army recruit a drink?"

"You can if you can explain to me your new religion. What is it you Protestants pray to—horses' asses?" Francis said, with Mathew putting him into a headlock as a result.

****

The next day, hungover, Mathew walked Francis to the army facility on Girard Street, the one they had passed after hiding Francis's sailboat. Francis went in and, after about an hour, came out and advised he had just been sworn into the United States Army. The Army had given him transportation money and reporting instructions for Fort Davis, Texas. Francis would be out of Philadelphia before sunset.

Francis advised, when the Army asked him his civil occupation, he had said hatmaker. "So, tell Mr. Whitney to keep that spot open for me." Mathew laughed.

Before leaving, Francis gave Mathew all rights and privileges to the sailboat. Francis asked whenever Mathew was aboard to think of their time together and to plan for when they would be together again.

"It is a deal," Mathew replied.

"So, this is it." Remarked an emotional Francis. Mathew gave him a hug and directed Francis to write.

The two brothers would never be closer than they were at that moment. Forces were in play, however, to drive them apart and to destroy them both.

Chapter Seven
The Frontier West

Fort Davis, Texas
1855-1856

After taking every mode of transportation that then existed to get from the East Coast to West Texas, Francis arrived at Fort Davis. Although he had marveled at the newer technologies of the streetcar, locomotive, steamship, and the stagecoach, the fact was he traveled nearly two thousand miles and was exhausted.

Fortunately, when he reported to Sergeant George Valentine as directed, Francis was told he would have a few days to rest and acclimate as the Sergeant was waiting on more recruits. Francis asked where he could find a soldier who was already there. A recruit named Michael Scanlon.

"A friend of Private Scanlon's? That is good. I'll bring you to him after I show you around the fort," informed Sergeant Valentine.

The fort did not look anything like Francis expected. In some ways it was beautiful, ringed on three sides by broad, textured canyon walls some 200 feet tall. The rocks in the canyon were a rich orange-brown color, among the oldest things on earth. Picturesque streams fed a nearby lake and the canyon floor was green with brush, vegetation, and trees that included cottonwoods and ponderosa pines.

It was less arid than the other parts of Texas Francis had seen on his trip into the fort. Francis also noticed the air did not seem as polluted as the cities he had called home on the East Coast, a distinction he deemed good for his health.

Valentine pointed out the facilities on the outskirts of the fort. The wagon yard, storage area, corral, blacksmith, armory, cookhouse, mess, commissary, and the guardhouse—which was not much more than a box. The Sergeant went on to reference the pair of powder magazines partially dug into the ground, the arsenal, and the officers' quarters. Then the wide parade grounds were highlighted as was the series of one-story wooden buildings housing the enlisted men's bunks.

Valentine informed that Francis was assigned to Company D and pointed to a bunk Francis could use in the building that the company called home. The Sergeant informed that after initial training Francis would be doing everything with the other members of the company. And by everything Valentine specified he meant eating, sleeping, shitting, and following orders as little else was of consequence to a frontier soldier.

"You can put your belongings in the trunk at the foot of the bed," Valentine advised.

Francis did not have much. He had the clothes on his back, the same he been wearing when he hastily left Norfolk, the fancy set of clothes his brother Mathew had purchased for him in Philadelphia, and two books. Sergeant Valentine took note of the books Francis had carried with him across the country. The history book which was a gift from his mother that he took from Ireland and the philosophy book Father Devlin had given him in Norfolk before the yellow fever outbreak. A recruit who could read, Valentine thought to himself, a good sign.

"You are now a member of Company D, 8th Infantry. We number, including yourself, two hundred eighty-eight enlisted men and officers. We should be around four hundred, so tell your off-the-boat friends back east to join." Valentine was not kidding. At the time, the Army's only fertile ground for recruiting of white men was the desperate Irish immigrants.

"Virtually everyone is on patrol now with the Colonel," explained Valentine, "when he leads in the field, he only patrols-in-force." That fact made Valentine contemplate yet again how he was supposed to defend the fort with the Colonel gone. He had one new recruit, the cooking crew, one inmate locked in the guard house, the doc, and the menagerie on sick call. They would not last a minute if an Indian war party of any size decided to waltz into the fort. The lack of a palisade and obstructions on the canyon walls drove the Sergeant crazy.

Finally, the Sergeant walked Francis to the medical building where the doctor, usually an assistant or two from the enlisted men, and all the soldiers excused from duty that day due to illness or injury would be.

A frontier soldier was much more likely to die from disease than Indian attack. Illnesses from tainted food and water, such as cholera and dysentery, were common. As were communicable diseases like tuberculosis, the disease that killed Francis's mother, sister and brother-in-law in Ireland. With germs and contagion theory not fully understood, all manner of illness and disease befell those living in the fort.

Sergeant Valentine had suggested they move the graveyard outside of the canyon ostensibly for sanitary reasons. But just as important to Valentine was mitigating the morale problem stemming from soldiers constantly looking upon the ever-increasing number of graves.

Inside the building, it took a moment for Francis to recognize Michael. Michael was pale and emaciated, even skinnier than when they had gotten off the *Hopewell* together nearly five years before. Wincing in pain, Michael did not immediately recognize Francis either. But that familiar smile returned to Michael's face when he heard Francis's voice. Sergeant Valentine noticed and was happy Francis could lift Michael's spirits. The Sergeant also took note of Scanlon calling Francis "Fireball." As a result, Francis would be teasingly called Fireball by those in his company, alternatively "Mac," and less frequently as McNamara or Francis.

Francis spoke to Michael for a few minutes and was even able to make him laugh although it seemed painful for his old friend. Sergeant Valentine left the building after talking to the regimental surgeon, Dr. Elkins. Francis ran after the Sergeant.

"Scanlon is seriously ill," Francis reported to Valentine. "He needs to go home to his family. Michael has a sister in Norfolk if the fever outbreak there has subsided and a brother, Thomas, in western Virginia. A place called Three Churches if I remember right. I can get more details if Michael can't provide them."

Sergeant Valentine advised that he was familiar with Michael's case. There was a recommendation that Scanlon be discharged already pending with the Colonel. Valentine assured Francis that in the meantime Michael would get the best treatment available from the fort's doctor.

Valentine did not say Michael would be made well. In fact, the Sergeant had serious reservations about the prevailing medical treatments at the time. The well-meaning Dr. Elkins followed all the established protocols of the day, carefully measured doses of arsenic, mercury, whiskey, and, of course, the occasional bloodletting. In Valentine's estimation, those interventions just made people worse. But then again what did Valentine know, he was no doctor.

The petition for Scanlon's discharge had been signed by Sergeant Valentine, Dr. Elkins, and Lieutenant James Longstreet. Private Scanlon had been an excellent soldier until he and two others contracted some type of illness that Dr. Elkins could not identify. Most illnesses at the fort went without a name or an understanding of its cause. The other two showed symptoms first. One died and the other deserted, apparently with the help of his family and fellow soldiers. Michael's condition was poor and getting worse.

When considering the petition, Lieutenant Colonel Lawrence Rogers, the regimental and fort commander, was under pressure from his superiors to keep up troop numbers. Although not so much an issue in Sergeant Valentine's company, the desertion rate for the regiment overall was nearly fifty percent. The illness and injuries among the remaining soldiers diminished the troop strength even more. Recruitment efforts were proving unable to compensate so Rodgers needed bodies, even Michael Scanlon's sick one.

Although the order had not been issued yet, the Colonel had already rejected the petition to discharge Michael. Instead, he granted Michael a few more days medical leave to get himself in order. After that, Private Michael Scanlon was to return to full duty or face punishment for being a malinger. When Sergeant Valentine heard of the Colonel's decision, he started selecting names in his head for the burial detail. Michael would not last long.

****

In the three days since Francis's arrival at Fort Davis, only one other recruit had arrived. Another famine Irishman named Kevin O'Brien from County Cork. Francis and O'Brien would undergo their orientation and initial training together. They were fortunate because their development would be overseen by Sergeant Valentine, and he was one of the best.

First and foremost, Sergeant Valentine knew a lot about soldiering along the frontier. Not just from life experience, which included fighting native tribes for years and being a veteran of the Mexican War. He was also well-read although not formally educated.

The Sergeant exchanged books with Dr. Elkins at the fort and other people Valentine knew throughout the Army. He read books on military theory and training, not just written by Americans, but military minds around the world. To keep himself balanced, he also read novels, poetry, and books on science as well as history. He had just read a book on a new way to increase soldier strength and endurance, a program called calisthenics. He planned to experiment with it in his training program for the company.

Just as importantly, Valentine was perceptive and knew how to tailor his communications to the audience at hand. In the case of Francis and O'Brien, Valentine adopted an irreverent, humorous approach to the training. He did not do so for the benefit of the students, but rather their collective survival. Francis and O'Brien needed to be capable frontier fighters or they, their fellow soldiers, and the entire fort would be in peril.

A tall, thin but wiry man, Valentine was approaching 30 years old. He looked much older than that for good reason. In 1840, when he was 14 years old, Valentine's family and several others formed a caravan and set out for the West Coast. They left behind Tennessee where they were unable to make a living.

Two months into their journey, outside of San Antonio, Texas, Indian warriors attacked the group. Indians Valentine would later come to know as Comanche. Valentine had gone ahead of the caravan with another older boy to scout for drinking water. They arrived back just in time to watch, helplessly at a distance, as the Indians scalped the men and older boys and left them for dead, eighteen in all. The women and remaining children were hauled away as captives. Valentine never heard from his mother and younger siblings again. He buried his father's butchered body where it fell.

Since then, Valentine had seen countless additional atrocities and injustices. Sometimes Indians were the perpetrators, often they were the victims. Valentine theorized that Indians and whites could not coexist; they would keep fighting until one side was annihilated.

His thinking was that God made him white, so he was bound to fight for that side. Valentine would therefore kill Indians when required, not out of revenge or hate but, in his mind, to end the insanity. If Valentine were to die in the process, that would just be God's will. And who was Valentine to question that?

Unfortunately for the Indians, Valentine was good at what he did. And what he did was not just kill Indians himself but turn inept recruits like Francis and O'Brien into real soldiers. A real soldier, in Valentine's mind, did not simply follow orders but was one who understood the mission, maintained situational awareness, and improvised as needed to be successful. Concepts ahead of their time. To get a recruit to that advanced state required some doing, at task Valentine found himself good at.

After the designated bugle call on Francis's fourth day at the fort, Francis and O'Brien met Valentine on the parade ground. Valentine started his lecture with the big picture: "Our assigned mission is to secure the trail between San Antonio and El Paso. We are also to survey and report on the surrounding territory and keep the peace. There are several obstacles in relation to that mission, not the least of which are the Apaches, Comanches, and Kiowa. More about that later."

Valentine then had the two new recruits layout their recently issued uniforms, equipment, and weapons on a canvas tarp the Sergeant had put on the ground. Valentine picked up one of the haversacks the pair had been issued and asked the two recruits what the uses of a haversack were. Francis and O'Brien looked at each other puzzled, with O'Brien eventually speaking up, "To carry things."

Sergeant Valentine hesitated a second, threw the haversack to the ground, and for dramatic effect walked directly up to O'Brien and leaned into his face, "Let me ask you this O'Brien, do you want your dick cut off?"

"No, Sergeant," mumbled O'Brien, confused.

"Well let me make this clear. The people we call savages out there," as Valentine pointed to the expanse of land beyond the fort, "are not savages at all. They are just desperate and determined to survive and it's their fighting style that is savage. Their war tactics are cunning and ruthless because they have to be, and they are not bound by the white man's ways or values. In fact, on principle, they reject our ways whenever they can."

Valentine continued as in a trance, "They run when we have the advantage and attack when we don't. They target our weak points and act at a time most opportune for them and least opportune for us. I fully expect to be killed by an Indian club to my skull while I am sitting in the outhouse."

Now looking over the two new soldiers' heads to the distant horizon, Valentine added, "They are willing to kill anyone when they deem it to their advantage. Soldiers, settlers, women, children, are all fair game under their rules. They cut off scalps, ears and, yes O'Brien—dicks, and keep them as trophies. I have seen it all with my own eyes." That was as close as Valentine would get to talking about what happened to his family.

"You, me, all of us in this fort have to be equally ferocious," said Valentine in an increasingly emotional tone. "Fort Bliss is to the north and Fort Lancaster is to the west, but each are several days' ride from here. If we cannot defend ourselves, the message we should send to them is 'assign a burial detail.' So, every item you are issued and everything that is around, for the duration of your tenure with this command, must be looked at as a tool to keep you alive and to allow you to fight."

Valentine hesitated and then asked the shocked pair of Irishmen, "Do you understand?" Both men responded in unison, "Yes, Sergeant."

"Now," Valentine continued, "tell me how you can use that haversack to defend yourself and your fellow soldiers in this fort?"

Francis volunteered that the haversack could be fashioned into a slingshot or a garrote to strangle an attacker. O'Brien suggested the haversack could be put over someone's head to disorient, even suffocate them.

"You boys may just keep those dicks yet," declared a satisfied Valentine. An ironic speculation in the case of O'Brien as he would go onto live to an old age and eventually have 21 children.

The day's training continued, spanning a wide variety of mostly administrative topics. The new soldiers were shown how to wear, clean, and store their newly issued uniforms. O'Brien remarked when putting on the uniform for the first time: "The ladies are going to love me in this."

Francis thought for a second and replied, "Well, at least the blind ones."

Sergeant Valentine, wearing his own uniform in pristine fashion, exceeding Army requirements, told the new recruits that the uniforms must have been secretly designed by the Indians to get a tactical advantage. The ensemble, made of wool and other heavy materials, was too hot for Texas, restricted movement of soldiers when working and fighting, and was uncomfortable on even the briefest of marches.

Valentine added, "Hell, they are ugly to boot and offer no camouflage in this part of the country."

Francis smirked at O'Brien when the Sergeant said the uniforms were ugly.

"Therefore, I will not be a stickler about your uniform or adherence to regulations in that regard," announced Valentine. "The exception is if officers are around. If you are caught out of compliance by an officer, you will be disciplined. Your crime, in my mind, will not be uniform violations but stupidity at being caught. You have to learn not to be stupid."

"Yes, Sergeant!" The pair replied.

"Tomorrow I am releasing you to construction detail. We have an ambitious schedule to build six new stone buildings to replace the shabby wooden ones now inside the fort," advised Valentine.

"Why do we have an ambitious schedule?" posed Valentine to the new soldiers with a leading tone. "So, we can keep our dicks!" Francis answered.

Sergeant Valentine was impressed and told the two men as much as he led them to the barracks to clean up before the call of the bugle for dinner. Along the walk, the Sergeant explained to the two young Irishmen the art of handling a pick and shovel. The tools were not there to simply move dirt but to allow them to get physically stronger and prepare for combat. More than once in history, the tools had been weapons themselves. So, technique mattered, focus mattered, and discipline mattered. The Sergeant used dirt as a training tool, no waste in that man's army.

****

The next morning the bugle call for assembly on the eastern portion of the parade ground brought out the entire 8th Infantry at the fort, many members having just returned late last night as the rearguard to the Colonel's patrol-in-force.

In his address to the troops, Colonel Rogers reiterated his commitment to have six new buildings constructed in the fort as quickly as possible. The buildings would be larger than the current structures and be made of stone rather than wood and have slate floors. The new building materials would make the soldiers safer, being more resistant to fire and bullets, and cooler during the triple-digit heat of West Texas summers.

Another advantage, the Colonel noted proudly, was that the buildings would be more aesthetically pleasing. Not to mention, Sergeant Valentine thought to himself, the more solid structures would tell the Indians the United States Army was here to stay. However, along that same vein, Valentine thought if he led the Indians, he would attack— and attack soon—before the buildings were complete.

The Colonel announced each company would be given construction plans and would work independently to build one structure each. The company that completed its building first would be granted extra leave.

What could go wrong with that? Valentine pondered. Speed over quality, companies sabotaging each other, were among a few possibilities that came to mind for the veteran. Although Valentine often used incentives in his own training, they usually centered around verbal praise and threatening to cut off soldiers' body parts. Incentives that could serve to promote undesirable as much as desirable conduct were to be guarded against in Valentine's book.

The Colonel neglected to mention that the construction project would not eliminate any of the soldiers' other duties. The burden of frequent patrols, escorting sensitive shipments, surveying, and acting as the region's primary law enforcement would not diminish. Nor would the more mundane tasks for the enlisted men of cleaning their own quarters and those of the officers. All this while the fort was significantly undermanned.

Another price would be deferral of projects recommended by Sergeant Valentine and other members of the noncommissioned staff. Projects such as the establishment of a defensive perimeter at the fort's entrance and better defenses should the enemy take the heights of the canyon walls were pushed aside by the Colonel. As was the request for a larger, more secure guardhouse.

Excitedly, the Colonel announced the construction would begin today with the labor-intensive task of digging foundations. The men were allowed to remove their covers and heavy frock coats. They could also strip back the upper portions of their long johns, as it was already surprisingly warm for that early in the day.

Francis kept an eye on Michael Scanlon the whole time at formation, fearing he would not be able to stand still that long while ill. Francis made his way over to Michael as Michael stripped to the waist like everyone else.

"Are you alright?" Francis asked of Michael.

"I have to be," Michael responded.

Committing himself to not leaving Michael's side, Francis thought back to the voyage on the *Hopewell* and Michael's kindness in sharing food when food was scarce and starvation the norm. Besides, Michael was Ellen's brother. In the event he ever saw her again, Francis did not want to say he left Michael alone so vulnerable.

Sergeant Valentine worked with Corporal Smith to scratch out measurements for the foundation. "Ok, Company D," the Sergeant said, "the plans call for a foundation and storage area, so we have to dig out this entire space four feet deep."

Sergeant Valentine looked over to the corporal who was holding the plans, the corporal nodded in quasi-agreement, neither man having any experience reading construction requirements. *Improvise*, the Sergeant thought to himself and doing something was usually better than doing nothing, so digging down four feet it was.

Four feet is nothing! Francis thought. While he had dug holes occasionally in Ireland, he had done it nearly every day while in Norfolk. Holes for pilings, holes for wells, holes for waste pits, holes for drainage, holes for supports to bulkheads and holes for retaining walls. He was never far from a shovel when working at the Rowland shipyard. And with all the men in the company chipping in, even discounting Michael, the task of the building foundation wouldn't be bad at all.

As one of the new men, Francis was chosen to be in the team to break ground. He grabbed a shovel looking forward to impressing everyone in the company and setting a blistering pace to get the job done. With the first plunge of the shovel, he hit a rock, and then another. Francis came to the realization he had been overly optimistic. Now he knew that he and his fellow soldiers were in trouble.

It triggered a flashback to his childhood in Ireland. His family farm seemed to be made of rock with some occasional dirt thrown in. On the trip to the United States, his friend, Mary Rowland had asked Francis what crops his family grew in County Clare. "Rocks, mostly," he told Mary, "We grew rocks." Rocks meant hard, backbreaking work and Francis grew concerned with the thought he may have grown soft digging in the sandy soil of Norfolk the past few years.

It was indeed slow going. Sergeant Valentine directed the men to dig in shifts to spread the work out and to keep the soldiers from exhausting themselves. When it was Michael's turn to dig, Francis pushed him back and took his turn.

Sergeant Valentine and other soldiers noticed but said nothing. This continued throughout the day.

****

The next morning, Francis reported with O'Brien for continued basic training. Francis was incredibly sore and had trouble moving his arms. Valentine said nothing but focused his initial lecture on how soldiers get stronger and how that strength is used to achieve the mission.

Valentine introduced but did not make Francis do the calisthenics and stretching program being adopted by the company. Valentine advised that periodically he challenged other companies to foot races, tugs-of-war, scaling up the canyon walls, wrestling, boxing matches, as well as shooting contests. He did not care who won, Valentine explained, he was just looking for improvement, improvement not just in Company D but the other companies as well.

"After all," the Sergeant explained, "they will be at your side when no one else will be." But that kind of activity would have to wait for Francis as Valentine knew that pushing an already spent soldier too hard could lead to injury and longterm problems.

In the afternoon, it was back to construction detail. Francis, his arms still aching from the previous day, was able to do one stint—barely. When it came time for Michael to dig, Francis again was about to jump back into the hole, but O'Brien stopped him, and jumped in.

"*Saothar foirne,*" teamwork, O'Brien said in Gaelic with a wink.

Again, Valentine saw and said nothing. Corporal Smith approached the Sergeant and was about the raise the topic, but Valentine's facial expression shut that down. *Must be another lesson*, the corporal thought to himself.

Eventually, other soldiers began to cover for Michael as well. It was clear he was sick, probably dying. More importantly, he was one of their own. Not just another Irishman lost in a new country, but a fellow soldier in the United States Army. Sergeant Valentine smiled. He was not making soldiers now; he was making a cohesive fighting force.

Later that week, Company D drew patrol duty. Although they were infantry, they used horses and mules for these patrols. They simply had too much ground to cover. The incorporation of horses led to officers to occasionally refer to enlisted men in the fort as troopers, a term usually more associated with calvary. Since they were not formally trained as cavalry, however, if fighting was to be done, they would dismount and use the infantry tactics they were taught by Sergeant Valentine and others. The tactics espoused by Valentine were both traditional and innovative, including the use of strategic movement, cover fire, diversion, flanking, and coordinated mass assaults.

"If the Indians attack us," Valentine lectured the men, "that is a pretty good sign we are not in a good place for defense. We will need to move quickly and as a group or, sure as hell, we will be picked off one at a time. That means generating consistent suppressive fire, undertaking real and feigned flanking movements and frontal assaults in a coordinated fashion. We have to keep them from pressing their advantage of surprise and positioning."

Valentine went on to advise, "And all that takes our keeping our wits about us. And you can bet your britches that the warriors will first try to separate you from your wits, because then separating you from your scalp and other parts becomes that much easier." O'Brien looked at Francis and covered his privates with his hands, as if that was his plan to save his genitals during an attack.

"One of their favorite strategies to scare you witless is the war cry," Valentine stated, following the statement with a half-human, half animalistic scream at the top of his lungs, making the troopers jump instinctively. "Yep, and I am not giving it justice. You will feel you are surrounded with all the dark angels of hell coming for your very soul."

With that, Valentine had the men break into small squads, moving from sitting and prone positions to the left, the right, backward, and forward as a group. Then he had them practice simultaneously shooting, loading, and moving— with some men in the squad providing cover fire. Then to make things even more realistic, he had each squad take turns trying to move and make decisions as the other soldiers charged at them, mimicking war cries, and even throwing rocks at the squad to simulate bullets.

Valentine told the men that a few welts in training was better than a warrior hatchet to the head later on. The last component of the training was having the troopers do all the exercises again, at dawn, just as they were about to eat breakfast, in the heat of day, and then once more in dark of night. Valentine would make them as prepared as possible.

But keeping them at a high state of vigilance would be difficult and that is what Valentine feared his adversaries were doing, trying to lull his soldiers into complacency. It has been a while since a warrior had been seen on a patrol.

To combat it, when the company seemed to be at its peak of preparedness, Valentine led them off on the portion of the vast, four hundred mile San Antonio-El Paso Road, onto a trail that he had been told by civilians that Comanches had been using for their livestock raids. Looking at maps he had annotated from earlier patrols, Valentine concluded use of that trail for raids would make sense in that it provided sufficient access to drinking water and feed for warriors and their horses, as well as relatively easy access to white settlements and ranches. However, the troopers found nothing, not even a recent hoof print or sign of a single night's encampment. The intelligence was either stale, wrong, or lost in the reporting. Or, as Valentine concluded, it was part of the native tribes' strategy to couple clever thinking with their mobility and knowledge of the terrain to be a threat to his mission, his life, and that of his men.

On the last night of the twelve day patrol, with Fort Davis now just hours away, Valentine announced sentry and picket duty assignments. Francis was assigned the first watch and would start close to the camp and rotate every 30 minutes to other positions until his 2-hour tour was done and he was relieved by another soldier. Valentine warned everyone not to let their guard down just because they were close to the fort.

"Wouldn't you attack when your enemy least expects it?" Valentine then directed those on watch to put pebbles in their shoes and back pockets, so the discomfort would keep them from dozing. They also were to set aside a portion of their canteen to rub water on their eyes periodically and to repeatedly remind themselves how severe the penalty could be if they were caught sleeping.

When O'Brien came to relieve Francis from guard duty two hours later the full moon gave the whole area an orange glow. If Indian warriors were going to attack that night at least they would see them coming. O'Brien was relieved he would have the advantage of the moonlight and remarked to Francis: "The one thing Valentine is not taking into account is that by keeping us on edge all the time we are eventually going to have a nervous breakdown. I hardly ate this whole patrol, figuring it would just slow me down with vomit and shit once the warriors came calling."

"I am with you," Francis replied. "Much more of this and I am going to develop a twitch and shoot myself or another soldier in the ass with my jumpy trigger finger."

O'Brien laughed loud enough for Valentine to hear as he was supervising the change in guard.

Valentine growled intensely: "Shut up or I will cut both your throats."

Unfortunately, that made Francis and O'Brien, both deliriously tired, laugh even harder. Valentine stormed over menacingly and was about to threaten the two Irishman yet again but knew that would probably make things worse.

"God damn it," Valentine mumbled to himself, why hadn't he seen he had driven the troopers to hysterics. He needed to push them to the line but not over it. Pushing too hard would defeat the goal of making them effective fighters. "O'Brien, go back to camp and put yourself together. I will take the first portion of your tour and you will get extra duty to make up for it when we get back to the fort. And either of you ladies have another giggle fit like that again..." But Valentine caught himself, remembering that he did not want to make the duo's laughing fit any worse and God forbid result in him joining in because of his own exhausted state.

When Francis and O'Brien returned to the camp they were surprised to see a fire, a luxury of warmth that Valentine did not allow outside of meals. There was also a surprising number of troopers still awake, they were overtired and excited about returning to the safety and relative niceties of a real bed and prepared meals.

No one spoke and the only sound was the crackling of the fire. That was until O'Brien decided to sing. He sang a song Francis had not heard before, for O'Brien had written it himself, his homespun poetry and songs he was normally too self-conscious to share. His exhaustion emboldened him.

In my dreams I see it,
A field that lies fallow,
And still the field will stay, until I escape this shadow

In the shadow my fate I know not
I endlessly endure burden, forced to risk and to gamble
No hearth, no place for me, in the dark only to ramble

All else of the past blur and the future forever unclear
Except for the faces of those I left, and those who left me
All those I hold dear

But in my dream the peaceful stream takes me
  To a cottage filled with laughter,
Filled with those who do not dread just to be

There I will see, clear as day
Those I left, and those that left me
In the cottage filled with laughter
And joy forever after

Until then, the field lies fallow
And I live, till I sleep, in the shadow

A sadness fell over the troopers. The song spoke to the Irish famine survivors, more than half the troopers, but the rest as well. All of them were lonely and it was hard luck that universally pushed them out to that West Texas desert. They were there to battle and suppress others as desperate as themselves.

****

Michael's illness abated for a while, but then returned with a vengeance. He became so weak that the option of deserting was totally gone, even if the whole fort was willing to turn a blind eye. Absent a discharge, Michael was going to die.

Dr. Elkins reported to Sergeant Valentine that Michael's symptoms were tracking those of Corporal Andrew Buchanan who had died two months earlier.
The doctor, and other officers, approached the Colonel to reconsider discharging Michael. The Colonel once again refused.

With desertion still running high and so many troopers asking for discharges, Colonel Rogers thought he could only put an end to it by being harsh and feared. He would make an example of Michael. By rejecting Michael's request for a discharge, which by all indication was justified, the Colonel was sending a clear message to everyone else: no discharges. The Colonel notified his officers that he planned to send an equally clear message related to desertion. "God help the next man caught attempting that," Colonel Rogers warned.

Often those caught trying to desert would spend time in the guardhouse and then get extra duty and lose pay. Occasionally, physical punishment of various sorts would be added. But the death penalty was never totally out of the question, and the kind of statement the Colonel thought may be needed.

The men in Company D would not be able to cover for Michael much longer as they were so shorthanded. The Colonel would eventually figure out Michael was not going out on patrol, doing construction detail, and other tasks. The doctor and Sergeant Valentine, in particular, were taking a great risk in creative paperwork to protect Michael. They were doing so because they felt it was the right thing. Uniting to help Michael, Valentine also calculated, was making the soldiers in the fort a more cohesive force and that is what he wanted.

Based on the Colonel's plan of making an example of Michael, once he was caught missing duty, the Colonel would likely have him thrown in the fort's undersized guardhouse. The "hotbox" the soldiers called it. In the box, Michael's physical movement would be restricted, and he would only be given bread and water. In a day or two, Michael would be dead. Just another mound in the graveyard.

Sergeant Valentine pulled Francis aside, knowing that he was Michael's friend. "This conversation never happened, and I'll deny that it did if questioned," Valentine establishing the terms, "is there any chance Scanlon's family would have contacted a congressman or Department of War official on his behalf?"

"I don't know," responded Francis, "I haven't been in touch with them." Francis thought of Ellen. Francis assumed Michael had been too sick to write his family, so they probably did not even know he was ill. Intervention from Washington, Sergeant Valentine advised, was the only thing left that could save Michael. Valentine feared the death would do more to demoralize the company than achieve the Colonel's goals, He hoped Michael would get a miracle for the fort's sake, if nothing else.

Francis would have fallen into a depression over what seemed to be Michael's imminent death, but for the constant distraction. The Colonel kept him and virtually everyone else incredibly busy on the fort's construction projects. Then there were the patrols, surveying expeditions, and the seemingly endless game of hide and seek with the natives.

Having been at the fort for months, Francis had yet to see a single Indian warrior. He would know one when he saw one based on Sergeant Valentine's repeated lectures on their physical characteristics, including their smell—which Valentine claimed mimicked the beef they ate and the horses they rode.

****

The resourcefulness that Sergeant Valentine had been drilling into Francis's head for military purposes, would now prove useful in other regards. Francis received his first letter since arriving at the fort. It was from his brother Mathew in Philadelphia. Before opening it, Francis thought through an exercise Valentine required upon receipt of anything new in the fort, large or small. How else could the item—in this case an envelope containing a letter—be used? As he pondered the possible applications, Valentine's words came back to Francis about intervention from Washington being Michael's only hope.

Mathew's letter said nothing about Michael or officials in Washington, but it would. Francis practiced copying Mathew's handwriting ensuring it matched the envelope with the postmark and rewrote the entire letter. He added in a crucial new paragraph with Matthew relaying that the Scanlon family knew about Michael's dire medical condition. The paragraph also indicated the family was determined to have him sent home and already spoke to local politicians and newspapermen and were heading to Washington to talk to even more. The last sentence had Mathew describing the family "as fiercely determined to protect their kin."

Francis was pleased with his handy work and thought with the authentic postmark the letter would be accepted as real. The problem was how to get the letter into the hands of the Colonel without it looking suspicious. Not wanting to implicate his friends in his scheme, Francis did not mention it to them. Instead, he approached Sergeant Valentine as earnestly as he could feigning illiteracy and asking the Sergeant to read him the letter. Francis's logic was that once Valentine knew of the letter's contents he would be obligated to share them with the Colonel because they related to the operation of the fort.

"Do you want me to read you a bedtime story too, Fireball?" Valentine barked at Francis dismissively, not even taking the letter out of Francis's hand. "I am a busy man, busy keeping you and that band of idiots we call a company alive. Go ask the chaplain to read the letter to you."

Panicked, Francis responded, "It could be personal. You know the kind of stuff a chaplain shouldn't see. Come on Sergeant, I never get letters—just this one. Tell me what it says and I'll be on my way. Never bother you again." Valentine was just about to kick Francis out of his office when he remembered, Francis was on his shortlist of troopers who could read. The Sergeant not only saw him with two large books the day he arrived at the fort but overheard him at times reading the books to others in the company. Something was a foot, and now realizing it, Valentine decided to play along.

With an eyebrow raised, Valentine started to read the letter. Not out loud but to himself. Then he said, looking at Francis with a smile, "The good news is that your brother has a wedding date set and will be opening up his own storefront soon in Philadelphia. The bad news is that you are not going to the wedding. You have a job to do here. But Michael Scanlon may just be in attendance."

With that, Sergeant Valentine marched out toward the Colonel's quarters. Three days later, Michael Scanlon was in the back of a wagon being escorted out of the fort by a squad of troopers. The troopers had been directed to intercept the next stagecoach heading east and to put Michael on it. He was going home discharge papers in hand.

Watching as the wagon pulled out from the fort, Sergeant Valentine turned to Dr. Elkins. "Scanlon looks like death warmed over; do you think he'll make it?"

"Make it?" The doctor responded, "To the Mississippi maybe, can't imagine much farther than that." Dr. Elkins had been amazed Michael had lived as long as he did already.

Michael Scanlon died of complications related to his illness. But only after they were coupled with those stemming from old age. Michael would pass away in West Virginia with his wife, children, and grandchildren around him decades after his departure from Fort Davis.

****

During the next few months at the fort there were occasional reports of Indian warriors wandering about, but the warriors vanished whenever government troops arrived. The word "vanished" was not an exaggeration. The warriors were literally covering over their footprints and the tracks of their horses. They would not camp anywhere close to white settlements, instead spent most of their time in the rough and remote areas of the Texas landscape. Their contact with whites seemed limited mostly to trade for necessities and some cattle rustling.

In response to livestock thefts, the regional cattle baron, Milton Faver moved his largest herd to just outside Fort Davis for protection. Sergeant Valentine had concerns about the new location of Faver's ranching operation. The Sergeant feared the closer civilians and cattle got to the fort, the closer hostile Indians could too without being detected. However, Faver was one of the richest men in West Texas so he could move his cattle anywhere he pleased.

The result was that the soldiers had two new tasks at the fort on top of their preexisting duties. One task involved rounding up and returning cattle from Faver's herd when they would occasionally wander into the canyon. The second task was to be more mindful where they were walking. The size and frequency of the cattle's droppings showed their mass, up to a ton each, and their skittishness. Any abrupt sound or movements made the beasts jump and add to the dung minefield the soldiers had to take pains to avoid.

With it more difficult to steal cattle from Faver's herd due to the relocation, Sergeant Valentine anticipated that the Indians would move onto another, easier target. He was surprised, however, when Lieutenant Longstreet returned from patrol and advised that Indians had raided one of the fort's building supply depots along the Limpia Creek. Indians had never been interested in building supplies before. When Longstreet added the Indians burned anything they couldn't carry away—which included supplies needed for the new buildings at the fort—Valentine's surprise turned to concern.

The Colonel dismissed the significance of the attack, attributing it to the random aggression of Indians on an unguarded depot. In support of his position, the Colonel noted that it had been more than a decade since tribes in the area amassed a war party of any significant size. They were no threat to the fort or to its soldiers the Colonel insisted. Instead, the Indians would continue to busy themselves with "nuisance crimes" and would avoid military engagement at all costs.

Initially, the Colonel denied Longstreet's request for two companies to conduct a sweep to look for Indians around the depot and to check on the settlers nearby. But then he relented explaining that seeing a military presence may help settlers in the area from getting too nervous once they got news of the attack.

The Colonel directed that Companies A and D proceed to the Limpia River the next morning. One company was then to head north and the other south but both units—the Colonel ordered emphatically—were to be back in the fort by nightfall. The Colonel advised that he follow the company strength patrols with one of his own "reconnaissance-in-force" the day after to further assuage residents' anxiety.

It was not long after the column of Company D split off on its own along Limpia Creek that it was intercepted by a lone horseman. Both horse and rider were soaked in sweat and clearly agitated. The rider stopped at the front of the column as Lieutenant Longstreet and Sergeant Valentine, in command of the patrol, made their way forward to question the man.

"There was an Indian attack at Limpia Station," the man blurted out first to the soldier riding point in the column and then again to Longstreet and Valentine. He was referring to the town beginning to form around a stagecoach watering stop on a trail off the San Antonio and El Paso Road.

Countering the rider's panicked presentation, Longstreet spoke back to him in a deliberatively calm manner.

"When did it happen?" Longstreet asked.

"Not more than a couple of hours ago." The rider responded, the redness of his face contrasting with the faded and earthen color of his clothes and broadbrimmed hat.

The man continued without further prompting. "A warrior came into town and had words with one of the merchants and shot the merchant dead with a shotgun."

"A lone warrior?" Longstreet questioned without showing any emotion.

"We only saw one," the man advised.

"Walked into town, you say?" Valentine asked puzzled. Indian warriors in that vast part of Texas were seldom far from their horses.

"Yep," replied the man. "He made his way over to Nathaniel Tyler who was prepping his sideboard to make deliveries. And as if he were dispatching a soulless muskrat, the Indian filled Nate's chest with buckshot—blasting him clear out of the wagon."

"What happened after that?" Longstreet pressed.

"That is the damnest part." The man said shaking his head as if in disbelief. "The Indian hopped onto the driver's seat of the wagon and meandered out of town as leisurely as you please. We brought Nate's body into the saloon, not knowing what else to do since we ain't got no doctor, not that one would have made a difference. And wouldn't you know it, after a spell that damn warrior came back."

"Came back, are you sure?" Valentine asked, now completely perplexed

"Sure as I am standing here," the man continued. "He figured out we were all in the saloon and came in himself, that old shotgun pointing at anyone who looked at him. We dared not do a thing. There were woman and children about including Nate's wife and kids who were crying up a storm. The feathered bastard looked around, took old Nate's top hat that was lying next to his corpse and a bottle of whisky off the bar and left once again back with Nate's wagon and team."

"Strange," Longstreet said, "Very strange. What direction did he head?"

"Toward San Antonio." The man added, "You won't have much trouble tracking him, just follow the fresh wagon tracks that break off on the trail about a mile down." The man pointed behind him.

****

The man was right. The column of soldiers caught up to the warrior inside of an hour. He was the only Indian on the trail. The only Indian, no less, driving a cumbersome wagon with a top hat fashionably tilted on his head, liquor on his breath, and a shotgun strapped to his back with the twin barrels pointing up to the sky.

While it would have been better to take the warrior to San Antonio where there was a proper jail, Lieutenant Longstreet directed his force to take the prisoner back to the fort. Longstreet had been ordered to return to the fort, no excuses, prior to sundown. They were already running late.

When the company arrived back, they were surprised to see several other Indians being shoved into the door of the spare storage shed.

"The guardhouse ain't big enough to hold all these cattle rustlers," advised a private from Company A. His unit had just returned from their own patrol about a half-hour before.

"You have room for one more in there?" Sergeant Valentine asked—nodding to his company's prisoner.

"Barely," the private said, and pushed the top-hatted warrior stinking of whiskey in as well.

The men of Company D were tired but they were instructed by Sergeant Valentine to situate themselves outside the makeshift jail and stay vigilant. Francis sat down where there was a small gap in the planks of the shed. After Valentine left, one of the Indians in near-perfect English said, "We are suffocating in here, we need more air."

Francis was about to approach the corporal for permission to vent the shed, as it must have been unbearably hot and stuffy in there. He thought better of it knowing the corporal, hating the natives, would have said—*let them suffocate*. Instead, Francis took it on himself to kick-in the lower portion of two boards in the back of the shed—opening up a space of a few inches on each.

The corporal, laying down on the other side of the shed, heard the noise and shouted, "What the hell are you doing Fireball?"

"Just checking the planks of the shed, corporal. They seem secure." Francis lied, not totally sure why he was helping the men held inside. Maybe because he, himself, despised tight and congested places.

"We need water," cried out the same voice.

The water Francis figured he could get permission to provide and began to walk over to the corporal. Francis stopped and looked back through the gap between the planks of the shed. Staring intensely into the face of the Indian who had been making the requests—the Indian still wearing the top hat. Francis started to suspect he was not drunk at all.

"Where I come from," Francis stated, "if you trick someone who is trying to help you it's a special sin and you go to the worst part of hell." Then, for added effect, Francis said gruffly, "And, if you are trying to trick me now so you can hurt my colleagues here, I'll kill you myself."

The answer came back, "Please, water."

Francis did get clearance to get the Indians water, but food would have to wait till the morning. With the water errand accomplished, Francis sat down in the same spot he was previously close to the shed.

"Where is it that you are from?" The top-hatted Indian asked.

"Ireland, you familiar with it?" Francis retorted cynically.

"Yes," the warrior said proudly, "A land with no snakes and has Lepers who hoard gold."

"Leprechauns, you mean Leprechauns." Francis said with a laugh.

"My name is Latee, my white friends call me Myles," volunteered the Indian.

"White friends? Like the guy you got that hat from?" asked Francis sarcastically.

"No, he was a thief, he was not my friend." Latee continued, "Sometimes when people treat you bad, you get angry. Sometimes, you get more than angry. Today, I got more than angry."

Francis could relate.

"I was taught English by the Irish priests who served as missionaries. They used to say my people and the Irish had a lot in common." Latee was now starting to impress Francis as overly chatty.

"Yeah, well, I think those priests were having some fun at your expense—both about the Leprechauns and being like the Irish. Total twaddle." Francis advised.

"You did not have your own tribes?" Latee asked in an earnest tone. "Your own land, your own spirits, and ghosts, your own ways until a different people came from across the sea and took them all away. Didn't your warriors die in battle, of disease, and from starvation until there was nearly none left?"

Francis said nothing. But he was now sure Latee was not drunk and nor was he stupid.

After a moment of dead air, Latee continued, "Then maybe we are the only ones to know what it is like." Latee glanced over past Francis eyeing one of the fort's cannons nearby, "To know what is like to be there at the end. When resistance and acceptance mean the same thing, destruction of your way of life."

Francis began to appreciate the comparison to the Irish. He wanted to say something reassuring to Latee but did not for two reasons. There were no reassurances that could be honestly offered, and secondly, he still had his suspicions Latee may be manipulating him.

"I'll tell you what, once I figured a way out for all the buggered people, Irish and Indian, I'll let you know." Francis said.

"There may be a way." Latee said but went silent once he saw Valentine return.

"Fireball, I didn't know that you had been appointed the new superintendent of Indian Affairs. You mind telling me what you and the Indian have been chatting about? Your favorite parasols and hoop skirts, maybe?" Sergeant Valentine glared at Francis disapprovingly.

"No, Sergeant, I just found the drunk Indian entertaining," Francis replied, embarrassed.

Valentine then gestured for Francis to walk with him away from the shed. "You open your mouth to a prisoner again, I'll knock you senseless!" Valentine was livid, and conveyed as much through his words, although his appearance was calm for the benefit of the Indians watching him through the boards of the shed.

The Sergeant then deployed a new group of four men to guard the shed, one man assigned to each side of the structure. That accomplished, Valentine walked over to the section where Francis had been. "Any of you try to distract my men again," Valentine said loudly enough for all the occupants and the guarding soldiers to hear, "I will burn this shed down with all of you in it."

Valentine then gathered the rest of the men close to the partially completed stone buildings and away from the shed. "The Colonel is going on his routine patrol tomorrow with most of the men," Valentine almost slipped and called it a parade instead of a patrol.

And it had a parade aspect to it. The Colonel would target areas to visit that were most populated by Indians but white settlers. He would lead the troopers in tight formation with flags flying and supply wagons and even artillery pieces following behind. It was a show of force calculated to give the civilians peace of mind. At other times, Valentine understood the need for putting on a show. But with the increasing Indian activity in the area, Valentine thought showtime over.

Making yet another concession to Longstreet, who the Colonel considered his most promising young officer,

Company D and elements of Company A were ordered to stay behind at the fort. Longstreet reminded the Colonel that there were still eight warriors to guard in a makeshift jail and the men had been on a long patrol the day before.

The real reason for Longstreet's request, which he discussed with Valentine, was to avoid the fort being left as vulnerable to attack as was the supply depot along the Limpia. Longstreet requested the fort's three artillery pieces be left behind as well so that the men could train with them. The Colonel left one, not wanting his parade being too diminished.

"We have been tasked with continuing to guard the prisoners," Valentine told the soldiers who would be staying at the fort. He wished he could have kept the mission at that but he was a big believer in telling soldiers all they needed to know. "Also, we have reason to believe the Indians may be up to something, possibly an attack on this fort."

Valentine went on knowing that he had to disabuse the soldiers of two notions. One that the threat he was communicating was not just one of his scare tactics for training purposes. Second that Indians did not have the fight in them any more to attack a manned military installation.

"For months now, Indian warriors have been reported all over our sector, yet we don't see hide nor hair of them." Valentine spoke directly to convey his sincerity. "Then the Indians raid a supply depot destroying the very things we need to finish the stone buildings. The same stone buildings that will afford us some real protection in this place. And just today, eight warriors go and let themselves be caught and hauled inside the fort." Taking a second to ensure he had all the soldiers' attention, Valentine asked, "What does that all tell you?"

No one answered so Valentine singled out Francis. "Fireball, you seem to have a friendly relationship with the natives, they tell you anything?"

"No, Sergeant." Francis said now mortified at the realization he had been duped by Latee.

"Really?" Valentine said mockingly. "They didn't mention wanting to cut your throat ear-to-ear? Funny, Indians are pretty straight forward about that sort of thing."

Moving on, Valentine said to all the soldiers, "If I were those Indians, I would have warriors up on the canyon walls right now surveilling us. When they see the Colonel leave in the morning on his routine patrol with the bulk of our troops, they will likely make their move."

Taking a deep breath, Valentine looked at his men intensely. "We will be the most vulnerable from when the Colonel leaves tomorrow at dawn until he returns at noon the following day. The Colonel is a creature of habit and I am sure the natives know his routine as well as we do. So, the Indians will have a window of thirty hours or so to do something, if they do—in fact—want to target the fort."

"But this is what we train for and I pity the Indians if they try to pull it off. I will work with Sergeant Coleman of Company A on assigning shifts to guard the shed. And do not be mistaken for one second. If we get attacked, those Indians," pointing to the men in the shed, "were planted here to kill us from the inside."

"If you are not selected for guard duty, go get some sleep. Tomorrow is going to be a very busy day." Valentine said while dismissing the soldiers.

****

In the morning, Sergeant Valentine did not assemble the men in formation. He did not want to make it easy for any Indians on the canyon walls to count their number. Instead, Valentine walked in and around the men as they moved about as well, readying themselves.

"Last night, I created an inventory in my head," Valentine advised each of the soldiers, "and if I trained you right you did the same. Give me your ideas now on how we can use what is around us and I will relay that to Lieutenant Longstreet who is in charge until the Colonel gets back."

Some of the ideas offered by the troopers were good and Valentine passed them along to Longstreet, who had a few of his own. He worked through with Valentine which would be the most practical considering the time they had and ordered Valentine to put the most promising into effect.

The first thing the Sergeant did was place wagons and other objects to obstruct the view of those in the shed. That was quickly followed by Valentine dispatching scouts on horseback and skirmishers on foot. The other soldiers, as they worked digging rifle pits, were told to study the canyon walls to look for any movement or other signs of Indians. Sergeant Valentine pulled Francis aside, well out of view and ear shot of the shed. "Mac," Valentine whispered, "I am going to assign you and a few others to give the prisoners breakfast and to let them out one at a time to stretch their legs. I'll have the cannon and men run by two or three times so hopefully the Indians will think we have more men and firepower than we do."

The Sergeant went on, "Watch them closely and see if they give anything away about a possible attack. Maybe they will look at places on the canyon walls or out to the entrance leading up to the fort. Talk to your friend and maybe 'chief top-hat' will let something slip."

"He is not my friend," Francis said, recalling as soon as he did so that Latee had said the same thing about the merchant murdered in town.

"Damn right, that Indian would bludgeon you to death and eat his lunch out of your skull as quick as look at you. That reminds me," Sergeant Valentine said dispassionately, "Do not take any weapons with you when you are near the Indians. If they overpower you, I do not want them taking anyone else down with your gun. Your second-tier security must do all the shooting. So pick your team and Mac."

Valentine continued with gallows humor, "choose somebody who is a good shot, you don't want one of Uncle Sam's bullets in your forehead."

The prisoners did not give anything away, leaving Francis impressed with their stoicism. A trait foreign to the temperamental Irishman. Francis suggested to O'Brien, one of the men he selected for his second-tier security, that they should never play poker with the natives.

Latee, top-hat still on his head, looked to engage Francis in conversation once again as he was stretching his legs. Francis simply stared at him, saying nothing. Latee just smiled, as if in understanding.

When Francis returned to the defensive perimeter after being relieved of his duties at the shed, he was amazed at the progress that had been made. A protective trench with rifle pits had been dug all around the partially completed stone buildings. The soldiers practiced moving from the rifle pits back to where, if necessary, they would make their final stand inside the partially constructed buildings.

The cannon was aimed at the shed and, if there was an attack, Lieutenant Longstreet wanted the Indians in the shed dispatched first because they were so close, only fifty yards from the perimeter of the trench. Measures were taken to ensure the troops, in their planned disposition, would be far enough away from the canyon walls and any rifle fire Indians could generate from there.

About twenty-five yards in front of the trench, slits were dug a foot or two into the ground. The slits were filled with brush, and from the assorted building supplies still around, pitch and other flammable items. The slits were to be lit on fire, forcing the attackers to funnel into areas where soldiers could concentrate their aim.

In one of the more ingenious defensive moves, a little behind the gaps in the slits, extra kegs of gun powder were situated with piles of nails from the construction site placed in front of them. A carefully aimed rifle shot into the kegs would detonate the powder, scattering the nails into the attackers.

Lastly, between the trench and the stone buildings, spare pieces of lumber had been partially dug into the ground leaving the top portions sticking out at an angle. The hope was that the wooden obstacles would impede any pursuers on horseback—slowing them down enough for soldiers to get an extra shot or two at them.

The only thing to do now was wait. Lookouts and skirmishers rotated in and out, none of them saw signs of a single Indian. Hours went by. The troops scouring the canyon walls saw nothing. Maybe this had all been for naught, some troopers thought. Others surmised that their preparations had scared off the would-be attackers, or that it was the Colonel and his column that were the real targets.

Lieutenant Longstreet became optimistic enough to authorize the men to eat an early dinner, meager fare of coffee, bacon, and hard bread. The same was given to the Indians in the shed. Valentine allowed one of the captives out to empty the chamber pots. All the other requests from the Indians to stretch their legs again was denied by the Sergeant and affirmed by the Lieutenant.

Night fell and no one was in the mood to talk. Everyone remained vigilant. More vigilant than when they had been offered protection by the light of day. The problem was that all that work and the intensified vigilance left the men exhausted. Some of the men were having a tough time keeping their eyes open. Even those on watch.

Those in Company D used all the mental and physical tricks they had been taught to stay awake by Sergeant Valentine. There were a handful of men from Company A guarding the shed. They did not have as many tools to stay awake and one young trooper leaned against a post and dozed. The others, while awake, were barely so and their senses were becoming dull.

A group of young and nimble warriors watched from the darkness having just scaled up and over the canyon walls. They were tasked with freeing their more senior warriors inside the shed and then, together, they would create as much mayhem as they could as a diversion.

One of the youngest warriors, Latee's nephew Qunah, sought to take advantage of the soldier sleeping and the others being glassy-eyed. In the darkness, he quietly sneaked passed the guards with a sack in hand. Inside the sack were knifes, hatchets, and two pistols, each individually wrapped in cloth to reduce the noise they made as Qunah carried them. He slipped the weapons one at a time to those inside the shed through the hole Francis had created to supply more ventilation. Latee was proud of his brave and enterprising nephew but feared his bravery bordered on recklessness. Then those inside the shed and the others in the nearby darkness waited for the signal.

The silence for Sergeant Valentine was deafening. If the Indians did not attack, the Colonel would mock him and Lieutenant Longstreet. Both men argued rigorously to a dismissive Colonel that an attack was imminent. The Colonel acquiesced to some of the defensive requests made through Longstreet but made clear he was among those who believed that the Indians no longer had the resources or tenacity to attack a fort.

At the same time, if an attack did occur, Longstreet and Valentine were not sure they had enough men to repel it. The

Colonel's compromise of leaving 42 men and one cannon against an unknown number of fierce natives coming against them could end in tragedy for the would-be defenders. While contemplating that thought, Valentine heard a shot.

It was a single shot. The signal from the skirmishers, who were disbursed in small groups, was supposed to be two shots if an attack was underway. A moment later, it came. The second shot. Then a third, a fourth and a whole barrage. The gunfire was terrifying enough but what made Valentine go pale was what he felt. He was only a few in the company who had felt that vibration before and knew the source of the increasing rumbling noise. Soon it echoed throughout the canyon, crowding out the clamor of the gun fire.

The ground shook so that the coffee in the tin cup at Valentine's feet began to hop out onto the vibrating ground. There was a low roar as if a train were coming from the canyon entrance.

"Man the cannon! Man the cannon," Valentine shouted, "Troopers take your positions in the rifle pits!" The soldiers, half asleep and scared senseless with the noise and the darkness, retraced the steps Valentine had them repeatedly practice during the day.

The cannon was already loaded and primed with solid shot and was aimed at the shed. "Shoot toward the front of the fort, fire and keep firing," directed Valentine.

"Shoot at what?" the cannon leader asked, glancing into the darkness.

"It doesn't matter, direct as much noise as possible toward the canyon opening."

"Light the fire pits!" Valentine directed the soldiers in the trench.

"What the hell is it?" Longstreet asked.

"They are driving Faver's cattle toward us. It's a stampede," Valentine knew from the ground shaking and noise. In the darkness, they could see nothing.

The rumble was now almost deafening. Faver had close to 5,000 longhorn cattle on his ranch outside the canyon. It seemed every single one of them was now heading toward the soldiers. A wall of them, tons of churning hooves and pointed horns five feet long. The frenzied animals were destroying everything in their path. The fearful noise and vibration were things soldiers would not face again until the advent of the tank decades later.

The cattle had been driven into a panic by the Indians startling them with pokes from spears, abrupt movements of their horses, and war cries. The Indians, on their horses, rode behind the cattle, ready to kill any soldier who managed not to be pulverized by the stampede.
The cannon crew worked frantically. The noise of the weapon likely to have a significant effect on the animals. But at best, the crew could get off two rounds per minute and the minutes were running out.

With everyone focused on the deadly stampede heading their way, no one noticed the Indians escaping from inside the shed. Taking the ground shaking as their cue, they burst out of the makeshift prison and set upon the guards, stabbing, and bludgeoning three soldiers at the cost of only one of their own shot.

The Indians made their way from the shed toward the cannon. Their goal, as directed by Latee hours before, was to disarm the cannon and then scale a designated portion of the canyon wall to escape the stampede. The Indians on horseback now following the cattle would take care of everything else.

O'Brien was the first to realize the gang of Indians was heading toward the cannon. He raised his .69 caliber musket. Adhering to his extensive training under Sergeant Valentine, O'Brien exhaled and calmly fired. The bullet hit the Indian closest to the cannon in the hip. It was Qunah, the fleetest of foot among the attackers inside the fort. He was 14 years old and would bleed to death from his wound.

As O'Brien attempted to reload, one of the Indians broke off from the rest of the group, seeking to avenge his younger brother who had just been hit, and set on O'Brien. Francis, seeing it, fired his own musket, catching the charging Indian center mass. In the process of reloading, Francis heard Sergeant Valentine.

"Protect the cannon!" Sergeant Valentine yelled as he sprinted to intercept the Indian group before they could reach the cannon crew. Francis joined Valentine. O'Brien was on Francis's heels. The three collided with the charging group of Indians. Other troopers jumped into the chaotic brawl after ensuring they would not leave too large a gap in the defensive line behind them.

Francis grappled with one of the Indians and the struggle drew them to the outer edge of the fracas. Francis knocked his adversary down and with the butt of his musket, cracked the warrior's skull. Francis worked then to finish reloading his weapon when Latee ran up to him, eyes wide, with a large knife in his hand.

Latee wrapped his leg around Francis, putting pressure on the back of Francis's knee causing him to fall. Francis used his musket as a barrier to push Latee back, but he knew it would not be enough. This was the end, Francis thought. But Latee pushed off and started to run toward Sergeant Valentine who was getting the better of another warrior.

Although the Indian pitted against Valentine had a knife as well, the Sergeant used his knee to pin the Indian's arm to the ground and pressed into his adversary's throat, choking him.

Valentine looked up, sensing the threat coming from Latee heading toward him, blade in hand. The Indian below him was still fiercely resisting. For a split-second, Valentine recalled what he told his students about multiple armed assailant situations. *Try to avoid them*, he would joke but he was not joking now. Valentine knew he had to get off his knees and move. As he did so, there was a sickening thud. The sound of flesh ripping and bones shattering. Latee collapsed, having been shot in the back by Francis. The Indian that Valentine had been fighting gave up when O'Brien's musket barrel was shoved in his face.

The threat from the Indians inside the fort had been neutralized. And the threat from the stampede was dissipating as well. The cannon and musket fire coming from the fort, coupled with the firepits, had caused the cattle to pull back upon themselves. Detonation of one of the powder kegs put an end to the Indian attack all together. The cattle now started to stampede back out of the canyon. The Indian warriors who started out behind the cattle were now in front of them, at least one seen falling and trampled after his horse was gored.

Sergeant Valentine was not going to take any chances. "Keep the Indians," referring to those inside the fort, "alive if you can. I need to talk to them." Valentine needed to know how many warriors were still out there and if there were plans for a second attack.

Francis made his way over to Latee. The bullet had made its way through his spine, lodging painfully in his stomach. Francis turned him over and could see the Indian's tears. Whether they were tears from the physical pain or mental anguish of the defeat, Francis did not know. What he did know, however, was that Latee was in a bad way.

Already responsible for the murder of a civilian and now the attack on the fort, Latee was going to hang. But worse, what Valentine meant by wanting to "talk to the Indians" was that he would torture them to get the information he needed to defend the fort. To Francis, all rebellions followed the same course. Promise, bravery, followed by defeat and rebel leaders being executed in some humiliating way to send a message. The book on Irish history his mother had given him was replete with the pattern.

Latee seemed to relax for a second, looked at Francis and simply said, "Leprechauns."

"Yes," Francis said, "Leprechauns" and took the nearby knife. The one Latee could have killed him with—and plunged it into Latee's side. Latee felt nothing, he had been paralyzed by the gunshot wound.

In killing Latee, Francis knew he was sparing the warrior harsh interrogation and the spectacle of a public hanging in his crippled state. Knowing his desperate attack had failed and the fate of his people was enough of a burden for Latee to take to the grave, Francis thought.

Francis, normally not one for praying, said a prayer of sorts for Latee. Not addressed to God but to Father John Murphy, the leader of the unsuccessful 1798 Irish Revolt—the same revolt ending at Vinegar Hill and in which Francis's namesake, John "Fireball" McNamara, had been wounded.

Quietly, Francis began to sing, O'Brien—who sat down beside him—accompanied thinking Francis was singing in honor of only the soldiers who had fallen:

At Vinegar Hill, o'er the pleasant Slaney,
Our heroes vainly stood back-to-back,
And the Yeos at Tullow took Father Murphy And
burned his body upon the rack.
God grant you glory, brave Father Murphy
And open heaven to all your men

"Look after Latee, Father Murphy, for he is one of your own." Francis mumbled to himself, tearfully gazing up into the night's sky. "The Indians are like us Irish."

****

The Colonel, looking at the carnage the next day, did not want to acknowledge his leaving the fort was a mistake and had opened the door for the attack. As a result, he did not elaborate on the incident in the fort's log. He simply wrote that the command engaged and countered a hundred Indians coming from Faver's ranch. No mention was made of the sophistication of the attack or the determination of the defense.

****

Thou shall not kill. But Francis had killed two people and seriously injured a third with a rifle butt to the head. The man was left, according to Dr. Elkins, permanently witless. He would be hung for his part in the attack anyway.

While Francis had shed many aspects of his Roman Catholic upbringing, a special form of self-loathing guilt still stuck to him like glue. Intellectually, Francis could cite self-defense and defense of his friends, O'Brien and Valentine, and the purported soldier exception to the First Commandment. His guilt, however, operated and destroyed at a more visceral level and Francis could not rationalize it away. He could not make it go away at all.

The anxiety and depression that plagued Francis after the yellow fever outbreak in Norfolk returned and returned with a vengeance. The physical and mental activity demanded by Sergeant Valentine that had stabilized Francis's mood before the battle, now only left the trooper exhausted. Valentine's Socratic questioning that Francis once found so stimulating began to strike him as pointless. It got so bad that Francis started to envy those that did not survive the battle.

Francis's best friend at the fort, Kevin O'Brien, worried about him. The only way O'Brien knew to get people out of their own heads was to get them out of their mind drunk. The next time the two were on leave, O'Brien dragged Francis into the saloon at the town closest to the fort along the El Paso Road. O'Brien purchased a bottle of whiskey and placed it in front of Francis.

"Drink the swill and let it chase the devil out of you, as my dear old mother used to say." O'Brien quipped. The two then drank, shot glass for shot glass, making a major dent in the whisky bottle. Eventually, Francis would smirk pleased at some of the things O'Brien would say. That grew into Francis laughing like he used to and O'Brien laughing along with him. For a while, at least.

Gradually, as the day turned to dusk, Francis became depressed once again evidenced by his drunken, brooding silence. He eventually walked out of the saloon without saying a word to O'Brien. At first, O'Brien assumed Francis left to relieve himself but when he did not return within the period associated with such an endeavor, O'Brien went outside himself. He saw Francis walking toward the El Paso Road on the town's main and only street. O'Brien shouted repeatedly for Francis to stop.

Francis turned around to look at O'Brien just as a man stuck his head out of a second-story window at the boarding house near the saloon. The man, agitated at O'Brien's shouting, yelled, "Shut up, you stupid drunk."

The man punctuated his demand by throwing a bottle that struck O'Brien in the back of the head. Seeing his friend injured, Francis ran back. He ran back right past O'Brien and into the boarding house. Francis stormed up the stairs and then kicked in the first door he came to. The inebriated Francis proceeded to beat up the room's sole occupant, a seed salesman from Fort Worth who had nothing to do with the assault on O'Brien. The guilty man hid quietly in his room two doors down, avoiding retribution.

When Francis sobered up, he found himself in the "box," the small and cramped secure section of the guardhouse. Hot, dehydrated, and hung over, panic overtook Francis. Having had bouts with claustrophobia before, they had never been as bad as this one. Francis kicked, pushed, and screamed to be let out.

"Calm down, Fireball," said one of the soldiers who had drawn guard duty. "The captain," the new commander of the fort, "ordered you in the box for three days." It would be three days of torture and at a time when Francis could least cope with it. It was so hot, and he was provided so little water, that Francis felt as if he could not swallow or breathe. It got so bad that he passed out several times over the three days.

When he was released, Francis never felt so physically and mentally depleted in his life. He staggered out of the guardhouse worse than he staggered in. Francis could not rid himself of thoughts of the battle, the death, and all the other hardships he seen dating back to his time in Ireland. Everything seemed futile and the only certainty pain and misery. Happiness, love, and laughter were flukes that some people would not know at all and no one would know enough.

Francis began to think it would be better if he just put a stop to it all. Finally, to take control, to put himself in charge of outrageous fortune. He was aware of others who had taken their own lives at the fort, the isolation, monotony, and terror of the place making the decision—for some—purely logical. Sometimes officers would attribute the death in the fort's log to an accidental gunshot wound, injury inflicted by Indians, or an unspecified physical malady. It would be yet another obstacle to recruitment if suicide became associated with army life.

O'Brien continued to worry about Francis and did whatever he could do to make him laugh—laughter being the layman's measure of mental health. One day, the early vanguard of what would be a herd of camels were brought into the fort. The Army was testing whether the camels were more efficient than mules in carrying supplies across the dry southwest territory.

Everyone at the fort marveled at the camels, a type of animal they had never heard of, let alone seen. "What in God's name is that?" asked Francis staring slack jawed. Without skipping a beat, O'Brien responded: "That, my friend, is what you get when a colonel screws a Texas longhorn heifer." The witty remark, at the expense of an authority figure, was too much. Francis laughed like he had not in some time. It would be the last time O'Brien would share a laugh with his friend, a friend he started his army career with and with whom he was bonded in combat.

****

Francis returned to his bunk to find mail at the foot of his bed. There was a letter from Jamie, his brother in New York.

The envelope felt bulky and there was a reason. In addition to carrying a letter from Jamie there was a smaller unopened envelope inside. It was from Ellen Scanlon, the woman that Francis loved. Not knowing where Francis was, she sent it to Jamie via the Rowlands and asked him to forward it.

Ellen's letter had been in transit for several months and Francis wondered how much had changed since she sent it.

In the letter, Ellen explained how Francis had been right and her husband, Martin, wrong about the severity of the yellow fever outbreak. Martin had been one of the many Norfolk residents to die in the epidemic. Things were now difficult for Ellen and her two sons with Martin gone, but she assured Francis they would make it through.

Ellen explained that she wrote, first and foremost, to check on Francis. Ellen reminded Francis they had not spoken since their trip to the barrier island and had not seen each other in over a year. She asked him to write back as soon as possible, if nothing else, just to confirm he was alright.

In the letter, Ellen also advised that she had sad news to convey. Abraham Simmons, the proprietor of the bait shop at Rowland Wharf and one of Francis's closest friends in Norfolk, had died. Ellen had tried to find out what killed Abraham, but the city medical examiner only offered supposition. The supposition was that Abraham had simply "seen enough of this life."

The letter provoked a complex mix of emotions for Francis, and he put it aside for several days. Eventually, Francis showed the letter to O'Brien and asked what he thought of Ellen's comments.

"Well, I think she wants you to write," remarked O'Brien.

"You should be a detective," sarcastically responded Francis, adding, "First of all she literally told me to write her and, between the lines, she says she loves me and wants me to come back."

O'Brien smiled, "For a depressed soul that is a tremendously optimistic interpretation you have of what she wrote."

Francis—undeterred—retorted, "I am convinced of it and what do you know about women anyway." O'Brien shrugged his shoulders in partial agreement. If O'Brien did not know anything about women, then he would learn. His feat, later in life of having twenty-one children, was not accomplished alone.
O'Brien then said, seemingly out of nowhere, "Suicide."

Confused, Francis asked what O'Brien meant.

"Abraham killed himself, or at least it sounds that way to me, based on the letter." O'Brien remarked in a solemn tone.

Francis became quiet. He questioned himself, how had he overlooked something so obvious? The answer came to him with a deep and sad insight. Francis did not overlook how Abraham died at all—he suppressed it. Losing his friend was hard enough but to suicide when Francis was trying to avoid doing that very same thing was too much.

The loss of Abraham was made even more painful because Francis had considered Abraham the most resilient person he knew. With most of his life spent in slavery and eking out only a bare-bones existence at the bait and tackle shop, Abraham was the one with a constant smile.

The rich and powerful of Norfolk would pass through Rowland Wharf often with scowls on their faces and a harshness to them, while Abraham—with every reason to resent, to hate, and to despise—was above it all. To Francis, Abraham was at peace with himself and accepted the world as it was, or so it appeared.

While Abraham did have the strength to overcome the pain of his hardships, he did not have the strength to do it forever. Francis feared no one did.

It was just too painful to think about Abraham anymore so Francis decided to apply all his own strength to push memories of his friend aside. To do so, Francis tried to focus his mind on what was directly in front of him. And what was in front of him was being a soldier. That strategy, however, failed miserably. He found himself haunted by the ghosts of those he had killed and injured.

The only thing that helped was Francis thinking about Ellen. Whether driven by his brain, his heart, or his desperation, Francis solidified his belief that Ellen both loved and needed him. The reality was he needed her. He needed hope. Hope that there was a better life out there for him, someone who loved and cared about him, and a place where he did not have to kill or fear being killed. That place was not Fort Davis.

With his fixation escalating to the point that Francis felt his sanity—his very life—depended on seeing Ellen again, the path forward came to him. He would desert.

In his time at the fort, Francis learned there were two ways to abandon his post. The right way and he would be back in Norfolk and likely never be caught. The wrong way and he would find himself back in the guardhouse, a fate he knew he could not endure a second time. Even if he did survive the box, it would likely be followed by years of hard labor with a ball and chain on his ankle.

The smart way was to wait until he had leave for a few days. That would delay notice of his absence and give him time to catch a stagecoach heading east to San Antonio. Once in San Antonio, he would figure out which path would get him back to the East Coast faster, overland as he had come into Texas or by steamship originating in the Gulf of Mexico. So as patiently as he could, Francis waited and planned until he earned three days leave.

****

Sergeant Valentine and O'Brien approached Francis in the barracks as he was preparing to depart. The pair asked Francis to pick them up things in town while he was there. When they tried to give him money for the purchases, Francis refused saying he would settle with them when he returned. At that point, O'Brien noticed the two books Francis always had on his bunk—one from his mother and the other from Father Devlin—were missing. Valentine noticed that the haversack Francis was taking with him looked heavy for just three days outside the fort. A good part of that weight could be contributed to something that showed the extent of Francis's desperation.

Francis had purchased an old, single-shot pistol from the fort's armorer. The armorer who periodically sold Army weapons he listed on inventory reports as lost, stolen, or broken—offered Francis a newer sidearm that held multiple rounds.

"A single shot is all I will need." Francis responded, determined not to be thrown back in the box if he were caught.

"Think you are that good a shot, huh?" The armorer teased Francis.

"I'll hit what I aim at." Francis said, abruptly ending the conversation, never having liked the corrupt armorer in the first place.

Valentine and O'Brien walked Francis to the wagon taking him and a few other soldiers into town for leave. Francis could not maintain eye contact with his friends, solidifying their suspicions he was about to desert. They said nothing and hoped, for Francis's sake, they would never see him again.

Chapter Eight
Returned to Sender

Norfolk, Virginia
1857-1859

As trying as Francis's journey had been from Philadelphia to Texas to start his army career, his escape from Texas back to Ellen in Norfolk was worse. An added wrinkle was that Francis arrived back East in the height of winter. It had been exceptionally cold, leaving him scrambling to stay warm and to find shelter between the legs of his trip.

As was his luck, Francis made his way to the outskirts of Norfolk on January 16, 1857, as a fierce snowstorm hit. Over the next two days, the Norfolk area was buried under snowdrifts, some ten feet high. Rivers froze in the bitter cold and the entire Chesapeake Bay was covered in ice.

Francis did not care; he made the last part of his trek on foot to where Ellen lived when he left Norfolk. He pounded on the door, nearly frozen to death. A large, aggravated man answered. Shocked, Francis heard him say, "Ellen Moriority moved." Francis thought he would faint. The man's words began to register again when he said, "She moved three blocks down."

Francis summoned his strength once again to run against the frigid wind. He headed in the direction pointed out by the man to a much smaller house. The size and condition of the home were evidence that Ellen had fallen into difficult times following the death of her husband. Ellen opened the door, putting her hand to her mouth in shock. A flood of emotions and thoughts overtook her.

Ellen recognized him in an instant, although he was now bearded and his once tan face was made bright red and dull blue by the cold. His greenish-blue eyes and his lost puppy expression were still the same and gave away the feelings Francis had for her. Feelings that she could not allow herself to reciprocate in the past.

Ellen thought of Francis often since their time together on the barrier island. She even thought of him in the way ladies at that time were not supposed to. Her guilt about those feelings was only starting to lessen with her husband gone for so long. But she had not heard from Francis in nearly two years. She took the bold step of writing him unsolicited, even though that required her admitting her feelings to her friend Sally Rowland.

Sally was Ellen's only means of reaching Francis. Ellen assumed—incorrectly—that upon leaving Norfolk Francis had rejoined his brother Jamie in New York. The only person she knew with Jamie's mailing address was Sally. Sally mentioned finding it among her late sister-in-law's belongings, along with a half-completed thank you note for a wonderful tour of New York. Playing the role of extortionist, Sally would only share it with Ellen if Ellen admitted to her feelings for Francis.

Once Ellen made the admission, an admission that was not needed because Sally already knew, the address was handed over with Sally giving some advice along with it.

"Be charming when you write him, brutes like Francis love charm." Then hugging Ellen, Sally added, "If that brute does not write back telling you he loves you too, I will thrash him!"

Francis did not write back. Ellen thought she had not been charming enough. She had been so self-conscious when writing, Ellen feared she had not been charming at all. Her self-doubt only grew when her brother Michael reported that he had been with Francis at Fort Davis. So excited at the news, Ellen blurted out before she could think better of it, "Did he mention me?"

Michael responded, "Why would he mention you?" A clueless brother, Michael went on to regale Ellen, oblivious to her feelings, with how Francis appeared at the fort as if from nowhere and saved Michael from sure death.

Now it was time for Francis to be at Ellen's door as if from nowhere. Ellen's heart raced at the sight of him and it was all she could do to keep a calm appearance. A challenge not just because she was thrilled to see him but because he looked half-frozen. It was her luck, Ellen thought, Francis would remerge just in time to drop dead in her doorway.

"Jesus, Mary, and Joseph!" Ellen exclaimed, "Francis, what are you doing here in the middle of a storm?" She brushed snow off him and pushed him toward the fireplace. Ellen instructed her sons, Timothy and Dennis, now eight and six years old, to quickly rub Francis's hands and feet to ward off frostbite. She put blankets on Francis and gently stroked his nose and ears to reestablish circulation.

"I came back," Francis said while shivering and trying to keep his teeth from chattering, "to marry you."

Ellen hesitated, surprised and not sure what to say. After an awkward pause, Ellen directed "We can talk about that ridiculousness later, just get warmed up before you die of cold."

Making eye contact with Francis, Ellen nodded her head toward the boys indicating it was not the time nor place to be talking relationships. While she was not sure if the proposal had been earnest or the product of frost delirium, it showed—at a minimum—Francis's feelings for her had not diminished. Also, that her feelings for him had not been for naught.

Later that night, when the boys were asleep and the color returned to Francis's face, he and Ellen sat at the small kitchen table drinking tea. "So, what was this madness you were talking about, getting married?" Ellen said with a smile, looking down into her teacup.

"I was serious," Francis replied and then pausing until Ellen looked at him.

"The very thought of you is what has seen me through more troubles than you can imagine. Not a day has gone by that I haven't thought of you. I loved you the first time I laid eyes on you and heard your voice. The time apart has only made me miss and want you more. I may not know much but I know I love you and don't care to know anything beyond that." Francis said it more earnestly than he had ever said anything before.

Ellen leaned over and kissed Francis, "The reason you thought of me Francis is because I hoped and prayed for it. I missed you too. We will be happy together and we will make things better, glancing at the sleeping boys, for everyone."

"Together, that is good because I tend to get into trouble on my own," Francis said only half-joking.

Francis interpreted the conversation to mean they would marry right away. Ellen interpreted it differently. Propriety was important to Ellen and in the Victorian Era that required her to mourn her late husband for two years and to have a formal courting period after that in relation to any suitors. By Ellen's calculations, the ceremony would have to wait a year. But since Francis insisted that he could not wait that long, they compromised.

The two were married on February 20, 1857, a little more than a month after Francis appeared at Ellen's door. It showed just how adamant Francis had been and how desperate Ellen was to stabilize things for herself and her sons. She craved stability although it always seemed to be knocked out from under her whenever she found it.

George Rowland and family attended the ceremony. Sally Rowland—Ellen's best friend—was the maid of honor. Michael Scanlon was the best man.

"This is the happiest day in my life," Francis whispered to Michael as the ceremony was about to begin.

****

Aside from the matter of the deadly yellow fever outbreak, Norfolk had been a good place for Francis. And in many ways, he picked up where he left off, this time with Ellen at his side. Francis was able to return to the work he enjoyed at the Rowland Wharf and Boatyard. The ever kind George Rowland made a place for him even though business was slow and had not recovered from the epidemic. Consequently, the work would only be part-time and its wages would have to be supplemented somehow.

The strain of rebuilding his family's finances was taking its toll on George. He now looked ancient to Francis, although the Rowland patriarch was only in his early fifties. More troubling was that George was struggling to find words when he spoke and seemed increasingly frustrated when trying to organize his thoughts. Today, he would be diagnosed with early-onset dementia.

George was as close to a hero as Francis would allow. The man was in a position of power and wealth yet comported himself with kindness and compassion for others. Not a frequent combination in Francis's experience. More importantly, Francis had seen the expansive nature of George's altruism. His daughter-in-law, Mary, was one of the kindest people Francis had ever met—and that, at least in part, had to be influenced by George.

To supplement his income at the wharf and boatyard, Francis reluctantly took a job at the slaughterhouse on the outskirts of Norfolk. The slaughterhouse was owned by William Collins, one of the larger butcher shop proprietors in the city. Among other retail locations, he had two stalls at the Norfolk Market House.
It was not that Francis disliked Collins or his coworkers at the slaughterhouse. Actually, he enjoyed their gallows humor. Collins would jokingly refer to his business

competitors as "giblets" and directed his men at the slaughterhouse to "put their back into the work, but not to back into the meat grinders—he wanted no behind in the operation." In the mid-19th century that was top-notch humor.

The problem was that Francis did not like killing animals. He hated the thought of it at the family farm in Ireland and he was particularly averse to it on an industrial scale at the slaughterhouse. It also reinforced for Francis that he was a murderer of man and beast. But he had to provide for Ellen and the children, and their family would be growing as Ellen became pregnant a few months into the marriage.

****

On Christmas Eve 1857 in Norfolk, Ellen gave birth to her third son, her first by Francis. They named him Stephen Michael McNamara. Stephen after his paternal grandfather, a tradition in County Clare for the eldest boy, and Michael after Ellen's brother and Francis's friend. Stephen Michael, as his mother would always call him by both names, was a beautiful, healthy baby. Francis would never feel as much love as he did the day his son was born; Francis had expected Ellen would change his life and she did.

In the months that followed, Francis applied himself at work harder than ever before. He analyzed everything his bosses did, hoping to one day to be a boss himself and to earn more for his family. One of those he studied was George Rowland, although Francis increasingly worried about the man's health.

For Ellen, there seemed nothing to worry about. Her husband was happy. Francis had never been in better spirits, no conflicts, no enemies, just happiness. She was happy too, with a family she loved immensely and everyone happy and healthy—what more could she ask for. She had found stability.

****

With nearly as much excitement as the children, Ellen was looking forward to a long-awaited family sail around the Chesapeake Bay. Francis was starting to reestablish his interest in the sea and had rented a sailboat. It would be the first time she and Francis would be sailing together since the yellow fever outbreak years before.

For the occasion, Ellen had sown matching nautical-looking outfits for all her boys, Timothy and Dennis, the infant Stephen Michael and—of course—for Francis. While Ellen was a talented seamstress and the outfits were in her own modest opinion "adorable," Francis grimaced at the thought of wearing a family "uniform." He acquiesced to Ellen's wishes but dreaded the thought of the teasing he would take from his coworkers who would be at the dock. But for Ellen, he would do anything.

Just a few weeks before, when discussing whether Francis should formally adopt Timothy and Dennis, Francis said something Ellen thought remarkable.

"Absolutely, they are my boys," said Francis, "but I will not be denying them their birth father. They must keep the Moriority name. I did not like Martin, I admit that, but only because I was jealous. He was with you and I wasn't. He loved you and did what he could for you and the kids. I owe it to him then to do the best I can by his boys. However, they need to know they are as much Martin Moriority' sons as they are yours and mine. You need to tell them about him."

Ellen had told her best friend, Sally Rowland, of the conversation. Ellen advised that she never had been prouder of Francis than at that moment. "He has an incredibly good heart," announced Ellen looking up to the sky as if in thanks.

"But he has the look of the devil," said Sally playfully.

Sally suggested that Ellen "should keep an ear on that good heart of his but her eyes always on his hands." Sally was discreetly trying to remind Ellen that on earlier occasions Ellen had described Francis as "brooding" and "like a pot about to boil over." A boiling pot was helpful at times in the kitchen, but it could also be dangerous. Sally was able to see the harder part of Francis, clearer than most people although she still liked him. Sally could appreciate contrasts in people.

On the day of the scheduled family sailing trip, Ellen made her way to the wharf with Sally helping with the children. Sally had to be there anyway for the expected arrival of her cousins from New York, Martin Van Buren Rowland and his new wife, Lucinda.

As if on cue, Martin and Lucinda docked just as all the workers on the wharf were gathering around to ooh and ahh over the McNamara children. As expected, Francis's coworkers entertained themselves greatly at Francis's expense related to him and the children being in matching sailor outfits.

"Laugh it up fellas, laugh it up!" Francis responded goodheartedly.

Lucinda Rowland, a few years from having her own children, gushed over baby Stephen Michael with his fat rosy cheeks and little belly sticking out beneath his sailor suit. Ellen handed Stephen Michael over for Lucinda to hold and the young woman from New York was thrilled.

Sally explained to the crowd, all friends and employees of George Rowland, that Martin and Lucinda had come to Norfolk to visit as part of their honeymoon. While in the area, Martin Rowland, an oysterman by trade, planned to get some samplings of Virginia oysters for bedding in New York. Martin, who went by Mat, had noticed the oyster stock in New York City and Long Island was starting to thin.

He attributed the problem to some kind of defect among the oysters native to the northeast region. The problem had nothing to do with the type of oysters, once more plentiful and diverse in New York waters than anyplace else on the planet. Instead, the decline was the result of a combination of factors. Factors including the ongoing dumping of sewage and industrial waste into New York waters, increased development along the area's shoreline, and overharvesting. A few added oysters from Virginia were not going to overcome those problems, but Mat had to try to save his livelihood somehow.

"Does anything from Virginia thrive in New York?" Teased Sally Rowland. "It sounds like a completely different world." Mat Rowland responded, "We'll find out."

Mat did not look anything like his cousin, George Rowland, but they both shared a kind, good-natured way about them. In the future, that good-natured way would change the life of someone else on that dock.

****

George Rowland's health continued to worsen. With his declining mental faculties, George—with the help of his wife, Abagail—took on a new business partner, Layton Sibbet. Sibbet had recently moved to Richmond from New Orleans. Sibbet assigned his eldest son, twenty-year-old Nathan, to be involved in the day-to-day operations at the wharf and boatyard. The business along the wharf represented the largest of the Rowland holdings and was where Sibbet planned to make his greatest investment.

Francis intended to give his new boss every benefit of the doubt. Borrowing a page from the book being written by his brother Mathew in Philadelphia, and the philosophy espoused by Sergeant Valentine at Fort Davis, Francis now considered his bosses as a means to an end. No longer as authority figures to battle against in a senseless world.

The problem, Francis was soon to learn, was that Nathan Sibbet was a spoiled rotten idiot. Nathan would belittle men who had been working at the wharf their entire lives, undo things that had worked successfully for years and steal ideas from others and run with them to his father as if they were his own. Nathan had been born the son of a boss, and that in turn entitled him to be a boss himself.

What particularly bothered Francis was when Nathan would make fun of George Rowland, behind the old, declining man's back. While George clearly was not the man he used to be, his lifelong generosity, fair business dealings, and development of a capable and faithful workforce were being cast aside by someone who accomplished nothing on his own.

Nathan's dismissiveness of George followed that of his father, Layton Sibbet. In entering the partnership with the Rowlands, the elder Sibbet intended to get inside knowledge of the business. With that information, he would secretly drive down the value of the enterprise and then buy the increasingly desperate Rowland's out. Once he owned the company by himself, Sibbet would take the breaks off its profitability and make a fortune. It's what he did successfully in New Orleans and why he needed to find new ground in Norfolk. All the initial cash investments Sibbet was making into the Rowland businesses were just for show and to throw off suspicion.

Nathan Sibbet had the lowly character of his father but not the sophistication. Contributing further to Nathan's unpleasant personality was his underlying insecurity. His frequent belittlement of others was more a coping technique than anything else. A technique that would bring him trouble.

The breaking point was reached during the Christmas party on the wharf in 1858. The men who worked on the wharf and in the boatyard had a few drinks beforehand. They all bemoaned what a tough year it had been with Nathan running things. Francis had a buzz on when he went into the large boathouse structure where George Rowland and the Sibbets planned to wish the employees a Merry Christmas. George being earnest in his wish, the Sibbets not as much.

It was sad to see George Rowland try to get through his speech, his wife, Abagail, at his side helping him. At times, George stuttered, became frustrated, and at other points pathetically asked Abagail what he was doing again. Abagail smiled at the employees as she gently guided her husband best that she could. Many of the employees, knowing her and George for decades, looked at the ground brokenhearted.

Nathan spoke next. His immaturity and lack of professionalism showed immediately. Even to his own indulging father's chagrin, Nathan used his speech to make fun of George's decline and to suggest George had been running the business into the ground. Nathan thought his comments would aid in his father's scheme.

George Rowland gave things away and got nothing in return, Nathan claimed to the workers who were quickly losing the holiday spirit. That would all change in the coming year, Nathan assured, making the older Sibbet furious. Not because his son was being heartless but because the boy may have been needlessly tipping their hand in terms of the scheme.

When Nathan started to stutter to further mock George, forlorned Abagail was standing next to her husband. The pain showed on her face. Even more sadly, the comments did not register at all with George who stood with a confused smile.

Watching it unfold, Francis lost all restraint. George Rowland may have been overly generous, even gave things away, but he would get something in return. In Francis's case, George got loyalty. And that loyalty prevented Francis from standing by idly any longer while George was mocked.

The patterns as to Francis's violence by then being all too clear. The strategic variety as with the Toobins in Ireland and Latee in Texas. Other times, Francis's violence was spontaneous, usually in response to an unanticipated slight or injustice. The assault on Captain Dixon in New York, the threat against the old man on the dock in Philadelphia, and now Nathan Sibbet.

Francis said nothing. He just stormed onto the makeshift stage that had been assembled for the event. At first, Nathan looked surprised by Francis's approach, then quizzical as he tried to recall the Irishman's name, and then Nathan looked rightfully fearful. Francis put his young boss into a strangling headlock and vowed not to release him until Nathan apologized to Mr. and Mrs. Rowland.

Abagail Rowland abhorred violence, even when intended to defend her and her husband. She begged Francis to let go but he would not. He was locked onto one person and one person alone, and that was Nathan Sibbet. Until Sibbet apologized or died, Francis had no intention of letting go. A fighting determination modeled by Francis's father.

The elder Sibbet threatened to have Francis arrested if he continued the strangulation, but again Francis held fast. It was only when a group of Francis's coworkers pulled him off and dragged him out kicking and screaming did Nathan know he had escaped death.

The group took Francis to a nearby tavern. Francis would not have to pay for another drink that night. He was the working man's hero. The group laughed, one of the carpenters exclaiming, "Nathan must have been really embarrassed, his face was so red. Or maybe that was because Francis was strangling him." One of the caulkers chimed in, "Nathan may have apologized to Mr. Rowland, but it was hard to tell with him gagging so much!"

But, like many working man's heroes, Francis was now out of a job himself and would be going home to Ellen, on the eve of his young son's birthday, completely inebriated. Francis did not drink much normally and never as heavily as he had in the past few hours. He would have to admit to Ellen that earlier in the day he had effectively undone all their hard work and sacrifice of the past year.

And it was undone for nothing. Nathan Sibbet would still be the boss, no matter how evil he was, and George Rowland's health would continue to decline, no matter how good he was. The world would not be righted by the likes of Francis McNamara.

Ellen tried to remain calm as her husband, in his drunken state, explained what happened. He had lost his job at a time when jobs in Norfolk were hard to come by. Adding to the problem, Ellen had just agreed a few weeks before, at Francis's urging no less, to let him quit the slaughterhouse. Ironically, full-time work on the wharf had been expected to come available for Francis due to the infusion of cash from the Sibbets. Part of their scheme.

The facts coupled with the whole incident being relayed by a drunk Francis proved too much for Ellen. Drink was the damnest of all poisons as far as she was concerned. But Ellen knew she had to push her anger aside, she had a growing problem she had to deal with then and there.

In his telling and then repeated re-telling of the incident, Ellen could see Francis was riling himself up against Nathan Sibbet. The matter did not appear to be over for drunk Francis. He started looking frantically through his things in their small home. If it were the pistol he was looking for, the one he had taken from Fort Davis, Francis would be out of luck. Ellen had gotten rid of it a long time before, not wanting it around her children nor her temperamental husband.

Francis, saying he was disgusted that Ellen did not want to kill Sibbet herself after all George Rowland had done for her, stormed out of the house.

Not knowing what else to do, and trying to protect her husband from himself, Ellen flagged down a police officer making rounds near the house. Her complaint kept Francis locked up long enough to become sober and to let his rage subside. In doing so, Ellen saved two lives and prevented even more misery for her family.

Chapter Nine
With the Bridge Burned Behind Him

Richmond, Virginia
1859-1861

Francis's former coworkers at Rowland Wharf tried to help as much as they could. They gave Francis the cash they could spare and secured him job referrals in his new destination, the City of Richmond.

The attack on Nathan Sibbet left Francis unemployable in Norfolk. Had that not been enough to prompt the move, there were rumors Francis was going to be indicted for assault. In a rough and tumble port town, a drunken headlock would not normally be an indictable offense absent it causing significant injury. Unless, of course, the victim was a person of status. And if there were any questions of the Sibbets' status, that disappeared with their campaign contribution to the local prosecutor. So, Francis decided to leave and to leave quickly.

Moving to Richmond made sense to Francis for several reasons. It was a large city, the third most populous in the South after New Orleans and Charleston. Francis could disappear among the masses, leaving his legal problems behind him in Norfolk. Richmond also had a growing immigrant presence, mostly Irish and German, so he would fit in.

The city offered the type of industrial jobs that often desperate immigrants could fill. There were also several low-cost areas to live in the city, although not necessarily desirable ones. Just as importantly, it would not cost Francis much to get there. Only the cost of tickets for the soot belching locomotive the McNamara family rode in for three hours to get to the new city.

Ellen was furious at Francis for having lost his temper and his job in Norfolk, the place she had called home since arriving from Ireland. But as Francis played with the children during the train ride, repeatedly making the boys giggle, Ellen realized she could not stay angry forever.

Once they arrived in Richmond, they found their way to the Oregon Hill neighborhood and the cheap apartment they arranged to rent through a mutual friend with the landlord, Kenneth Coale. A kindly widower in his fifties, Coale showed the family their small apartment on the top floor of the three-story, rickety old, wooden building.

Coale seemed happy with the children moving into the house. He lived by himself in the back room of the ground floor, renting out every other square space to sustain himself and to send money to his daughters. The four girls were now married and living on the outskirts of the city. They seldom visited him and Coale only saw his grandchildren when he walked the many miles to their home. Even then, the grandchildren treated him like a stranger. But Coale understood. They had their own lives and it was a privilege just to be able to see his progeny. A privilege his wife was denied having died years before.

On the job front, Francis remained anxious even with the references his coworkers gave him. It had been drilled into Francis's head that jobs were hard to come by for poor whites in southern cities like Richmond. And for a long time that was true. Slave labor undercut job prospects for everyone else. But by the time Francis and his family arrived in Richmond, that trend had been changing. At least when it came to industrial jobs.

The large agricultural plantations took up an increasing amount of the slave workforce, leaving the South's flour and cotton mills, tobacco warehouses, and ironworks open to hire from the mix of poor whites, recent immigrants, and free blacks desperate for work. Twenty percent of the blacks in the city were free and as in need of paying jobs as all the other groups.

The collective desperation of the poor working class kept wages low. And since they involved no upfront purchase price as with slaves, the mix of free blacks, immigrants, and poor whites offered a workforce that was also easily disposable. In some ways, more desirable to employers than slaves when it came to the most dangerous jobs.

Fair labor laws and unions were still decades away and the courts were geared more to protect the interests of the wealthy. So, when a worker was injured or killed on the job, a risk inherent in the industrial work of the time, the employer simply replaced them with little or no consequence. There was always more desperate people out there.

Through his references, Francis was able to find two parttime jobs in Richmond. Most of his hours would be as a laborer for the Tredegar Iron Works, a company that produced locomotives, train track, and fabrications for bridges and large buildings. The second job was at the McCloy Masonry, owned by Bill McCloy—brother of Jack McCloy who Francis worked with at the wharf. Francis picked up hours at the masonry when the ironworks was slow and had no work for him.

The contrast between the two employers could not have been more pronounced. The ironworks was huge and impersonal with hundreds of laborers, including a relatively large slave contingent recently brought in by the company to defeat a rumored strike planned by free black and white workers. The masonry was small and staffed exclusively by Irish immigrants—most related to the owner. The masonry offered a degree of comradery and good humor among the employees, the ironworks did not.

It struck Francis odd that although the employees at the ironworks were similarly situated in many ways, very few of them bonded as friends. Even on lunch breaks there was very little banter or good-natured ribbing. The employees would just break into groups based on their race, status, and ethnicity. The slaves stayed together, free blacks apart from them, the Irish amongst themselves, and so on. Within their groups, they would often talk to each other in whispers, use heavy slang or talk in their native tongues to bind their group at the exclusion of others. Each to their own tribe, Francis rationalized it.

Not long after he had started at the ironworks, Francis was assigned to a special project. He was tasked with hollowing out the cores of large metal blocks for structures to be used as retaining walls for a large bridge being built. It was a laborious task that had never been undertaken before. Normally the blocks weighed several hundred pounds but once Francis hollowed them out they were deceptively light.

When the whistle blew for lunch one day, Francis decided to take advantage of the novelties of his project. He entered the crowded area where workers had broken into their groups for lunch pushing one of the hollowed metal blocks as if it were still filled. Francis leaned into the block, grunting and groaning to make it skid slowly across the floor to the middle of the break area. Then Francis effortlessly flipped the block over, pulled out his lunch from the hollowed-out core, and turned the block back over once again and used it as a seat while he ate. Some of the workers laughed at the gag but not for long and continued to chatter in their small groups. It would take more than one laugh to unite the workers. That is the way the bosses liked it.

Between the two positions, Francis worked six days a week, usually 12-to-14 hours a day. To keep him connected to the boys and in effort to re-instill some religious faith in Francis, Ellen insisted he read Bible passages to the boys when he came home at night regardless of how exhausted he was. The readings were from a palm-sized Bible that Ellen had received as a gift from the Rowlands when she first arrived from Ireland.

Francis often tried to extricate himself from the chore, coming up with one excuse after another. Ellen would just stare at him and periodically ask, "Is the baby done whining yet?" Inevitably, Francis did the reading. Sometimes, he even supplied commentary.

After recounting the Book of Job, Francis remarked that he had thought only the Devil caused the world's troubles. Adding that Job makes clear that God jumps in on the action too, at least when dared by the Devil like a little boy in a schoolyard. "Isn't that comforting boys? Not just one deity trying to trick you but two!" Francis said with sarcasm.

Ellen suspected shenanigans were afoot and listened in closely one night. She heard as Francis improvised the Book of Daniel. Daniel not being eaten by the lions had nothing to do with his faith or God's intervention, but rather the offensive vapors from Daniel having eaten too many beans and day-old fish. The moral of the story, Francis explained to the boys, was that even excessive bean and bad fish consumption can be a good thing under the right circumstances.

As Francis handed Ellen back the Bible, she said, "Really, beans and bad fish?"

"That's not how they teach it in that highfalutin Protestant church of yours?" Francis asked, before passing out from fatigue. As much as Ellen enjoyed Francis's sarcastic wit at times, she worried his harshness would diminish the joy of life for him. She also worried it would rub off on the boys, for they all looked up to Francis.

****

The 1860 census confirmed that Francis and Ellen had not made much progress financially. Ellen became demoralized by the fact when responding to the census taker's questions. "No," is all she kept saying to the questions related to assets and financial holdings.

The financial pressure was only getting worse despite how hard Francis was working and all that Ellen was doing to keep expenses low and the family together. Adding to the stressors was that Ellen was pregnant. She was going to tell Francis that night when he came home from work. As she saw the census taker out, Ellen noticed the sky looked as if a storm was coming in and indeed there was.

Hoping the rain would hold off till he made it home, it began to pour as Francis and a coworker, Joe O'Toole, left the ironworks. They took shelter under a wooden awning connected to a blacksmith's shop closed for the day. O'Toole was new to the ironworks. Being from County Mayo in Ireland, he and Francis exchanged stories about the old country. And with that, O'Toole produced a flask. He and Francis drank, exchanged stories, laughed, cried, and sang a rebel song or two. The longer it went on, however, the more the two slid into an underlying sadness. The realization that either Ireland had failed them, or they failed Ireland, and the quality of their lives in the United States still left much to be desired.

It got to the point that Francis thought it better to take on the rain than wallow in the dower thoughts. O'Toole understood and waved him off with an encouraging, "Don't let the bastards get you down!"

By the time he arrived home, Francis was soaked through, exhausted, and still very drunk. Ellen was furious. It was his drinking that had driven the family to their sad financial state and here he was drunk again.

"Spending money on spirits while I barely have a penny for the children!" Ellen yelled.

"I didn't buy any liquor!" Francis yelled back, then hiccupped at the most inopportune time.

"Ah, so you have me thinking it's raining whiskey? Well then, I should stick my head out the window because you have driven me to drink." Ellen shouted.

The more she stared at Francis in his drunken state, the angrier she got. To the point that Ellen let totally loose, "We were making progress in Norfolk and you threw that all away you selfish bastard! You wanted to be the big man, show off to your friends, get drunk, and beat up some jackass. If it is your God-given mission to beat up people who are jackasses, you should have started with yourself."

Ellen was livid, the hormones of pregnancy adding to her understandable frustration. She meant, but did not want to mean, what she was saying.

Frustrated himself, tired, and inebriated, Francis responded with hurtful observations as well. "That is right, you and the boys were living high on the hog before I came around. How close were you to being evicted from that shack you were living in? What prospects did you have? If it weren't for me, you would have starved."

With that, Ellen smacked Francis's face. Francis, enraged, smacked her back.

The ongoing yelling and screaming prompted the landlord, Mr. Coale, to summon the police. Two officers arrived, a young one, tall and skinny, the other older and heavyset who pointed with his billy club as he spoke, water dripping from his squared blue hat due to the persistent rain.

"What do we have here? A drunken Irishman slapping around his wife. Now I have seen everything. Let me guess," the older officer continued in an antagonizing tone, looking at Ellen, "You don't want us bringing any charges against your darling. Until maybe next time when he knocks your teeth out?"

The younger officer started to speak, wanting to soften what his partner had just conveyed, but the older officer stopped him. "Not a word, Barkley!"

Now aggravated at the belligerent cop as much as Francis, Ellen put her hands to her hips not sure on who to release her wrath upon. She glared at Francis, having made her decision. Francis had hit her. His own wife while pregnant no less, although he did not know that at the time. *Simply unforgivable*, she thought.

"Francis McNamara, you shall never raise a hand to me again." Then glaring at the older police officer, Ellen announced, "Take him away, I will press charges."

The older police officer smiled and approached Francis who was now seeing red he was so angry. Without question,

Francis knew he was wrong for hitting Ellen and was embarrassed by it. In the heat of the moment, however, it was just easier to shift blame and rationalize. Ellen had disrespected him and hit him first, she accused him of being a drain on her life while he had been breaking his back to support her and the children.

But worst of all, Francis felt Ellen had just betrayed him. Like Judas handing over Jesus to the Romans, Ellen had surrendered Francis into the hands of an Irish-hating authority figure. In Francis's mind, unforgivable. Yes, Francis's self-justification had gone so far as to analogize himself to Jesus.

In terms of resisting arrest, Francis's anger only got him so far. Exhausted and drunk, his opposition to the police was as futile as it was pathetic. He would do better in the future. The two police officers beat Francis, the older officer more than the younger. Then they dragged him by the arms down the wooden steps out of the house and off to jail.

Ellen, having time to think about it, did not go to the courthouse to pursue the charges. She was still angry at Francis but regretted empowering the haughty police officer. It was just that she was upset, angry, and hurt.
Also still upset, angry, and hurt was Francis, and he had every intention to pick up the encounter with Ellen where it was left off. He was released after two days, two days to stew in subjective juices. Francis marched home, his mind so twisted with anger that he was blaming Ellen—the woman he loved—for anything and everything that had gone wrong in his life.

As fate would have it, Francis was intercepted by the landlord, Mr. Coale, outside the residence. At first, Coale intended to tell Francis to gather his things and leave. Coale would not tolerate violence among his tenants. But what came out was something entirely different.

"I miss my wife," Coal said so earnestly it stopped Francis in his tracks. "Even if I had to listen to her complaining the rest of my days, I would do it in a heartbeat rather than have her gone."

After a moment's pause, Coale added, "And what I would do for a chance to set a better example for my daughters. The irony is that when you get older and wiser, and learn to appreciate things, there is no time left to do anything about it." Coale looked down, shook his head, admitting to himself for the first time exactly how lonely he had become.

The old man's words made Francis think, breaking the cycle of superficial, defensive emotionalism that had been driving him.

"Thank you, Mr. Coale." Francis said softly, "You are a good man."

"Wait, wait!" Coale said as Francis started to head up toward Ellen. "You may want these." And then Coale disappeared into his room and reemerged with a handful of flowers, freshly picked bluebells. "I saw them this morning along the river during my walk. Maybe Ellen would like them. A little piece of old man wisdom, 'flowers never hurt,' when patching things up." Coale said with a wink.

****

The domestic incident that could have very easily ended their marriage ironically made the bond between Francis and Ellen stronger. They realized their relationship did not cause their hardships. Instead, being a family gave them the strength to endure life's challenges. They were a team, a couple. Apart, or worse at odds, life's woes could overwhelm them. Together they had a chance. Together they had hope.

The positive dynamic between Francis and Ellen translated to the benefit of the boys. Timothy and Dennis Moriority had begun their schooling at the local parish and were doing well. Stephen Michael was approaching three years old and modeled everything his older half-brothers did. The sight of the boys together made Francis think of his own brothers, Mathew, Jamie, and Patrick. He would never tell Mathew and Jamie, but he missed them terribly. Patrick had already been dead a million years it felt to Francis.

Francis and Ellen now recognized Ellen's pregnancy for the blessing that it was, financial gods be damned. Ellen happily wrote her brothers in Three Churches in western Virginia and her best friend Sally Rowland in Norfolk of her expected due date. They all planned to come to Richmond for the birth and to help Ellen set up for what would be her fourth child. Ellen did not want to be so bold as to pray for a girl, but *a girl would be nice* she thought.

In November, Ellen began to have contractions. Shortly after, she went into full labor, but something was clearly wrong. The baby, a boy, was born alive but was struggling. Ellen too was having difficulty, she was bleeding badly and burning up with fever.

Sally Rowland arrived as the midwife, really just an older Irish woman who had children before herself, was struggling to care for both Ellen and the infant. Sally, taking the initiative, scooted the baby away so the midwife could focus on Ellen. Ellen called out, pain in her voice, to see Francis. Francis rushed in from the other room where he had been waiting anxiously with his brothers-in-law, Thomas and

Michael. Unable to hide his alarm at Ellen's pale appearance, Francis just listened at Ellen's side.

"You must be strong Francis. Accept help. The world is not yours to fix, just do what it takes to fix yourself," counseled a weakening Ellen.

"Why are you talking like this?" Francis asked with his voice quivering in anxiety.

Ellen went on, "I think we should call the baby Francis, after the man I love with all my heart." She winced in pain, although she tried not to show it. "Francis Thomas would be nice. Two of my boys with middle names after their uncles."

"Yes, of course, anything you want. Just don't leave me," pleaded Francis. But she would leave him. The Lutheran minister had been called for by Michael Scanlon and the minister entered the room. Francis recognized him but could not recall his name, but he knew Ellen liked the minister from the Sunday services she attended regularly—but not with Francis who continued to resist religious indoctrination. The minister gave Ellen Last Rights and then asked to baptize the baby as soon as possible.

In the room that served as a kitchen, living room, storage space, and spare bedroom, baby Francis Thomas McNamara was baptized a Lutheran. After the somber ceremony, Francis stepped outside. He looked up at the darkening sky and prayed for the first time since Latee's death at Fort Davis.

As in the case with Latee, Francis did not pray to God directly. Instead, he invoked a spirit, this time of his own father. "I am naming him Francis not after me but you Da," referring to his father's middle name. "He needs to fight. I need him to live so Ellen has more to live for. Please Da,

245

please. Give him your fight, give him all your fight," tears rolled down Francis's face.

To provide an offering, Francis went on to assure his father than if everyone lived through the threat, he would bring the baby to the Roman Catholic Church for a proper baptism, trumping the Lutheran protocol done under duress.

But there would be no Roman Catholic baptism. Francis Thomas McNamara died on November 20, 1860, the same day of his birth. His mother would die just hours after him. They would be buried together in the paupers' section of Mount Calvary Cemetery in Richmond in a plot maintained by the Little Sisters of the Poor.

Prior to her death, Ellen asked that her sons Timothy and Dennis Moriority go to western Virginia with her brothers, Thomas and Michael. Her younger child, Stephen Michael, should go with Sally Rowland to spread out the financial burden of caring for the children. Ellen knew Francis would not be able to care for the young boys by himself. In fact, she feared Francis would not be able to take care of himself after yet another hardship in the loss of his family. She asked her brothers and Sally to pray for Francis. "I worry for him so," Ellen said.

Ellen's worry was warranted. Without her, Francis was lost. He was also angry, heartbroken, bitter, but mostly lost. After the funeral, he declined an offer to go "drown their sorrows," with Thomas and Michael Scanlon. Instead, Francis went to McCloy's Masonry shop. He needed a mission and he gave himself one, saving his wife and young son from oblivion.

Francis pulled a slab of the prettiest stone he could find from the large pile behind the shop. After bringing it to the workbench, Francis prepped the stone for engraving. Bill McCloy instructed the rest of the employees to stay out of

Francis's way. Bill, himself, gave Francis advice on the project, but only advice. He never touched the stone. It was sacred. McCloy had to make his own wife's tombstone, so he knew.

When it was done, Bill McCloy was in awe. It was the best work he had seen from someone of Francis's experience level. Francis installed the headstone himself, tears in his eyes. He figured it would not be long before he too would be in that grave. But people plan and God laughs.

Chapter Ten
Rich Man's War, Poor Man's Fight

1861-1862
Virginia and Maryland

The next few months were a blur for Francis. When he was not working, he was drinking. When he was not drinking, he was depressed. When he was not depressed, he was angry.

With Ellen's death and the children gone, everything changed for him. Even the hue in which he saw the world, how he registered sound, his sense of time, the very feeling of his body was different. Francis could not understand how other people were able to go about their lives as if nothing had happened. Something did happen, something horrible. The love of his life had been taken from him. The family he had was no more. He was no longer a husband or a father. He was nothing.

Francis could not get himself to write directly to his brothers to advise of Ellen and the infant's death. Instead, he just paid to have death notices posted in newspapers in Norfolk, Philadelphia, and New York. Mathew and Jamie saw the notices and their sincere letters of condolences were left unopened on the floor of Francis's small and increasingly unkempt apartment.

Also gathering dust in the apartment was the history book that had previously given Francis comfort when he left Ireland and the philosophy book that offered him solace after the yellow fever outbreak. Reminders of more death including that of his mother and the priest, Father Devlin, who had given him the books. There was a third book now, Ellen's small, palm-sized Bible that she made him read to the children. He would never open it again. Instead, he just spent hours staring at it, closed in his hand.

In several of the unopened letters, Francis's brother Mathew talked about the war that was brewing between the states. Mathew advised that he convinced their brother Jamie to come to Philadelphia and join an army regiment being partly funded by Mathew's father-in-law. Francis remembered the pompous Gordon Whitney well; an example that luck and fate may explain success more than brains and hard work.

Mathew pleaded for Francis to come to Philadelphia and join as well. The three McNamara brothers would make short work of the war, Mathew assured, and their success would catapult them into the upwardly mobile portion of American society.

Francis, had he seen the letter, would not have gone anyway. There was the small matter of him having deserted the United States Army just a few years before, and besides Francis had no means to escape from the South, which was now insulating itself from its northern neighbors.

The idea of secession from the Union was not universally popular in Virginia. There were abolitionists in the western part of the state, and people in that region associated themselves with free state farmers, not the rich, slaveholding plantation owners pushing the drive for succession.

When Virginia voted to secede from the Union, many in "West Virginia" protested, even going so far as threatening to break off from the rest of the commonwealth and rejoin the Union as a new state. A threat, eventually, they would carry through.

Secession from the Union, in contrast, was popular in the City of Richmond. It would eventually become the capital of the Confederacy shortly after the war began in earnest with rebel forces shelling Union troops at Fort Sumter outside of Charleston, South Carolina.

Francis could not escape the fanatical state-oriented patriotism running rampant in Richmond. It seemed the allegiance of everyone around him ran to the State of Virginia—what they perceived as their home—rather than to the United States. Francis, however, had no such allegiance. He stood for, and affiliated with, nothing.

On April 21, 1861, Francis was passing through the heart of the city. There were bands playing, all sorts of signs and banners being carried about by happy citizens. There was much excitement about the *Second War of Independence,* as some were calling it. A large crowd cheered whenever men approached a table marked "recruitment." The call for volunteers was for one of the better-known regiments, the 1st Virginia Infantry, which had its roots in the American Revolution and the colony's militia before that.

Francis could not have cared less in his depressed state. People would periodically stop him as he walked by and encourage him to join. "You look like a scrapper, join the fight!" One man yelled at Francis. Francis decided to keep walking rather than clobber the man for being an idiot.

Just then, Timothy Purcell, the friendly apprentice from Bill McCloy's stonecutting shop, grabbed the distracted Francis by the arm. "They want Irishmen, Francis." Purcell advised, "This is our chance. We win this war for them and they must look at us differently. We will be on the inside rather than the out. Besides, America always gives land to their soldiers who win wars, farmland. I would love to take a hand at farming here. I am told the sod is so rich in the western part of the state that lifting the abundant crops into wagons is the only hard part."

None of this, which might as well have been said by Francis's brother Mathew in the North, registered with Francis. What did catch Francis's attention, however, was a well-dressed banker standing next to the recruitment desk.

The banker, a vice-president at the Commonwealth Bank, shouted: "Any soldier who signs over their $100 recruitment bonus to my bank today will have an additional twenty-five dollars deposited in their account! Yes, you can turn $100 into $125 that quickly," the banker added. The fine print, which was not discussed by the banker, was that the $125 would only be payable upon successful discharge from the military.

It did not matter because what really caught Francis's attention was the banker's claim that the beneficiary of any soldier who deposited his bonus and was killed in the line of duty would receive an extra $250 as a death benefit.

Francis did the math in his head; all that money together would take him four or five years to save through the jobs he had now. He could provide his kids, particularly Stephen Michael, a nest egg. A nest egg that would never exist otherwise. So, Francis enlisted as a private in the 1st Virginia Regiment and was assigned to the primarily Irish unit, designated as Company C, the Montgomery Guards.

The Rowlands knew what to do with money, so he made them the beneficiary of his death benefit and bank account on behalf of his son, Stephen Michael, and to help support his two stepsons. Francis divided up the last of his earnings from the ironworks and the masonry shop and sent it off to the Rowlands and the Scanlons for the boys' sake. Now,

aside from getting his belongings from his apartment, all
Francis had to do was get himself killed in the war.

Before reporting for duty at the city parade grounds, renamed
Camp Instruction by the Confederate government, Francis
approached his landlord, Mr. Coale, for the return of his
security deposit. Coale explained he would return the deposit
once the mess of an apartment was cleaned out.

In undertaking the task, with the aging Coale helping best he
could, Coale mentioned once again how sorry he was at
Ellen's passing. Coale also said he had concerns about the
war and that it may not be the easy victory people thought it
would. He did so in an effort to have Francis rethink his
enlistment, Coale having lost his brother as a soldier during
the Seminole War and a cousin in the Mexican War. Francis
just forced a smile toward the old man, who he liked but was
too weary to engage in a serious or emotional conversation.
It was then that Francis came across his brother Mathew's
letters.

It dawned on Francis, for the first time, that he had signed up
to do battle with his very own brothers. As far as Francis
knew, he would also likely be taking up arms against his old
friends, Sergeant Valentine and Kevin O'Brien.

Francis consoled himself thinking that he nor the war would
last long. His brothers, Valentine, and O'Brien were smart
enough to keep themselves alive, Francis assured himself. If
there were to be a casualty, Francis decided—as if it were up
to him to decide—that he would be the one to fall and not
those he cared about.

****

A month of basic training and drill at Camp Instruction went
by in the blink of an eye. Francis was shocked by how
seemingly impractical everything was that they were being

taught. The new recruits were told by their commanders to stand clustered together in tight formation, march shoulder to shoulder, and shoot flatfooted, and stand up straight while reloading—making themselves perfect targets for the enemy.

Sergeant Valentine back in Fort Davis told Francis that the army was usually smart enough to learn from the last war but stupid enough to have to learn from the next one. The tactics the Civil War soldiers were being taught, North and South, would have been effective in the War of 1812. But it was not 1812 and infantry weapons had become more accurate and easier to load, and newer artillery shells were specifically designed to wipe out swaths of soldiers marching together. The lessons from this war would be painful and deadly, and bourn mostly by men who were better at being waiters, clerks, and farmers than being soldiers at war.

Even the uniforms, the 1st Virginia in all grey, while a little more comfortable than those at Fort Davis, left much to be desired. They were made of just enough wool to be extremely hot in summer and insufficiently warm in winter. Their boots fell apart after a few weeks of marching, taking chunks of soldiers' blistered feet with them.

The madness of it did not bother Francis at all, he was just there to cash in. More specifically, to let his sons cash in on a quick and socially acceptable death. Francis felt carefree in his assignments, which ironically allowed him to do them better than anyone else.

Francis did not care about winning the war, it was not his war in the first place. Anti-war mumbling had already coined the phrase, "rich man's war, poor man's fight." That phrase was spot on for the South, the North as well, and its truth would become more apparent in time. Francis had no slaves.

He had nothing. He was familiar with the argument that participation in the war would lift his social and economic standing. He dismissed it as little more than propaganda. Somebody had to be on the bottom, and to have a solid base most people had to be there. Society was not a circle; it was a pyramid.

The thought of it made Francis recall a book Father Devlin had given him at one point about Egyptian history. It included an in-depth discussion of the symbolism of the Pyramids of Giza. For Francis, the shape of the pyramids represented society with the poor and working classes making up the base. The merchant and professional classes constituted the smaller, middle part of the pyramid, and the super-wealthy and privileged the capstone. If those at the bottom moved around it would destabilize the whole structure and everything would be left in rubble. No one would benefit as even the poor would be crushed by the falling stones from above.

If anyone had bothered to ask Francis who would win the war, he would have unhesitatingly said the North. Not only because he was under the impression that squads of Sergeant Valentines were training their troops better than how he was being trained in the South, but because he had seen New York and Philadelphia. Their populations, their industry, and their shipping exceeded, by far, anything he saw in the South.

However, the smart money at the beginning of the war was on the South. One or two decisive battles and the whole thing would be over. The South had a disproportionate number of West Pointers, veterans, hunters, and people familiar with guns. Europe was dependent on Southern cotton and would pressure the North if the war went on too long. So, it looked like a quick war and a quick war was a Southern war. But the conflict was, in the end, long, bloody, and costly by every measure. Europe got by with cotton from Egypt and India and sat back, more than happy to watch American influence dissipate with its internal struggles. It was to be a Northern war.

The 1st Virginia started the war 570 men strong; they would end it with fewer than twenty. By June 1861, they had moved from Camp Instruction in Richmond, mostly by train and foot, to Fairfax County in Northern Virginia. The soldiers built and settled into defensive positions around the small town of Centreville.

The positions were not like the military installations Francis had become familiar with at Fort Davis in Texas. Ironically, that fort had been named after Jefferson Davis who was then United States Secretary of War. Now he was President of the Confederacy. Fort Davis had huge canyon walls to protect it, in contrast the positions in Centreville were exposed on an open plane on all four sides. Francis feared they could be surrounded and annihilated by a few Union cannons.

Another veteran of Fort Davis, now a Confederate general, James Longstreet reached the same conclusion as Francis. Longstreet, with the goal of protecting the nearby railway hub in the City of Manassas, had his troops fall back to the Bull Run—a watery tributary to the Occoquan River. The Bull Run offered the Confederates a strong natural defense.

A relatively wide stream, at points upwards of a hundred feet wide and several feet deep, the Bull Run had a mucky bottom. Its banks were mostly overgrown and led to steep hills. Consequently, the Union army, with its long supply train and artillery, would find it difficult to cross. The only vulnerability along the Bull Run was a handful of fords where the water was shallow and bottom rocky enough for troops and wagons to pass. Recognizing the weakness, Longstreet concentrated his forces along the fords, especially those near roads leading into Manassas.

Francis was annoyed to have to abandon all the defensive works they had built in Centreville, but he knew it was the right move. He would not tell Longstreet that out of fear Longstreet would recognize him as an absconder. Granted an absconder from the enemy's army, but an absconder nonetheless. So, Francis just followed orders and went about patrolling in and around the Bull Run, using old Indian paths and part of a road dating back to the Revolutionary War. Francis was struck by how beautiful the calm waterway was, hemmed by green foliage and rolling hills. The water meandered down to the Occoquan River which, in turn, linked to the Potomac River a few miles south of Washington, DC.

On a hot and humid morning, Thursday, July 18, 1861, Francis and his regiment were mulling around their temporary camp in a forested area next to a dirt road. The road led from Manassas down a decline to a narrow, shallow portion of the Bull Run called Blackburn's Ford. The road resumed on the northern side of the water, up an incline, and onto Centreville.

There had been rumors spreading of a sizeable Union force nearby, but Francis was doubtful. Such rumors had been as frequent as they had been wrong since he had enlisted. All the fighting to date, no more than skirmishes and posturing really, took place along the coast or to the west. The Union would not be fool enough to waltz right into the main strength of the Confederate Army in a good defensive position. Francis argued to his fellow soldiers that the Bull Run was as fine a moat as surrounded any castle in Ireland,

and he should know because the McNamaras had been castle builders.

"I don't know, Francis?" Challenged Tim Purcell, Francis's friend from Richmond and now fellow member of Company C. The two were prepping for lunch and then would be off to picket duty on the northern side of the water. "Some boys returned to camp last night saying Union troops were just a few hours away looting and burning Germantown and Fairfax Courthouse." Purcell referring to towns above Centerville that stood between Blackburn's Ford and Washington, DC.

"That only strengthens my argument," Francis responded trying to allay his young friend's concern that combat was coming his way. Purcell was 18 years old and looked up to the older Francis, nearly 10 years his senior.

The deference Purcell showed was not just because of age. Purcell, always asking questions, knew Francis had been a soldier previously and that he could always be counted on to explain the "why" for things. Those explanations were often wrong but at least he offered them. In contrast, the officers controlling Purcell's fate only barked out orders, seldom giving explanations because they had none. Most of the time they were just trying to keep soldiers busy because idle hands do the devil's work. And the devil particularly liked large groups of armed and bored men.

"They probably took to looting and burning just to get a rise out of us. To bait us into coming out from behind our defenses. If they had their way, we would drag all our stuff in this heat up to fight them just in the place where fighting suits them best. Don't you worry, Longstreet is too smart to fall for that. After waiting around for a while, Union troops will move onto someplace else rather than attack us here where we have the advantage."

No sooner did Francis complete the sentence that there was the jolt of a nearby cannon blast. Purcell and the others in the company jumped to their feet with worried looks on their faces. Their panic had, for some reason, a calming effect on Francis.

In effort to share his calm, Francis assured his colleagues, "Don't soil your pants boys, it's probably just those crazy gunners from Louisiana again getting in some practice." But even Francis became alarmed when someone pointed to the heights on the other side of the ford where soldiers in dark colored uniforms were scrambling about. Any doubt as to who the soldiers were vanished when, in the distance behind them, flags could be seen. Among them the flag of the United States.

The stripes of red and white with a field of blue waved in the soft summer breeze. There, but not as visible from the Southern side of the water, were stars in the field of blue. Stars representing each state in the Union, including those that had seceded. The North's position was the Union could never be broken, the South arguing back that all bonds eventually break. If it were not the case, both sides would still be paying homage to a king.

With the presence of the Union troops confirmed, the only question was their intention. That became clear enough with an additional volley of cannon fire with the white smoke drifting up adjacent to the Union flags and the projectiles whistling over the heads of Francis and company.

A third round of artillery was fired, this time with the aim lowered so that the shells beheaded trees directly above the position of the 1st Virginia. Additional rounds followed, coming in lower and lower until the gunners over adjusted and shells embedded themselves deep into the red clay of the incline between the Confederate camp and the Bull Run.

Amid the bombardment, the Confederates scattered in panic. One company, some ninety men, tried to stay together. They did so in single file hiding behind the biggest tree they could find. In the shade of the immense three-headed poplar, they squeezed as tight as they could to the tough textured bark of the three-headed growth that was more than a hundred feet tall and twenty feet around. It did appear to be the safest place in the vicinity until a cannonball struck it dead center. The ancient tree, which had lived its life in nothing but peace and quiet, swayed unnaturally and emitted a sickening sound as parts of its root system ripped through the ground like arms and legs from the grave. The men of the company abandoning its cover like a besieged colony of frantic ants.

Francis continued to find himself strangely calm and sympathetic to his terrified colleagues. As if to make them laugh, Francis called out to those around him now hugging the ground for dear life: "You know, now that I think about it, maybe the Yankees would be crazy enough to attack us here after all."

With that, Francis took a deep breath, picked up his rifle and began to walk down toward the water. Across the stream he could see Union infantrymen preparing to attack along the ford. The Confederate pickets that had been on the northern side of the stream had just taken up positions along a tree line on the southern side. Francis joined them thinking this would be the place where his struggles would end. *As good a place as any*, Francis thought to himself and braced for the likelihood he would be killed in the Union infantry attack.

What Francis did not realize is that by calmly walking down to the tree line to face the Union forces, other Confederates in the camp assumed they had been ordered to do the same. Now there were hundreds of Confederates along the tree line that offered them cover and protection from Union fire. The Union troops, not afforded as much natural protection on their side of the stream, fell back after a half-hour of fighting. They reformed about a hundred yards up the incline on their side of the Bull Run.

The Confederates watched, unsure what the Union troops would do next and not wanting to leave the protection of the tree line. The Union plan was to buy some more time and then retreat altogether in an organized fashion. The whole exercise had been intended by Union commanders to be a probing action to determine if Blackburn's Ford was well defended. Now they knew.

General Longstreet arrived on the scene and, from a top his horse looking across the Bull Run, he saw signs that the Union troops were preparing to retreat. To take advantage of their backward movement, Longstreet ordered a frontal counterattack. His decision was bolstered by the Confederates artillery now being engaged and able to respond to Union cannons with equal vigor.

Officers moved down the southern slope toward the tree line and ordered Francis and his unit, and all the other Confederates nearby, to form up into lines and cross the river in pursuit of the Union troops. As the 1st Virginia Infantry marched to the north side of the Bull Run the cannon fire on both sides intensified. In all, close to seven hundred shells would fall onto the battlefield which was only a few hundred yards in size.

With the sound and vibration of the artillery rattling their bones and recognition they had lost momentum, the eyes of the Union forces grew wide at the sight of the Confederate bayonets glistening in the sun in advance of the counterattack. Random assignment had Francis in the second line of men in the Confederate formation. He noticed that the young man in front of him was visibly shaking. It was the youngest member of Company C. Because he was much younger than the sixteen years he claimed to be, the other soldiers called him "the infant."

Francis grabbed the young man by the shoulder and switched positions with him, Francis now being at the very front. An officer yelled, "You there, stay in formation!" Francis ignored him.

It was then that Francis heard it. The order to begin the attack shouted down from behind him, having started with Longstreet. There was no denying it now, he was poised to meet his fate.

Not looking back, Francis sprinted toward the Union line. As he did so, he found himself letting out a whoop and holler, mimicking the war cry of the Indians of the west that he had been taught by Sergeant Valentine and heard firsthand at the battle of Fort Davis. He mixed with it a *Banshee* wail, the frightening call of spirits in the Irish countryside who foretold death. It was more instinctive than anything else but it caught on.

His fellow Confederates added to the war cry, a bastardized combination of Comanche, Banshee, and piss-in-your pants panic. The German immigrants in the Confederate unit running alongside Francis and his company rounded out the din with their own ancient war cry, a guttural moan that went from low to high, sounding as if a horrible storm were rising.

The Roman Legions called it the *Barritus* and appropriated it for themselves after first being terrified by it when they entered the dark forests of ancient Germania.

All the war cries, honed by generations of soldiers to unite their own troops and terrify their enemies, had the intended effect at Blackburn's Ford. Not because those cries were foreign to the shaken Union troops but because they were familiar. Many of the Union enlisted men opposing the Irish and German Confederates were Irish and German immigrants themselves, recruited by the Union in New York and Massachusetts. The northern immigrants hoped too that by fighting in the war they would be accepted as Americans but now feared their ancestors, with the call of the *Banshee* and the *Barritus*, were punishing them for their change in allegiance.

The first step back by Union troops at the sight and sound of the charging Confederates led to several more. The training they had received was just as lacking as that endured by Francis and his fellow Confederates.

The Union infantryman had never practiced falling back on uneven ground or while under aggressive attack. As a result, they awkwardly attempted to fire, reload, and fire again all while tripping and falling on the incline. Francis heard the hiss of countless Minie balls flying around him but then the odd sound and sensation of a swirling object passed overhead. The noise came from one of several ramrods that Union soldiers failed to remove from their gun barrels in their haste when shooting.

The only thing slowing the Confederate attack was the angle of the incline, it being all uphill once they crossed the Bull Run. It gave the Union infantrymen enough time to reform and let loose a volley into the oncoming Confederates.

Francis was shocked he was not hit and that even more of the Confederate soldiers around him did not fall wounded or dead. It reflected poor training, faulty equipment, and panic among the Union soldiers. But there was also another factor. Some of the soldiers, now that the moment had come, could not bring themselves to shoot another human being. Instead, they shot over the enemy's head, their bullets being more of a threat to trees and birds on the other side of the stream than the attacking soldiers in front of them.

Although Francis did not know it, he had been spared by not one but two Union soldiers who had him in their sights. Not everyone was so lucky. When the Union line reformed and let loose yet another massive volley, Captain James K. Lee of Company B and the 1st Virginia's Colonel, Patrick Theodore Moore, were shot. Lee's torso was riddled with bullets and he died instantly, Moore had been hit in the forehead and laid on the ground moaning. Blood from both officers having splattered over men in Francis's company. Attempting to cope with the horror, the infantrymen would later joke in gallows fashion that Captain Lee and Colonel Moore led from the front but ended up all over the place.

Before the Union troops could reload for another volley, Francis reached their line and charged at them yelling in Gaelic, "*Gaugh a Ballagh!*" Make way! Again, he expected at any minute to be struck down but, miraculously, it did not happen so he ran on deeper into the Union ranks. He did not care if any other Confederates followed him. In fact, he hoped no one would. Francis wanted all the enemy fire for himself. He wanted to be blown to smithereens, not languishing with painful wounds. He just wanted to be gone altogether.

But the other Confederates did follow him, including the remaining officers although they were initially slowed by the sight of Colonel Moore. Moore, in a state of shock, tried to stand and rejoin his regiment despite his ghastly head wound. He collapsed just as soon as he got to his feet and he was left for dead.

The Union troops fell into full retreat, their officers desperately trying to form a rearguard below the safety of their cannons now filled with canister that would decimate the Confederate attackers once their own troops were out of the way.

A young Union soldier bravely stood his ground directly in front of Francis. He hurriedly tried to reload his musket while also eyeing Francis's approach. The threat posed by Francis was enough distraction for the Union soldier to miss the gun barrel entirely with the ramrod. Instead, the long metal piece came down with such force that it ran through the soft tissue between the soldier's left thumb and forefinger. He cried out, dropped his gun in pain, and turned to run away. Francis heard that same horrible sound he heard when Latee had been shot at Fort Davis. This time the sound, one of blunt impact and tearing flesh, came from the young Union soldier. The soldier fell to his knees, crimson streaks of blood coming from his mouth. He looked up to the sky, as if seeking divine help.

Francis moved around him, so did the infant—now horrified by the realities of war and wanting to stay as hidden behind Francis as he could. One of the other Confederates eventually bayoneted the young union soldier, a compassionate *coup de gras* or simple cruelty—it did not matter.

With its rearguard dissolving, the Union forces began abandoning the field to Confederate control. There were some lingering cannon exchanges and Union soldiers shooting over their shoulders as they left, but then silence came marking the end of the Battle of Blackburn's Ford.

With the reality that it was over and the Northerners were in flight, the Confederates cheered and threw their hats into the air as if they had won the war. Francis looked around him and saw close to one hundred bodies lying prone or moaning on the ground wounded. Others who had been wounded but still able to move had already left the field or were being carried away to field hospitals. Yet Francis himself—the one who wanted to be struck down once and for all—was left unharmed. He was more surprised and confused by that than anyone.

After the battle, Francis volunteered for the unpleasant task of burial detail. He looked closely at each and every face. He hoped not to see either of his brothers, Sergeant Valentine, or his friend Kevin O'Brien. He did not see any of them but did come across the bluing face of twenty-three-year-old James Silvey.

A Union recruit from Massachusetts, Silvey had been shot twice with one of the bullets traveling through the width of his body, slightly above his hips, and lodged inside a fist sized ball of leather, yarn, and hardened cork in his haversack. Also in the haversack was a pair of canvas shoes with metal spikes that Francis stared at, puzzled.

Another member of the burial detail, a Union prisoner, explained to Francis that Silvey was a *"rounder."* An enthusiast of the new sport of baseball who carried around the ball and cleats in hopes of a pickup game wherever he went. The prisoner teared up and advised that Silvey was "as nice as a fella as you could find" and would have preferred that the outcome of the war been staked on a baseball game rather than a bloody battle.

The prisoner and Francis buried Silvey—with his beloved cleats on and the baseball in his hand. That grave, and that of five others next to him, would remain undisturbed for more than one hundred and fifty years until unearthed and moved to make way for a McDonald's restaurant.

****

It would not take long for Francis to have an opportunity to volunteer for burial detail again. Three days later, on July 21st, Union artillery shelled the 1st Virginia's position again on the Bull Run, resulting in a handful of casualties. The shelling, however, was a diversion. The firing stopped as soon as it started, and the rumble of more intense and sustained cannon fire could be heard several miles to the west, following the upstream path of the Bull Run.

Known as the First Battle of Manassas, it was a rout for the South as was the Battle of Blackburn's Ford. The difference was a matter of scale. Francis and his unit had been relieved of their defensive position and allowed to harass Union troops as the Northerners fled back to Washington, DC.
Some companies of the regiment went into Centreville in pursuit, others—like Francis—were directed to the hills overlooking Warrington Turnpike and Sudley Road, where most of the day's fighting occurred. They were there to help with the wounded.

In horror, Francis looked out over the remnants of the battle and its four thousand casualties. Francis could not fathom all the death and destruction. Bodies of men and animals were spread as far as the eye could see. Half destroyed wagons, often with horse and mule trains still attached, lay sprawled about. There were men walking about dazed, many with physical wounds visible and most with psychological injuries even more damaging. The smell of gunpowder still thick in the hot, humid air.

Francis was struck mute by the carnage and he was a man who had seen cruelty of almost every sort: famine, epidemic, crime, poverty, death of loved ones, and even previous acts of war. He carried wounded men to hastily erected hospital tents where, to Francis's eye, doctors were doing little more than feeling around in soldiers' open wounds searching for bullet fragments and hacking off limbs. Francis vomited at his first sight of discarded arms and legs piling up outside the tents.

With nothing left to heave, his brain then focused on the screams of those with mangled bodies and in dreadful pain. He feared their shrieks would never stop echoing in his ears. But he kept going back to the field to retrieve more of the wounded and looking at the faces of the dead, all the time hoping his brothers and friends would not be among them. They were not. At least not yet.

As the sun fell and night came, Francis continued to do what he could for the wounded, Union and Confederate alike. The next day, in a driving rain, he helped transport those wounded well enough to travel to more established hospital facilities in Manassas Junction about ten miles away. Once there, Francis was reassigned to help carry medical and food supplies from the train depot to the hospital facilities.

He continued to work in that capacity for a few weeks until he started to cough incessantly, and he developed a sore throat. He dismissed it as being run down, but it was more than that.

One of the doctors at the train yard where Francis was helping put patients on trains for transfer to Richmond noticed red spots along Francis's neck and hairline. He directed at once that Francis be restricted to an area reserved for contagious patients.

Francis protested to no avail, the doctor directed a sergeant and guard to make Francis comply. He had measles which were running rampant among the troops North and South. It and other contagious diseases would kill more soldiers than all the bullets and artillery of the war combined. But it would not kill Francis and he was fortunate not to be among those left blind or deaf from the disease. He felt more guilty than thankful at having survived, as so many with more to live for than him had been struck down.

When Francis was sent back to his unit in December 1861, the enlisted men of Company C were glad to see him. He had higher stature than most, being older than the other enlisted men and having been a veteran of the Indian Wars in the West. Adding to that the soldiers huddled in that cold hut in Centerville had already discussed amongst themselves what they deemed as Francis's fearlessness at the Battle of Blackburn's Ford. His willingness to take on the difficult tasks of burying the dead and caring for the wounded, coupled with his surviving a disease that killed and maimed so many others, elevated Francis to almost legendary status.

Little did the men know what they attributed to Francis's bravery were actually signs of his insanity. His suicidal ideation and a morbid fixation that his loved ones would die were his motivators. Had they asked, Francis would have told them as much.

The *de facto* leadership status the men bestowed on Francis had both beneficial and deleterious effects on the military discipline of his company. Notwithstanding his own chronic depression, he could lift the morale of those around him. Usually with a quip or a funny story.

He told one story of a patient next to him in the hospital who had been delirious with fever for weeks. When the fever broke and he came to, the patient asked Francis "Are we in hell?" Francis responded, "Worse, Richmond."

Singing was one of the ways the soldiers occupied themselves and Francis could be counted on to sing some Irish songs, particularly interesting because the lyrics were never the same twice. The trauma in his life and periods of malnutrition during his formative years left his word recall diminished. His choice in word replacement, when not puzzling, was often humorous.

The soldiers particularly liked Francis's deadpan version of "Camptown *Races*" with his version subconsciously reworked as "Claptown Ladies," the clap being a sexually transmitted disease running rampant among the troops at the time. He would end the song, none the wiser to his malapropisms, belting out: "All the Doo Dah Day!"

The drain Francis created on unit discipline stemmed back to his dislike for authority figures. Smart enough not to challenge officers directly, he did it through passive aggression. His antics amused the other enlisted men, they did not like being bossed around anymore than Francis did. And then there was the occasion when Francis led a group of the men, without permission, to a tavern in nearby Clifton, Virginia.

When the provost marshals arrived at the tavern to arrest and return the soldiers to camp, a drunken Francis ran out of the backdoor with all the marshals following him. The other men returned to camp without getting into trouble, as did

Francis—reporting that he lost his pursuers, who he referred to as "jackasses," in the thickets and fields of adjacent farms.

In the spring, as they prepared to leave winter camp, the enlisted men nominated Francis to serve as a flag bearer, taking the unit's battle stars and bars into combat. Most considered it an honor, Francis viewed it more realistically. The flag bearer was a magnet for enemy fire, and for Francis when it came to bullets the more the merrier, for they would put an end to him and his misery. The officers in the unit felt it may put an end to their misery too.

But his tenure with the flag coincided with a lull in the fighting. When it came time in June 1862 for Francis to hand the flag over to another man there was a ceremony attended by General Longstreet. Making eye contact with Francis after the ceremony, Longstreet tipped his hat and smiled in recognition. "Good to see you, Fireball." Longstreet said before riding away.

Captain Dooley, one of the few officers in the regiment that Francis liked, heard what Longstreet had said. He asked Francis, "You know the General?" and followed quickly with, "Why did he call you Fireball?"

Francis shrugged his shoulders, letting Dooley think the General may have mistaken Francis for someone else. Nonetheless, some in the unit took to calling Francis "Fireball," and Francis said nothing to discourage them.

****

As time went on, Francis continued to struggle mentally, yet paradoxically his status among fellow soldiers continued to grow. In the skirmishes that followed, Francis again helped care for wounded comrades, reassured those who had cowered during battle—telling them it was a sign of intelligence—and helped the sizable number in his unit write letters home, many soldiers, particularly the immigrants, being illiterate.

When rations were scarce, as they often were, Francis shared what he had with others. As he did so, he remembered back to the generosity Michael Scanlon had shown him aboard the *Hopewell,* sharing food with him when he would have starved otherwise. As much as Francis ruminated over the negative things in his life, the kindness stayed with him as well. And when he could be kind to others it somehow gave him a reprieve from his depression.

When helping at a field hospital after one skirmish, Francis came upon Michael Scanlon's brother, Thomas, serving in another Virginia infantry regiment. Thomas was suffering from what may have been the first, but not the last, selfinflicted gunshot wound of the war. The chaos of battle and flowing from his inexperience and the inadequate training he received, Thomas had shot himself in the leg while trying to scale a fence and had to be dragged away by other Confederates to avoid being captured by Union troops.

Thomas, not wanting to go into too much detail with Francis as to how he had been injured, told Francis about his stepsons, Timothy and Dennis Moriority. They were doing well, Thomas reported, and they were proving themselves very valuable in helping maintain the Scanlon family farm while Thomas was gone to war.

More than just relieved that the boys were doing well, Francis was proud that they were able to contribute to the family at this difficult time, notwithstanding their young ages.

When Francis asked about Michael Scanlon, Thomas smiled. "You know," Thomas advised, "Michael has been sick off and on since he left the army in Texas. As much as that has been a curse for him, in the end it turned out to be a blessing. When the South seceded, the richest and most politically connected man in our town, Elias White, formed an infantry unit for the Confederacy and expected every man around to enlist, fit or not. When Michael said he was too sick to play a soldier again, White belittled him something awful. I was fuming but Michael—ever the patient one—just let it roll off his shoulders."

Thomas continued, "Since White commanded the regiment and just about everything else in our county, he had it that Michael had to serve as his personal attendant, getting him tea and doing other stupid menial things. That was until White, so big and round, got himself shot dead in our very first encounter with the Yankees. Didn't know how a bullet could miss him to be honest, he was that large. Michael took it on himself to lead the burial detail and when old Colonel White could hardly fit in the pine box, Michael took the initiative to jump up and down on the top lid till it could be nailed shut. Michael acted as if he didn't enjoy it, but justice prevails in the end as the good Lord directs. And with that, Michael made his way home and that is where he stays. God willing, with that peaceful way about him, he'll be dancing on all our graves."

"Amen to that." Francis replied, feigning the religious favor that Thomas actually held. But sincerely Francis hoped his friend Michael would remain out of harm's way. Thomas Scanlon would not be so lucky. He would return to his unit just to be shot yet again, this time by a Union soldier and taken prisoner. After the war, he would have to start over again with his residual injuries and as destitute as when he got off the boat from Ireland with his sister, Francis's deceased wife, Ellen.

****

Francis's kindness was not limited to those in his unit and those he knew. He would also talk, console, and help Union soldiers wounded and taken prisoner as well. In doing so, Francis would always ask the northerners if they knew of his brothers, or of the fate of the 8th Infantry that he had been part of at Fort Davis. The answer was always no. The Union Army started the war with less than twenty thousand regulars but that would swell to two million during the war. Outnumbering the Confederates two to one. On both sides, despite the massive size of the forces, most soldiers were restricted to their own small worlds and only knew those in their company and regiment.

The kindness Francis displayed, however, often stopped at the officers who controlled his fate and that of his comrades. Again, his innate animosity toward authority figures was part of it. But also many of the officers were proving themselves incompetent and Francis had little patience for that when lives were at stake. It was not that the officers chose to be inept. Most had no combat experience coming into the war, received little formal training after their commission, and were often appointed more because of their financial and social standing than their military acumen.

Also underlying Francis's friction with officers was that he thought they should at least consult the men for ideas before making decisions, like Sergeant Valentine had and, at one point, so did General Longstreet. Instead, in seeming insecurity, the officers simply drew up orders and sent them down, never looking back.

Several enlisted men—like himself—had been soldiers before and had seen combat. A handful of men in his company alone had been in the Crimean War in Europe less than a decade before. Others, like Francis, had seen fighting on the frontier. Even more of the enlisted men had been hunters, mechanics, and engineers of various sorts and had other experience that could help them formulate good solutions. Francis would say, "even a blind squirrel finds a nut once in a while," acknowledging that a good suggestion could come from any quarter. Francis recognized that someone had to be in charge, but he thought that someone should get as much input as practicable before acting. That, however, was not the way things worked.

The officers would have loved to rid themselves of Francis somehow. The problem for them was threefold. First, the enlisted men looked up to Francis. If they dealt with him too harshly, it would hurt morale and feed resentment against the officers. Second, the unit was becoming desperately short of men because of casualties and an increasing number of desertions. Third, Francis had proven himself to be more than competent once the fighting started. It was when Francis was on the verge of death that he was thought to have his greatest societal value.

The dynamic between Francis and the officers would take a turn for the worse, and then the better, on April 16, 1862.

****

When he enlisted, Francis agreed to serve for a little more than a year to defend Virginia from Union attack. He was scheduled to be discharged on June 30, 1862. The way things were looking, Francis felt he was not only on the wrong side of the war but more likely to take the life of someone he knew in the North than be killed himself. He wanted out. Upon his discharge, he would be entitled to his signing bonus and extra amount added by the Commonwealth Bank.

Francis had been sending much of what he earned as an infantryman, $11 a month, to Sally Rowland in Norfolk and

the Scanlons in western Virginia, a place called Three
Churches, for the care of Stephen Michael, Timothy, and
Dennis. With the bulk of the bonus money when discharged,
Francis would pick up Stephen Michael and join his brother
Mathew in Philadelphia. Once he found work there and
could establish a home and childcare, Francis planned to
send for his stepsons. He would resurrect his family from the
ashes, or at least he would try to do so to make Ellen—
wherever she was—proud.

The war would be over by summer, Francis surmised. The
North had already launched a massive sea and land
campaign. They were now driving up the Peninsula from the
Chesapeake Bay toward the Confederate capital of
Richmond. Union troops were laying siege to the
Confederate forces at Yorktown, the same place Washington
laid siege to the British at the end of the Revolutionary War.
If they took Yorktown, and it looked like they would, Union
troops would be within sixty miles of Richmond.

Francis's assessment was strengthened by the fact that he
and his company were currently digging defensive works in
the old colonial capital of Williamsburg, expecting to
encounter Union troops there after Yorktown fell.

On April 16th, the drumbeat sounded for assembly and
Francis lined up with the rest of his regiment. Officers
advised they had an important message from President Davis
and the Confederate Congress. To assure a Confederate
victory, the officers announced, a draft had been instituted to
increase troop strength. In addition, all current enlistments
would be extended three years.

Francis was shocked, and the other men were not happy
either as mumbling increased up and down the line. The
officers were then foolish enough to enumerate the

exceptions to the draft and extension: Persons with the means to pay for substitutes and who had large estates with twenty or more slaves. Rich man's war, poor man's fight, for sure.

The officers explained it was not their job to debate the law but to fight the enemy. Many of the men were no longer sure who the enemy was.

One soldier shouted, "Was this a ploy to enslave us all?" Another accused the Confederate Army of fraud. "This is nothing more than the old bait and switch. Join on one set of terms, stay—because you have to—on other terms altogether." The statement coming from a position of knowledge, the soldier a known huckster.

The men figured they would talk as a group later to see what they should do. In the meantime, there was the rote exercise of roll call after announcements. Each soldiers' name was called and the soldier was to step forward and crisply call out, "Here!"

The rote nature of it changed when they got to Francis. He stepped backward instead of forward and said nothing in response to his name. He was protesting.

One of the captains came over and threatened Francis. "If you do not answer, you will be considered absent without leave," snarled the officer.

Francis said nothing and did not move. The officer threatened again, "You will be docked pay and subject to discipline, up to and including execution." Again, Francis said nothing.

The roll call continued, and several other soldiers followed suit—stepping backward and refusing to respond when called. The day was a disaster for the regimental leadership. Morale had already been declining among the troops. Desertion was becoming more common. The legislation, especially with the rich man exceptions, only made things worse. Casting may be the largest cloud of all was that a bigger, better equipped, Union army supported by a powerful navy was closing in on them. A massive force that had been designed for the sole purpose of wiping the Confederates there on the Virginia Peninsula off the face of the earth.

As the men were dismissed to go about their duties, Captain Dooley—then maybe the only officer Francis trusted—called him over. "Colonel wants to speak to you." Dooley led Francis over to Colonel Frederick Gustavus Skinner, then in charge of the regiment.

The Colonel, known as Franklin to his friends, got down from his horse and in a sympathetic tone acknowledged that he too had issues with the Conscription Act that had just been announced to the troops. "The politicians are terrified," said the Colonel trying to explain the situation, "The Yankees are only days away from hanging them all as traitors. Frightened people do stupid things."

The Colonel looked Francis in the eye, "I need you McNamara. You can fight and you can lead. Put aside what those panicking politicians have done. Tell me what I can do to keep you here and the regiment together? Otherwise, we all may be facing the gallows unless we can beat the Yankees back and secure better terms."

Skinner was under no delusion that the Confederacy still had a chance to win the war. He anticipated that Francis understood that as well. No benefit in making believe. Well negotiated terms were the South's only hope. "We bloody their nose a few more times, they may decide the cost of total victory is too high and come to the table. With all the sacrifice we have already made, now is not the time to give up."

Skinner had sought Captain Dooley's counsel on how to communicate most effectively with Francis and was following that advice to the letter. It worked, Francis was given a say in matters affecting his life and often that is all he wanted. A say.

"My wife died and I have kids to take care of. I must get back to what is left of my family. My enlistment goes through the end of June. Let me go then and you have three months of me giving bloody noses starting today." Francis countered.

"I am not going to lie to you," said Skinner, "I don't have authority to discharge people contrary to statute, but I do have friends. One of them is Attorney General Thomas Bragg. He is a good man. I promise you this, and Captain Dooley here is my witness, I will write a personal note on your behalf. If there is a way out for you, Bragg will find it. And you help me here, when I desperately need it, I will find you decent work in Richmond when this is all said and done."

"It's the best deal you can get," advised Skinner. Adding: "If you desert, I will authorize your execution myself. If you malinger, you will be punished severely."

"And if I stay?" Francis asked, with the implication being that the results would be equally bad.

Skinner avoided answering the question directly, just saying again that Francis was needed and that an unconditional loss by the Confederacy could be bad for everyone, as no one knew what kind of retaliation the North had in mind. With the odds increasing that things would not work out well for him, Francis found himself for the first time in a while wanting to survive.

To see his boys again and to take on civilian life with a new perspective, Francis thought that maybe there was still a chance of happiness for him after all. He had pushed the concept of happiness out of his head for a long time after Ellen's death, thinking it never again achievable. He still missed Ellen but in the two years since her death his grief had lessened from intolerable to just agonizingly painful. That coupled with signs that the war was coming to an end, offered him a sliver of hope.

Again, following Captain Dooley's advice, Colonel Skinner looked directly into Francis's eyes to convey earnestness and offered his hand for Francis to shake on the deal. Skinner was desperate, if he lost Francis and a few others to desertion or open insubordination, the regiment would cease to be an effective fighting unit. The Union troops would march right into the Confederate capital and everything Skinner had known in his life would be lost.

"A letter from you urging the Confederacy to honor my original commitment and let me go with no strings attached. And you will get me a good job once I am out of the army." Francis said, seeking confirmation on Skinner's end of the deal. The Colonel gave the requested assurance and Francis shook his outstretched hand. Not much of a deal considering the situation, but a deal nonetheless. A deal struck just in time for the Battle of Williamsburg.

****

Yorktown fell a few weeks later, on May 4, 1862. The bulk of the Confederate forces withdrew up the Peninsula to stage ongoing resistance to what seemed like an inevitable end.

What the South needed was time, and the plan to provide it involved a delaying action at Williamsburg. In and around the old city, more of a town really, Francis and his colleagues had worked day and night to construct defensive works and redoubts.

Those structures and Francis's unit would be at the center of 70,000 troops clashing the day after Yorktown was in Union hands. The battle went back and forth, Northern attacks pushing forward only to be repelled, and the same for the Southern counterattacks. It was a stalemate and a stalemate the Confederate leadership desperately needed. But the cost was immense, nearly four thousand casualties in one day.

Another casualty was Francis's neutrality. He was no longer there seeking a painless death, he now fought to impress Colonel Skinner in hopes of getting out alive. Fighting to live, Francis would find, was more difficult than fighting to die.

Adding to Francis's woes was that just days after the Battle of Williamsburg, Norfolk fell to Union forces and would stay under Union control the rest of the war. Francis's son, Stephen Michael, was in Norfolk with the Rowlands. The boy, therefore, was behind enemy lines. Then West Virginia—where his stepsons Timothy and Dennis were housed—formally and permanently withdrew from the Confederacy and joined the Union. Whereas his grief and lack of resources kept Francis from the boys before, now he was separated from them by a massive army, the army now setting its sights on the Confederate capital.

The Union pushed forward one costly battle after another. They were within five miles of the Richmond city limits when General Robert E. Lee launched a counter-offensive. The Seven-Days Battles that followed, and that involved the

1st Virginia Infantry, produced more than 35,000 casualties—with the Confederates suffering most. But the desperate fight did put an end to the Union's Peninsula Campaign. A bloody nose but not enough to produce the negotiations Colonel Skinner had hoped for and that Francis banked on.

It was June 1862, when his enlistment should have expired. Francis sat, filthy, bloody, and exhausted. He was not alone. His company had fought for a month straight, marching hundreds of miles and digging enough trenches—he thought—to reach hell itself. Often, they had little in the way of food, no medicine for the wounded, and dwindling stores of ammunition. Francis did not even have shoes. The ones he had—along with his socks—fell victim to the mud of the Chickahominy River during a surprise attack on a Union position.

With Richmond visible in the distance, the place where most of Francis's regiment had been recruited, many of the enlisted men—upwards of 30 percent—deserted. Some left temporarily while others abandoned the army altogether. Among those in the latter group included most of the men from Francis's company.

Colonel Skinner had hoped by convincing Francis to stay with the regiment others would follow suit, just as they had followed Francis in protest at Williamsburg. It was a major miscalculation. The Irishmen in Company C knew the war was lost and unilateral altering of their enlistment terms proved the Confederates government had no respect for their rights. There was nothing justifying them staying with the Confederate Army. The fact that Francis got a deal to stay only sped up the exodus, many of the men resentful they were not offered anything.

Francis understood and would have left too but for the deal. That did not stop him, however, from leaving for short periods of time when desperate enough. As he looked at Richmond in the distance, he decided to go there on his own seeking socks, shoes, and food—things the army was proving unable to supply him. As he made his way into the heart of Richmond, the town was uncharacteristically quiet except for a tavern operating out of what had been an art studio before the war. Francis went in and ordered a drink and just sat, running his fingers through his hair, not wanting to have a single thought.

At the table behind him, Francis heard a commotion. He turned to see three Confederate officers, in pristine uniforms harassing the barmaid. She was an Irish woman about Francis's age, who looked like she had as much heartache as he did.

The officers, staffers at headquarters, had obviously not seen any of the hardship of the recent battles. That was ironic because they looked to Francis like the rich, slave-owning type. The people who had the most at stake in what was going on.

One of the officers said, "Come on, give us a peek," and tried to pull down the top of the barmaid's blouse. She pushed the officer away forcibly and gave him a disgusted look.

"Leave her be," Francis said monotoned yet conveying determination. "She is just trying to make a living."

"How about you shut up? Private, is it? Is that what you are, a private?" questioned the officer who made a go at the blouse.

With that response, Francis's trigger had been pulled and there was no going back. The harshness of the war made

Francis's propensity for violence generally bubble to the surface with ease. The thought of striking out against a pompous authority figure gave Francis a jolt of adrenaline. A hormone his body had become fine-tuned to in all the battles he had seen.

As he walked toward the officer, Francis said nothing. The officer stood up from the table, as did his colleagues. Francis walked to within inches of the officer's face.

"Are you trying to intimidate me, a superior officer, private?" Asked the officer with a smirk on his face. He was larger and in better condition than the worn and battered Francis. Besides, Francis was by himself while the officer had two others with him.

Inherent in intimidation is a threat of harm and Francis did not intend to make threats. He had already committed himself to inflicting harm on the officer directly, no matter the cost to himself. It would pale in comparison, in Francis mind at that moment at least, to the cost to his self-respect if he backed down.

In approaching close to the officer's face, Francis was taking measurements. With the measurements in mind, Francis bent his knees, grabbed the officer by the lapels and pulled down while launching headfirst into the officer's nose. The officer instinctively brought his hands to his face and bent forward in pain, at which point Francis yanked the officer's upper body down further and kneed him in the face. If the headbutt did not break the officer's nose, the knee surely did.

Francis quickly slipped behind the officer and kicked him in the back of the knees. Francis fell to the floor pulling the officer's body over him as cover. Using his own arms to pin the officer's arms, Francis wrapped his legs around the officer's legs. The officer's shiny boots stood in stark contrast to the filth of Francis's bare feet.

The other two officers tried to get at Francis but had a difficult time doing so because of the positioning. A trick Francis had learned from Sergeant Valentine. It worked great, for a while. Then, one kick with a wooden soled boot caught Francis above the right eye. Another kick caught him in the temple, and everything went black.

A higher-ranking officer seeing the ruckus intervened shouting: "Save it for the Yankees boys! Save it for the Yankees!" Francis heard none of it. He woke to the smiling, pretty face of the barmaid. Bridget Maloney.

"You need some stitches or you will bleed to death," Bridget advised. Francis looked down at the blood stains on his now shabby grey uniform. She took him to the back of the bar, sat him down, and left to get a needle and thread. The bartender brought over a bottle of whiskey. "On the house," he said, "Bridget is good people and should not have to put up with bullshit like that."

Bridget had a confident way about her, although Francis wondered how often she was in the business of stitching up people.

"This may hurt a bit," she said, "if you are the little girl type. Just keep looking into my eyes. My beauty will hypnotize you." She was right, Francis did not wince once.

"There," she said, "same stitch as I put on my skirts when I want them to drag in the mud." Francis would be left with a noticeable scar above his eye. Bridget was no seamstress. He would thereafter run his finger along the scar whenever he wanted to think of her.

Bridget Maloney was a widow with no children. Her brogue had softened more than Francis's had, but it was still there, as were her Irish eyes, her Irish wit, and her Irish heart. Francis and Bridget were married two days later, on June 26, 1862, in Richmond.

Francis returned to the 1ˢᵗ Virginia, albeit reluctantly. He needed money and his soldier's salary was all that was currently available to him. Francis planned to draw his infantryman pay for a little longer, and then resume his life as a civilian without fear of provosts chasing him as a deserter once Colonel Skinner came through on his promise. Francis wondered how Bridget would get along with the boys, Stephen Michael in particular, once he could reunite the family. Splendid he assumed.

****

The fighting for Francis was more sporadic over the summer of 1862, although it seemed other people were shooting each other wholesale elsewhere in the country. The quiet gave way for the 1ˢᵗ Virginia at the end of August.

As if everything was going full circle, the Confederates met a large Union force in nearly the identical place as First Manassas a year before. The fighting was fierce yet again. In the end, the outcome would turn on a counterassault led by General Longstreet. It was the largest, simultaneous mass assault of the war and Francis and the 1ˢᵗ Virginia were in the center of it.

Northern troops put up a brave fight, but they were overwhelmed by the speed and tenacity of the Confederate attack. In the encounter, Francis and his company confronted the 12ᵗʰ Massachusetts Infantry. Francis was struck by the gallantry of its Colonel Fletcher Webster. Webster stayed with his men and directed resistance until he was struck down.

The Colonel, Francis would learn, was the son of the famed New England lawyer and statesman Daniel Webster. Francis would hear it from a fellow Virginia soldier, Ludwell Hutchison, who gave water to Webster as he lay dying. Webster, knowing his time was at hand, gave his personal effects to Hutchison asking that they be returned to his family in Massachusetts. The Confederate would do what was asked but would have to wait years until the war was over and communication reestablished between the states to do it.

Francis was just as impressed by the heroism during the battle of his own colonel, Franklin Skinner. He too remained beside his men in the thick of the fighting. When Union cannons threatened his Virginia regiment, Skinner did not run but charged the artillery instead. Gravely wounded in the process, Skinner was carried from the field. Francis assumed the deal for a discharge from the army was as dead as Skinner appeared to be.

The Battle of Second Manassas was a Confederate victory. There was no celebrating, however. There was no end to the war in sight and the battles were just becoming more costly. When Francis wandered the Manassas battlefield for the first time, a year before, he was horrified by the nearly five thousand casualties. Now, at Second Manassas, the toll was four times as great, with 22,200 dead, wounded, missing, or taken prisoner.

Adding to the carnage, hundreds of partially destroyed artillery pieces, wagons, and assorted military wares laid about. So did many dead and dying animals drawn in by humans to serve and suffer in the conflict with no stake in the war or its outcome.

Glassy-eyed, Francis did what he always did after a battle. He studied the faces of the dead hoping his brothers and Union friends would not be among them. As on the other occasions, none of the faces looked familiar to Francis but oddly they were all beginning to look the same. The only difference this time in the brutal August heat was the intensity of the stench from the battle. The vile mix of gunpowder, rotting flesh, singed hair, and of death itself was stronger there than any other place Francis had been. He feared he would never rid his nostrils of it.

The war was madness and Francis felt once again as if he would break. He thought about desertion but knew the Confederacy was now aggressively dealing with its deserters. In the previous month alone, he had witnessed two soldiers savagely flogged and three others executed by firing squad for desertion. The executions had been ordered and carried out with great fanfare by General Stonewall Jackson. The men selected by Jackson for the most severe penalties were chosen because they were liked and respected by the other soldiers. The desperation that drove them to desert was irrelevant, all that mattered was the message: desertion would no longer be tolerated. Be killed on the battlefield or be shot by your own on the parade ground, the choices had become that grim.

The Confederate government increased its bounties for the capture and return of deserters. The provost marshal and home guard patrolled the roads with specific orders to forcibly apprehend any soldier without a pass. Even if a deserting soldier could elude capture and physical punishment, finding employment once they returned home was nearly impossible. The Southern economy was in free fall. The Richmond newspapers were replete with stories of deserters who resorted to begging and petty theft to survive. There were no good options.

Lost in his thoughts on the bloody Manassas battlefield, Francis glanced to the west where the sun was setting. He could see the outline of the beautiful Blue Ridge Mountains. The mountains, part of the Appalachian chain, started in Pennsylvania and ran south straight through Georgia. One of the officers on a horse rode up to Francis, "That is where you are heading McNamara, to the mountains. We leave at first light so get some sleep."

The officer started to ride away when he looked back over his shoulder at Francis. "You were really something today, Mac." Francis acted like he had no idea what the officer was talking about. For Francis, there was nothing to be proud of, or embarrassed over, on the battlefield. There were only things to be endured and he was not sure he could endure much more. He wondered what Bridget was doing and desperately wanted to see her again.

The next morning, Francis collected his haversack, knapsack, tent, bedding, cooking gear, canteens, rifle, and ammunition. The equipment weighed upwards of fifty pounds, adding more than a third to his declining body weight as he marched. Francis also carried with him, as he had the whole war, three books. There was the history book given him by his mother in Ireland. The book on moral philosophy he received from Father Devlin in Norfolk. And the small Bible he had taken from Ellen's hand in Richmond when she died. Francis had the first two all but memorized, the Bible had remained closed—the way it was when Ellen took her last breath.

****

The marches during that previous summer had been brutal due to the heat. The trek deep into the Blue Ridge lasted into September and there was finally a hint of fall in the air. The journey was also made easier by the beauty of the surrounding countryside. They marched past open meadows with tall green grass and flowers, trickling streams, and followed roads lined with majestic old trees. There were gentle twists and turns through the foothills that made Francis pleasantly wonder what was behind each curve.

Francis thought back to the day he enlisted in the Confederate Army. His coworker from the masonry shop, Tim Purcell, had said at the war's end soldiers may get land grants. Farmland. Purcell had been in the same unit as Francis from the very beginning, but Francis could not remember what happened to him. Had he deserted, been transferred, killed, or wounded? Francis was starting to forget about the loss of those he knew, a self-preservation mechanism he assumed.

Nonetheless, Francis daydreamed of surviving the war, receiving a land grant, and building a homestead in one of the passing meadows. It would be beautiful and peaceful. Francis promised himself that he would come back to the area because it was that picturesque.

****

On September 14, 1862, a little more than two weeks after the Second Battle of Manassas, Francis and his unit walked onto yet another battlefield, this one along South Mountain in Maryland. The day-long struggle left five thousand casualties and was a Union victory.

The outnumbered Confederate soldiers retreated to their camp, quickly grabbed their belongings, and left. They did not go home, however, they stayed in Maryland—Union territory.

The next day, September 15th, as part of Kemper's Brigade, the 1st Virginia Infantry arrived at the town of Sharpsburg, Maryland. They were assigned to camp on an elevation above the town, ominously called Cemetery Hill.

Fate would not afford them a single day's rest. On September 16th, the Confederates heard the roar of Union cannons once again. Union infantry could be seen forming up across the nearby Antietam Creek. There were clearly more Union soldiers than Confederate, at least twice as many. Outgunned, outnumbered, and in Northern territory, Francis feared this would be a slaughter. As if on cue, the weather turned colder and it started to rain. The battle would have to wait to the next day. The soldiers on both sides would spend a miserable night in anticipation of yet another blood bath in the morning.

At dawn, on September 17th, with fog thick in the air, Union forces began to cross the Antietam Creek that, up until that point, had been separating them from the Confederates. More bothersome for Francis than the noise of the supporting cannon fire aimed in his direction was the haunting echoes from Union drums.

The drummers, often just boys, used beats to communicate orders and to signal the positions of their units. At Antietam, the drum's percussion also heralded death. The death of not only infantrymen but drummers too.

The youngest Union fatality of the day was thirteen-year-old Charlie Edwin King, a Union drummer from Pennsylvania, who was killed in a shrapnel blast. The youngest Confederate on the field was 9-year-old drummer Richard "Little Berry" Binford of the 9th Alabama Infantry. While

Binford would survive the war, the mental stress of his military experience contributed to his premature death in his thirties.

Once the fighting started around Antietam Creek, it continued at an intense pace for twelve hours. The bloodiest twelve hours in American military history with nearly 23,000 casualties.

When Francis first fought at Blackburn's Ford, he could have counted artillery shells in the hundreds. By the Peninsula Campaign, the shell count was in the thousands. At Second Manassas, tens of thousands. At Antietam, five hundred artillery pieces rained down more than fifty thousand shells of ruin. If that rate of destruction continued, Francis feared that the earth itself would eventually be a casualty. He envisioned pockmarked and scorched fields, forests reduced to stumps, cities in rubble, and dead bodies floating in the water. World Wars on the horizon.

With all the horrible sights and sounds around him at Antietam, Francis found it necessary to put himself into a mindless trance. He did what he was trained and told to do, and that was nothing short of inhumane for Francis and those he fought. When the battle was over, Francis sat once again covered in dirt, sweat, and blood. This time, he was catatonic and unresponsive to officers and enlisted men alike. It looked as if he would just sit there even as the other Confederates were retreating to Virginia and the Union was establishing control of the field.

Then, abruptly and without saying a word, Francis stood up and started to walk. He paid no attention to any other soldier, alive or dead, on the battlefield. He just walked deliberately back to where he had left his knapsack and other belongings that morning.

Joining other stragglers in a similar mental state, Francis stayed at the rear of the retreating Confederate Army of Northern Virginia. From a distance, they looked like a rear guard. Up close, everyone could tell the group was mentally spent. They had simply seen, heard, and done too much.

It took weeks for Francis's zombied state to diminish. None of the other soldiers would remark on Francis's mental condition. They all had battle fatigue or what they called "soldier's heart" themselves. The fear was that if one person spoke about it, they would all break. It was a torment they and their generation would have to deal with on their own. The medical profession could not help them and even religion, for most of the men, now sounded hollow.

****

In October 1862, the Confederate Army of Northern Virginia was solidifying its defensive position in the Blue Ridge Mountains. They expected Union forces to press their advantage after the Battle of Antietam. What little was left of Francis's unit was assigned to monitor a railroad line that ran from Harpers Ferry, then in Union hands, to Winchester, Virginia where the bulk of the Confederates were based. The Union, it was feared by Confederate leaders, would use the railroad to bring in troops and supplies for an attack.

When Francis returned from a patrol and approached his tent, he was stopped by a corporal he had never seen before. The corporal asked Francis to declare his name, rank, and unit. When Francis did so, the corporal handed him a document, saluted, and walked away. It was Francis's discharge. Although he did not know it because communication was so slow, Francis had been out of the army for a month.

True to his word, Colonel Skinner, who survived his wounds at Second Manassas, had written the Confederate Attorney

General on Francis's behalf. The discharge order was actually a special directive from Attorney General Watts, not Bragg, so Skinner's influence—bolstered by reports of his heroism at Second Manassas—was significant.

The Attorney General took a provision of the Conscription Act, designed to have immigrants subject to the draft, and spun it on its head. The law, and related regulations, said an alien domiciled in the Confederacy was subject to draft and enlistment retention. Francis just had to attest that he was not a citizen of the country and that he had no domicile. The result was an official separation from the army, albeit an unceremonious one.

Francis's appearance and brogue corroborated his claim not to be a citizen. It was the only time those traits worked to his advantage. As to the domicile question, Francis had no idea what a domicile was, but he would not let it keep him from going home to Bridget in Richmond.

As to Skinner's promise to find Francis a job, with the discharge papers was a copy of a letter of recommendation Skinner had sent to an acquaintance, Abraham Myers, the Confederate Quartermaster. The letter urged Myers to hire Francis as a civilian, describing Francis as capable, dependable, and has having better appreciation than most of the Quartermaster's importance in supplying the troops.

The beauty of the Blue Ridge Mountains now became crisper to Francis's eye as his spirits soared at the thought of having survived being a soldier once again. As he made his way back to Richmond via supply wagon, train, and foot, Francis took in every tree, each leaf changing color, and the texture of the gravel and dirt beneath his feet. Yes, he thought to himself, he would come back to this beautiful place and start over with Bridget and the boys.

Chapter Eleven
A Civilian with a Mission

Virginia
November & December 1862

Once back in the capital, Francis made his way to the Commonwealth Bank on the north side of Cary Street. Francis waited in line and then spoke to a teller about collecting his signing bonus and matching funds deposited at the bank. Francis planned to pool the money with the back pay he was given upon his discharge, for nearly three hundred dollars total. He would not have to show up to his wife, Bridget, empty-handed.

A middle-aged teller, with her hair pasted flat and parted in the middle as had been the style before the war, asked Francis for the paperwork related to the account. Francis stuck his hands down the back of his pants. He had sewn a waterproof leather pouch into the seat of his pants for all his important documents. Francis concluded that keeping the paperwork in his haversack was too risky, as would be leaving it in his jacket which he often had to take off in the heat. The seat of his pants went everywhere he did, and no one could rifle through there without him knowing. The paperwork had stayed neatly folded and perfectly safe in his "behind pocket," as he called it, for a year and a half.

The teller looked in disgust on the counter in front of her. She refused to touch the papers as they smelled as bad as Francis did.

"Not a lot of time for bathing where I have been," Francis said with a smile. "But everything you need is right there," Francis said pointing to the documents. "Once you give me my money, I'll get out of here and take a long bath, I promise." Giving the teller an incentive to quickly process his request.

Fighting back the dry heaves, the teller summoned over the assistant branch manager. She explained the situation to the manager and then excused herself to get some air. The manager examined the documents that Francis provided. It appeared as if the manager was going to ask a question but then shook his head and returned to his review of the papers. Eventually, he looked at Francis and said, "I don't have authority to release these funds."

"Good to know. Who does have the authority?" Francis asked surprisingly not agitated by the bank employee being useless.

"It has to be one of our vice-presidents." The manager advised, and then signaled for the attention of an older and better-dressed man sitting at a large desk in the back of the bank. The man did not introduce himself when he arrived at the teller station. Instead, he heard the manager explain the situation and then began his own examination of the documents—in virtually the same manner the manager had.

Without saying a word, the man turned away and started walking back to his desk, the documents in hand. Francis followed him. The man stopped abruptly and directed Francis to go back to the teller station.

"Only employees are permitted in this section of the bank." The man made the statement with such an authoritarian tone most people would have sheepishly returned to the counter in front of the teller station. Francis did not.

"I go where the documents go until I get my money." Francis said sternly but calmly.

"I am a vice-president in this bank, you can entrust the documents to me to look into the matter." The man responded dismissively.

"Well, I entrusted this bank with my money," Francis said, "and so far, it hasn't turned out well. You are the third person I am speaking to and the cash is still nowhere to be seen. And no offense but I don't know you from Adam. I do not even know your name. So, until I have my money, I am not letting those documents out of my sight. Being a bank vice-president, I am sure you understand that."

"Alright then," the man said with a sigh. He directed Francis to follow him to a conference room at the far end of the bank, near the vault. Along the way, the man asked one of the secretaries to have other people—Francis did not hear the names—to join them in the conference room. What Francis did hear was the secretary refer to the man walking around with Francis's documents as Mr. Blidge.

More people, more trouble, Francis thought to himself as he and Blidge sat in silence waiting for the others. But Francis had expected, and prepared himself for, some resistance. It was inherent whenever trying to collect money, so he decided to remain calm as his right to the funds were indisputable.

A Mr. Sagget and Mr. Tolner introduced themselves properly, not like Blidge, and advised they too were vicepresidents of the bank. They read over the paperwork, conferred in whispers to each other, and then handed the documents back to Francis. Somehow Tolner drew the short straw and spoke up, giving Francis assorted reasons why the funds could not be released.

"Mr. McNamara, you are among the first to seek withdrawing funds from what are special accounts created to support the war effort and our fighting men. The accounts are designed to be payable at the end of the war, and as you know the Yankees haven't surrendered yet."

Based on Francis's down and out appearance, Tolner assumed Francis wasn't literate and even if he was, it would not be to the level to understand the complex financial documents. But Tolner was quickly disabused of that assumption when Francis began pointing to, and quoting from, key phrases in the documents related to withdrawals.

"Funds payable upon successful discharge, says it right there." Francis cited as he pointed to the provision on one of the documents. It says nothing about the end of the war and thank goodness because only God knows when that will be."

Blidge spoke up, annoyed that Francis had the audacity to challenge the bank officials, "You received a *special discharge,* Mr. McNamara, according to the very documents you provided. You did not earn the requisite s*uccessful discharge*." Blidge looked at his coworkers pompously as if to convey the case was closed and yet another lowly customer outwitted.

"There is no such thing as a *successful discharge,* Mr. Blidge." Francis responded with sarcasm beginning to surface in his tone. "The bank made up that phrase. It is not used by the Confederate Army, and it is them that does the discharging. Sloppy language is on the bank, not me. And *what I earned*, Mr. Blidge, is payment of $125. And maybe a thank you for having kept the Yankees from shoving a bayonet up your ass while they looted this bank."

With the situation beginning to spin out of control, Tolner tried to defuse things by saying, "Mr. McNamara, we are not questioning your service to Virginia, it is just that these are special accounts and involve special considerations." Just as Francis was about to say all the considerations were in the paperwork and there was nothing special about them, yet another bank official entered the conference room before Francis could get the words out.

Clarence Ramsford was the most senior in both age and rank among the vice-presidents in the bank that day, which also served as the institution's headquarters as well as a branch. The other men seemed relieved with his appearance, Francis sensed just another obstacle and said, only half-joking, "How many vice-presidents does this bank have and do we need all of them to get this done? It is not that complicated; I have money deposited at the bank and I want to withdraw it. That is how banks work, isn't it?"

Ramsford stared at Francis in a condescending way, literally looking down his nose before asking the other vice-presidents for a summary of the situation. Francis began to speak but Ramsford put his hand up in front of Francis's face to silence him, and that brought Francis close to the breaking point.

Instead of losing his temper, however, Francis began folding up the documents in his hand and once again returned them to the seat of his pants. The sight of him doing so brought all the bank vice-presidents to silence.

"Gentlemen," Francis announced, watching to see if Ramsford would be stupid enough to raise his hand again— he wasn't. "You need time to consult with one another and to think it over. I understand. You were not expecting me today. I just ask that you keep in mind that while $125 may not be a lot of money to you or this bank, it's all that I have for my family."

Francis continued in a slow steady tone, "You should also remember that for more than a year now I have been shooting and bayonetting people. Perfect strangers. I have done so, in part, based on representations made by this very institution. I am sure some of the poor souls I killed were nice people, maybe even a few bank vice-presidents among them. I trusted this bank. And so did many of my fellow soldiers still in the army and they are going to be quite upset to hear of difficulties related to withdrawals. I can tell you, the last thing you want is them coming back here to create a run on this bank—because the Yankees will be right behind them. And I imagine the Yankees won't be submitting paperwork for their withdrawals."

With that, Francis made a point of saying goodbye—out loud—to each vice-president by name. He stared at their faces as if incorporating them to memory. That night, Francis slept in an empty lot around the corner from the bank and was first in line when the bank opened the next morning. He was greeted by the same teller as the day before, who grimaced at the sight and smell of him. Francis again smiled at her, "No cash, no bath." Francis said.

The teller notified Blidge, who looking at Francis from his desk, took out a ledger. He wrote and ripped out what looked like a check. The teller took the check, proceeded to her station, counted out cash and then recounted it. She waved to Francis to come over, gave him the slip of paper to sign as a receipt and gave him the money he was owed.

Francis recounted the cash himself, slowly. Periodically looking up at the teller cringing at his stench. "Bath time." Francis said, winking at the teller. He then placed the cash into the pocket in the seat of his pants and left the bank.

****

Francis went to one of the city's bathhouses. He stripped down, transferring the money from his pants to inside the history book his mother had given him. Francis put the book along with other valuables, including his discharge papers, in his haversack and placed the strap across his naked body as he washed his clothes and took a bath. Afterward, Francis got a haircut and a shave at what he thought were ridiculously high prices. He was not familiar with the inflation plaguing the city.

Once he was cleaned up, Francis proceeded to the small room Bridget rented in what was more of a shack than a building, just around the block from the tavern where she worked. She was so surprised and excited to see him, Francis could not help but laugh. He did not leave her side for three days.

As they caught up with each other, having been apart for months, Francis brainstormed with Bridget how he could reestablish communication with his son and stepsons—the three of them still being in Union controlled territory. He had set aside a portion of his cash to forward to the Rowlands and Scanlons for the boys' care, but there were no means to send the funds. Feeling guilty keeping the money himself, Francis handed the cash to Bridget. When she advised she would deposit it at the bank where she kept her meager savings, Francis advised: "If it is the Commonwealth Bank, don't tell them you got it from me." Bridget was afraid to ask why.

Once Bridget left for work, Francis found himself quickly becoming anxious and uneasy. Thinking a walk would help, Francis only became more unsettled seeing just how much the city had deteriorated during the war. The Union naval blockade and repeated land invasions targeting the Confederate capital, left the city short on most things.

Once flourishing businesses were boarded up everywhere Francis went, including Bill McCloy's masonry shop where Francis worked before the war. The Tredegar Iron Works, however, seemed busier than ever. Its smokestacks covered everything nearby with filth, including its now mostly slave workforce who labored around the clock producing war goods.

Only the businesses that serviced the military, including bars and houses of prostitution, seemed to be surviving. The other things, the things that made life worth living in the city— were starving or already dead. Most street corners had groups of beggars, former soldiers missing arms and legs, and equally desperate women and children in rags. The sight of it made Francis think back to Ireland amid the famine.

Adding to the sadness, Francis went back to his old apartment, the one he shared with Ellen. There he learned his kindly old landlord, Kenneth Coale, had passed away.

When Francis visited Ellen's grave, and that of his infant namesake, he brought flowers and cleaned off the tombstone he had made for them. Francis spoke to Ellen about what he had been through since she died, and admitted he was unsure of the status of her sons. There was no reply, although he secretly hoped there would be. She was truly gone and couldn't help him nor the boys.

On his way back from the graveyard, Francis went into one of the countless taverns filled with soldiers that he had passed earlier in his walk. With the pocket money he had kept for himself, Francis got ossified drunk. While in his drunken state, Francis started picking fights with anyone in uniform and when thrown out of the bar, he threatened to burn down the home of a man innocently standing nearby, Joseph Stukenburg, because he looked like a Toobin.

When he eventually made his way home to Bridget, Francis was still drunk. Bridget was terrified by the sight and sound of him. He was out of control, and seemingly out of his mind. He wobbled, mumbled, and periodically shouted as he threw things at random targets. Bridget tried to hold Francis to calm him down but he threw her to the ground, shouting "I will kill you all, leave me alone, I will kill you all!"

A police officer on foot patrol, waived down by a neighbor, entered the room but backed away upon seeing how wildly agitated Francis was. Back in the street, the officer whistled frantically for backup. It was only when there were three officers, aided by some passersby, that Francis was subdued and he started calming down. One of the police officers told Bridget that they were seeing this type of behavior often now with soldiers coming home injured and on furloughs.

"Poor bastards," the officer said, and then seeing how shaken Bridget was, he added, "I am sorry Ma'am, I am sure it is just something they have to get out of their system and then they will be fine. Just keep him away from the liquor. That seems to make things worse for many of them."

The police hauled Francis away in a wagon, a paddy wagon as it disparagingly came to be known, and when arraigned in court he was charged with *Mistaking his family for the enemy and making terroristic threats*, in relation to the arson comment he had made to the Toobin lookalike. Francis apologized profusely to the judge and everyone in the courtroom, particularly the elderly German, Mr. Stukenburg, whose home Francis had threatened to burn down.

"You look nothing like an Toobin, I am truly sorry," Francis said to Stukenburg as if the comparison to the Toobins was the most problematic aspect of his crime. Then to the judge, Francis explained, "I didn't realize how drunk I was. It has been a while since I touched the stuff and it will be a while before I touch it again based on all the harm I did. I didn't mean to do it. Again, I am sorry."

The judge looked at Francis's discharge papers confirming that he was not a deserter, which would have been an aggravating factor in his case and a reason to turn him over to the provost marshal.

"I have never heard of anyone released from the military upon a special order of the Attorney General like you have been, you must have done something very good or very bad." "I did what was asked of me," Francis responded.

After the judge asked Francis what battles he had been involved in, he asked if Francis had killed any Yankees. Francis became uneasy and hesitated to answer and showed signs of becoming upset.

"I take that as a yes." The judge said with a smile and ordered Francis released and the charges dismissed to the chagrin of the German mistaken for an Toobin.

While the courts may have been done with Francis, Bridget was not. She lectured and questioned him about his conduct for what seemed to Francis like hours, but he remained contrite—because he truly was sorry. He was also embarrassed by what he had done, which made him think of his father and the day the old man came back to the family cottage looking for forgiveness. The last day of the old man's life.

What Bridget was most concerned about was not what Francis did but what he would do in the future. Had the war driven him insane? Was he a danger to her or to himself? Francis blamed it all on being drunk which he told Bridget would not happen again. She knew that was a lie but his face was so forlorn and there was that scar above his eye he got defending her when they first met.

The drinking excuse resonated with Bridget for the same reason it resonated with so many others. It was simpler to attribute things to drink rather than try to wrestle with the black hole of the human psyche that prompted the drinking. The symptom more visible than the cause. Francis drank in a misguided attempt to self-medicate. His ability to cope had been overwhelmed by the harshness and arbitrariness of his life. It was the same coping tactic used, with similar results, by his father. But what else was there? Religion and medicine both fell horribly short. So, it was easier for everyone to think the problem started and ended with the alcohol.

****

Just as things were beginning to look bleak for Francis's civilian life, he got a break. He landed a steady paying job— an increasingly rare commodity since the Union was making more progress against the Confederate economy than its military. Colonel Skinner's reference to the Quartermaster paid off. Hired as a porter, Francis's pay was not much different than his infantryman wage—which Francis originally thought a good thing. But again, he had not fully grasped the impact of inflation and it was rising rapidly throughout the Confederacy. Francis and Bridget found themselves quickly losing ground monetarily. The only saving grace was that so was everyone around them. They were not alone.

Francis's work with the Quartermaster varied. At first, he was assigned to the Clothing Bureau receiving and distributing shipments of uniforms and boots from the main warehouses in Richmond. Then, for a week, he loaded and unloaded supplies of all sorts at the city's train station. After that, Francis was assigned a wagon and mule team to go into the field to act as a procurement agent.

His job was to scout about and obtain needed supplies any way he could and deliver them to Quartermaster facilities or to Confederate combat units, depending on the nature of the item and the desperation of its need. With the Confederate currency plummeting in value, no one was willing to sell Francis needed items large or small. He resorted then, in concert with army troops, to seize items that were needed and leave behind a tax in-kind certificate that was even more worthless than Confederate currency.

In doing so, Francis knew he was ruining small businesses and effectively stealing from civilians. It troubled him but he did not know what else to do. The war was destroying everything and everyone, that was not his doing even though he was one of those doing it.

****

In early December 1862, Francis's supervisor summoned him back to the main warehouse in Richmond. When he arrived in the Confederate capital, Francis could feel the tension in the air. People with somber looks more pronounced than usual scurried in the streets, families packed their belongings on wagons and carts—anything that would move, and the warehouse was a hive of activity. Francis deduced that the Union Army was once again threatening the capital.

"Sounds like everyone in the North has put on a blue uniform, grabbed a gun, and is heading this way from Washington, DC." Nathaniel Parrod, Francis's supervisor advised.

Parrod had worked in the same warehouse before the war counting bales of cotton and sacks of cornmeal but was now responsible for getting as many mechanisms of death to battlefields as possible. Of late, most things were being shipped via the Richmond, Fredericksburg and Potomac Railroad to a place called Guiney Station. The supplies were then being carted to a small Virginia town along the Rappahannock River called Fredericksburg. That is where the Confederate Army was setting itself up across from the Union Army, whose next move was still unclear.

Most thought the Union troops were settling in for the winter on the north side of the Rappahannock, others that they were just organizing themselves before a final push onto the Confederate capitol just sixty miles away. Either way, the Union Army was too close for comfort to anyone living in Richmond aside from the slaves for whom the Union Army represented freedom.

Only months before, Parrod had been a good-humored, potbellied man with a head full of curly black hair. Now he was a drawn, balding, middle-aged man who wore a grimace constantly. The stress of the war would kill him, if a bullet would not.

"Here is your paperwork," Parrod said, thrusting the hastily completed documents in Francis's hand. "Load up those boxes of shell fuses, the dock chief will sign off on the quantity, and get to Fredericksburg as fast as you can."

"I will just check on my wife, and I'll head right out." Francis replied.

"No time for that," Parrod countered, "we already shipped nearly every artillery shell we had but the fuses got left behind!"

Logistics was a war within a war, and the Union was winning. The Confederate infrastructure in terms of manufacturing, railroads, and shipping could not compare to that of the Union. And that was pushing the conscientious Parrod to an early grave. Notwithstanding his deteriorating state, Parrod still had the mental faculties to know it was important to make the urgency of the situation personal to Francis.

"If you don't get this ammunition up to Fredericksburg by tomorrow there is a good chance those soldiers you used to serve with are going to be massacred, and we will all be singing Abe Lincoln's praises by the end of the week. If you press hard enough, you may make it in time. If you don't, you will be dooming this God-forsaken city and everyone in it, including that wife of yours. So, Godspeed."

****

Francis did press hard enough, he made it to Fredericksburg by the evening of December 10th. Unlike Richmond, there was an eerie quiet in the town and the surrounding area. The soldiers who greeted him at the hastily fashioned supply depot outside the town were stoic, hiding their anxiety.

"Any sign of the Yankees yet?" Francis asked the pair of soldiers from Louisiana at the depot entrance.

"Yep." One of the soldiers responded with a deep drawl. "I am not good at counting, but I'd say there is about a million of them right across that river." The soldier gestured with his thumb over his shoulder.

The estimate was off, the actual number massed on the northern bank of the Rappahannok River was one hundred twenty thousand. The growing Confederate force opposing then was nearing eighty thousand and being organized around the heights overlooking the town. Only a token force and officers enjoyed the comforts of the town itself.

The most recent intelligence spreading among Confederate troops was that the Union forces did not have boats or materials for bridges to cross the river. Nor would the river freeze over for passage due to the strength of the current. Coupled with the fact that winter weather was bogging down the roads that would be needed for any flanking maneuvers, odds were increasing that the Union Army would be staying put until spring. At the same time, seasoned Confederate scouts did not see signs that the Northerners were constructing the types of defensive works consistent with winter quarters.

The mystery of what the Union would do was soon solved. There would be no peaceful winter with soldiers singing Christmas carols to each other across the river. It would be bullets and artillery rather than exchanging gifts and season's tidings.

After unloading the fuses from his wagon, Francis prepared to head back to Richmond and reunite with Bridget. Those plans were dashed by the sound of a rifle exchange in the town and an ill-tempered Confederate officer directing that Francis and his wagon had to stay. If a battle was on every resource had to be marshaled, the officer advised.

"Start loading up those barrels and crates over there and bring them to the heights." The officer commanded.

"Where are the heights?" Francis asked.

The officer dismissingly instructed Francis, "Take the one and only road right there. That road leads into town and once there look for the area that is higher than the rest. Can you do that?"

With sarcasm of his own, Francis replied, "I'll do my very best."

Over the next three days, Francis made the trek between the heights and supply depots on the outskirts of town more times than he could count. Often the sights, smells, and sounds of the battle were too close for his liking. He thought he had left those horrors behind him but now feared they would follow him always. Francis grew tense and his stomach became nauseous, the toll on his body and mind simply picked up where it left off after the Battle of Antietam just months before.

On the fourth day there at Fredericksburg, Francis was reassigned by Confederate officers to help move wounded Confederate soldiers from a triage area in the back of the battlefield to a hastily erected hospital behind the town. Men missing limbs, others their eyes. The wounded that Francis transported seemed to disproportionately include soldiers struggling to breathe—suffering from chest and face wounds. Francis tried to comfort them as much as he could when he placed them into the wagon.

"The worst is over, boys. Just hang in there." He found himself saying it repeatedly, not knowing what else to do to help them in their misery.

It was only after he unloaded the last of the wounded at the hospital and he was by himself, staring at the blood-soaked floorboards of the wagon, that Francis allowed his emotions to get the better of him. He collapsed to the ground and cried like he never cried before. *Life is too brutal,* he thought to himself, *just too brutal.*

When he ran out of tears, not knowing what he was to do next, Francis decided to return to Richmond and distance himself from bloody Fredericksburg as much as he could. Officers and orders be damned. After all, he was not a soldier anymore anyway. For a war supposedly about rights, freedom, and individual liberty, those concepts were being trampled upon at every turn.

As he prepared his wagon to leave, Francis realized that the din of battle emanating from the direction of the town had stopped. Coming down the dirt road toward him was a somber looking Confederate soldier dragging his rifle behind him, a bloody makeshift bandage on his left hand.

"Did the Yanks withdraw?" Francis asked.

"What is left of them." The soldier replied. "They abandoned thousands of their dead and dying back on the field. To be honest, I thought their Irishmen were going to break through. They got that close before we cut them down."

"Irishmen?" Francis questioned.

"Yeah, Irishmen like you." The soldier recognizing Francis's brogue.

"At least that is what our own Micks from Georgia said they were. The poor devils were left out in the field all night, stuck their bleeding between our lines and those of the Yankees. They called out in that language they have," the soldier reported.

"Gaelic," Francis advised.

"Yeah, you're an Irishman, you would know. It pushed some of those Georgia boys to tears, saying their former countrymen were praying to God for an end to their pain, while others called out to their mothers and fathers in their death throes. Awful."

The thought of his brothers overwhelmed Francis, along with a sinking, sickening, feeling in his stomach. "Were those Irishmen from Pennsylvania?" he asked the soldier.

"Don't know but with so many of them covering that field I imagine they came from all over the North." The soldier then ended the conversation by shuffling past Francis and continuing wherever he had been heading in his exhausted state.

Richmond was no longer Francis's destination; he steered his wagon back toward the plumes of smoke. In the cold temperature, he would not be led by the smell of blood, entrails, and decomposing bodies until he got closer to the sight of the battle itself. Francis headed up the southern slope until debris from the battle made it too cumbersome to navigate with the wagon. He tied up the mules and went up the heights on foot.

When he reached the crest there was still enough sunlight to see it. There were hundreds, if not thousands, of bodies clad in blue winter uniforms of Union soldiers. Most gathered in small groups, others sporadically scattered about but most in front of a stone wall and a narrow road that divided the downward slope, heading east to west.

"There are no live ones left." Francis heard from behind him. The remark came from a blood-covered Confederate, Richard Rowland Kirkland. Kirkland, from South Carolina, mistook Francis for one of the ambulance drivers he had been working with earlier in the day. Francis said nothing, still shocked at the sight of the carnage. Kirkland, unbeknownst to Francis, was a distant relative of the Norfolk Rowlands to whom he owed so much. He let Francis be. Kirkland had been driven to near madness by the sight of it himself and risked sniper fire in no-man's-land to bring water to the wounded and dying, Union and Confederate alike.

Part of Francis wanted to move no further, yet his feet propelled him forward. He climbed over the stone wall awash in broken rifles and remnants of ammunition. His eye was drawn to the body of a Union soldier, the soldier's cap partially covering his face and in the cap a sprig of boxwood. He did not appear to be an officer but, unlike most of the other enlisted men, he had a custom-made uniform, consistent with someone with ties in the garment industry. His size, his hair color, and even the way his body lay gave it all away.

Francis knew but he did not want to know.

When he got close enough, the face was bloated and blue but undeniable. But Francis tried to deny it anyway and searched the pockets on the corpse eventually finding papers confirming it was indeed his brother, Mathew.

Francis let the papers blow out of his hands and disappear into the growing darkness. He stared at what must have been the fatal wound, a Minié ball to the abdomen. There was blood all around and on Mathew's hands, with his jacket and shirt ripped open—so he must have lingered.

With Mathew's suffering and death already too much to endure, Francis was shaken by another terrifying thought, Mathew and their brother Jamie would have undoubtedly been together. Francis began rapidly moving from corpse to corpse nearby, inspecting the face of each looking for his brother, Jamie. But Jamie was not there, at least not among the bodies in the immediate area. With the darkness of night falling ever more quickly, there was no chance for Francis to expand his search.

Finding his way back to his wagon, Francis was lost in a surreal torrent of emotion and pain. The deep depression that had plagued him periodically since his arrival in the United States had returned and this time he feared it would envelop him completely.

****

Bridget could see it in his face when he returned. Melancholia, some called it, but Bridget knew it as the damage to the heart and mind that would have a survivor of the famine take his own life just as he reached the relative safety of the New World. Just as her brother did. She found him, having hung himself not three months after they had immigrated together from Ireland.

Seeing that look in Francis's face terrified her. What made it all the worse was that she had more sad news for her husband. News that she could not keep from him even in his darkened emotional state.

Days before, Sally Rowland—now Mrs. Sally Beaumont— visited Bridget. Sally like so many others in Richmond was leaving the city in anticipation of the Union attack and to rejoin her husband. Sally had traced where Francis was living through his last mailing address.

Although Sally could have talked for hours of her own heartache, that is not why she came looking for Francis and spoke to Bridget. At the outbreak of the war, Sally married a rich and dashing Confederate officer from New Orleans. An engineer, he had been in Norfolk assessing the defenses there. At a party celebrating the Confederate victory at First Manassas, he met and was smitten by Sally, as she him.

While he secretly hoped his engineering background would keep him from the front and close to Sally, it would not. Sally would be trapped behind Union lines in Norfolk while her husband would lose both his legs in one of the many small and nameless canon exchanges during the Peninsula Campaign.

A high-ranking Union officer in Norfolk, in part because he was charmed by Sally but also because he had a brother who had lost a leg in battle, gave Sally special permission to reunite with her husband at a hospital in Richmond. Her husband was in the process now of being moved to

Petersburg with other invalids, again anticipating the capital would be attacked. Sally was going with him but needed to get information to Francis about his son, Stephen Michael.

"The boy is with my cousins, Mat and Lucinda Rowland, in Norfolk. But they secured permission to return to New York. They hope to join one of the regular flotillas that transport Union wounded to the north in a month or two. They will take Stephen Michael with them unless there is someone else to care for him." Sally said this knowing that there was not much Francis could do at this point to keep his son from being moved even farther away from him. But Francis had a right to know, she thought.

Fearing the news of his son's departure would push Francis's depression to the breaking point, Bridget was instinctively reluctant to tell him about his son. But like Sally, she knew he had the right to know. So, Bridget told him in a matter of fact manner, even before he got off his coat or could say a word about Fredericksburg. His reaction was not what she expected.

"I have to get him back," Francis said, the mission of saving his son zapped his depression into determination.

"My brother Mathew is dead." Francis advised, generating a gasp from Bridget who loved the look on Francis's face in the past when he told stories about his brothers. "Jamie could be dead too for all that I know. I'll be damned if I am going to lose anyone else to this damn war."

"But how?" Bridget asked, fearing Francis was being reckless. "He is in Norfolk and will soon be in New York."

"I have been moving all around with my job and there are holes all over between the Union and Confederate lines. I will go through one of those holes to Norfolk and bring

Stephen Michael back here." Francis said, more to himself than Bridget.

Bridget thought the idea madness but with the look on her husband's face, there was nothing she could do about it.

"Winter is here and he is only a child so keep him as warm as you can." Bridget said handing Francis blankets, trying to be supportive. "And promise me if it gets too dangerous, you will turn around and come back home to me."

Bridget added, "You will be no use to Stephen Michael dead, and I won't be able to take it if something bad happens to either you or Stephen Michael."

Francis took the blankets, kissed Bridget first on the lips and then the forehead and left. She feared she would never see him again. Francis leaving her life as abruptly and dramatically as he came in.

****

Approaching his supervisor at the warehouse, David Parrot, Francis asked to make the next delivery to the Confederate outpost closest to Union lines outside of Norfolk. Parrot would have asked why but someone volunteering to take on the dangerous task of hauling supplies close to enemy lines made his life easier, so Parrot gave the authorization.

On Christmas Eve 1862, Stephen Michael's fifth birthday, Francis left Richmond heading for Norfolk. He had a wagon and mule train courtesy of the Confederate government along with passes that would get him through Confederate checkpoints. To get through the Union checkpoints, however, Francis would have to improvise.

When he arrived at the rebel encampment closest to Norfolk, Francis offloaded the quartermaster's supplies acting as normally as he could. He discreetly solicited information from the soldiers at the outpost regarding how tightly the roads and access points to Norfolk were guarded by Union forces.

"They will shoot and let the buzzards eat you if you are thinking about sneaking in," advised one of the grizzled Confederates.

The veteran, who looked as worn as Francis, advised that the Union used a combination of fixed and roving patrols. The northerners had Norfolk and were determined to keep it.

The only option, Francis thought, was to bluff his way in. Take the main road with the wagon, claim he lived on a farm on the outskirts and report that he was heading to Norfolk for supplies.

Francis removed anything from the wagon and his person that would identify him as Confederate. The grizzled Confederate soldier, now on picket duty on the edge of the camp, saw which direction Francis was heading. "Nice knowing you!" The Confederate shouted sarcastically.

Trying to stay positive, Francis kept reminding himself that he was getting closer to Stephen Michael with each creak and movement of the wagon. At the same time, the obstacles to his success kept creeping into his mind. He had no Union identification, no Union money, and no familiarity with how the Union operated things around Norfolk. He was not even sure where the Rowlands were staying within the city or even if they were still there.

The time for anticipation was over. About an hour into his ride Francis observed Union soldiers at a checkpoint. They had a felled tree blocking the road. The soldiers had ropes attached and would drag the tree out of the way if a traveler had permission to enter or leave Norfolk. Virtually no one had that permission, so the tree was rotting in place.

As soon as Francis reached the Union soldiers, they demanded to see his pass. He had none. They asked who authorized his travel and his answer, in effect, was no one. They asked his business in Norfolk and by then even Francis saw the weaknesses in his story. To his surprise, however, the soldier asking the questions nodded and made a face as if he was convinced and passage would not be a problem.

"Just wait here a minute," the soldier instructed as he walked toward a cabin about twenty yards further down the road. The soldier entered the cabin without looking back at Francis and came out again in what seemed like a minute at most. Francis gave him a friendly smile as he returned.

"Yep, just what I thought. Corporal wants us to take you into custody, you stink to high heaven like a spy." Francis was going to protest but stopped himself. Unless he was talking to the corporal or whoever else was in charge, Francis would be wasting his breath.

For two days, Francis sat shackled to a tree behind the cabin near the checkpoint, hungry, thirsty, and exhausted from the anxiety he felt. If they truly believed him a spy, the soldiers could hang him or shoot him on the spot. On the morning of the third day, a soldier came out of the cabin and placed an old flour sack over Francis's head. The shackles were removed but Francis's arms were tied behind his back with rope and he was tossed in the rear of a wagon. The same wagon he had driven to the checkpoint.

"You run Johnny Reb and we'll just use it as an opportunity for target practice," threatened one of the soldiers in the front of the wagon. Another soldier pressed a bayonet into Francis's stomach just so the Irishman would know he was not alone in the back of the vehicle. Francis said and tried nothing.

****

At Fort Norfolk, an old stone installation built in the Chesapeake Bay, Francis was repeatedly interrogated—being asked the same questions by different people. Francis decided to be honest, as the Union officials could verify the presence of the Rowlands and his son in the city. It did not seem like his interrogators cared at all whatever Francis said. He was just thrown into a windowless blockhouse, part of an old ammunition magazine. It was cold, dark, and dank, with scores of other Confederate prisoners as fraught as Francis.

With no windows in the blockhouse. Francis could not see the water or the flotilla with his son sailing past. Stephen Michael, with the Rowlands, would be in New York before Francis would see the light of day again.

Chapter Twelve
The Wandering Prisoner

Virginia & Indiana
1863-1864

Over the next several months, Francis was moved within the fort and around to other holding facilities used by the Union. He was eventually transferred to Camp Morton outside Indianapolis, Indiana, more than seven hundred miles from where he had been captured. The Union strived to separate suspected spies from their networks, which in the paranoia of war, Union intelligence deemed everywhere in occupied territory.

While in transit, Francis was often shackled, kept in dark cattle cars and covered wagons, and fed only the rations rejected by his guards. In Camp Morton, he was exposed to the elements in a large walled pen, with inadequate clothing, little food, and rancid, unsanitary conditions. The mortality rate at Camp Morton was twenty percent, with more than half the Confederate inmates sick or dying at any given time.

Francis and his fellow inmates debated the reasons why the conditions at the camp were progressively getting worse. The minority argued it showed that the Union too was experiencing massive supply shortages because of the war. The more commonly accepted argument, and the one adopted by Francis, was that the Union was overwhelmed by the sheer number of Confederates giving up on the war and surrendering. At that point, there were more Confederates in Union prisons than Robert E. Lee and all his generals could amass in the field.

As a practical matter, the war was over and Francis knew it. With his survival so tenuous, however, he chose not to espouse his beliefs in the camp. Why make enemies out of the rabid successionists who remained? Why choose to make enemies at all? Fate was doing a good enough job of that for him without his help.

Fortunately for Francis, he was able to get along with other inmates better than most. His penchant for gallows humor would generate a smirk among the desperate people around him, as close as you could get to a laugh under the conditions. On a particularly hot and humid day, the horrid stink of the camp was unbearable for inmates and guards alike. The noise of coughs and those gagging echoed throughout the camp. Francis shouted up to the palisade where the guards were looking down.

"Out of curiosity, are the solitary confinement accommodations out there up or downwind from the camp?" Francis asked only half-kidding. Solitary confinement was used for punishment, one of the many harsh mechanisms to keep order in the camp. But if it were away from the sickening smell, even complete isolation in a hot, dark shed would be welcomed.

One of the guards shouted back, "If the hole was upwind, I would be dragging the lot of you there myself!" An hour later, the same guard tossed a bushel of fresh apples over the wall to the inmates. A token effort to show humanity. A rare thing in that place and time.

Many of the inmates were giving up hope of ever seeing their families and homes again. Prisoner exchanges had been abandoned in 1862 because the Confederacy refused to treat black Union soldiers for what they were—soldiers—rather than slaves. The result was the number of prisoners on both sides swelled, overwhelmed facilities, and contributed to the deaths of more than 60,000 people while imprisoned. More than any single battlefield of the war.

The Union did offer Confederate inmates release if they agreed to join the Union Army and fight. Not against former brothers-at-arms but against Native American tribes who were using the war as an opportunity to secure their own rights. Thousands took the offer and became what they called "Galvanized Yankees."

Francis considered joining them but when the nightmares of him killing Latee at Fort Davis returned, Francis realized he had no desire to fight anymore period. Besides, Francis hoped the fact that he was among the few prisoners taken while a civilian would increase his chances of being released compared to those who had surrendered as combatants.

Francis was right. Union and Confederate officials had resumed discussions for prisoner exchanges in 1864 because of the humanitarian disaster playing out in prisons on both sides. While those discussions petered out, it was not before gestures of good faith led to handfuls of prisoners being released, Francis among them. Exactly why he had been chosen was not clear, and Francis did not care.

He first learned that he would be released during one of the "prisoner counts" held at Camp Morton. To get their modest daily rations, the inmates had to line up and one by one approach a wagon brought into the camp. The inmates gave their name, the unit they had been assigned to before being taken prisoner, and responded to whatever other questions the guards posed.

Francis gave his name and said "civilian" in response to the unit question as he usually did. He was handed a piece of bread and hard cheese but instructed to wait by the front gate with a handful of other inmates rather than return to his normal designated eating area. The camp commander, hoping more to pacify those in the camp than actually give them hope, loudly announced that Francis and the handful of others were being released. Negotiations between both sides were continuing in relation to more prisoner exchanges. That is all the commander said. Francis nearly fainted.

Although he was on his way to be released, he was not released yet. He traveled via a series of cattle cars on locomotives and wagons in ankle chains for more than two weeks until reaching a place his guards advised was City Point, Virginia. City Point was a sprawling Union complex of interconnected forts with every type of supporting facility imaginable.

The fort walls were high and thick, the hospital was immense, the warehouses even bigger, and there were vast train yards, corrals, and wharves. Now Francis knew the war was all but over. The South could not have assembled anything near as grand when the war started, let alone now after years of fighting. *Good*, Francis thought to himself, *the sooner this thing is done, the better*.

Francis was given paperwork to sign, including an oath to the United States and a promise not to take up arms again against the Union. After signing, he was put in a line with other prisoners being returned to the Confederacy. They crossed paths with people being released from Confederate prisons. The men in both lines looked starved, beaten, and, in some cases, near death. The difference was that one group was going back to a world about to win a war, the other to a world about to lose it.

Chapter Thirteen
Witness to the Fall

Richmond, Virginia
1864-1865

Although the Union appeared to have limitless resources at its disposal, the Confederacy could not even scrape together enough wagons to carry the recently released inmates, many of them ill, to Richmond. Rather than sit and wait for the limited number of wagons to go back and forth, Francis began the twenty-five-mile trek to Richmond on bare feet. He struggled to keep his near skeleton frame moving forward.

Along the way, Francis heard one report after another about the deterioration of the Confederate capital. Crime and looting were said to be rampant, price gouging common, and social order gone. Disaster was in the air and had been for some time. Food riots started in 1863, not long after Francis had been taken prisoner.

Francis was angry at himself. He went on a hopeless, foolish mission and left his wife, poor Bridget, behind to fend for herself in a collapsing city. In his weakened state it took him a day and a half to arrive in Richmond after his release. He arrived at the shack of a building he had shared with Bridget only to be told by a neighbor that Bridget had moved. The neighbor estimated that she left six months or so after Francis had disappeared. Francis went to other neighbors, the post office, and stopped anyone who would make eye contact with him asking if they knew where Bridget was.

By the end of the day, Francis learned that Bridget was staying in the home of Beatrice Sands on Floyd Avenue, near the old Scuffletown Tavern. As the tavern had been a mainstay in the area before the war, Francis knew exactly where it was. Although having just endured a harsh imprisonment of over a year, and a long trek to the city on foot, Francis ran with all the speed he could generate to the address he was given.

At the house, Francis was greeted by the aging widow, Mrs. Sands. The kind old woman reacted with earnest excitement upon hearing Francis's name.

"Come, I'll show you," Mrs. Sands said adding that Francis should call her "Bea" as she ran deeper into the house. Bea had to step around the group of cats and dogs, all of them extremely thin, she kept as pets. Francis was seeing how extreme the scarcity in the city had become, every living thing now little more than skin and bones.

There was Bridget, her face brightened with surprise boarding upon shock when she saw Francis. Bridget was holding an infant closing in on a year old.

"This is Patrick," she said proudly referring to the child. "You spoke so fondly of your brother in Ireland, I thought you would like to name your son after him."

Tempted to tease Bridget because her father's name also happened to be Patrick, Francis was too thrilled to say anything. He hugged and kissed Bridget. She was all right, better than alright.

When Bridget filled Francis in on what had transpired while he was gone, he was struck by the kindness and generosity of Bea. The widow had taken Bridget in, having seen Bridget so pregnant she was about to burst. Bea had already taken in a traumatized youngster, about three or four years old, she found wandering the streets. Her generosity exercised at a time when one half of the country was trying to kill the other half.

With the war, the rioting, and everything else, Bea advised that no one was investigating reports of missing children. No one cared. The city had become that harsh. The boy's trauma was only slowly resolving, and he was beginning to speak again, meekly disclosing that his name was John. Either John England or John from England, they did not want to press him in his vulnerable state. He would get nothing but support from Bea, Bridget, and now Francis.

In Francis's absence and her pregnant state, Bridget had run out of money. The cash from the Commonwealth Bank that Francis had given her did not last but a few months with the rampant inflation. She could no longer work in the final term of her pregnancy. Even now, she and everyone else in the house would be starving but for the garden Bea had on her roof and the essentials Bea was buying with the last of her savings. Earlier in the war, Bea had a fruitful garden in her backyard but, as time went on, anything that grew was stolen before Bea could harvest it.

Periodically, Bea would splurge on buying protein, in one form or another, for John, Bridget, and by extension the infant, Patrick. Bea refused to eat it herself, claiming old women did not need much in terms of calories. But Bea, at one-point Rubenesque, was now emaciated and weak. Bea's pets, which she loved as if they were her children, now looked as thin as she did. As much as she loved them, the animals, like her had to share with the others in the house in need.

Francis remarked on Bea's generosity, but Bea dismissed it. "Bridget, John, and the baby saved me," she would say. Bea's husband, Joseph, had died from a heart attack two years before. He had been a livery driver and the couple met and fell in love later in life.

Bea would say her husband died of a broken heart more than a heart attack. The war, the hatred, the slavery, the poverty, all grew too much for him. "He was the kindest man I had ever known," Bea would say. Francis started to suspect that her husband did not die of a heart attack at all. He thought of his friend Abraham in Norfolk.

"Well, that is ironic," Francis told Bea, "Your husband Joe was the kindest person you have known and you are the kindest person I know, saving my wife as you did. I just wished we could have met in better times," although Francis was at a loss as to when those better times would have been.

The reality was that Bea felt useful and part of a family with Bridget, the children, and now Francis. Without them, she shuddered to think what she would do.

Francis went back to seek work with the Quartermaster, as it was the only job he knew of in the dying city. Upon his arrival, those in the Quartermaster's Office looked shocked to see him. He had been on the lengthy list of people absent from duty without permission and accountable for missing property, namely the mule team and wagon that he took with him to Norfolk. Francis was told he would have to explain his absence and loss of the property to the General and was escorted to the General's office by a pair from the provost marshal.

Upon entering the office, Francis recognized the General at once. He had been the colonel with the 1st Virginia Infantry before Franklin Skinner. Francis assumed Patrick Theodore

Moore, P.T. to his friends, had died from his wounds at the Battle of Blackburn's Ford.

Moore had a thick and jagged scar running from the middle of his forehead up through his receding hairline, evidence of the wound three years later. But as Moore, a native of Galway, liked to joke, it would take more than one bullet to penetrate his thick Irish skull.

After Blackburn's Ford, Moore recovered at his home in Richmond where he had been a successful merchant before the war. He was eventually strong enough to return to the army holding a series of administrative positions that he handled so well that he was promoted to general. The self-effacing Moore downplayed how hard he worked to make himself useful again, attributing his qualifications for the higher rank to having lost sufficient brain matter when he was wounded.

"It is good to see you McNamara, it has been a long time," Moore said, his memory miraculously still intact. With a smile to Francis, Moore dismissed the provost marshal guards with a nod of his scarred head.

"It's a good thing we didn't know then what we know now, wouldn't you say Mac. I can see you haven't had it easy," Moore observed. The crisp and clean uniform Francis had when Moore saw him last was long gone. Instead, Francis stood before him now in little more than rags that hung loosely over his gaunt frame.

At Blackburn's Ford, Francis weighed a muscular 180 pounds at a tad under 5'10". Now, due to the hardship of the war and his imprisonment, Francis was lucky if he weighed 120 pounds. And like the General, Francis now sported a prominent scar. Francis's courtesy of kicks to the head by

Confederate officers and the wanting artistry in Bridget's stitch work.

Moore ripped up a piece of paper, saying it had been the warrant for Francis's arrest for the missing mule and wagon. Francis took out his parole papers to explain his absence and loss of the wagon, but Moore waived him off.

"The fact that you are back here and the look of you is proof enough that you have had a rough time of it. I won't insult your sacrifice by accusing you of nonsense." Moore said.

"But I do need to add to that sacrifice," Moore advised, staring somberly at Francis. He went on to explain, "My job here is not to run the Quartermaster's Office. It is to bolster the defenses around Richmond drawing on all the municipal employees, postal workers, prison guards, ambulance corps, and just about anyone else with a pulse."

Bringing his hand to the back of his neck, the stress of his position keeping him constantly tense, Moore stated, "As you can imagine, they are not shaping up to be an elite force. There are boys not tall enough to hold a rifle and old men so deaf they could not hear a cannon go off right next to them. The rest are office workers who would pull a muscle running in any direction except to the rear. And most of them don't have the brains to be the village idiot." Moore let out an exhale in exasperation.

"But you are trained McNamara and have proven yourself in combat. You can help the sorry lot defend themselves because God knows they cannot do it on their own. And the better you can help them be, the less likely this city will be left a smoldering pile of bricks." Moore did not wait to give Francis an opportunity to respond.
"Everything now Mac is conscripted service so welcome back and welcome to the local defense force." Moore moved

back behind his desk and began looking at paperwork, signaling Francis that he had been dismissed.

"General," Francis spoke up anyway, "there is a misunderstanding. I have been discharged from the service already. On top of that, I had to sign an oath not to fight when the Yankees paroled me." Francis looked desperately at Moore as he spoke but Moore did not look up from his desk.

"None of that matters," Moore responded, "no exceptions."

"But General. . .," Francis began only to be interrupted by Moore attempting to put the matter to rest.

"You can serve or spend the rest of the war in Libby, Belle Isle, or wherever they are leaving people to rot these days." Moore referring to the notorious prisons in Richmond along the James River. "Report to the clerk outside for your paperwork." Moore's once pleasant tone now gone.

Dazed, Francis walked out of the office. The clerk at the door asked Francis a few questions and had him fill out forms for his second induction into the Confederate military. He was being assigned to Company A of the 2nd Battalion, Virginia Infantry, Local Defense. They were known as the Quartermaster's Battalion because most of the unit was made up of porters and clerks from the Quartermaster's Office.

Francis filled out the forms with the first name of "Frank" and surname spelled "McNemarra." While he could not totally falsify his name because the General knew who he was, Francis wanted to at least mask it a bit. Otherwise, once Union forces won the war, and they inevitably would, they would know he violated the oath made when he was paroled. So Frank McNemarra was the best he could do.

He assumed the penalty for breaching his oath would be hanging and that the Union would be vengeful at the end of the war and hanging a lot of people. It was not the type of death Francis preferred although he knew something had to kill him.

Francis had marched past a man hung and left dangling from a tree during the fighting in 1862. Even with all the death around him, the grotesque corpse with hands bound left Francis particularly disturbed. The assumption Francis and his fellow soldiers made as they marched by was that the man had been a spy or a deserter whose body was left as a message. The man could have also just been unlucky as one of the casualties during the fighting was due process.

****

Fortunately for Francis, the Quartermaster's Battalion was proving itself so inept as a fighting force that it was kept far away from the front lines. They were assigned to man forts near the city when they were not under siege and patrol areas not likely to bring about an engagement. Instead, the men were directed to focus on their primary job handling supplies at Quartermaster warehouses. Most nights, Francis was able to go home to his family.

But there was still reason for Francis to be anxious. If things continued to go badly for the Confederacy, his unit would eventually be thrown into the violent fray. And if that happened, they were sure to be slaughtered. That assuming they did not starve to death first. The city was becoming increasingly unlivable.

What little food there was, the prices were astronomical. Inflation was destroying the purchasing power of Francis's pay from the Quartermaster. As a result, he and his family were constantly going hungry. The strategy of the Union Navy to blockade Southern ports was helping speed an end to the war. A collateral consequence, however, was that the old, young, free and slave, combatant and civilian, were on the verge of starvation.

Although materially the family was in dire straits, Bea and Bridget somehow kept the tenor of the house upbeat. Francis was in awe of the women's internal fortitude and force of will. Although they were driven to protect the children first and foremost, they may have helped Francis most of all.

The women modeled the kind of resiliency and inner calm Francis could never master on his own. The women only talked about pleasant topics and avoided discussion of the war and its hardship. They understood they had no control of much that was going on around them and dwelling on it would do them no good.

Francis did his part for the family. He brought home as much money as he could and took to stealing from the Confederate warehouse at every opportunity to sustain the family. Bridget knew what he was doing and the risk he was taking, as pilfering from the war effort could end with his execution. She would not discuss what he was doing with him, but simply say "thank you," and gently stroke the scar above his eye he bore for her.

When in the home, Francis—like Bridget and Bea—would force himself to smile and play as if carefree with the children. When his stomach would growl in hunger, which was often, he would tell the children it was a sign he had a story to tell them and he would act out one of the scenes from the history book his mother gave him which seemed a lifetime ago in Ireland. And there were also the fallback stories of Seas the Explorer.

****

There were always rumors of a renewed Union attack on the city. Northern troops had been close enough three years before, during the Peninsula Campaign, to hear the church bells in the capital. Then just two years after that, in 1864, when Francis was still a prisoner of war, Union forces got within six miles of Richmond. In both cases, only desperate, last-ditch efforts by the Confederates forced the Union troops back. With winter still heavy in the first months of 1865, Francis could hear the faint din of artillery from Petersburg twenty-five-miles to the south. The capital was being threatened once again and was close to being encircled.

While the meager trickle of supplies into the capital stopped altogether due to the Union presence at Petersburg, the flow of Confederate wounded into Richmond became a torrent. The intensity of fighting at Petersburg showed the Union forces were pushing hard against Richmond's back door. Then there were rumors that key cities in North Carolina and Georgia had fallen, and some sacked. The end seemed near yet Confederate leaders continued everyone to fight on. They still had hope of a negotiated peace and dread the cost of unconditional surrender.

In late March 1865, Francis noticed the artillery fire getting louder. The fighting was nearing the city limits. His auxiliary battalion was called into full-time service just as he had feared. Francis did not show. He risked being shot as a deserter but he decided he would rather make his final stand with his family rather than be slaughtered pointless at the gates of Richmond.

Ironically, General Moore made the same decision as Francis and left the Quartermaster's Battalion on their own to face the overwhelming Union forces at Sailor's Creek just outside the city. The clerks, old men, and boys of the battalion were outmanned, outgunned, and outpositioned. So, they gave up without much of a fight. They weren't so stupid after all.

****

Shortly before dawn on April 3, 1865, not six months since Francis's return to the city after being a prisoner of war, Confederate cavalry rode through the streets of Richmond shooting into the air and shouting at the top of their lungs. The noise woke Francis with a start. He was unsure whether the troops were drunk, were signaling an attack, or notifying the residents of something else.

It was something else. The city was on fire. Walls of flames were spreading from the warehouse area. Whether the fire was set by fleeing Confederate soldiers, advanced Union troops, or looters, it did not matter. The flames were such that the whole city would turn to ashes, and quickly.

"Francis, get Bridget and the boys out right now!" Bea shouted anxiously from the front door—seeing the flames.

"Ok, you hurry too Bea, just take what you absolutely need." Francis said and then raced around the house frantically throwing things into his haversack that would prove to be necessities for the family.

He could not expect the others to carry much. So once his haversack was filled, Francis had to take things out to make room for items that may prove even more vital to their survival. Among the items Francis removed were the books he had been given by his mother and Father Devlin, books he had kept with him for years and that he would carry no longer. He also took out Ellen Scanlon's small Bible but rather than dropping it to the floor like the other items he was discarding, he forced the Bible into his jacket pocket. With his son Stephen Michael gone, the Bible was the only thing Francis had left of Ellen Scanlon.

With Bridget and the children with him, Francis exited the house, but Bea was not there. He ran back into the house to find Bea going through the drawers of a bureau. "Come on Bea, we have to get out of here. The fire is getting close."

"Yes, Francis you have to go but I am old. I will slow you down and I cannot risk me being the cause of anything happening to Bridget or the boys. You have to get around the fire and then two armies, you cannot do that with an old woman bringing up the rear." Bea spoke slowly in effort not to show her own panic at the decision she had made.

She placed the last of her cash in Francis's right hand. Into his left hand, she placed her wedding ring and that of her husband. She also gave him her husband's watch. "Godspeed" she whispered to Francis, "and explain it to Bridget. In my heart, she is my daughter and I love her so."

"What will you do?" Francis asked Bea with his eyes welling up. He knew. She smiled and said, "I have missed my Joseph long enough."

Francis dragged Bridget away from the house, his wife screaming for Bea to follow. Bea just waved to them, crying, shooing her pets out of the house. The sky now orange behind her with the glow of the flames and trimmed in black from the smoke.

They had not gone more than a mile with Bridget still calling out Bea's name and the toddler, John, and infant, Patrick, crying at the commotion that they were knocked to the ground by the shockwave of a huge explosion. One of the largest of the war. The arsenal where the Confederacy kept stockpiles of gunpowder and artillery shells had exploded, breaking every window in the surrounding area and even blowing over the tombstones in the graveyard, including the tombstone Francis had made for his first wife Ellen and his namesake son.

Coming to with intense ringing in his ears and nausea from the shock wave, Francis staggered to his feet. He got everyone else up and moving again. He knew there would be soldiers and fighting to the north, south and east of the city so he moved his family west, toward the James River. They crossed on a makeshift raft and continued onto one of the main roads with other fleeing civilians. Just as Francis thought they may escape both armies, the pathetic line of people on the road stopped moving. They had been cut off by Union soldiers on horseback.

The soldiers demanded the civilians clear the road, which they did with the men, woman, and children and the miscellaneous items they carried with them settling onto the sides of the dusty thoroughfare. The horsemen then continued on toward Richmond. They were followed by what seemed an endless parade of Union soldiers on foot, with the civilians remarking to each other how well-fed the soldiers looked.

Eventually, a Union supply train arrived. The commander, taking pity on the civilians, gave them some food. He advised that a refugee camp was being established several miles up the road and the civilians should go there. But he made clear everyone should get off the road in the presence of Union troops. If it was thought the civilians were impeding the troops, it could end in tragedy the commander advised. There was still a war on but not for long. It would only be a few days before Robert E. Lee surrendered and, after that, Confederate President Jefferson Davis would be captured and imprisoned.

The seven miles to the refugee camp the commander had reported was more like twenty-five miles, taking the civilians three full days to get there. But it would be worth it. A conglomeration of churches, with federal government assistance, ran the camp. Seeing all the volunteers from different religions and denominations work together made Francis think he had witnessed the fall of the Confederacy only to see the beginning of the apocalypse.

It was not the end of days, however. Francis and his family survived thanks to the kindness and abilities of those who ran that camp. Camp officials also helped Bridget contact her brother in New York to see about relocation. Staying in Virginia—or anywhere in the South—would be difficult, the war had done that much damage.

Based on the extent of the damage he could see just in Virginia, Francis guessed it would take several years for the South to be fully functional again. That was assuming the North, which itself had lost a fortune in blood and money in the war, would be willing to help rebuild the South. Francis's estimate was off by decades. The South had started a war that left it in complete and utter ruin, making the recovery slow and painful.

As refugee administrators were arranging Francis and his family's transit by ship to New York, Francis toyed with the idea of returning to Ireland. A smile came to his face thinking of fishing on the Fergus and Shannon again, particularly to a spot he and his father used to frequent. But his father was gone, so was his mother, and his siblings. There was nothing there for him even if he had the money for the trip for himself and his family. It was charity that was getting him to New York, and beggars cannot be choosers.

Chapter Fourteen
Second Bite at the Apple

Greater New York City Area
1865-1871

Back in 1851, when Francis first arrived in New York City from Ireland, he had no money nor prospects. He was also fresh from the trauma of living through a horrible famine. Against this, he had a new beginning in a growing new world. He was also energetic and young, and as a bachelor had only himself to worry about.

Now, more than a decade later, Francis was returning to New York City. It had doubled in size and was even more imposing than when Francis arrived the first time. Once again, he was destitute and had little in the way of prospects. This time, he was older, in his thirties. He was also worn down having been a veteran of the frontier and Civil wars. In addition, he spent a year as a prisoner of war in a failed attempt to regain custody of his eldest son, Stephen Michael.

Also, while in Virginia, Francis had to bury his first wife and namesake newborn son. He had also witnessed a deadly yellow fever outbreak that killed thousands in the only city in the United States he considered home, Norfolk, Virginia. He endured all this while maintaining manual labor, back breaking work that kept him from starving but not far out of poverty.

Adding to the pressure this time around, Francis had to care for his new family, his second wife Bridget, his infant son

Patrick, and a boy named John who Francis and Bridget effectively adopted after the boy was abandoned during the Civil War. The added pressure, trauma he had lived through and his running failure to better his financial condition proved too much. For lack of a better description, Francis suffered a nervous breakdown.

It started on the steamship taking him and his family from Virginia to New York. Francis paced the steerage area repeatedly, would not eat, hardly slept, and periodically would have fits of uncontrollable tears. His wife, Bridget, when she was not taking care of the children, offered Francis words of encouragement, would rub his back and just be the stable presence he needed to keep from breaking all together.

Shortly after their arrival in New York, she even tried using sex to break him out of the depressive spell, the result was another son, Joseph, born nine months later, adding to the family's financial pressures.

At the docks on New York's westside when they first arrived from Virginia, Francis and family were met by his in-laws, Thomas and Mary Maloney. Thomas was Bridget's younger brother and worked as a tinsmith in the nearby City of Brooklyn. Thomas and Mary would temporarily put-up Francis and his family in their small apartment in the heavily Irish populated section of Fulton Landing, close to the Brooklyn waterfront.

As the first order of business, Francis took to looking for work. His chances were best to secure something as a day laborer, so he frequented the nearby taverns and churches were those looking for such work gathered. He met with little success for several reasons. One was that a deep postwar recession had developed and with the *laisse-fare* economic policies of the day, it persisted for a number of years unchecked. Secondly, Francis no longer had the appearance of a man capable of intense physical labor. Instead, he looked what he was—a man who had been beaten down physically and emotionally.

It produced a vicious cycle, the more defeated Francis looked, the more he was passed over for work. The more he was passed over for work, the more defeated he became.

At Bridget's suggestion, Francis moved his job search a little farther northeast, to the neighborhood of Vinegar Hill, or as the nativist disparagingly referred to it: Irishtown.

On a crisp morning in late 1865, acting on his wife's suggestion, Francis stood among a large crowd outside one of the taverns in Vinegar Hill, just a few blocks from the main entrance to the Brooklyn Navy Yard. A balding man, a few years Francis's senior, came out of the tavern wearing a weary look and a bartender's apron. He looked around the crowd, stroking his beard, and pointed to a handful of men in the gathering.

Those chosen, knowing the routine, began to follow the bartender into the tavern to get instructions for their day's work. The rest of the crowd, with a collective moan of disappointment, disbursed. Not Francis, his mind and body resisting the realization he had been passed over yet again. He just stood there in front of the tavern and stared blankly.

Upon seeing Francis, the bartender barked out, "You there, move along now, no more work to be had here today."

But Francis did not move, it was as if he was frozen in place.

"You heard me!" The bartender now clearly agitated and approaching Francis, "Move along or I'll. . ." But the bartender stopped midsentence, tilted his head as if trying to get a better look at Francis's face.

"Where are you from?" The barkeeper asked.

At first Francis did not answer, still in the disappointment generated stupor. But then he said, "Ferry Landing," referring to his temporary residence with his in-laws.

"Before that!" The barkeeper pressed.

"Richmond." Francis stated, regretting it instantly. Most of the men on that street were either Union veterans or had family members who were, and too much of their blood was spilled in and around the Confederate Capital. Francis knew his being a former Confederate would win him no friends in Vinegar Hill.

"Jesus," the bartender responded in frustration. "Where in Ireland, are you from!"

Embarrassed at no longer instinctively thinking of himself as an Irishman, although his brogue and looks gave him away, Francis advised: "The Village of Clare, along the River Fergus."

"Would you be knowing then a lad by the name Mathew McNamara?" The bartender asked.

Shocked at hearing his brother's name, Francis responded with some excitement, "My older brother." Francis informed.

"I knew it, you have the look of him," the bartender said with a growing smile. "Good people, that Mathew. I haven't seen him since I left the old sod. How is he?"

"Dead." Francis advised, the momentary positive emotion in his voice giving away to sadness. Francis only added one more word, "Fredericksburg," but to New York Irishman it was more than enough to explain Mathew's fate.

"And who did you serve with?" Asked the barkeep.

"I was down in Richmond when the war started and ended up mostly with the 1st Virginia Infantry and spent part of the war as a prisoner." Responded Francis.

Hearing what Francis said about being a prisoner clearly piqued the bartender's interest, bordering on alarm. He stared at Francis's face no longer looking for similarities to Mathew, but to nameless and countless others.

"Where were you held?" The bartender inquired, lowering his gaze as he did so as if to brace himself for the answer.

"Camp Morton." Francis disclosed.

"Hard cheese." The bartender retorted, using the old phrase denoting bad luck. But at the same time the bartender seemed relieved at Francis's reply. He stuck out his hand to shake with Francis.

"Thomas Kearns is my name. I am sorry for the loss of your brother. We were both lent out, Mathew and me, as lads to help old man Touhey with his fields." Francis recalled his brother working some harvests on other farms when they were growing up.

Kearns served the Union as a noncommissioned officer guarding Confederate prisoners in Elmira, New York. "Hellmira," the inmates called it. With mortality rates rivalling those Francis knew at Camp Morton. Kearns had seen hundreds, if not thousands, of Confederates grow weak due to neglect, contract disease, and then die. The prison was overcrowded, filled to three times its designed capacity, and there was never enough food, medicine, nor adequate clothing for the harsh Elmira winters.

With the conditions out of his control, Kearns focused on protecting his own soldiers and himself. They were vastly outnumbered by the desperate Confederate prisoners and at risk from the same diseases running rampant among those confined. As a result, Kearns announced to the Confederate prisoners that he and his men would shoot any inmate who dared come within fifteen yards of a guard house or a prison fence.

For added effect, Kearns vowed to leave any rebel so shot to lay where they fell as a reminder. If there was any doubt as to the seriousness of Kearns's threat, he personally put that to rest shooting the first inmate who got even close to the demarcation line. Kearns rationalized that by shooting that one inmate, he may have deterred countless others, and in the end saved lives. But the guilt gnawed at him, and he continued to have nightmares about the man he killed and the faces of all the prisoners he watched die slowly. All at a distance of fifteen yards or more.

"Come inside." Kearns instructed.

Kearns peppered Francis with questions, starting with his given name and then moving on to what vocational skills he had, beyond those of a laborer—for which Francis was no longer fit. Upon learning that Francis could read, write, and do basic arithmetic, Kearns smiled and inquired if Francis had ever done bookkeeping work.

Not wanting to lose an opportunity, Francis avoided answering no and instead advised: "I have done all kinds of warehouse paperwork and can learn just about anything that can be taught." The answer was perfect for it showed Kearns that Francis was smart enough to keep himself in contention and that Francis did not have any perceived notions of how bookkeeping should be done. Orthodox bookkeeping could be a liability in relation to the type of numbers Kearns wanted tracked.

Francis followed Kearns as he walked past the bar, squeezed through an overstuffed storage room, and reached a small office at the back of the building. The area had a distinct odor as it was not far from the outhouse and back alley where the more impatient drunks chose to relieve themselves.

"Don't worry about the smell, they will be cleaning out the privy shortly." Kearns advised.

There were three men sitting in the office. They had been talking but went silent at the sight of Kearns.

"Gentleman, we have ourselves a new bookkeeper." Kearns announced, nodding his head toward Francis.

"Francis, these are my junior associates who also happen to be my sons-in-law." He then introduced them: Thomas McCleary, the oldest in his mid-twenties, followed by Brian Burke and Patrick Lally, a baby-faced teenager.

Kearns had all daughters with three of them now married to the men whose only similarity to their father-in-law was that they were deep thinkers. They did not think alike, but they all thought deep. McCleary, Burke, and Lally depended on Kearns for their livelihood and Kearns did not run his family or his business like a democracy. So, the trio kept their opinions to themselves when Kearns was around but never shut up when he was not.

The sons-in-law were mystified as to why Kearns acted so pleasantly around Francis. To them he was often gruff and directive. Underlying Kearns favorable view of Francis was beyond them simply being from the same area of Ireland.

Kearns did desperately need help with the bookkeeping duties. His business was becoming increasingly complex with the tavern itself requiring two sets of books, one official and one real. The duplicity to defeat the sizable tax on alcohol used to paydown the debt of the Civil War and to finance reconstruction.

Then there was tracking his fees from the employment referral business with Kearns shaking down employers and employees alike. Also, with his growing capital, Kearns had begun loaning money to other Irishman with fledgling but promising businesses. Mainstream banks often refused to lend money to the Irish, creating an opportunity for Kearns.

While Kearns could have entrusted the books to his sons-inlaw, that would have lessened his leverage over them. He also thought they were not ready yet for such responsibility. So, the sons-in-law would be kept cleaning up the bar, running errands, and other menial tasks, while Francis did the books.

In hiring Francis, Kearns felt he had a blank slate that he could help shape. A blank slate that had the same positive attributes Kearns associated with Mathew McNamara, trustworthiness, commonsense, and an easy, practical demeanor. More subconsciously, Kearns also hoped against hope that by helping Francis he would finally be rid of the guilt he felt toward the Confederate prisoners at Elmire.

****

With the job, things steadily improved for Francis. He was able to move his family into their own apartment in Vinegar Hill. Bridget, for the first time she could remember, did not have to worry where the next meal would be coming from. The children had the luxury of going to school, rather than having to work like many other neighborhood children, and they had presentable clothing and could even go to the doctor if they needed one.

Eating regularly allowed Francis to regain most of his physical strength, adjusting for him now being in his midthirties. His mood stabilized, although some underlying anxiety remained as he suspected something would eventually go wrong, it always did.

Francis enjoyed the mental stimulation of his work, especially compared to the back-breaking physical labor he had done previously. The growing complexity and quasi-legitimacy of Kearns's business endeavors required Francis to be creative and extremely careful with his analysis and recording of the numbers. Kearns also consulted him about potential business investments, a sign that Kearns both respected Francis and valued his opinion.

That closeness initially created a divide between Francis and his three office mates—Kearns's sons-in-law, McCleary, Burke, and Lally. They initially resented Francis because Kearns treated them as subordinates to be directed, not equals to be consulted. Uncharacteristically, Francis was patient with the situation and did not force things. He would wait for opportunities to arise for him to reduce the tension with the three sons-in-law.

Deeming McCleary as the most influential of the three, Francis paid the most attention to him. McCleary often read the Tribune, one of the more leftist newspapers of the day. Francis also noticed pamphlets sticking out of McCleary's jacket pocket one day, pamphlets with titles associated with the most radical political thought of the day, socialism, communism, and anarchism. Reading up on the topics himself: Francis began to discretely float concepts related to them during the banter in the office. At first, McCleary would respond with awkward silence. Francis's decided to abandon the effort thinking it was making McCleary even more guarded but then, unexpectedly, McCleary invited Francis to take a walk with him.

To justify the invitation, McCleary noted the office was getting unbearably hot in the rising summer heat and the stench from the back alley was particularly bad. They walked less than a half-mile to one of the few remaining vacant lots along the quickly developing shoreline of the East River. The two other sons-in-law, Burke and Lally, were waiting for them. Francis looked around the vacant lot and began to suspect he had been taken there to be killed.

It was not a murder plot but a test. McCleary asked Francis how he thought the Irish should best assimilate in America. It was not atypical for McCleary to ask theoretical and philosophical questions, but this was the first time he posed a politically loaded one to Francis. Based on how all three brothers-in-law stared at him intently, Francis concluded the three were of the same mind and they wanted to see if Francis thought the same.

To hedge his bets, Francis did not answer directly and instead articulated the risks and benefits he saw to the prevailing views of assimilation. There was the approach of using the vehicles society provided for upward mobility. Change from within, slow and steady, with concession and compromise being the key. The approach expounded by Kearns. Then there was the revolutionary, potentially violent approach. Not assimilate to the world but make the world assimilate to them. Forcibly demand the Irish be accepted as they are and the country start sharing resources more equally. The approach that McCleary had been studying.

"That is all fine and good," Burke said dismissively, having no interest in Francis trying to walk a tight rope. "Which approach is better?"

"It depends," Francis replied, speaking calmly as he truly saw pros and cons of both approaches. "You have to take in account the opportunities that present themselves, how people are thinking today, and how they might think tomorrow."

"Right now, which approach would work best right now?" Burke insisted.

"Neither, most Irish are too busy just trying to survive. They are not inclined to be thinking about political and economic ideology. Nor do they have much in the means to effectuate change. So now is the time to wait and prepare."

"Wait for what?" Lally, the youngest of the trio asked.

"For the fertile ground of change to show itself." Francis responded. "And it will."

"Nonsense!" McCleary shouted. "We have to create the opportunities, not wait for them. They will never come otherwise. The rich and powerful will see to that." The earnestness of his reaction let Francis know McCleary truly believed what he had been reading. He was an extremist ideologue and not just inquisitive, or someone conducting counterintelligence as to what the radicals were thinking. The reaction of Burke and Lally to McCleary's outburst confirmed they too were revolutionaries.

What followed was part debate, part shouting match. To the surprise of all, it ended with everyone having a greater appreciation for how difficult their situations were as first and second generation immigrants. Francis found himself moving closer to McCleary's position about the need to make change happen, ironically while McCleary and his inlaws gained greater appreciation for Francis's point of cultivating the ground and looking for the right time and opportunities to act.

From that point forward the four of them constantly discussed how best to fix the world, but always out of ear shot of Kearns who would have shut the discussion down and directed them to think like him, as if his position as primary bread winner translated to Devine declaration. His attitude however made him the personification of what his sons-in-law wanted to fight against.

****

The relationship with McCleary, Burke, and Lally turned into a friendship for Francis. The feeling was mutual, and the trio offered to help Francis look for his brother, Jamie, and son, Stephen Michael, whom he had been looking for since his return to New York.

On his own, Francis had not made much progress. Letters he sent to Jamie's last known address had been returned unopened. His visits to the Five Points, where Jamie had been living before the war, turned up nothing. Francis scoured the lists from the war of dead and wounded, praying he would not see Jamie's name there. His prayers were answered but he did not take much solace in that knowing those lists were notoriously incomplete. His other brother Mathew, who Francis knew was killed at Fredericksburg, showed up occasionally on lists of missing and wounded but in reality lay at the bottom of an unmarked grave.

As for his son, Francis looked for the Rowlands who were caring for him in city directories and newspapers. But there was no mention of the family head, Martin VanBuren Rowland, at all. It seemed all the Rowlands scattered into the wind.

McCleary had friends in the Five Points from whom he learned that Jamie had not been seen there since before the war. Jamie's girlfriend, Eileen Brady, also disappeared without a trace from the Points at the beginning of the conflict.

Edward Fitzpatrick, the only other person Francis knew from his first trip to New York, had moved to New Jersey but no one was sure where. He was said to periodically come back to New York but had not been seen in over a year.

Lally had worked previously as an oysterman and knew many people involved in the trade and that gave Francis hope. Francis recalled Martin Rowland had also been in the oyster business and had planned on taking Virginia oysters back to Brooklyn. Asking around, Lally was able to find out that the Rowlands had indeed returned to Brooklyn near the end of the war but had since moved once again. Some thought they went out east on Long Island or to Connecticut, others thought they had returned to Virginia but no one was sure.

Francis refused to concede that his brother and son could be lost to him forever. At the same time, he was at a dead-end and could not take any more disappointment. So, he took what he described to Bridget as a temporary break from his search. He vowed, and she agreed to support, renewing the search once any clue as to their whereabouts surfaced.

****

Things went along relatively uneventfully for Francis and his family for a few years. That was until the summer of 1871, six years after his return to New York. It was then that the ideological divide between his employer, Thomas Kearns, and his sons-in-law would explode. Not just for them but the entire Irish-American community in New York.

While there had long been tension between Irish Catholics and Nativists who were often identified as Protestant. That tension had been increasing in New York where Irish Catholics, like Thomas Kearns, were starting to make inroads in American society and desperate Irish Catholics took more and more of the unskilled jobs from other groups. The St. Patrick's Day parade, which had been a relatively peaceful event in Manhattan for a hundred years, was starting to encounter resistance and resentment from Nativists.

In 1867, for example, Nativists used wagons to block Irish Catholic marchers from finishing the parade route. The marchers became incensed and a brawl ensued leaving scores of Irish-Catholics, Nativists, and police bloodied and bruised.

Things got worse in 1870 when the Nativists inaugurated a parade of their own. Ripping a painful page right out of Irish history, the Nativists chose to celebrate William of Orange. The man who had subjugated Roman Catholics under Protestant rule in Ireland centuries before. If that were not provocative enough, the Nativists selected a parade route that would take them right through the increasingly Irish

Catholic Hell's Kitchen section of Manhattan. The parade started with marchers taunting the locals, Irish-Catholic hurling insults back, and after reports that marchers urinated on one Catholic church and shot through the window of another, ended with a melee that left eight dead and many more injured.

The Orange Day Parade, as it was called, was to take place again in 1871. In anticipation, Irish Catholics debated how to respond. The majority argued that replying with violence would only play into the Nativist's hands, as they had been trying to portray Irish Catholics as violent, undisciplined drunks.

Others argued that not meeting the parade with violence would only embolden the Nativists to oppress them further. The Nativists would only stop when they were forced to, the thinking went. For Thomas McCleary, Brian Burke, and Patrick Lally this was the opportunity they were waiting for. If the parade resulted in violent chaos, that could be the spark for the anarchist, socialist revolution they wanted.

Leading up to the parade on July 12, 1871, Kearns became increasingly vocal that the marchers should be met with empty streets. "Give them no attention at all!" Kearns shouted at his tavern, trying to convince those around him with the sheer intensity of his voice. "Show them we act when and how we choose to. Not at their whim or provocation. We are too smart to fall into their trap."

One of the more vocal patrons shouted back, "What would you have us do, let them walk all over us? Maybe instead of ignoring the parade we should show up and bend over so they can kick us literally in the ass."

"Get out of my establishment!" Kearns screamed, his face red as he teetered on the very violence he was advocating against.

The patron left, his feet not touching the ground, as McCleary and Burke had him by the elbows and Lally cleared the way to the door. All for their father-in-law's benefit. Once outside, they gently put the man down and said that if he were true to his convictions, he would show up the next night to a meeting at the newly opened Prospect Park. The trio advised that plans were being made to foil the marchers and stout Irish-Catholic men were needed.

Once back inside the tavern, Kearns thanked his sons-in-law for their support. "It means a lot to me," Kearns said. "If we respond to this parade like a bunch of violent *bodachs* then that is the way the rest of the country will treat us. Everything we sacrificed for since coming here, the back-breaking work, the war—it will all be for nothing."

Francis watched the encounter and remained silent, but he knew the brothers-in-laws were up to something. Later in the office, when the three were alone with Francis, they pressed him.

"Now is the time, Francis." McCleary said as he sat beside Francis at the desk where he did his bookkeeping work. "You always preach to us we should look for opportunities, well here one is gift wrapped for us by the Orangemen and Nativists. There is not an Irish Catholic in New York who isn't angry about the parade and what it represents. They are mad, fighting mad. Kearns is delusional, he would have us living forever off the crumbs the rich decide to throw at us.

If we want respect, we have to take it. They want to march through our neighborhoods, they are going to have to do it with our fists in their faces. You with us Francis?"

"What are you planning?" Francis asked.

When the three started to explain what they had been working on with radical members of the Ancient Order of Hibernians and the more secretive Ribbonmen, Francis had to conceal his alarm. Storming an armory, arming the masses with rifles, and trying to take over parts of New York City was too much for Francis liking.

Francis somberly reminded the trio they would be arming and unleashing a mob. He tried to make them think.

"If you were the government, how would you respond to all that?" Francis did not wait for an answer. "I imagine with the national guard, the whole Union army maybe, throw in some gunboats to boot. Maybe they will starve you out or force you out at the end of a bayonet, but they will push you out. Doing nothing will not be an option for them. They will crush you faster and harder than they even did the Confederacy and the Confederacy had its own army, navy, laws, and regulations. You will have an untrained, undisciplined mob. Real soldiers will run through you like a hot knife through butter. Some of your recruits will die, most will give up, and if you survive the fight, it will be just to be hung as a criminal. That is the way it works. You should study your history." Francis thought of Latee in Texas.

"The Confederacy didn't have a moral cause but we do, to help the downtrodden." McClearly countered. "And beside we don't have to win. We just have to inspire. The exploited people around the world will see us stand up for ourselves and they will do the same. We will be the spark that starts the fire."

"A fire that could destroy everything and everybody!" Francis exclaimed. "The rich and entrenched own the newspapers. The rest of the world will only hear that you are treasonous criminals, not martyrs. You need to be more sophisticated than taking over a few neighborhoods for a week or two if you can even keep them for that long."

The debate went on until Burke cornered Francis with one basic question. "Do you want things to stay the way they are? Today, most people have nothing, a few have some crumbs, while a handful hoard everything else. Is that what you want Francis? You want your kids and grandkids to know only the squalor and struggle you have known. There is no perfect time to stand up for yourself, there is only today and what are you going to do with it?"

"No," Francis said somberly, "I don't want things to stay as they are." Francis was many things, but a hypocrite was not one of them. He had preached to look for opportunity and he had to agree this parade was an opportunity. It offered a wild card he and people like him could play to change things up, but to go all in on a wild card alone would be foolhardy. So, Francis unenthusiastically agreed to help. But quietly to himself, he would help make the resistance to the parade a clear statement to oppressors, but at the same time he would keep it from becoming a bloodbath.

****

On the morning of July 12, 1871, Francis was with the three son-in-laws and hundreds of other Irish Catholics. They were heading for an armory on Avenue A in Manhattan that was said to have hundreds of rifles and ammunition. If successful, they would graduate from being a mob to a self proclaimed militia very quickly. However, there was a sizable police presence in and around the armory. The police had been tipped off, which surprised everyone except Francis.

Now Francis despised informants as much as the next Irishman, and if he were exposed as one he would be good as dead in Vinegar Hill. But Francis felt he had no choice. It was the only way to save lives and to keep the resistance to the Orangemen parade from getting out of hand and setting back the Irish-Catholic cause. So, off the anonymous letters went to the police, with steps taken to avoid anything being traced back to Francis.

Frustrated, the group of Irish Catholics proceeded further uptown in Manhattan, where they were joined by thousands of other likeminded Irishman. The horde was mulling along 8th Avenue, filling up the streets between West 23rd and West 30th Streets. Some were overturning vendors carts and garbage bins and throwing other things in the streets to block the path of the parade, the marchers scheduled to be heading down the avenue shortly. Other Irish Catholics took to lining the roofs of the tenements and businesses along the avenue, with bricks, rocks and bottles in hand.

Some police in advance of the parade tried to clear the street but were jeered, pelted with rocks, and were close to being surrounded until they retreated back up the avenue. The sight of the running police officers sent a jolt of energy through the Irish Catholic crowd, they had muscle and were flexing it.

The sheer number of protestors, in combination with the message just sent via the retreating police, gave Francis hope that the marchers would be intimidated enough to back down. They weren't, in good part because the marchers were not alone.

McCleary pulled Francis and Lally aside. "The marchers will be gathering on 29th Street to start the parade. Run up there, count how many there are and report back to me. I'll stay here on 24th Street and start organizing things." McCleary was fancying himself a general of the revolution he saw developing.

In light of the increasingly belligerent tenor of the crowd, Francis thought McClearly was deluding himself about organizing things. But he and Lally followed the general's command anyway. It took them a while to make it up to where the marchers were assembling, the crowd of Irish Catholic protestors so large that Francis and Lally found it faster to move uptown via 7th rather than 8th Avenue.

Once on 29th Street, Francis ran up the stoop of a tenement across from the Lamartine Hall to get a better look. Lamartine Hall was the headquarters of the Orangemen and various Nativist groups. Francis could see the marchers with their sashes, banners, and drums, but he was surprised how few there were—about 150 in all. What there was a lot more of, however, were police and national guardsman. Putting his bookkeeping skills to work, Francis counted the number of police and national guardsmen in a single formation and then multiplied it by the number of formations that he could see. Five thousand men, all heavily armed, some atop horseback.

Most of those guarding the marchers were, ironically, Irish Catholics, Francis could tell by just looking at them. McCleary and others assumed many police and guardsman would call in sick rather than protect the Orangemen marchers. A horrible miscalculation. Those that had joined the police and enlisted in the guard were there to make a statement themselves. They gave an oath to uphold the law, and they were going to keep it. The courts decided the marchers could march, so they would march.

"Oh my God," Francis mumbled. He then shouted for Lally who had moved from the stoop to the curb to look more closely at the marchers. Francis told Lally, "Run back to McCleary as fast as you can. Tell him to call it off, there is literally an army heading toward him. The opportunity we thought we had, we don't."

Lally ran back toward McCleary as directed, and Francis continued to watch the marchers and their escort getting ready to start the procession. Lally returned, red faced, and nearly out of breath from his sprints back and forth.

"What did he say?" Francis asked.

Lally opened his jacket to show two pistols beneath. "He wants us to show them we mean business. They have to turn back now or face the consequences." There was fear now showing on Lally's young face, they were not talking political theory anymore.

"Damn it!" Francis replied. "Give me these." He took both pistols and secreted them underneath his own jacket. "Get out of here, go home. I'll take it from here."

"No," Lally said. "I am no coward," although there was a quiver in his voice. "I will see this through with you and the others."

Not wanting a debate, Francis moved away from the crowd to conceal himself behind a stoop. He then shot both pistols into the air just as the procession started to head down the avenue.

With the upward angle, Francis figured the bullets would reach their zenith a mile up and then tumble down harmlessly into the Hudson River or the New Jersey marshlands beyond. The police horses jumped at the sound of the gunshots, and momentarily the parade stopped. Then there were shots fired from other Irish Catholics across the street, except they were not aiming into the air. A guardsman fell to the ground wounded. Another guardsman fired his rifle seemingly in response but it was an accidental discharge, the guardsman's hands were shaking that much. No one was sure where guardsman's bullet landed.

"Steady boys!" Shouted one of the officers among the guardsmen. "We have our orders, do your duty. Show arms and forward march."

The Orangemen's drummers set the slow, methodical tempo for the march. The fact that the guardsmen left their wounded comrade behind with a medic was evidence of the specificity and priority of their mission. The governor of New York had pushed aside public safety concerns of the city's mayor and police chief. Citing his support of the marchers' First Amendment rights, not mentioning campaign contributions from Nativist and Protestant groups, the governor had assured the march would take place and directed his law enforcement and guardsmen leadership to make it so.

The marchers stayed bunch together, and some crouched behind those protecting them. The relatively small group of marchers were rattled by the size of the crowd protesting them, as well as the flood of threats, bricks, rocks and bottles the crowd was hurling at them. "Irish confetti" as the debris came to be called.

The line of police at the front and sides of the parade shoved protestors back and menacingly displayed their billy clubs and bayonets. The crowd responded with even more bricks, rocks, and bottles, as well as expletives that bordered on the poetic in their obscenity.

Francis and Lally made their way back to McClearly as quickly as they could, both to update him and to avoid being pointed out as those who fired the initial shots.

"Are they still coming?" McCleary asked, looking over the other two men's heads trying to look for the marchers himself. Sure enough, the banners of the marchers could be seen, along with the police on horseback. The echo of the beating drums could also be heard, along with the low rumble of thousands of feet and hooves of horses on the cobblestone avenue.

"Yes, they are coming. A lot of them," Francis answered. "And they are armed to the teeth. Since we shot at them, they are madder than a March hare. This is going to be a disaster; you have to call it off!"

"And squander such a fine opportunity?" McCleary said, either feigning bravery or actually displaying it.

The three men then moved over to the side of one of the overturned carts. A top it was a boy, no more than 12 years old. "Edward Halsey," Francis heard someone call, "Get down from that wagon and get in here before I tell your mother!" It was a woman calling out from one of the windows of the three-story tenement behind them.

The boy looked at the woman and gave her the raspberry, a disrespectful sputtering noise made by pressing his tongue and lips together. Then he took a slingshot from his pocket and loaded it with a rock. He looked up the avenue, drawn there by the increasing noise of the approaching marchers and their armed escort.

The drum beat of the marchers gave Francis a shudder, as he thought back to the battlefields of the Civil War. Death was coming. He could feel it.

As the mass of police and guardsmen neared the overturned carts that demarked the strongest line of resistance, they had to slow down. When they did, the torrent of rocks, bricks, and bottles from the rooftops and the crowd lining the avenue intensified.

Several police and guardsman fell when hit by projectiles. The marchers started to panic but could not escape, hemmed in by those protecting them and those wanting to assault them. A squad of guardsman raised their rifles, aiming at the rooftops. Their officer intervened and instructed them instead to move the wagons out of the way so the bottleneck could be broken.

As the guardsmen moved to do so, shots rang out from among the crowd of protestors. One bullet struck the officer in the shoulder who had given the order to remove the wagons. Another guardsman fell to the ground clutching his thigh, another still held his hands over his blood spirting eye. It was then that a single shot came from among the guardsmen in return. Then another, and then a series of volleys, guardsmen in the back mistakenly assuming an order had been given to open fire. Instead, nerves, fear, and confusion resulted in hundreds of bullets indiscriminately hitting and ricocheting along the congested avenue.

When the smoke cleared, there were bodies—some moaning, some not—lying in the street and along the curb. Cries came out from the apartments lining the avenue where occupants had been hit. Store front windows had bullet holes, with employees and patrons injured inside, people who had nothing to do with the parade or the protest.

Francis noticed the boy who had been a top the wagon was now on the ground behind it, bleeding from his chest. Instinctively, Francis ran to him, picked him up and then looked around for help. As he did so, he saw McCleary on the ground shot dead with a bullet to the head. Burke was bent over, spitting up blood, having been shot in the stomach. Lally lay missing part of his lower jaw that had been shot off. He was unconscious, if not dead.

Not knowing what else to do, Francis decided he had to help the wounded boy. He better secured the boy in his arms, turned his back toward the guardsman—half expecting another volley to come his way—and headed south along the avenue. On the corner of West 20th Street and 8th Avenue he spotted two nurses from a nearby doctor's office tending to others who had been wounded but able to make their way from the scene of the shooting. One of the nurses made eye contact with Francis and noticed the bleeding boy. "Bring him here," she said, and Francis laid him down on the sidewalk. The boy groaned.

"Is he your son?" The nurse asked.

"No, he was in the crowd but I think he lives in the neighborhood." Francis answered and added, "He is just a kid. I have boys at home close to his age." It was only then it fully dawned on Francis the risk he created for his own family by his involvement with the protest. Life was tough enough in New York for working class kids, it would be tougher without a father. While his intentions had been to save Irish Catholics from continued oppression, and to keep people of all stripes from being hurt in the process, he had failed miserably.

The nurse looked up to say something to Francis but noticed behind him police —mad with emotion and adrenaline—had broken through the line of wagons and were now clubbing any man they came across, affiliated with the protest or not.

"Go now!" The nurse directed Francis with a compassionate but commanding tone. "Go home to your own sons while you can. I will take care of him." She looked down at the injured boy and spoke to him in a reassuring manner. "It will be alright; it will be alright." Although she knew it would not.

****

When Francis arrived home to his Brooklyn apartment, Bridget screamed. His shirt was covered with the boy's dried blood. Francis's despondent countenance only added to her alarm.

"What happened, Francis?" She asked, the concern deep in her voice.

At first, Francis said nothing. He sat down and Bridget pulled his shirt over his head fearing there was a horrible wound underneath. There was none. None that she could see anyway. She kept questioning him until he finally spoke.

"There is no mercy in this world. All is arbitrary, all is capricious." A phrase he had read in some of the anarchist material he had been given by McCleary. The now dead McCleary. Then there was a cry from out in the street, a boy running on the sidewalk shouting the news: "More than sixty people killed, hundreds injured, even more arrested at the parade!"

"Where you there? Were you part of that?" Bridget asked with a tone of judgment and distain.

She watched as Francis's despondency turn into rage. His face and body tensed as if he were about to explode. But he said nothing. Francis got another shirt and left, slamming the door behind him.

Chapter Fifteen
A Coping Compromise

Greater New York City Area
1871-1880

The next few days were a blur for Francis. He got drunk, wandered the streets of Brooklyn, even walked as far as Queens at one point. Eventually, he made his way back to Vinegar Hill and Kearns's tavern.

It was still early, a little after ten in the morning. Kearns, a man of habit, was at the bar alone, as he usually was—deep in thought. He was normally a tea drinker, but this morning, he had a glass full of whiskey in front of him and a half empty whisky bottle aside that. When he saw Francis enter, Kearns face reddened.

"You have some nerve coming back here." Kearns growled. "I knew they were naïve and had crazy ideas, but I hoped they would grow out of it. I hoped that you would be a good influence on them. Well, McCleary is not going to grow out of it now, is he? He is dead and my daughter a widow. If Burke lives it will be without most of his intestines and Lally, the only handsome one in the lot, is disfigured. And for what?"

Kearns reached for his glass of whiskey. Francis had never seen him drink before. Although he owned a tavern, Kearns thought drinking foolish. Just a way to make yourself think and act stupid. He never understood it, until now. He wanted to think and feel nothing. But the anger and frustration he felt could not be muted, and he focused it on Francis.

"You were older than them. Old enough to remember what the violent revolts in Ireland got us—more oppression and more violence. You, Francis, more than anyone else around here knew how dangerous idealistic ideas can be. How did they get you to fight for the Confederacy? What did they tell you? State's rights? Defend your home? Defend your honor? It was all bullshit, they wanted you to fight so plantation owners could keep their slaves. They didn't put that on their recruitment posters, did they?"

Kearns shook his head. "Those three idiots saw none of that. They fancied themselves intellectuals. Back-alley revolutionaries. They were going to change the world. It was our job, me and you, to save them from themselves. I was going to leave everything to them one day, better than how I found it. And they would improve things for their kids in turn. But now one is a corpse, another is a cripple and the third a mute with half his face missing. How are they going to improve things now?"

Beginning to tear up, Kearns looked away. Francis approached him in consolation, but Kearns stiffened. He stood up with a wobble for he was not used to the alcohol, and Kearns shouted at the top of his lungs: "Get out of my sight, Francis, and never come back. You have brought nothing but ruin to my door after I helped you."

Just as when they first met, Francis did not move. This time though Kearns threw his whisky glass at him and then the bottle. Missing with both. Then, taking a deep breath, and Kearns said with all the calm he could muster, "Go this instant and never come back." Francis knew what that meant. Things said emotionally could easily be retracted and forgiven. Things said deliberately would seldom be withdrawn.

****

If having witnessed friends killed and injured was not bad enough, and losing his job, the riot reawakened Francis's depression and anxiety. The visions of the riot merged with the death and destruction that he saw while in the military. Death always around him. The yellow fever epidemic, the loss of Ellen and newborn child, his father's murder and the famine.

Not knowing how else to cope, Francis drank which—not surprisingly—only added to his problems. He would wake up in strange places, sometimes with bruises on his hands and face from fights, and his pockets empty.

He could not go home, at least not empty-handed and he could not go back to Kearns. He could go, however, to someone he knew with some resources in Vinegar Hill. That person was Gerard "Ginger" O'Sullivan. O'Sullivan was Kearns's illicit whiskey supplier. Not that whiskey was illegal but supplying it in a way that circumvented excise taxes was.

Taxes had been raised on alcohol, temporarily the government said, during the war. But O'Sullivan had once jokingly told Francis that: "There is nothing more permanent than a temporary tax." He was right, the tax continued after the war and was markedly increased to pay down the war debt, finance reconstruction, and fund the Freemen's Bureau to assist recently emancipated slaves. The net effect was driving a once legitimate industry, and a reasonable amount of government income, entirely underground and making criminals rich.

O'Sullivan heard the despondent Francis out, often nodding his head in understanding. He reached into his jacket pocket and took out a wad of cash and handed it to Francis.

O'Sullivan said: "Take this home to your family and take it easy for a few days. I'll be in touch. While I can't take you on because that would offend Kearns, I know people who can use a good man like you."

As Francis turned to leave, O'Sullivan added ominously, "Francis, you know it may be rough work. But I know you are desperate. We all have to do what we have to do for our families."

Francis understood all too well what that meant. O'Sullivan's business was in the black market, putting him in touch with all the other components of the underground economy. O'Sullivan was close to the numerous criminal gangs that roamed Vinegar Hill and the waterfront. He hired them to firebomb and intimidate other distillers who tried to steal his staff or customers. He also used the gangs to intimidate revenue agents and police he could not bribe, and to even oppose the military's attempts to destroy his stills and bring him in as a tax evader.

Since 1867, the United States Army and Marine Corps had repeatedly launched regimental size attacks and sieges on *Irishtown*, searching house to house and effectively imposing martial law on the residents, all to stamp out criminal distilleries. The Irish resisted, more specifically the

Irish distillery owners resisted, producing the *Brooklyn Whiskey Wars*.

The gang that O'Sullivan referred Francis to was like most of the others of the time. A combination of young, desperate toughs and down on their luck Civil War veterans. Most Irish gangs chose names reflecting their turf, like the 19th Street Gang or the Battle Row Gang, but the group Francis fell in couldn't be bothered. That would prove problematic as others would create names for them.

The newspapers took to calling them the Leonard Street Burglars, after several members, including Francis, were arrested for breaking into textile and clothing factories along that street in Manhattan. The newspaper stories added the gangs stole silk ladies' garments and underwear, prompting rival gangs to refer to Francis's group as the *Girdle Gang* and *Brassiere Boys*.

Francis counseled the younger members who chaffed at the disparaging name while they served their three-month prison sentences. "Let's use it to our advantage. The less of a threat we appear to the other gangs—and it will be pretty easy to dismiss the Girdle Gang as harmless—the more free we are to do what matters, and that is making money. Let the other gangs fight it out for bragging rights, counting cash is what matters."

And Francis truly wanted to avoid any more violence in his life, but what he wanted did not matter. All the gangs in Vinegar Hill were summoned by Ginger O'Connell and others to combat yet another military attack on the neighborhood. This time it was a joint amphibious and land attack. Ironically, it was United States Army soldiers arriving by boat while Marines attacked from the gates of the Brooklyn Navy Yard. The pincer movement sought to capture the distilleries lock, stock, and barrel, and to arrest those that worked in and owned them.

On top of the tenements that lined the streets leading to O'Sullivan's operation, Francis was with members of other gangs throwing yet more Irish confetti in front of the troops to slow them down.

"You know what would help us throw these rocks further?" Francis asked the leader of one of the other gangs. "Brassieres," Francis said, answering his own question and getting a smile out of the gang leader who had been one of those giving Francis's group the disparaging names.

Periodic pistol shots from other gang members slowed the troops just enough for O'Sullivan to get his skilled workers and most of his inventory and equipment out. While the government heralded the seizure of the things O'Sullivan left behind, he was operating once again at full capacity in less than a week.

With a lull in the work trying to foil the United States military, the gang returned to its routine criminal existence. Most of those crimes did not pay well, at least not for Francis. But whatever he did make, Francis sent on to Bridget through a mutual friend. Unresolved distress over the Orangeman parade and embarrassment kept Francis from going home. That was until one day he found himself drunk enough.

Bridget was livid at the sight of him. He had been gone for weeks without a word. The little bit of money he sent did not make amends for much, and now he was back stinking of liquor. This did not bode well and Bridget tried to play it out in her head. Francis would be around less and less. The support money would eventually stop and she would be left alone to care for three young boys.

The oldest boy, John, now barely 10-years old, had been struggling in school. He was a sweet child but cognitively never fully recovered from whatever trauma he experienced before his adoption. So, Bridget was making arrangements for him to work at a factory making rope for the Navy Yard.

To further supplement the family, Bridget had been making inquiries about taking on sowing work herself. She did not have high hopes for that, as the nasty scar above Francis eye was evidence Bridget was not much of a seamstress. But it was something she could do in the home and that would allow her to simultaneously care for the two younger boys.

But her immediate problem was Francis standing sheepishly in the doorway. It was all Bridget could do not to wring his neck. *How could he have left the family in such straights?* She wondered to herself. But she knew it was not the time for her to vent.

While most other people considered Francis a rough character, Bridget knew that he was dreadfully fragile. He tended to ruminate over life's shortcomings and any missteps he made. The result would be, if the process was not interrupted with a dose of understanding and compassion, that Francis would become anxious, depressed, and volatile.

Bridget had witnessed his nervous breakdown onboard the ship taking them from war torn Virginia to New York. Bridget understood that her job was to build Francis up. She could not afford to lose him. Not so much for her own sake but for that of the boys.

Once Francis stabilized and they were back on their feet, then Bridget would vent. In her mind, she would rehearse that venting over and over, until venting day came. Until that day, she had to be the bigger person and forgive Francis his many faults. She did get some instant gratification, however, by kicking Francis out of the apartment because he was drunk. There was no talking to him in that state.

"You are not welcome in this house while in a drunk." Bridget declared unequivocally. "I can't have the boys seeing you like that."

"They are right there." Francis said, pointing to the boys who were waving at him from the back of the small apartment.

"What I meant," Bridgit clarified, "was that I can't have the boys seeing me tolerate you while drunk. So come back when you are sober." And with that, she pushed Francis out and closed—but did not slam—the door in his face.
Francis came back an hour later, while not totally sober—he was definitely less drunk than he had been. At their small kitchen table, he told Bridget everything. The riot, the boy, about McCleary, Burke, and Lally. Getting fired by Kearns and the shady work he was now doing.

The pragmatic Bridget took it all in, with a mix of horror, anger, and sympathy that she had to suppress. She then gave Francis what he needed. A path forward. A path based on priorities and grounded in the realities of what was around him.

"Understand this, it is no longer about me and you. It is about the boys. Our job is very simple: help and protect them as much as possible. With any luck, they will not have to live as desperately as we do. You will do whatever you have to in order to provide for them. But what happens outside the home—if it is bad—stays outside the home. One mention of crime to the boys or bringing them into it, I will throw you out. And if you come home drunk again, I will throw you out. From now on, you will act like a civilized human being at all times in this house no matter how uncivilized the world outside gets. Do you agree to all that?" Bridget finished, placing her hands on her hips and staring sternly at Francis—awaiting his answer.

Not responding instantly, Francis stroked the scar above his eye.

"Don't you dare!" Bridget screamed. "This is serious, no cutesy stuff. Just because you did a nice thing a long time ago doesn't give you the right to hurt this family now. Do you agree to the terms or not?"

"I do; I do," Francis said. And he did.

****

Ironically, the dichotomy that Bridget established between the streets and the home would help not only the children. It allowed Francis a respite at home from the real world he operated in, a world that was harsh and unforgiving. A world where it was seemingly easier to move down the economic

ladder than up. A world where you had to do rotten things just to survive and feed your family. Francis thought back to when he was a child and his father explained that in order for humans to live, they had to kill other living things.
It was just the way the world was.

With his criminal endeavors remaining unsophisticated, Francis got caught often. He became well known to prosecutors, judges, and particularly to police—as Francis often resisted arrest. He blamed those in authority for his problems, and police were authority. Francis also hated being handcuffed and locked up. It triggered his claustrophobia and made him think back to the nightmare of being put in the box at Fort Davis. Whenever he saw a police officer approaching him, his stomach sank and adrenaline shot through his body.

Some of Francis's criminal exploits earned mention in the local newspapers—one reporter giving him the moniker of *Fierce Francis*. He stayed loosely affiliated with the gang in Vinegar Hill and there were benefits to that. His associates often posted bail for him, helped him brawl with marks and police alike, and provided Bridget with money when Francis was in custody. But it was not the kind of friendship he had enjoyed with his brothers, Michael Scanlon, Abraham Simmons, and so many others. In fact, Francis lamented this time, when he was literally surrounded by a gang, was the loneliest period in his life.

For the most part, crime continued to afford Francis only a subsistence income. Consequently, he and his family learned the fine art of skipping out on rent. Their frequent and abrupt moves still kept them within the handful of Brooklyn neighborhoods that the Irish seemed to be confined. They just swapped one small tenement apartment for another, using different names for each until all the landlords knew their faces.

Francis and Bridget would pretend to be excited about going to a new place whenever they moved for the children's sake. But the strain on their schooling and friendships due to the moves eventually made the negatives of the moves very apparent to the boys.

Even with ongoing financial pressures, home disruptions, and the demoralizing nature of Francis's work, he stayed true to his bargain with Bridget. The couple were able to keep the home relatively upbeat for the children. As far as the three boys were concerned, their father was a laborer—which was true one or two days a week when Francis could find that kind of work. Bridget maintained various side jobs and kept the household. She also led the family in prayers at meals and before bed. Francis would bow his head but say nothing during the rituals.

On Sunday nights, the boys were expected to put on a show of sorts. Read a poem, sing a song, tell a story and—welcomed most of all—tell a joke. Making Francis laugh was the measure of success. And when Francis would laugh, Bridget would eventually smile as well—she couldn't help it. Two for one, the boys knew.

Alcohol was still a problem for Francis, but he only drank outside the home. As a result, a few *drunk and disorderly* charges were added to his rap sheet. The drinking also required him occasionally to sleep on the streets and in parks. In his mind, he would look up to the night sky from the park bench or whatever he slept on and think back to the beautiful

Blue Ridge Mountains he had seen during the Civil War. The lush rolling hills and majestic trees and greenery helped him relax and fall asleep, usually with the reminder to himself that he needed to go back to the Blue Ridge. He never would.

Francis would not go home drunk or even hung over, again he had promised Bridget. Returning from one absence of a few days, his youngest son Joseph asked him where he had been. Not wanting to lie to the boy, nor prematurely introduce him to the darker side of life, Francis replied, "I was on a toot."

After that, whenever Francis was gone for a prolonged period, all three boys, John, Patrick, and Joseph, would ask: "Where you on a toot, Da?" He would respond, "Yes, a toot." And he would often add, "But none of these toots have provided answers to life's mysteries yet boys."

Chapter Sixteen
The Prodigal Father

Brooklyn, New York
1880-1883

One of Francis's "toots" would take him to Canarsie Pier in Brooklyn and it would bring hurtful consequences.

It was a hot August day and Francis was sitting on the stoop of an abandoned building in Vinegar Hill. The building was formerly a flower shop and three-story tenement that had been gutted by a fire—a hazard in the overcrowded tenements lit by lanterns and heated by coal and wood stoves.

The shell of the building had become the meeting place of the Vinegar Hill gang that Francis now depended on for his meager livelihood. From the vantage point of the stoop, Francis noticed a man approaching wearing a neckerchief over his mouth and lower face. He was pushing another man in what looked like a makeshift wheelchair.

At first, Francis did not recognize them, they were mere shadows of their former selves. But eventually he was able to recognize Brian Burke's face, and then Patrick Lally's blue eyes above the neckerchief to cover his missing jaw.

"We found them!" Burke exclaimed, bypassing any greetings though they had been a part for so long. "The Rowlands, we found them—and your boy."
Francis was silent with shock and surprise.

"Martin Rowland returned to Brooklyn not too long ago with crates of oysters from Virginia for bedding. He is hoping they will take better than the previous bunch he brought up a few years ago. Canarsie Pier, that is where you will find him and your boy." Burke explained.

Finding himself tearing up, Francis wasn't sure if it was because he had just been given the first break in more than a decade as to his son's whereabouts or that Burke and Lally— with all their own problems—kept looking on his behalf when he himself had given up.

"How did you find that out?" Francis asked.

"It was Patrick," Burke advised and Francis could see Lally's eyes light up in pride above the neckerchief.

"We don't get out much," Burke stated, "everyone treats us like freaks. But once in a while Lally checks on his friends from his oysterman days. They still treat him like a human being, although he can only talk to them through his blackboard and chalk due to his injury." Lally took the items out to show Francis.

"We knew you were still in the neighborhood somewhere, so I asked around and here we are," Burke summed up.

"I can't thank you enough." Francis said wiping the tears from his eyes. "I can't believe you remembered and that I may actually see my son again. Francis could sense both Burke and Lally were proud of themselves. They felt useful again for the first time in a very long time.

Just as it seemed Francis had completely regained his composure, he lost it again looking at the condition of his old friends and their ongoing suffering. Lally made his way over and put his arm on Francis's shoulder. He then withdrew his hand to write on his black board. *Gud Luck*, he wrote— having only had a second-grade education. Burke looked at what he wrote and smiled; he could not read at all. It occurred to Francis as the pair left that he had no idea how the two communicated with each other, but they clearly did—somehow.

****

Francis was a ball of emotions. There was the guilt and sadness at having seen Burke and Lally along with the possibility of getting his long-lost son back. Then there was the question of how he could provide for another mouth to feed, his family already struggling.

Could he even ask Bridget to take on yet another person in the household—a small, two-room apartment in a rundown tenement. His son John was already working and Patrick was getting ready to. Maybe Stephen Michael would be able to pay his own way. He was a teenager at that point and could find work.

The stress of the thinking and of the possibilities made Francis crave for a drink. That led to him getting drunk. While drunk, he took horse drawn street cars and walked to Canarsie Pier. There he was pushed toward the Rowland's new home on Remsen Place, several blocks up from the water.

What Francis did not know was that as much as he had been looking for the Rowlands, they had been looking for him— for Stephen Michael's sake. They suspected that Francis may have been looking for them in Brooklyn because that is where they were before the war, and they still had connections there.

The Rowlands asked their web of cousins and friends to keep their eyes and ears open for a Francis McNamara. And what those people saw and heard in relation to the name was not flattering. One cousin worked as a clerk in the Brooklyn courthouse where Francis had been arraigned on various charges in recent years. There were also others who read the newspaper accounts of his crimes, resisting arrest, and public intoxication. They knew about Fierce Francis, as if it was not bad enough that Martin Rowland recalled that some in Norfolk had referred to Francis as Fireball.

To protect their adopted son from what they reasonably concluded was his troubled father, the Rowlands signed Stephen Michael out as a deck hand on a ship carrying cargo up the Hudson River. They also took to calling him Michael Rowland, rather than Stephen Michael McNamara although he, and they, knew his true name.

Now, the boy's disreputable biological father was pounding at the Rowlands' front door. Martin, known as Mat to his friends, answered and remained calm—as was his nature. In response to Francis's demands to see his son, Mat explained that Stephen Michael had begun training as a sailor and was at sea.

He also advised Stephen Michael was in good health and good spirits. Mat proudly explained how he had provided for

Stephen Michael's education and the boy could read, write, and was exceptionally good at arithmetic.

Mat then tried to subtly remind Francis that the Rowlands were the only family Stephen Michael had ever known, and he was close to Emma and Edwin, the Rowlands' biological children that were a few years younger than himself. Mat Rowland hoped that would help Francis realize that it was in his son's best interest that he stay with the Rowlands. It did not seem to sway the still intoxicated Francis.

Fearing Francis may have already heard that his son had been introduced to the neighborhood as Michael Rowland, Mat sought to contextualize things: "He knows you are his father, and Ellen was his mother—we told him that. And he knows that he is Stephen Michael McNamara. He may go by Michael Rowland at times but that is only for expedience's sake, people know his association with us, and he didn't want to keep rehashing his life story for people."

Mat knew Stephen Michael retaining his birth name would be important to Francis. "My cousin Sally told us," Mat continued, "it was important to you that your stepsons keep their surnames out of respect to their biological father. So, it was important to us that Stephen Michael keep his."

The mention of his stepsons, Timothy and Dennis Moriority, is what sobered Francis up more than anything else. He had completely failed them. The boys were in the care of his inlaws, the Scanlons, in West Virginia. He had their address but hadn't written in years, embarrassed that he was unable to send along any money for the boys' care. He could not even send them money now as he was that broke. He couldn't even support Bridget and his three other sons in

Brooklyn. Bridget had to work cleaning homes, sowing in addition to doing all the shopping and cooking at home. His oldest son John had been working for a few years at the rope factory to help keep the family afloat and Patrick was about to be pulled out of grade school as well to secure another income.

Staring at Mat Rowland, Francis had to admit to himself that the man had done more for his son's welfare than Francis himself had done. Not out of neglect on Francis's part, but capacity. Not that the reason mattered, the support did and Rowland could give it and Francis could not. With that realization the aggressiveness Francis first arrived with dissipated and was replaced with sadness.

Detecting progress had been made and trying to leverage it, Mat dug into his pocket and pulled out bills to give to Francis. That had the anger quickly come back to Francis's face.

"You think I am here to sell my son?" Francis growled.

Now alarmed that he made things worse, Mat replied: "No, I think you want your son to be happy and to have a good life. I can assure you that is what he has here. You have sacrificed greatly to make that happen and I respect you for that, as will Stephen Michael. I am just giving you what I can, just as I am giving Stephen Michael what I can."

Refusing the money, Francis stormed away but then stopped. He turned to face Mat Rowland once more.

"Him being happy is what his mother wanted, and I loved his mother, you know." And after another pause, Francis said with his eyes starting to glisten with tears: "Thank you. It is a good thing what you and your family have done for my son." And Francis left and made his way back to the pier and looked out over the Jamaica Bay that surrounded it, the late afternoon sun sinking in preparation for evening. With no one else around he let himself fall completely to tears. He would not get his son back, and the worst part was that was in his son's best interest. Fierce Francis was brokenhearted.

****

After leaving Canarsie, Francis got drunk yet again. He arrived home later that night not just inebriated but still sipping from a bottle of bootleg whiskey. By doing so, he had broken the agreement. And for Bridget that meant it was venting day. She started shouting at him which prompted feeble attempts at explanations from him. But in his drunken and emotionally raw state he made the mistake of calling Bridget by his first wife's name, Ellen. Before he could finish the slurred sentence, Bridget hit him with a steel burner cover from the stove. She knocked him unconscious and left him with a gash at his hairline. Yet another scar memorializing their relationship. This one, however, he would not be able to gloat over.

With all his brawling and rough street existence, Francis had been knocked out before. But this time his heart and pride would hurt more than his brain. Had the blow come from anyone else in the world he would have fought back and continued to attack until he had nothing left. With Bridget, however, he just took it and felt guilty.

Neither Francis nor Bridget would mention the violent incident ever again, not even in jest. He was too embarrassed, and Bridget felt her actions had spoken clear enough. Francis did tell Bridget, however, about finding his son, Stephen Michael, and the conversation he had with Mat Rowland. Her heart broke for her husband, and she told him as much. But ever the insightful and practical one, she assured him that he was doing the right thing by leaving his son where the boy was doing well.

She reminded him, "It is not about us, it is about the children. You are noble one, Francis, by putting his interests ahead of your own." That praise was just what Francis needed to hear. He did face a difficult choice and made the right decision. That did not happen often for him.

Chapter Seventeen
The Brother's Mystery Solved

Greater New York City Area
1880-1882

Ironically, it took a prison sentence to move things in a better direction for Francis. In court, the judge asked him how he pled to the charges of theft and resisting arrest. Francis being unable to afford an attorney, represented himself. He answered the judge as honestly as he could, "I probably did it, I can't remember anymore," pointing to the scars on his forehead.

His confusion stemming from all his crimes starting to blur together as much as the head trauma. The judge, taking pity on Francis and his scars, gave him only a one-year prison sentence. Absent that sympathy, Francis would have spent closer to a decade in prison. His criminal history had gotten that bad.

After sentencing, bailiffs brought Francis to the large holding cell in the basement of the courthouse. He was to stay there until he could be transported to the Brooklyn Penitentiary. In that holding cell was none other than Edward Finnegan.

The same Edward Finnegan that Francis had met on his first day in New York when he arrived from Ireland. The same Edward Finnegan who was a trusted friend of Francis's brother, Jamie. At first, the two did not recognize each other with more than twenty years having passed, and it was another inmate who inadvertently prompted the reintroductions.

Roberto D'Antonio was a small but wiry Italian just arrested on charges of extortion. While a growing percentage of the population in the poorer parts of New York, Italians were still not as numerous as the Irish. With strength being in numbers, D'Antonio was getting rough treatment by a handful of Irish thugs in the holding cell. It was clear, with his stance and fists clenched, that if D'Antonio had to catch a beating, he would go down fighting. That is what caught Francis's attention.

With the Irishmen's harassment getting louder, Francis spoke up in an authoritarian tone, "Leave the Guinea alone."

Being older than the others and having the look of someone who had scraped by most of his life, the harassing Irishmen yielded. It was then that Edward, sitting across the cell, saw the resemblance to Jamie McNamara, in body and tenor of voice.

"Be jiggers, Francis!" Edward cried out. Francis took a double take and then recognized Edward. They hugged each other.

"The man with balls enough to steal a policeman's horse!" Edward remarked. Looking Francis in the eye, as if to confirm that he was there.

Edward added, "We thought you were dead. Your brother had me hire a detective and a lawyer to look for you in Virginia. They searched in Richmond and Norfolk. They monitored refugee reports in the newspapers, all with no luck. I should have known those southern legal folks were swindling us. Here you are alive as can be!"

There had been no swindle. With such a large number of refugees during and after the war, the incomplete and easily lost nature of the hand-kept records, tracking people was a hit and miss endeavor at best.

"Is Jamie alright?" Francis asked nervously, but excited as Edward's use of the word "we."

Edward looked around and pulled Francis aside so no one can hear the rest of the conversation.

"There is no more Jamie." Edward said and Francis's heart sank. "But there is a Lawrence Smith." Edward referring to the identity Jamie had assumed upon his discharge from the army. "He is living well in swanky Brooklyn Heights, just a few miles from this very spot. I will pass along to Mr. Smith your address, Francis. And exactly how long will you be at the Pokey Hotel?" Edward asked Francis, using the slang for prison.

"A year, maybe less with good behavior." Francis replied.

"Yes, a year. I will tell him that, assuming he will not be too perturbed by my own little legal issue." Edward then turned and shouted at the policemen grouped outside the cell: "When did they make it a crime for a man to attend the theater!"

The policeman who arrested Edward shouted back, "When the man attends drunk and sings louder than the main act!"

"Louder *and better*," Edward snorted to Francis, "Louder *and better*."

Francis laughed, which felt good on a day when he thought he would be doing anything but laughing.

"Now about Mr. Smith," Edward advised, "he keeps a very low profile, he does. And you should know, since the war, Mr. Smith sometimes has a tough time of it. There are some days on end when he falls into a funk and won't talk to a soul or even come out in the light of day. But eventually, it fades and he is his old self again."

It was at this point, D'Antonio came over to express his appreciation for Francis's help with the bullies. Had Francis not intervened, Roberto would have likely been beaten to a pulp. His bold stand in that dingy jail cell for nothing. But Francis understood, we all fall in the end, the only question is whether you choose to fight or not. And now that he was getting older, Francis even wondered if the decision to fight was consequential.

D'Antonio introduced himself, but in an odd way. He spoke dramatically with his thick Italian accent and advised that he was a descendant of the men who made Rome great, the ones who brought water to the cities and the sewage out. Family history details most in the cell would have preferred to do without.

"And you turned out to be an extortionist?" Francis asked, having listened to the police processing D'Antonio when he came into the cell block.

"A temporary necessity," D'Antonio replied, adding that "My destiny is to make America as great as Rome."

The conversation continued with Francis teasing the colorful Italian. They had a totally misinformed discussion as to why the Romans never conquered Ireland. Francis claimed the Irish were smart enough to send false reports to the Romans that Ireland was full of angry giants, sex-crazed shemonsters, and belching cannibals.

"You mean it is not?" Roberto questioned with a smile, looking at his former bullies.

Roberto then proceeded to recite from memory, or imagination, a list of Italians and their accomplishments, including Columbus discovering the New World. Two Scandinavian brothers in the lock up for fighting with each other took umbrage and countered with the claim Leif Erickson—a Viking—discovered America centuries before Columbus. The argument was won by the overwhelming number of Irishmen in custody who asserted that the New World was discovered by a drunken Irishman in the crow's nest of a ship captained by Saint Brendan. The rest of the crew misinterpreting his shout "I am a drinker" to be "America," hence the name.

In the end, they all laughed. Laughter in a prison. A place where inmates were previously about to attack each other over nothing other than their ethnicity when, in reality, they all had more in common than not. It had been a while since Francis could make people laugh like that, but Roberto brought it out in him. Which was good, because as fate would have it, they would be cellmates in the penitentiary for the next year.

Chapter Eighteen
The New Beginning

Brooklyn, New York
1880-1882

As the penitentiary doors closed behind him, making him a free man once again, Francis braced himself for the long walk back to the apartment where Bridget and his boys would be waiting. There was a carriage, a fine one, at the curb. A well-dressed man exited and approached Francis. Knowing right away who it was, Francis could see past the weight Jamie had put on, the full dark beard with hints of grey, and the expensive, well-tailored suit. This time tailored to him and not some corpse.

"I am Lawrence Smith," Jamie introduced himself, adding that, "You can call me Lawrence or Mr. Smith but either way names are extremely important," with Jamie nodding back toward the driver of his carriage. Francis understood. Things were going well for Jamie under his alias, and trouble could follow if his true identity resurfaced. In those days, people could simply move to another town, adopt a new name and they were an entirely new person. The Jamie McNamara who had left the Five Points in 1861 for Philadelphia and the war, was no more except maybe in his own mind and Francis's heart.

"I understand," Francis replied, nodding knowingly.

"Extremely nice to see you, Lawrence. It has been a very long-time." The brothers hugged, having a hard time not laughing and crying in the process.

"Let's go someplace where we can talk," Jamie said. They entered the carriage and they proceeded to Jamie's brownstone in Brooklyn Heights. Eileen Brady, Jamie's common-law wife who now went by the name Mrs. Allyson Smith, greeted them, along with she and Jamie's teenage daughter, Nancy.

Eileen escorted them to Jamie's library where there was tea waiting. "Lunch is on its way," Eileen advised, "I'll leave you two to talk." Eileen allowing the brothers to catch up, as she had done once before on Francis's first day in the United States.

"You read all these?" Francis asked, looking around the luxuriously furnished library with shelves of books waist high to the ceiling. The books alone must have cost a fortune, Francis thought with them all being leather bound and some with gold trimmed leaf. With that kind of investment in the books, Francis could only imagine what Jamie spent to buy the spacious brownstone itself.

"I only consult these few here and only on special occasions," Jamie replied, putting his hand on a stack of four books atop the large rolltop desk Jamie was leaning against.

"Glad to see you so well-settled and partially well-read, Mr. Smith." Francis said with a smile.

"Yeah, about that and all this." Jamie referring to the house, his appearance, and everything else.

"During the war, Allyson found us a nest egg," Jamie said referring to Eileen, the couple now well entrenched in the habit of referring to each other by their aliases. And by found, Jamie meant stole. When Eileen accompanied Jamie to Philadelphia at the beginning of the war, she hoped they would get a new, legitimate start in the City of Brotherly Love—leaving the toxic world of the Five Points behind them. And that hope seemed to be shaping into a reality—at least for a while.

Eileen found work as a correspondence clerk, and being as bright as she was, she quickly moved up the ranks. Within a year, she was the assistant to the company owner, Mr. Tyler Voyhees. Maybe as smart and savvy as Eileen, Voyhees had none of her other positive qualities. He was devoid of compassion and sympathy for anyone other than himself. In fact, Eileen thought him as heartless as the Five Points, just without the stink of the slum or the bluntness of its violence.

Voyhees was a fixer. A middleman, of sorts, making a fortune during the war putting together profiteers and corrupt government procurement officials. The result was the Union Army got marginal quality goods and Voyhees and associates made obscene profits. Eileen would cry at night reading Jamie's letters telling her of the horrors of the war, knowing she was helping Voyhees exploit the very same situation.

In his letters, Jamie told Eileen everything he was seeing and feeling. He never held anything back from her, in part because he thought if his problems could be fixed it was Eileen who would figure out how to do it. The unfiltered disclosures, however, took their toll on Eileen. She worried incessantly—not just for Jamie's physical safety but his mental state at seeing all the horrors of the war firsthand.

She knew others thought of him as a cavalier, tough guy hardened by the famine and urban life, but he was more accurately a sensitive, little boy adrift in a world he could not make sense of. She loved that innocence and vulnerability about him and the selfless kindness that often went with it. He would send her nearly all his wages from the front and tell her to do something nice for herself.

But if anything were left over, Jamie would add, there was a comrade returning home maimed who may need a little help, and there was always a new widow and orphans of comrades who would not be coming home at all. If there problems too could be fixed, Eileen would be the one to do it for them too, Jamie thought subconsciously.

When they first met, many years before in the Five Points, Eileen was working as a prostitute. Not by choice but necessity, as she arrived in the United States with nothing but a pretty face, desperation, and a fierce determination to survive. An occupational hazard in her line of work, Eileen was subject to every lude remark and vile comment imaginable wherever she went in the Five Points. Her own customers, partners in moral compromise, would often speak to her as cruelly as the "Bible thumpers" who seemed not to heed the very book they bandied about.

Sundays were particularly bad for Eileen as everyone else, including the thieves and criminals who were the majority of the populace, were both out-and-about in the neighborhood and feeling holier than thou on that day. In the hierarchy of sin at the time, as a prostitute Eileen was left near the bottom.

And it was on a Sunday morning that Eileen met Jamie. He happened to be walking toward her on the street, tipping his hat as he did so, when a woman behind him started berating Eileen. With a child in her arms and two more holding onto her long, worn skirt she yelled in Eileen's direction, "You harlot, you whoring mawk, you should not show your face on the Lord's day."

"Forgive them for they know not what they do!" Jamie said to Eileen, smiling and moving out of Eileen's way so she could pass him. He snarled at the yelling woman in the process.

Instead of passing him, however, Eileen stopped directly in front of Jamie.

"I didn't expect to meet Jesus Christ himself today." She said looking closely at his face, trying to decide if he too was demeaning her but in a more sophisticated way.

"I can understand your confusion, but I am not Jesus." Jamie responded, "In fact, Jesus is not Jesus if you are expecting someone who walks on water, rises from the dead and that sort of thing. Hell of a thinker, but I imagine he sank like a rock in the water and stayed dead as dead can be. But as an admirer rather than a follower of the man's philosophy, I take your mistake as a compliment."

And it progressed from there, Eileen having found the most spiritual but unreligious man she would ever meet, and Jamie finding the smartest, resourceful, and resilient person in his life. Together, they were whole, and they knew it. Together, they just may have a chance to survive the Five Points.

That is why when she was working for Voyhees, Eileen felt she was betraying her love. She wrote Jamie when he was in Virginia with his regiment and told him as much and advised that she was going to quit her job with Voyhees, "I can't stand the man and hate everything he stands for."

Jamie wrote back conveying his unshakable confidence in Eileen and any decision she chose to make. "Your gift is always finding a way to make something good out of something bad, and if you can't do that with that job then move on. Don't think twice, I love you no matter what."

It was the phrase *make something good out of something bad* that made Eileen hesitate and rethink her situation. She did not quit, rather she doubled her time in Voyhees's office. She needed that extra time to develop a second set of accounting ledgers, to open bank accounts in Voyhees name without his knowledge, and to falsify a series of financial documents. Then, when the war was over and Jamie was at her side once again, Eileen siphoned off a sizable portion of Voyhees's fortune—giving most of it to charities that helped the very widows and orphans Jamie asked her to look out for.

Then, to keep Voyhees from undoing the transfers, Eileen leaked the story of Voyhees's generosity to the press. He could not nullify the donations without making himself a public pariah and bringing attention to how he made the money in the first place.

Keeping enough money for herself and Jamie to comfortably re-establish themselves in New York, close to their Five Point connections if they were needed but far enough away to live anonymously otherwise. Coming with them to New

York would be Nancy, a young girl orphaned during the war who Eileen fell in love with on-sight when visiting one of the orphanages in Philadelphia operated by the Catholic Church.

Eileen knew she could not bear children herself, but at the same time she could not bear the thought of not having a child's love in her life. Nancy would fill that need, be the beneficiary of Eileen's love, and get Jamie as a doting father as well.

"And money begets money." Jamie explained to Francis, with Jamie's hand still on the stack of books on his desk. "We keep a low profile but that is a small price to pay. There are only a handful of people that know us from the old days, Edward being one of them, but I trust all that know." There was some honor among thieves in Jamie's circle.

After other topics came and went, with the brothers laughing at times but then getting somber at others. The latter emotion evoked by discussion of their parents and the loss of their older sister, Patsy, and youngest brother, Patrick.

It was after lamenting those losses that Francis disclosed to Jamie: "I know about Mathew. I saw his body at Fredericksburg."

Jamie went silent, and for a moment looked out the window at the tree in his backyard, bare in anticipation of spring. "We were told he was missing at first," Jamie said, "and I tried to make myself believe he was alive, maybe taken prisoner, but I knew better. That bastard father-in-law of his had Mathew declared dead as soon as he could to marry his daughter off again, making sure this time it was not to an

Irishman."

The father-in-law's insult went beyond that. Ostensibly to protect his daughter from ongoing pain, while the bodyless funeral was underway, Gordon Whitney had his lawyer and household staff remove everything of Mathew's from the residence. Whitney told his daughter the items were put into storage, but they were actually sold. Whatever could not be sold was thrown away —including the still frame photograph of Mathew and Jamie together in uniform. The ragged old sailboat Mathew had maintained, the one Francis had taken up from Norfolk, was gone too—broken into kindling.

Emily Whitney got a fresh start while any trace of Mathew in Philadelphia, as in Ireland, had been washed away. Even record of him in Fredericksburg would become lost over time, his body decomposed in an unmarked grave.

There was a painful silence, which Francis broke by explaining how he had made his way to Fredericksburg in the first place and found Mathew's corpse.

"I was terrified I would find you dead there too." Francis said earnestly to Jamie.

Jamie shook his head as in disbelief, "Yeah, well, the army thing was a disaster from the very start. I enlisted and Mathew was supposed to join right after me as an officer in the same company. But his cheap father-in-law backed out of buying him a commission at the last minute. Mathew came in instead as a sergeant for a different unit altogether. It took some maneuvering and a transfer for me, but at least we eventually ended up in the same company. Just in time for Fredericksburg."

Recounting how they were marched into Fredericksburg with the battle already raging, Jamie described the town in rubble in such detail Francis felt he was back there.

"Between artillery exchanges and street fighting, buildings were riddled with bullet holes if not destroyed altogether. The streets were littered with the former contents of homes and businesses that had been abandoned by residents and looted by Union soldiers the day before. The cold December air was thick with the smell of gunpowder and fear," Francis could almost see Jamie's nostrils flare as he said it.

"The sight of it made me remind Mathew of our agreement," Jamie said. "We promised to stay together no matter what. We crossed the Atlantic together and we would do the same with the River Styx if it came to that."

"Orders were for us to sit and wait at the outskirts of the town," Jamie continued, "which should have tipped us off then to how bad things would get. We were stationary targets for rebel artillery as we sat there. The position also gave us a front row seat to units ahead of us being wiped out one after the other trying to take the heights overlooking the town. For hours it was like that, company and regiment being destroyed in front of our eyes. Our only hope was the rebs would run out of ammunition before it was our turn to attack."

Jamie's body and face tensed as he continued his recollection. He ran his hand through his hair, an attempt to soothe himself—a McNamara trait Francis himself had when nervous.

"Our captain was already out with dysentery, the luckiest case of the trots if there ever was one." Jamie said, generating a faint smile from Francis. "And the rest of the officers were either nursing or faking shrapnel wounds from the artillery we were taking. As a result, Mathew had to take command of our company in the field."

Suspecting this may have been the first time Jamie discussed Mathew's fate with anyone other than maybe Eileen, Francis just listened—fearing any interruption could foil the exorcism of Jamie's ghosts.

"Mathew's stint in charge did not start well." Jamie advised. "A messenger handed him a note and a satchel full of boxwood cuttings. Mathew read the note and gave his first command. Each of us was to take a sprig of boxwood and place the evergreen in our caps. The stupidest thing I ever heard." Jamie lamented.

"The boys in the company lit into Mathew something awful. Some saying if it was all the same to Mathew they preferred to hide behind entire trees—the sprigs didn't even offer them shade. Others said if Mathew was hoping the rebs would mistake them for bushes and not shoot at them, even the rebs weren't that stupid." Jamie shook his head saying it. "Mathew said nothing in response, but I dropped my rifle and went after the closest guy mouthing off." Jamie advised, raising his voice. "I wouldn't let 'em talk to Mathew like that. But Mathew ignored the brawl and calmly walked over to the officer in charge of the next company. They seemed to exchange pleasantries and when the officer pointed at us fighting, Mathew waved it off as if we were just warming up to fight the rebs. Then Mathew started to walk back toward us, writing something down on a piece of paper and stuffed the paper into an envelope and sealed it."

Continuing as if he were talking to himself as much as to Francis, Jamie said. "Mathew shouted out until he got the company's attention. He then explained that General Meagher had ordered the wearing of the evergreen sprigs. It was supposed to remind us, the Irish Brigade, of our heritage, which was ridiculous because we knew who we were, and where we were, and what was about to happen to us, and we were all terrified."

Picking up intensity in his speech, Jamie was coming to the critical juncture of the story and Francis knew it, bracing himself for what Jamie would say next.

"Mathew called me to come forward, referring to me not by my first name but as Private McNamara." Jamie recounted, his back to Francis and staring out the window of his library. "He handed me the envelope and told me, loud enough for others to hear, to get the message to Lieutenant McLauglin of the 1st Pennsylvania Light Artillery and return back as quickly as possible, the company could be ordered forward any minute."

Jamie then turned around to face Francis. "I told Mathew to make someone else his errand boy and he looked at me like Da would when he was tight and on a rampage. For a second, I thought Mathew was going to strangle me. But just as quick, Mathew calmed himself down, the mantle of leadership was on him"

"Mathew took a long pause and looked at me," Jamie continued with emotion rising within him. "And then looked at the rest of the company. He smiled at us and then, of all things, took to reciting a poem."

> *Into the valley of Death rode the 600. Theirs was*
> *not to reason why. Theirs was just to do or die.*

The 600 included companies of Irishmen, Mathew advised the men, immortalized for their heroism against incredible odds. *Theirs was not to reason why*, Mathew reiterated the phrase, as he gestured once again for Jamie to go.

"As I began to walk to the artillery units to deliver the message," Jamie relayed starting to fight back tears. "I looked at Mathew as he turned away to glance at the heights where the rebels were. I saw it, he was scared but when he turned back to look at the company it was as if he was getting ready for a picnic. In fact, he started to sing, sang as loud as he could—as if he had a few drinks in him and was trying to drown out the sound of the rebel artillery and fighting going on in front of us on the heights."

With that, Jamie sang there to Francis the same song Mathew had sung, the song the entire company joined Mathew in singing, the last thing Jamie heard uttered by Mathew and so many of his comrades.

> *The minstrel boy to the war is gone*
> *In the ranks of death you will find him*
> *His father's sword he's girded on*
> *And his wild harp slung behind him*
> *"Land of Song" said the warrior bard*
> *"Tho' all the world betrays thee*
> *One sword, at least, thy rights shall guard*
> *One faithful harp shall praise thee"*

The minstrel fell but the foeman's chains
Could not bring that proud soul under
The harp he loved never spoke again For
he tore its chords asunder
And said, "No chains shall sully thee
Thou soul of love and brav'ry
Thy songs were made for the pure and free
They shall never sound in slavery

When he reached the end of the song, Jamie went quiet bringing his hand to his eyes to stem the tears. When he was able to compose himself, Jamie asked, "Do you know what that stupid sonofabitch Mathew wrote in that message?" Francis shook his head, not knowing.

"It told McLaughlin—Mathew's friend from Philadelphia who owed Mathew some favors—to hold me back, tie me to a cannon wheel if needed. Mathew assured McLaughlin that Mathew himself would be adequately representing the McNamara clan on the battlefield that day, and I would just get in the way and steal some of his glory." After saying it Jamie looked up to the ceiling, as if Mathew were watching and looking down.

Then Jamie looked ashamed as he finished: "So, I watched from a safe distance as Mathew and company marched out and joined the rest of the brigade. Together, they approached the heights and disappeared into the smoke. The few that made their way back told me that they did not see Mathew fall but knew he could not have survived. He was at the very front of the formation and that suffered the brunt of the rebel fire." Jamie broke down altogether, saying through his tears, "I let him cross the River Styx without me."

With tears in his own eyes, Francis put his hands on Jamie's shoulders and said, "You didn't break your promise, you were relieved from it by your commanding officer and older brother. Mathew is with Ma and Da, and the rest of them in peace now, and he knew I and others would need you—that is why he did what he did."

So emotionally charged, Jamie did not know what to do or say next. He instinctively went back to the pile of books on his desk, the only books he told Francis that he consulted in the entire library. He opened the books, which had been hollowed out to hold a bottle of whiskey and shot glasses. He filled two glasses and slid one toward Francis.

"I only drink when the recollections come calling." Jamie confessed, referring not just to the loss of Mathew but the entire war, his sordid existence in the Five Points, and—of course—the famine.

"Me too," said Francis as he lifted the glass. "To Mathew and his trials and tribulations being over, and for him giving me back my brother Jamie."

"To Mathew," Jamie said lifting his glass and looking to the heavens.

****

Jamie started to provide Francis select job referrals, not wanting to be too associated once again with the McNamara name. Consequently, the work was on the fringes where people did not overly focus on names. As the older brother, Jamie also gave Francis life advice of all sorts, including cutting down on drinking. Jamie heard from Edward that

Francis could reduce his legal entanglements if Francis spent less time drunk and belligerent.

"If I had decent work," Francis responded, "I wouldn't need to drink as much to drown my sorrows." Neither brother entertained the thought of giving up alcohol altogether, as they viewed teetotalers as obnoxious as drunks. And life was too hard to cope without some form of medicinal aid.

Progress was made and Francis found himself joining Jamie with one foot in respectable New York and the other in the darker side of the metropolis. It was not an even split of his time, however. More time was spent in the shadows. For a good portion of the 19th century, the world was trapped in what became known as the "Long Depression." For New York City and Brooklyn that meant thousands of businesses failing and an unemployment rate hovering near 25 percent. If not for the diversification of Jamie's legitimate and criminal connections and the work it created, Francis feared he and his family would have starved to death.

Being true to his word, with steady work, Francis kept his drinking well controlled. Francis also handed over his entire pay to Bridget for management. Bridget was able to open a savings account at the Dime Savings bank, a bank she chose for the beautiful design of its branches. It made her think the bank would be more resistant to runs, and that she was a person of substance simply being there to do business.

Each Sunday, Jamie and his wife Eileen had Francis and his family over for dinner. Bridget, who liked Eileen immediately, would always make dessert. Francis would bring two bottles, homemade wine that he got from his friend and former cellmate Roberto D'Antonio, and a bottle of gin, as gin cocktails were then all the rage. Making Francis and Bridget proud, Francis would drink moderately, if at all.

Whenever Francis was at Jamie and Eileen's house, he made a point of checking on his favorite and only niece, Nancy. Always able to make Nancy laugh with one silly remark or another, Francis's visits were lighthearted. In turn, Nancy made Francis smile with her little idiosyncrasies and mannerisms that showed she was a McNamara—nurture over nature.

An indicator of how fast time was moving, Francis was shocked when Jamie advised Nancy had become engaged and would be married quickly, although she was only 16 years old. Francis thought of her younger than that, and the quick marriage made Francis assume she was pregnant. She wasn't and was holding out for marriage before hazarding such a thing, hence the interest in the quick ceremony.

Jaime was not fond of his new son-in-law, Patrick Connell. He thought Connell pushy and ambitious to a fault, but he didn't have to like the young man. He just had to tolerate him. And for Nancy, he could tolerate anything. So, over time, Jamie began introducing Connell to the family business ventures and investments. But not fast enough for Connell's liking.

****

It was a rainy day in October 1882 and Francis was uncharacteristically late for a meeting with Connell. *Better to be an hour early than five minutes late*, Francis would tell his sons. Even in his drinking days, Francis was always prompt for any appointment although the other attendees wished he wasn't. But today the delay was unavoidable. His youngest, Joseph, was sick and Bridget was stuck at the pharmacy in the rain. She instructed Francis to wait until her return with the medicine for the teenager, so he waited.

"You alright in there, Joseph?" Francis called into the boy's bedroom from the kitchen.

"I *loved* you, old man!" Joseph cried, using the past tense to melodramatically imply he was dying. He did have a fever and infection of some sort, but most illnesses went without a name in those days and Joseph would survive it—although true to character he would act like he would not until he was fully recovered.

Roberto waited in the kitchen with Francis. He was both nervous about being late but glad for the extra time to go over the business pitch once again. His pockets were full of newspaper articles and pieces of paper with cites to municipal reports and budget proposals. All the material told of the looming environmental disaster facing the New York metropolitan area.

"New York is drowning in its own shit." Roberto started his spiel, memorized to the last word and hand-gesture. Roberto was melodramatic enough in his delivery to rival the antics of young Joseph in the next room. The Italian was melodramatic but not wrong.

The metropolis, the cities of New York and Brooklyn, were generating more than one hundred tons of sewerage every year, all of it dumped into New York harbor and surrounding waterways. The risk of disease, damage to fishing industries, and other concerns was obvious. Roberto was not alone in arguing that a significant investment was needed in water and sewer treatment systems. That need had to compete for capital funds for transportation infrastructure. And a relative fortune was being spent to build what would become known as the Brooklyn Bridge.

"Why should we build a bridge?" Roberto asked rhetorically as part of his pitch. "Soon the East and Hudson Rivers will be thick enough with sewerage to walk across."

That and similar arguments resulted in bond referendums in multiple jurisdictions to fund miles of water and sewer pipes, and completion of the Croton Reservoir project. While advanced sewage treatment would have to wait, there were still millions to be made laying pipes and creating the infrastructure for more rudimentary water and sewer systems. A dream come true for Roberto, allowing him to fulfill what he thought his destiny.

"The Emerald Coliseum Water and Sewer Pipe Company," Roberto went on in rehearsal, "is a profitable and reputable company that can help create the needed infrastructure." The company was indeed profitable, netting a grand total of $11 in its single year of existence. Nonetheless, the business venture held great promise for Roberto, having partnered with Francis and secured the backing of Jamie and Eileen as investors. Jamie would prove particularly important as he had connections with Tammany Hall, the center of political influence in New York City—influence that could nudge lucrative municipal contracts toward the fledgling company. In his excitement, Roberto had business cards made up with his title, *Owner and Chief of Operations*, and gave the cards to everyone he met. His mailman had several.

"Will you stop worrying already, you crazy *wop*!" Francis told Roberto, using the ethnic slur as a term of endearment and to show their closeness. Anyone else who used that term toward Roberto would have had a knife at their throat. "We have Jamie and Eileen in our corner; they know the potential. Connell just wanted to get more experience crunching numbers and examining documents. That is all this meeting is about." Francis assured.

Roberto was still nervous; he was not sure why.

Once Bridget returned with the medicine for Joseph, Francis and Roberto ran to catch the horse-drawn streetcar towards Brooklyn's city hall. They were already an hour late to meet Connell at Calihan's pub just off city hall on Remsen Street.

While in the streetcar, Roberto spotted Connell running not toward Calihan's but away from it. He elbowed Francis to look.

"It is not raining anymore, why the hell is he running?" Francis asked, producing a shrug from Roberto.

They got off the streetcar and watched from a distance as Connell met up with members of the Smoky Hollow Gang. Both Francis and Roberto were familiar with the Smoky Hollows as they were considered an up-and-coming criminal organization. The city's newspapers had begun recounting some of their violent capabilities and growing control over the Brooklyn waterfront.

Most people were puzzled by the gang's name and Francis— with a particular interest in gang names since his *Brassiere Boys* days— learned that the gang founders met in a park by that name in upstate New York. They had been brought there as juvenile delinquents as part of a rehabilitative retreat for city youth by naïve but well-meaning social reformers, who helped facilitate rather than prevent crime.

"Why the hell is Connell meeting with the Smokey Hollows?" Francis asked. Had Connell been connected to the gang, surely he, Roberto, and Jaime would have gotten wind. And whatever he was talking about with the gang, Connell was certainly animated about it.

"We better talk to Jamie about this, it is really odd." Francis said starting to make his way toward Jamie's brownstone about two miles away in Brooklyn Heights. Roberto carefully kept looking back to ensure they were not spotted by Connell as they left.

When Francis and Roberto arrived at Jamie's brownstone, police officers were on the steps leading up to the home. The police eye-balled them and were about to stop Francis and Roberto when Eileen shouted from the doorway.

"That is my brother-in-law and our friend Roberto, please let them in." Eileen asked of the police, and the officers stepped aside.

"What is going on?" Francis asked.

Roberto noticed Nancy, Jamie's daughter, looking blankly out of the window as if she had been crying.

"Francis, I need to talk to you alone for a minute," Eileen said. Roberto got the message and stepped back and toward

Nancy to check on her. Eileen led Francis into the kitchen, closing the door behind her.

"Jamie has been shot." Eileen blurted out, trying to hold back the tears. "He is gone, Francis. He is gone." And then there was no holding back the tears and Francis found himself comforting Eileen, although he wanted to ask a million questions. The first being, "Am I dreaming this, is this a nightmare?"
Eileen had been crying off and on for close to an hour. The police had told her that a group of young men, boys one person described them as, broke into Jamie's business office a few blocks away on Montague Street. Jamie must have confronted them and he was killed. Eileen focused herself and relayed what her analytical mind had already processed.

"It looks like they targeted him," Eileen said. "Police found Jamie's wallet still on him and this," and Eileen held up a whistle. A police whistle, the one Francis had given him the night when Francis first arrived from Ireland.

"Jesus, he kept that thing?" Francis asked, emotions now overwhelming him.

"He had it with him every day since you gave it to him. Claimed it was his lucky charm during the war. I am surprised he didn't tell you." Eileen remarked.

How many other things had Jamie not told him, like was there someone out there who was a threat to him? But who and why?

The mystery would not last for long. As Francis and Eileen left the kitchen, a red faced, nervous looking Connell ran in.

When he made eye contact with Francis, it was as if he was looking at a ghost. Watching it, Roberto knew. He could spot a guilty man, having been one himself long enough.

"What is wrong?" Connell asked in an unconvincing way— leading Francis to join Roberto in the assessment of Connell. Nancy ran into Connell's arms. "My father has been killed," she cried.

"What? How can that be? Who killed him?" Connell asked, his acting skills leaving much to be desired. His reaction only fed Roberto and Francis's suspicions which they communicated by merely looking at each other.

"The police think it was a gang, the Smokey Hollows." Francis said slowly, gauging Connell's reaction.

"The Smokey Hollows, who are they?" Connell responded.

Eileen was puzzled too and was about to say the police had not mentioned anything about Smokey Hollows but Francis squeezed her hand. Then Connell said he needed air and hurried out of the house, leaving Nancy behind. Dread made its way through Eileen.

"What do you know, Francis?" Eileen asked trying to hold herself together.

Francis did not have the heart to answer, especially in front of Nancy. Implicating Connell, Nancy's husband, in her father's murder would be too much for the young girl to process.

Roberto did not have the same hesitation. "That sonofabitch would have killed us too had we not been late to the meeting. He is probably running to find the Sleepy Hollows right now to finish the job."

"You are not suggesting Patrick had anything to do with this?" Eileen asked in disbelief. "Why would he do such a thing?" And the motive was unclear, but it was safe to assume it was one of the oldest known to man, greed. Connell figured he would control rather than learn about Jamie's estate.

Nancy, already devastated at the loss of her father, could not even entertain the thought her husband was responsible for the murder.

"You are wrong!" Nancy shouted at Roberto, running up the stairs to the bedroom she shared in the house with Connell. Eileen followed her daughter to console her.

"I am not wrong," Roberto said confidently to Francis. "And we better get out of here because Connell should have those Smokey Hollows here any minute." Roberto and Francis left, not just the brownstone but Brooklyn. At least until they could figure out how to deal with the threat against them— they were unfinished business for Connell and gang.

****

In the weeks that followed, the logical Eileen studied every move her son-in-law made. She adroitly stymied his increasing efforts to seize exclusive control over the family's business accounts. Eileen had never been a figure-head partner in the family's finances but a driver, and very capable of running things even in the absence of Jamie.

Where that absence took its toll was on her emotionally. Unfortunately, for Connell, the primary emotion she felt would switch over time, going from heartache to anger. The anger engendered a thirst for revenge. But also underlying the interest in revenge was fear. Eileen considered Connell an ongoing threat not just to Francis and Roberto but to her and Nancy.

Eileen kept in touch with Francis who was staying with Roberto in Bayonne, New Jersey at a location arranged by Jamie's, old friend, Edward Fitzpatrick. Eileen did so using a relatively new invention, the telephone. Pharmacies in both Brooklyn Heights and Bayonne had public phones.

"The Smokey Hollows are little more than a bunch of knuckle draggers," Eileen advised Francis over the phone. "The newspapers take on them is exaggerated. People I know in the police department say gang the gang lacks the kind of sophistication needed to orchestrate coordinated murder attempts to take over a business enterprise. It was all Connell. We get to Connell, the gang will cease to be a problem."

"Alright, tell me where Connell is and me and Roberto will return the favor he showed Jamie." Francis advised, holding the receiver with both hands—not yet comfortable with the phone concept. No one was.

On November 1, 1882, Patrick Connell was walking along Henry Street in Brooklyn Heights. He noticed Francis and Roberto approaching him and began to sprint away. Francis and Roberto gave chase with Roberto crossing over onto the other side of the street to cut off Connell if he went in that direction. Francis thought he had a clear shot with no one around, so he pulled a revolver from his waist band and fired twice. One bullet grazed O'Connell the other embedded in a wagon the younger man hid behind. At forty-seven years old, Francis was not the shot he once was and feared that his eyesight was starting to diminish. As a result, he decided not to take any additional shots until he closed in on his target, out of fear he would hit some innocent person.

Seeing Roberto closing on him from the other side of the street, Connell left the cover of the wagon and resumed his sprint. To his good fortune, he ran into police officers investigating the sounds of the gun shots. Now it was Francis's time to run, but again being forty-seven years old, it did not take much for the police to catch up to him. Francis was not too old, however, to resist his arrest. He kept the officers engaged long enough for Roberto to escape.

Connell happily swore out a complaint against Francis, who was charged with attempted murder. At his arraignment, the prosecutor told the judge of Francis's extensive criminal record—which included previous acts of violence.

That coupled with the strength and uncontradicted nature of the testimony of the intended victim, Patrick Connell, the prosecutor urged was more than enough to justify holding Francis pending trial. Francis said nothing in his defense, and the judge ordered Francis remanded.

But when Connell repeatedly failed to appear for subsequent preliminary hearings, the charges against Francis were dismissed and would only be reinstated when Connell reappeared. But he would not reappear. The one thing the chief operating officer of the Emerald Coliseum Water and Sewer Pipe Company could do was dig a ditch. And a ditch and sewage would ensure Connell would never be found.

****

When Francis was released from Brooklyn's Raymond Street Jail, it was not with a full sigh of relief. Without his brother Jamie's connection to Tammany Hall, he and Roberto had little chance of getting a piece of the large city contract that was expected to be issued shortly. It seemed like even their reliable business referrals were drying up, word was spreading that even if Francis and Roberto were not dead, their primary benefactor was.

Francis's wife and family were getting financially by with the help of Jamie's widow, Eileen. But Eileen was planning on getting her daughter, Nancy, out of the city to help her move past the death of Jamie and disappearance of Connell. They were moving to Goshen, New York.

****

When Bridget and Francis visited Eileen's new home, they were taken by the beauty of not only the house but the area. Although it was only sixty miles north of New York City, it had the feel of a rural oasis.

It had picturesque farms and horse stables. The Victorian architecture was remarkable and provided the area with a relaxed but regal atmosphere. Aside from its popular horse track, a favorite of Ulysses S. Grant who had just left the presidency, Goshen was quiet and low key. Francis could not get over how everyone in the town waived at him, a perfect stranger.

Francis could tell his own wife, Bridget, loved the place. She would never ask for anything herself, but Bridget deserved a lovely home in a beautiful place. She had been in Brooklyn tenements long enough. Bridget was jealous of Eileen for having the nice home, and ironically Eileen was jealous of Bridget for still having her husband. Jamie's death weighed heavily on Eileen, who was resilient to just about everything else that had confronted her in life.

Seeing the melancholy in Eileen's eyes, and knowing what was causing it, Francis placed something into her hand. It was the police whistle he had given Jamie years before. The whistle Jamie had carried with him until his death. In the same grandiose way his father spoke when emotional, Francis spoke to Eileen.

"You know, the name McNamara means 'Hound of the Sea.' Some people think that is because we come from Vikings or that we fought the Vikings off, but that is not it. The name comes from us having the loyalty and hearing of an always faithful guard dog." Francis continued staring into Eileen's eyes, "If you need anything, you just blow that whistle. Either I will run up here or Jamie's spirit will—and he will bring an army of McNamaras with him. You are one of us, Eileen."

Eileen rolled the whistle around in her hand, she was truly struck by the gesture. Prompting her to simply state "you are an ass" to Francis. Using the humor to defuse the emotions that were overwhelming them both.

"Good timing," Eileen said to Francis, "because I have a gift for you too."

She went to a heavy-duty safe in the basement she had installed when she moved in. Eileen took out a large package wrapped in plain brown paper and tied in twine.

"It's from both me and Jamie," she said but with the ominous warning that Francis should not open it now. Nor, she advised, should he discuss its contents with anyone he did not trust. And she added, "Francis, I am out. I can't do it anymore. Use the gift as you see fit but I need to leave that kind of thing behind me now."

Francis was confused but did not push. He knew Eileen and trusted he would understand what she was saying when he eventually opened the gift.

In the privacy of his tenement apartment back in Brooklyn, Francis opened it up the gift. It was a ledger and folder filled with documents. It did not take long for Francis to figure out that what he had could result in the indictment of half the politicians in the New York metropolitan area. There were documents showing corruption of various sorts, the location of slush funds and bank accounts under aliases. There were also details and even photographs of politicians' illegitimate children. It was the culmination of Jamie and Eileen's work dating back to their early days together in the Five Points. *You could never have too much insurance*, Eileen liked to say.

Eileen's note said, "use these documents right, and you'll be free and clear like me. Your brother loved you very much, and I love you too. Bridget is like a sister to me and I adore your kids."

Francis had to think about how to use the information he now had, but first he needed a good place to hide the ledger and documents. He could not sew it into the seat of his pants like he did with his important documents during the Civil War. He wanted to keep it in a place where he stayed often, so he could keep an eye on it, but not be seen by anyone else. He also needed to protect it from fire, water, and anything else that could damage it. He decided to pull out some of the bricks from his kitchen wall and seal everything back inside, painting over the bricks to conceal that work had been done. Roberto remarked, upon seeing the handy work, an Irishman had no business touching bricks.

The contracts for the water and sewer systems in the cities of Brooklyn, New York and surrounding jurisdictions were delayed in disputes over bonds being issued and other matters. So, in consultation with Roberto, Francis decided they should wait before trying to use the information he had to influence politicians and have them steer business to the Emerald Coliseum Sewer and Main Company. They would wait until what could be steered was more substantial.

The problem was that they were extremely short on cash and Francis could not hit up Eileen again after what she had just given him. They just needed something to tide them over, and Roberto thought he found it.

Chapter Nineteen
The Girdle Gang Revisited

Cities of Brooklyn and New York
1883-1884

The opportunity that availed itself for Francis and Roberto to sustain themselves and their families involved a department store. One of the first and largest in Manhattan, B. Altman and Company located at 621 Sixth Avenue, between 18th and 19th Streets.

One of the night watchmen at the store frequented a bar in Roberto's neighborhood. The bar patrons called the man "Yap Yap" because he talked so much. While his incessant chatter drove most people crazy, Francis and Roberto could listen to him all day long—especially when he complained about his job and the security protocols at B. Altman's.

With an investment of no more than a few drinks at the bar, Francis and Roberto got Yap Yap talking about the store, how it worked, and what he did—and did not do—as a night watchman. Yap Yap reported having liked the work originally. He did nothing more than sleep away most of his shift and subsidized his salary by selling items he stole himself from the store. A new store detective, however, a Scotsman named Danwitter, was ruining everything.

"On his first day, Danwitter told us that he knew employees were responsible for most of the thefts from the store. What a pair of balls! If he really knew that he would have fired us all, if not had us arrested. Instead, he went about changing everything. New inventory procedures, new supervisors, shift changes, everything. He even convinced the store management to buy newfangled security equipment and supposedly had undercover detectives roam the store and pose as clerks and other employees."

The new technology particularly irked Yap Yap, as he was convinced it would eventually take his job. "A few months back they outfitted every single external window and door with an electro-magnetic alarm," Yap Yap advised between sips of his beer. "I don't know what electro-magnetic is but it must be some kind of sorcery because you open a store window or door just one bit and an alarm screeches so loud it can wake the dead."

Yap Yap continued with his rant.

"When that prick Danwitter leaves for the day, he turns the alarm system on and us night watchmen are locked inside until morning. We can't open a window. Not even on the upper floors, no matter how hot it gets. A fella can't sleep if he is covered in sweat."

As Roberto offered an understanding nod, Francis flagged down the bartender to keep the drinks coming. With more drinks came more of Yap Yap's carping.

"Even the floors of the jewelry department and the business office have alarms now, you just step on them and you'll be holding your ears with all the racket it makes." Yap Yap shook his head, "So now there are even places inside the store we—the night watchmen—can't go!"
"Why would they have such a fancy alarm in the business office?" Francis asked, feigning an innocent tone.

"They keep payroll and some cash in there, but mostly because Danwitter is giddy over technology," Yap Yap answered, beginning to slur as he finished his fifth drink.

This guy is bottomless in every sense of the word, Francis thought to himself.

Yap Yap continued to volunteer more information. "The stupid moron Danwitter had them buy a new massive safe for the office. They had to reinforce the floor to make sure the damn thing didn't crash all the way down to the basement. The kicker is that no one yet has figured out how to open the damn thing, and the office staff had to resort to using an old strongbox to hold everything."

Roberto asked: "How much money do they keep in there? Don't they use a bank?"

"They do, but the last bank run is at two in the afternoon before the bank closes for the day. So, all the store's proceeds from then until closing time goes into the strongbox. And they keep our pay envelopes in the strongbox on Wednesday nights before they pay us on Thursdays." Yap Yap said rubbing his face gruffly with his hands.

"Who keeps the keys to the alarms and the strongbox?" Francis asked beginning to wonder when Yap Yap would catch on as to why they were asking all these questions and demand a cut.

"Who knows, Danwitter probably hides them up his ass." Yap Yap replied, amusing himself in the process. "Or one of his kiss-ups that he brought in to supervise us watchmen. The boss now on the night shift is a big Swede named Larsen. The stupid Swede won't let us do anything. But he must have the key to the alarm now that I think about it. He was able to turn the alarm off one night when it went off accidentally during a windstorm. Good thing too because me and the boys were about to piss ourselves thinking we were being robbed."

With all the drinking Yap Yap was becoming tired, as evidenced by his finally tailing off in his talking and he started asking Francis and Roberto questions to let them talk. He asked them what they did for a living. Francis claimed to be a poet and told a dirty limerick as proof. Roberto claimed to be an opera singer. Francis had heard Roberto sing before and was glad the Italian did not break out in song and totally discredit himself. Not that Yap Yap would have noticed. He had passed out.

****

The next day, with Yap Yap's information in mind, Francis and Roberto went to the store to look for themselves. They put on their fanciest clothes to try to mix in with the high end shoppers. Francis had to fight the temptation to shoplift something nice for Bridget. But there were bigger fish to fry.

The two men wandered through the four stories of the store, trying not to be conspicuous as they looked around so intensely. They eventually had to apologize to the store manager for entering the employee-only section on the top floor. They left immediately with innocent smiles but not until determining the exact location of the business office with its very large and secure-looking door.

Once done casing the store, Francis and Roberto walked around the block talking quietly to each other. As they did so, Francis noticed that the building adjacent to the store running along 18th Street was vacant. The two buildings were nearly identical with the only major difference being that the vacant building was one story taller than the department store.

The sight of the additional floor gave Francis an idea. "All the security precautions are designed to keep people from entering the store through windows and doors. What if we came in through the roof?" Francis posited. "It would just be those floor alarms that pose a problem." Francis said looking up beyond the buildings to the sky above, as if seeking an answer from God. The answer, however, came from Roberto.

"My wife is never going to forgive me." Roberto declared after articulating his idea on how to defeat the floor alarms.

"Risky but brilliant," Francis labeled Roberto's idea.

****

It had been a while since Francis had been involved in a commercial burglary, and he had no experience at all with newfangled security alarms. So, he decided to reach out to those who would have more recent experience for advice. He was long overdue to check on his former gang members in Vinegar Hill anyway.

In some ways, the old neighborhood looked the same. It was still very much Irishtown. Two huge construction projects were underway, however, that would fundamentally change the area. Along the western edge of Vinegar Hill workers—many from Vinegar Hill itself—were nearing completion of the longest suspension bridge in the world. Its stone buttressed towers and massive anchorages were in the process of dwarfing everything else in the area.

At the same time, there was an increasing shadow from the southern edge of the neighborhood. Work had begun on an elevated train line. Portions of the track already stood thirty-five feet in the air. Soon the rails would be transversed by a pair of steam locomotives, adding to the noise and air pollution from the scores of factories and processing plants already burdening the residents.

The mass of faces Francis saw were familiar in the general sense, but foreign in the specific. The neighborhood was now increasingly second generation Irish or post-famine immigrants. The survivors of the famine were conspicuously missing. Although some had moved out of the neighborhood, most had died. Their life expectancy cut short by decades due to the trauma, malnutrition, and ongoing poverty they endured.

Now in his late forties, Francis was a relative novelty in his longevity. As he asked the current residents for whereabouts of one person or another that he knew, the answer was most often they never heard of the person or knew them to be dead. Francis former coworkers at Kearns's tavern, Burke and Lally, were among those long forgotten—both having succumbed to their injuries from the Orangemen Parade ten years before.

Upon hearing so many gone, Francis began to feel as if he was on borrowed time. Soon, he too would be among those no one remembered. The pressure felt by Francis to make a go of the B. Dalton job and the Emerald Coliseum Company only grew more intense. Francis had long given up any hope of a magical ending for himself, but if he could make things better for Bridget and his boys then maybe his life would have been worthwhile.

In the end, Francis's canvassing of the neighborhood resulted in him finding only two of his old gang members. Fortunately, from Francis's perspective, the pair still retained some degree of burglary expertise and were willing to share it. Kevin Gallagher and Mark McGraw were their names.

Without specifying the target, Francis told Gallagher and McGraw of the type of obstacles he would need to overcome at B. Dalton's: electronic alarms, security guards, and a strongbox. Their advice was to find a softer target.

"How old are you now Francis, a hundred something?" Gallagher asked teasingly. "Thievery is a young man's game and any old timer who stays in too long is an idiot."

"But you are still in it," Francis reminded Gallagher.
"Exactly!" Gallagher responded, "If I didn't have gambling's longest losing streak, I would have been out of the racket years ago."

McGraw was more to the point in terms of offering advice. "Some of the rules from the old days still apply. Get in when others are not around, take only what you can run with, have an exit plan, and always keep a cool head. These new alarm systems are making things harder but they have their vulnerabilities." McGraw went onto provide insights into the alarms currently in use and the tools that would be needed to defeat them.

"And Francis," McGraw said when getting ready to leave, "People have vulnerabilities too, being blinded by a big payday is one of them. I don't know what you have in mind but if it is too risky, just don't do it. You have survived this long. Don't push your luck."

Francis would push his luck. The question was whether he would have the *luck of the Irish*, a popular phrase of the day meaning no luck at all.

Chapter Twenty
The Last Job

Manhattan, New York
May 24, 1883

The city was abuzz. It was opening day for the East River Bridge, later more commonly known as the Brooklyn Bridge. In celebration, one of the largest fireworks displays in the city's history was scheduled for that night. Every spare police officer would be downtown for crowd control. That, and knowing the strongbox at B. Dalton's would contain payroll as well as store proceeds, was why Francis, Roberto, and Roberto's 14-year-old son, Leonardo, prepared to enter the store via the vacant building.

Posing as workers doing renovations in the vacant building, the trio acted nonchalant as they brought in tools that were going to be used not for renovations but to enter the department store. Once inside the vacant building, they waited until nightfall and after the store closed for the day, they went to work. As quietly as they could, they made their way to the roof of the vacant building. Once they exited the tented door on the roof, they placed wedges beneath the door so no one could come up behind them. They wanted no surprises.

The trio then scaled down the one story to the roof of the store. On top of the store, Roberto paced out what he calculated to be the center above the business office. He placed a crowbar and ax to mark the spot and turned around and started over, recounting his steps, happy to arrive in the exact spot where he left the tools.

"Measure twice, cut once." Roberto counseled his son. He was always trying to relay wisdom to the boy—his eldest.

Then Francis and Roberto got to work cutting a hole in the roof. They were careful not to let any heavy pieces fall into the business office that could set off the floor alarm. Leonardo, at his father's direction, spent the time doublechecking that everything he needed was snuggly secured to his belt. The heaviest item the boy carried was a carbide lamp that he would use for light. While it was not heavy enough to set off the floor alarm, it could make enough noise—if it fell—to alert the night watchmen. Not to mention dropping the lamp could start a fire that would burn the whole place down.

With the hole complete, Roberto tied one end of a rope to his son and spoke to him in Italian.

"Last Rights?" Francis asked Roberto, who normally appreciated gallows humor but not on this occasion involving his son. Trying to remedy the mistimed humor, Francis spoke reassuringly to Leonardo, "You are a good boy helping your father like this. It is all going to be fine. We have a good plan. Just do everything like we practiced." Francis smiled at Leonardo, with the thought back to his own early introduction to crime courtesy of his brother Jamie.

After measuring out a few feet of slack in the rope, Francis and Roberto lowered Leonardo through the hole until the boy's feet dangled about three feet above the floor in the middle of the business office. Roberto looked at Francis and said, "This kid drove me nuts for years, climbing everything. I would always have to say 'Leonardo, act normal, stop climbing the furniture, stop climbing the fire escape, stop climbing the church pew. Always climbing. Little did I know he was training for this."

"Ok, swing me to the right." Leonardo whispered up through the hole and Francis and Roberto did so. Leonardo was able to stabilize himself on a desk. He lit the lamp and spotted the large, malfunctioning safe and not one but two strongboxes beside it. The strongboxes were stacked one on top of the other, each having four legs a few inches tall. The legs of the bottom strongbox were directly on the floor. Leonardo advised his father about the additional strongbox and then asked a question they all should have thought about earlier.

"If the alarm is based on weight, will removing the strongbox off the floor or removing what is inside it trigger the alarm too?" Leonardo asked in a hushed tone.

"No." Roberto responded instinctively, having no idea if weight displacement had any impact on the alarm. He looked at Francis who was embarrassed at not having anticipated the issue. They had taken into account so many other things. They went so far as to ask around and learned that most strongboxes weighed about 75 pounds empty. Removing two of them would be like pulling an adult man off the floor. They had gotten skeleton keys from several different strongbox manufacturers, locksmiths, and fellow thieves. They brought all the tools they would need and had practiced lifting a strongbox using ropes and a small pulley, and even had brought explosives to blast the strongboxes open either there at the store or at the undeveloped lot in Brooklyn they planned to go to after the burglary.

"Wait, wait, let's think this through," Francis said. He and Roberto then exchanged ideas—most of them bad. Leonardo eventually called up advising that his legs were going numb with the harness Roberto had fashioned being too tight.

Roberto answered his son, "I knew I should have taken your sister instead of you with all your crying."

The plan they settled on was only a slight variation from what they were going to do originally. Leonardo, the calmest of the three, checked to confirm that the strongboxes were, in fact, locked. There were no wild oversights by store staff. Leonardo then tried the skeleton keys but none of them worked. That left a big decision to be made. They could either lift the strongboxes out of the business office and carry them away or blast them open in place with the explosives. If there was to be blasting in the store, they were going to wait until the fireworks display started at the bridge in hope it would cover the noise. But dealing with not one strongbox but two complicated things.

What else did Yap Yap forget to tell us? Francis thought to himself.

At Roberto's suggestion, they decided to haul out one box to see how it went and decide about the second box after that. Leonardo secured the top strongbox with another rope his father had handed down to him. Francis and Roberto then pulled the boy out in case the alarm went off. Also, so he could help in lifting the strongbox.
At first, they struggled with the weight of the strongbox. That weight was magnified by the fact that it dangled at the full length of the rope. But they found it easier as they pulled it closer and through the hole. The alarm did not go off to the trio's relief.

Francis and Roberto inspected the strongbox and decided to move it to the parapet of the roof overlooking 18th Street. They would place the second one there too once it was out. Then, if the alarm remained silent, Roberto and Leonardo would go down to the street and get their horse and wagon. They would park on the 18th street side and Francis would push the strongboxes down. If the fall broke the strongboxes open, fine, Roberto and Leonardo would be there to pick up the contents. They could do so in relative anonymity as the streets were vacant that time of night and with all the activities further downtown at the bridge.

Looking down to where the strongboxes would be dropped, Roberto said only half-joking: "Do not drop those things on my head!"

"Fine." Francis replied, "I'll aim for the horse."

The trio returned to the hole in the roof, and they lowered Leonardo down once again to secure the second strongbox. This time, for some reason, he flipped over as he was lowered and was left hanging upside down. Fortunately, Roberto had tied him so tightly Leonardo did not slip out but he could not stay upside down for long. With the blood rushing to his head, he had much more difficulty threading the rope around the second strongbox than he did the first. As he struggled to do so, Francis and Roberto froze in fear. They heard voices emanating from the doorway on the roof that led up from the store. They had not wedged that door, assuming it was alarmed and no one would use it.

It only occurred then to Francis that the stores guards would come up to watch the fireworks display. They would have to turn off the alarm to do so, so maybe the supervisor Larsen was not as much of a stick in the mud Yap Yap had described. Indeed, all three nightwatchmen—including Larsen—were in a line approaching the door and only moments from arriving on the roof.

Francis and Roberto pulled Leonardo out of the hole with such force he flipped right-side up again—just in time to hit his head on the outer edge of the hole, gashing his scalp. Already dizzy from having been upside down, Leonardo was wobbly as he tried to stand up and Roberto had to lead him toward the roof of the vacant building so they could escape. Francis did not follow; instead, he made his way over to the door that the watchmen were nearing.

"Sonofabitch," Francis mumbled to himself upon hearing Yap Yap's voice—talking nonstop to the other approaching watchmen. Francis turned his back against the door and pressed into it with all his might. He felt the push against the door from the other side and could hear Yap Yap once again.

"It must be stuck, when is the last time someone used this door?" Yap Yap complained to the others with him.

"Are you an idiot or a weakling?" Was the response from another voice, a voice with a Swedish accent.

Then the door was pushed once again from the other side, this time with much greater force and it opened partially until the resistance from Francis shut it again. Francis looked over as Roberto was finishing pulling Leonardo over onto the roof of the vacant store.

Roberto and Francis made eye contact; they were in trouble. There was a good chance all three of them would be caught.

But if Francis could just hold the watchmen back for just a little longer, maybe Roberto and Leonardo could get away. Francis remained against the door, continuing to press into it with all his weight. It partially opened and then closed again twice more before the collective strength of all three watchmen pushed it open. It swung open with such force that it nearly sent Francis flying into the hole in the roof.

For a split second, Francis thought about jumping through the hole and trying to escape through the office below. But the door out of the office was likely locked and Francis could be trapped inside. With Roberto and Leonardo already out of sight and presumably safe, Francis sprinted instead toward the roof of the vacant building. The watchmen, shocked at seeing Francis, the tools spread out on the roof, and the hole into the business office, took a second before pursuing Francis. Not as fleet of foot as he once was, Francis was caught by the watchmen as he was trying to climb the wall separating the store roof from the vacant building.

It was over and Francis knew it. And this time he was looking at a very lengthy prison sentence. Rich, influential people did not like their stores being broken into. But Francis was facing other consequences as well. Yap Yap turned ashen upon recognizing Francis. It was only then Yap Yap realized he had been disclosing information that could be used to rob the store. Worse still, he could easily be misconstrued as a coconspirator if Francis talked. Francis looked at Yap Yap and then away as if he were a total stranger.

Larsen, the supervisor, planned to turn Francis over to police. Not before, however, sending a message through Francis to all other would-be thieves. Danwitter had made clear to Larsen that anyone caught stealing from the store should be roughed up. The courts in New York were too lenient for Danwitter's liking in terms of creating a deterrent.

With Yap Yap and the other guard holding Francis's arms, Larsen punched Francis in the face. It hurt, but Francis had been hit harder over the years.

Looking off into the distance, Francis could see the fireworks starting over the East River.

"Oooh, ahhh," Francis said of the fireworks as if he was totally unphased by Larsen's punch. Enraged by the slight, in front of his subordinates no less, Larsen took out his billy club and struck Francis over the head. Then again and again. For Francis, everything went black.

When he came to, Francis was not sure how much time had lapsed. But his instincts were still intact enough to jump at the sound of a loud explosion and to attribute it to the fireworks display. But it was not fireworks, it was an explosive charge detonated by Roberto.

"I have more," Roberto barked out to the three watchmen. But between the lit cigar in his mouth and thick Italian accent, the watchmen looked at each other puzzled. But when Roberto held out what appeared to be a stick of dynamite and knowing he had just set off one previously from the roof of the vacant building, the watchmen stepped back. Keeping his eyes on the watchmen, Roberto helped the bloodied Francis up.

"We are not going to prison, understand? I will blow us up and take all of you with us before I let that happen." Roberto took the cigar out of his mouth and kept it close to the fuse to make the watchmen nervous. He also spoke slowly, American cadence Roberto called it, to ensure he was understood.

"You," Roberto said, nodding his head toward Yap Yap. "Collect everyone's handcuff keys," with each guard having a set on their belts next to their billy clubs. "Bring them over here," Roberto demanded, and when Yap Yap got close enough, Roberto whispered to him, "We get caught, you get caught."

"Ok, move back and handcuff yourselves around the chimney" referring to one of the several chimney shoots and pipe extensions on the rooftop. At first it, looked like Larsen would resist and try to charge Roberto. In response Roberto walked toward him and lit the fuse on the stick of dynamite saying, "I will look forward to taking you to hell with me, beating up my defenseless friend like that!"

Larsen thought better of it and began stepping back toward the chimney with the others. Roberto extinguished the fuse with his fingers, with the fuse having burnt down more than he realized, his threat that close to becoming a reality. With that, Roberto made his way over to the strongbox on the parapet.

Looking down and seeing the street still empty below, he dramatically looked back at the watchmen and he leaned against the box intending to push it over the side of the building. It did not budge. Roberto then pushed it with all his might and again it did not move—generating a laugh from Larsen. With that, Roberto went back to the handcuff keys where Yap Yap had placed them on the tar of the roof and threw them over the side, generating a groan from the watchmen who knew they were going to be stuck standing around that chimney shoot for some time.

Roberto then led Francis, still dazed from the beating, to the strongbox and whispered directly into Francis's ear, "Help me push this thing."

In his semi-conscious state, Francis heard the familiar voice that he trusted and pushed as much as he could in his injured condition. The strongbox started to move, the problem not being its weight but that it was pressed against the lip of the cast-iron façade of the building. With Francis's added weight, the front two legs of the strongbox made their way over the lip and the box started to tip over the side. The back two legs caught the lip once again and with momentum tore a huge piece of the façade off that fell along with the strongbox. The strongbox landed with a thud; the façade crashed shortly after with a metallic din.

Roberto led Francis to the door leading down into the store. The two made their way out to the street. Propping Francis up against the wall of the store, Roberto ran over to look inside the strongbox which had broken open upon contact with the cobblestone street. There were a few ledgers and a few blank bank deposit slips but not a dime in cash. It had all been for nothing.

Having no time to sulk, Roberto went back to Francis and the two made their way around the corner to their wagon. Roberto had sent Leonardo home already on foot. Francis was bleeding badly. Francis had long streaks of red running down his face. Roberto helped him into the back of the wagon, propped up his head, and then covered him completely with a tarp.

"Just rest, don't try to say or do anything. I will get you home." Roberto told Francis. Roberto changed his clothes, a prearranged part of their getaway plan in case anyone gave physical descriptions to police. Then driving the wagon downtown, Roberto mixed in with the throng of people and carriages making their first trips across the newly opened bridge to Brooklyn.

****

By the time the wagon arrived in front of the tenement that Francis and his family called home, Francis had gone from semi-conscious and periodic groaning to complete silence. Roberto pulled back the tarp, afraid of what he might find. He put his hand to Francis's neck and was relieved to feel a pulse. Two neighbors helped Roberto carry Francis to the third story apartment and to Bridget.

Bridget tried to conceal her shock and panic at seeing her husband. He was completely unconscious as he was carried in, the left side of his face now grotesquely swollen. Intermittently, Francis's body would jerk and twitch. Bridget directed her boys to summon the doctor. She would figure out how to pay for the medical services later, the priority now was getting her husband help. The doctor, however, proved useless. He could only advise that Francis had been severely injured and would either die from his injuries or be permanently disabled by them. Bridget, angry and afraid, turned on the doctor.

"Really?" She asked. "It is your medical opinion that he is injured and may or may not die? Can you look at him a little closer and this time take the bone out of your nostrils"

The doctor left, insulted at the witch-doctor reference.

Chapter Twenty-One
The Only Advantage to Knowing

Cities of Brooklyn and New York
1883-1884

Unfortunately, the doctor's prognosis was not far from the mark. Francis hovered near death for several weeks. He would improve for a while and then relapse. It took three months before it appeared more likely than not that he would survive. Although it was clear he would be left incapacitated. Francis was blind in his left eye. The retina had detached during the beating. His headaches were constant and the nerve damage made it difficult for him to walk, although Francis insisted on at least trying to walk a little further everyday. He hoped he could work himself back to health.

It was false hope. His remaining days would be painful and involve more bad days than good. Yet Francis's mood and demeanor never seemed better. Some viewed it as Francis, in his maturity, accepting his fate but it was really him knowing the end was near and he no longer had to struggle.

Once Francis's condition stabilized, Bridget went back to work cleaning homes in the more upper-class section of Midwood, Brooklyn. The couple's three boys, John, Patrick, and Joseph, being in their early twenties and late teens, were now starting lives of their own. Just as Francis and his brothers had done, they provided their mother as much money as they could spare. They never offered money directly to Francis, nor would he have taken it. He was the father.

Showing the kind of friend he was, Roberto visited Francis every day. When he would leave the apartment, Roberto would discretely leave money on the kitchen table for Bridget. Not much but whatever he could afford after taking care of his own family obligations.

Rounding out the financial support, Francis and Bridget's sister-in-law, Eileen, always made sure the rent and the tab at the grocery store of her in-laws never got too far behind. She provided the money directly to the landlord and grocer, to minimize the embarrassment to Francis and Bridget.

As he was essentially restricted to the small apartment, Francis tried to make himself useful by cleaning up and making dinner for Bridget. His culinary skills were such that Bridget suggested he focus more on the cleaning and leave the cooking to her.

One early spring day, Bridget came home from work expecting to see Francis in his usual spot in the bedroom but he was not there. In recent days, he had graduated to being able to make his way to the tenement's outhouse and a short walk around the block, but little more than that. Before she could go completely frantic wondering where he was, Francis limped back into the door of the apartment. He was carrying flowers.

"Where in God's name did you go?" shouted Bridget, both relieved and angry.

"I thought you would like some flowers," Francis responded, using only three quarters of his mouth—the paralysis seeming to spread.

"You never bought me flowers before, and now you choose to wander out to bring me some damn daisies," Bridget countered, now mostly angry with her focusing on Francis scaring her so.

"I always should have brought you flowers. In my mind, I always did. It is just that we were so always. . ." and, with that, Francis put some money on the kitchen table and then collapsed back into his bed. The money had come from Roberto who had visited earlier in the day.

The outing left Francis out of commission for a week. From his bed, he stared at the flowers in a vase thinking of the kindly old landlord, Mr. Coale, back in Richmond. When it came to relationships, flowers never hurt was the old man's advice.

As time went on, it became increasingly hard for Bridget to watch Francis in so much pain and so limited. In the beginning he spoke a lot of his head and body aches, and problems stemming from his now useless eye. He eventually stopped complaining but the dreadful discomfort continued to show on his face. But again, his spirits were remarkably good and he would often joke, frequently at his own expense.

Whenever someone knocked on the door, Francis would respond, "I'll get it," in jest. On good days, it would take him an inordinate amount of time to make his way to the door. On most days, he could not make it at all.

Bridget found it easier to speak to Francis now than almost any other time in their marriage. That made her watching his physical pain that much more difficult.

Eventually, it got too much. One night, as Francis tossed and turned in bed futilely trying to make himself comfortable, she placed a bottle of whisky in front of him. Francis could not remember the last time he had a drink, but Bridget could. She hated when he drank but it was the only thing she knew that could mitigate his agony.

As she released the bottle, Francis reached out and held her hand. He said nothing, only pointing to the scar over his eye he got defending her when they first met.

"How long are you going to milk that?" Bridget said with tears forming in her eyes.

"Smartest thing I ever did," Francis responded. After a moment's silence, he went on: "I never thanked you for all you did for the boys," Francis referring to their three sons they raised together.

"If not for you, they would have been lost like..." and Francis stopped himself. He was going to say they would have been like Stephen Michael, his son by Ellen Scanlon, who was raised by another family. Totally out of Francis's life.

"Don't be getting all soft on me, Francis *Fireball* McNamara," Bridget said, emphasizing his nickname trying to invoke his toughness. In her difficult life, she never learned how to deal with sentimentality. It made her uncomfortable. At the same time, she feared this kind of conversation was a sign her husband knew his end was at hand.

"And if you take off on your own again like you did today, I'll strangle you! You hear me?" Ellen barked at Francis trying to break the intense emotion that was building.

Francis gave no assurances, and just a weeks later—when he felt he had built up enough strength—he left the apartment again. When Bridget returned to an empty apartment again, she anxiously scanned the street below hoping to see Francis coming home again with flowers. He would eventually return but not with flowers. He would have something else reflecting his sentimentality.

It was July 4th, Independence Day, although Francis did not know that. He had lost all sense of time since his injury. But he felt better than he did on most days and he decided it was time to press his luck. Francis took streetcars and a very slow walk to Canarsie Pier. He sat on a bench along the pier. As he sat, the image came to his mind when he last saw his mother on the quay in Limerick.

From the bench, Francis could eye the slip used by a small commercial vessel called *the Duane*. Originally, *the Duane* was used by its captain exclusively for oystering but now served as a charter vessel for day fishing trips along Long Island. The captain's name, as reflected by the handprinted sign posted at the slip, was Michael Rowland. The same Michael Rowland who also went by Stephen Michael McNamara. Francis oldest son, his only by Ellen. At this point, Stephen Michael would be close to the same age as Francis at the outbreak of the Civil War.

No one was near the boat and it was neatly tied and covered up, so there was the possibility Stephen Michael would not by anytime soon. Francis thought back to the time he waited anxiously in Philadelphia hoping to see his older brother Mathew. Luck was on Francis's side in Philadelphia and it would be for him on Canarsie Pier as well.

It was just as he was about to give up and start his trek home that Francis noticed two figures approaching. A man and a woman. Even with his impaired vision, Francis recognized his son. He had the look of his late wife, Ellen, and that made Francis smile. The woman's figure and how she walked gave away that she was pregnant. Pregnant with Francis's first grandchild. The woman was Stephen Michael's wife of nearly a year, Lottie Mae Doyle.

Trying to clear his throat because he knew his speech was impaired and hard to hear, Francis called out: "Are you Stephen Michael McNamara?"

"Yes, I am." was the answer, Stephen Michael puzzled by the older, obviously down on his luck man.

"Your mother would have wanted you to have this," Francis handed Stephen Michael a palm-sized Bible. The same Bible Ellen had made Francis read to Stephen Michael when the boy was no more than a toddler. The Bible Francis had carried with him for years and the only thing, other than the clothes on his back, he was able to carry out of Richmond the night the city burned.

"And here is a list of the last known addresses of your halfbrothers and relatives in Three Churches, West Virginia. Your mother's people were Scanlons. They are nice folks. You should reach out to them," suggested Francis—a suggestion Stephen Michael would indeed act on.

Francis did not know it but as he spoke to Stephen Michael his step-son, Timothy Moriority, raised by the Scanlons, was on his way to California where he would eventually work his way up to become a bank president. Charles Scanlon, the son of Francis's friend and brother-in-law, Michael Scanlon, was making his way up as well, running for President of the United States on the Prohibition Party ticket, so he would not likely get Francis's vote. There was also talent among the Moriority boys that went unrealized. Francis's remaining stepson, Dennis Moriority, had been killed a few years before in a work-related accident.

With the Bible and list in his hands, and a puzzled look on his face, Stephen Michael asked Francis: "Do I know you?"

"No, just an old friend of your parents, Frank Redmonds is the name," Francis stated, using his favorite alias that he had used on occasion when booked by police.

"How about my father, did you know him?" Stephen Michael added to his questions.

"A bit, a bit." Francis responded looking away with his good eye. He was not a good liar.

"Was he as bad a person as they say?" Stephen Michael asked, sitting down next to the old man, and making room for his pregnant wife and introducing her at the same time.

Francis saw an out and started with his own questions: Was this their first child? It was. How was Lottie Mae feeling? Extremely well. Did the couple prefer a boy or a girl? It would be a girl, and they named her Ellen, after Francis's first wife and Stephen Michael's mother. The child would not survive infancy.

Stephen Michael brought Francis back to the topic he wanted to discuss. "Please, about my father?" The young man urged.

"I can tell you this for certain," Francis responded, "Your father loved you very much and thought of you every day without fail. If he had his way, things would have been different. But he did not have his way. I can understand that you may think that you were abandoned by your parents, but you were not. In their hearts and minds you were always with them, and always will be. They didn't just leave you with anyone. They placed you with the Rowlands, the best people they knew."

Francis then thought of Mary Rowland for the first time in years, and how influential she was although he only knew her from the voyage over from Ireland and a brief time before her death.

"Look at you and how you turned out. You and the Rowlands have done a fine job. I am sure that would have not been the case had you stayed with your father." In saying it, Francis sadly thought of the hardship his sons John, Patrick, and Joseph had to endure. The poverty, their father at times being a criminal, a drunk, and inattentive—sometimes all three at the same time.

"We are taking a little sail into the harbor for Independence Day, would you like to join us?" Lottie interjected, having recognized Francis as Stephen Michael's father.

She found herself sympathetic to the ailing, older man. Her own father, John Doyle, had the same brogue and been worn down by famine, hard labor, and the horrors of the Civil War as well. John Doyle had passed away at the age of forty-six the previous October, and Lottie's heart still ached.

"What interesting eyes you have," Lottie made the remark in part to signal her husband. She always had admired her husband's blue eyes with hint of green, eyes she now knew he inherited from Francis.

"My eyeballs are more ornamental than anything else these days," Francis responded with a smile, "but thank you."

Stephen Michael picked up on his wife's hint and had already reached the same conclusion, Francis was his father. This battered, pleasant old man was Fireball McNamara. Fierce Francis. Not the monster Stephen Michael had envisioned and feared that he, himself, would turn into due to the blood in his veins.

Wanting to talk more to his prodigal father, even if it involved still going along with Francis posing as someone else, Stephen Michael echoed Lottie's invitation for Francis to join them on the boat. It had been a long time since Francis sailed, he thought back to the barrier island off the coast that he enjoyed so much when he lived in Norfolk.

"Yes, I would love to join you." Francis said with a crooked smile, having only partial control over his facial muscles. Lottie wrapped Francis in a blanket as her husband helped the ailing man aboard the boat. She intuitively knew that Francis's temperature regulation, among other things, was failing him.

Once at sea, Francis raved over the quality of the boat and Stephen Michael's handling of the vessel—he navigated the congested New York harbor with aplomb. Stephen Michael was a seasoned sailor at that point, a captain of his own ship. A dream Francis once held out for himself while in Richmond. If the dream had to come true for just one of them, Francis was glad it was for his son.

When they closed in on Brooklyn Bridge, still sparkling new, Francis marveled at its size and majestic design. He had never seen it from the water before. Francis told Stephen Michael of having seen the Girard Street Bridge in Philadelphia, many years before, when it too was less than a year old. Adding that at the time he had been in the company of Stephen Michael's uncle, Mathew McNamara.

Looking back at Manhattan, Francis recounted for Lottie the first time he set foot there, at Battery Park, when he arrived from Ireland. Then looking at Stephen Michael, Francis added "I was greeted there by another of your uncles, Jamie McNamara. Right there, at that very spot," pointing to the southern tip of the city.

Taking that as a hint, Stephen Michael steered the boat south along the East River until eventually mooring just off the Battery. From there they could see the festivities already underway for Independence Day. Francis marveled how much the city had changed since his arrival some three decades before.

The population had more than doubled, cementing New York's title as the country's most populous city. Brooklyn, just across the East River, was the third largest and together

could take being disappointed now without feeling the need to find and beat anyone causing him frustration.

Overhearing the encounter was a man named William Blagheen, born in England to Irish parents. "Stay with me," said Blagheen to Francis, as Blagheen straightened his old blue jacket with a single medal on it, the Congressional Medal of Honor.

"Most of those folks who just passed judgement on you never saw a day of combat, at best they may have spent a day or two in a whorehouse in Washington." Blagheen laughed.

"What did you do to get that?" Francis asked, referring to the sole medal on Blagheen's chest. Blagheen had just the one while many of the other veterans seemed to have several, along with ribbons presumable symbolizing their bravery during the war.

"Well, for most of the war I was a navy cook but on one day I was more than that." Blagheen, who habitually minimized his own heroism, delivered highly explosive artillery shells to Union guns while under intense enemy fire, and continued to do so even after fellow sailors around him were killed and wounded.

His actions helped turn the Battle of Mobile Bay. "I would have got the medal earlier, but I deserted before they could give it to me. I had run home because I was scared and missed my family, and they dragged me back in chains just to give me the medal." Both he and Francis laughed at the irony. Francis thought of what his brother Jamie used to say: "A hero today, a coward tomorrow."

A young soldier handed Blagheen a folded flag for the ceremony. Blagheen interlocked his arm with Francis's and said, "We are on," the two men carrying the flag together to the pole at Battery Park to be raised.

In respect for Blagheen's medal, the highest honor that can be awarded for United States military service, the group of men who had to just rejected Francis had to salute in his direction. For Francis, it felt like redemption. He had been on the wrong side and fought against the wrong people, people like Blagheen.

Stephen Michael and Lottie watched from a distance, surprised by Francis being given the honor of helping raising the flag. When Francis made his way back, he apologized for stepping away.

"Were you a soldier?" Stephen Michael asked.

"I have been a lot of things," responded Francis, his exhaustion clearly overwhelming him.

Francis began to have trouble keeping up conversation, repeatedly asked the same questions of Stephen Michael and Lottie, and seemed on the verge of falling asleep though it was only mid-afternoon. Francis had pushed himself too far. While he had accomplished what he wanted to, connecting with his eldest son, he was spent.

Francis never mentioned his ill-fated attempt to secure custody of Stephen Michael during the Civil War, and the year Francis spent in a harsh Union prison as a result. Francis just needed to see for himself that his son was alright, and he was. Francis could share the good news with Ellen, Stephen

Michael's mother, should he see her in heaven or wherever it was he was going.

Stephen Michael invited Francis back to his and Lottie Mae's home in Canarsie. Francis responded weakly but with a degree of urgency that he needed to get back to his wife, Bridget.

The surprise Bridget got looking out her window was the sight of her husband being carried by his eldest son. Francis's weight had decreased to the point that Stephen Michael had little problem carrying his father in his arms. It was hard for Stephen Michael to picture Francis as he once was, a muscular and strong young man himself.

Bridget instinctively knew who was carrying her husband. When Stephen Michael came to the door, Bridget thanked him for bringing Francis home. "You are a good man," she said looking into Stephen Michael's eyes, eyes she too noticed matched those of his father.

"You are obviously a gentleman; you were raised well." She added, looking at her husband. Stephen Michael smiled. He wrote down his address and handed it to Bridget saying, "In case he needs it." Nodding his head toward Francis.

****

As if relieved of all the loose ends, Francis's health rapidly worsened afterward. He never left the apartment again. Bridget stayed with him, letting him drink heavily to lessen the pain. She would smile to herself when, even in a drunken stupor, he would stroke the scar above his eye.

****

Having retained her Catholic faith, Bridget was a parishioner at St. Stephen's Church in the Brooklyn neighborhood of Carol Gardens. In light of Francis's decline, Bridget asked one of the new priests, Father Peter Harrigan, to administer Last Rights to her husband. Bridget was surprised to see Francis smile at the arrival of the priest and saw him gesturing with his weakened arms for the priest to sit down.

Bridget left to give them privacy but stayed close to the apartment fearing that Francis still had enough strength and contrarian temperament to offend the priest. Her concerns were unwarranted. Francis treated people—including priests—with respect when he could afford to. Any cruelty that came from Francis was out of necessity. Besides, seeing the priest made Francis think of Father Devlin, the caring and innovative priest who gave his life trying to care for the victims of the 1855 yellow fever outbreak in Virginia.

Father Harrigan, however, looked more like an altar boy than a priest. If he were not wearing a collar, Francis would have put him at fifteen-years-old. The nerves in his voice and shaking hands made clear that Father Harrigan had not performed Last Rights before, at least not on his own.

"Ba, ba, ba." Francis said, in response to Harrigan commencing prayers in Latin. He then put his hands on those of the priest and said: "Let's just tell my wife you gave me the Last Rights. I don't want to meet God, should there be one, as a hypocrite. I have been about the least Catholic as a man can be, in part because I don't believe in God—at least not in the way he is portrayed in the Bible. So, no last-minute conversions here, Father. No offense."

To the young priest's credit, he did not answer right away. Francis reminded him of his own father who was near death when Harrigan left for the seminary. Instead, the priest took the time to view the situation from Francis's perspective and to figure out how best to negotiate with him.

Then, leveraging Francis's love for his wife and the assumption Francis needed a say in the process, Father Harrigan stated: "Mr. McNamara, I think we can work something out."

With more and more time having passed, Bridget grew anxious in the hallway and put her ear to the apartment door. She could hear a weak and muffled laugh from Francis, followed by a coughing fit. Then the priest would laugh. This went on for over an hour. Eventually, the priest opened the door and Bridget nearly fell into the apartment—she had been straining so hard to hear.

As the priest picked her up, with whiskey on his breath, he smiled at the red-faced Bridget. "Your husband has been given absolution, and the way he tells it—Mrs. McNamara—you have done enough good in this world to get both him and you into heaven. That being the case, God bless you, Mrs. McNamara," and the young priest stumbled a bit upon departing.

With the priest gone, Bridget shouted at Francis, "Did you give whiskey to that man of the cloth?"

"The poor lad was nervous," Francis responded as he tried in vain to make himself comfortable in the bed that had become his world. "I gave it to him before absolution, so I am still good," Francis added as if to ease Bridget's mind.

Bridget shook her head, how odd that among her husband's few virtues was his honesty about being a non-believer. He rejected the only thing in her mind that could save his soul.

As she fixed the pillows beneath Francis's head, she hoped his acceptance of Last Rights for her benefit rather than his own would be enough. Her hope also rested on the knowledge that her husband did good things when he could, and his sins stemmed more from the hardship thrust upon him than anything else.

Bridget contemplated how different her life would be without Francis. A man who made her life anything but boring. She loved and understood him, but he did not make life easy for her or himself.

Knowing that he had been far from a fairytale husband, Francis often acknowledged his weaknesses to Bridget. Nonetheless, he would still boast to her: "You will curse the day I am gone," as if his charm and his love for her would vindicate him in memory.

In his own mind, all faults of his first wife, Ellen, who died nearly twenty-five years before, had melted away. Now he hoped his own faults would do the same.

With his last day close at hand, Bridget knew she would indeed curse the day Francis was gone. While most of their life together had been an unromantic and desperate struggle to survive, they always had something special to sustain them. Their bond was the makings of a romantic tale. Bridget thought back to all those years ago and that miserable bar in Richmond during the war. She thought she had been abandoned by God to a life of loneliness and indignity. But she was not alone and someone would fight for her honor.

For one day at least, Francis McNamara was a chivalrous knight. A knight who took on his foes. Not clad in armor but rather while he was shoeless and in rags. To Bridget, Francis's humble appearance made him all the more noble and brave.

Had Francis amassed a vast fortune during his lifetime, his proudest possession still would have been the sizable scar above his right eye. The scar he incurred defending Bridget. It reminded him of one of the day he fought for something truly worth fighting for.

Francis wished he could leave the scar behind to his sons. To remind them they too had it in them to fight when they needed to. And they would indeed need to fight. He would be leaving them nothing but debts—scars not being transferable.

Francis told the boys, John, Patrick, and Joseph, as much. He knew he had been like gravity to them, a force felt more than seen. He apologized for his inability to help them financially and his many absences while in jail and on benders. Francis advised that as much as he loved the three of them, he knew at times they were better off without him. But he was smart enough, Francis reminded them, "To marry your mother, because I knew she was parent enough. Watch after her," he asked.

Looking out the window to the rooftops of neighboring buildings, Francis said sadly—not realizing he was saying it out loud, "I wish I could have been a better father."

"You were a fine father," Joseph, the youngest, responded.

"God damn it!" Francis replied. "I am not an idiot. I know I should have been better!" As if Francis wanted to use his potentially last interaction with his sons to offer direct evidence of his failings as a father.

His ill-tempered lapse showed how much pain he was in, and that even on his death bed he had little tolerance for insincerity and sugar coating the truth.

"I am sorry, Joseph. You are a good boy, the three of you are," Francis said straining to look at his sons with his good eye. "But the truth is, I failed you in many ways. Not because I wanted to but because the means to be better always eluded me. But I will promise you this: if I can help you from the hereafter, I will do it. I owe you that much."

The boys, having more their father's religious views more than their mother's, said they appreciated the sentiment and assured Francis they knew he did the best he could. They made clear they did not confuse that with doing a good job, they did not want to set him off again. The three boys would go on to do the best they could with what they had in their own lives; they had learned that from their father. He did leave them something valuable after all.

****

A few days later, on November 5, 1884, Stephen Michael McNamara visited Francis as he had periodically since the two reunited. The rest of New York was transfixed by the results of the Presidential election the day before. New

York's own Grover Cleveland had won by the narrowest of margins, less than one percent. It had been a particularly vile campaign with sex scandals and mudslinging overshadowing substantive issues. Pundits questioned if ever a presidential election would be as ugly again.

Stephen Michael loved discussing politics with his adopted family, the Rowlands. He decided, however, to avoid the topic with Francis. A good choice because Francis had little patience for politics and politicians. And now that he was on death's door, he had no patience at all.

Francis knew more than most the damage political machines, inflammatory media, big-monied interests, and a gullible populace could do. He had seen the corpses and limbs on the battlefields of the frontier and Civil War. He had been witness to one of the country's leading cities being laid to waste. Francis had been among the starving masses in prisoner of war and refugee camps, he had seen people enslaved and workers exploited. Failings that fell at the feet of politicians in Francis's mind. His thinking still not far from that brought him to resist the Orange Day Parade more than a decade before. Resistance that left his friends Brian Burke and Patrick Lally maimed and Thomas McCleary dead.

Sitting down in the small apartment beside Francis's bed, Stephen Michael committed himself reluctantly to continuing the charade started by Francis months before. It was Francis's fear that he, due to his bad reputation, would undo the advantages his son gained by being raised by the Rowlands. Consequently, Francis's claim to being merely a family friend to his son would have to do. It was at least one selfless thing he could do for his own flesh and blood.

Respecting the older man's wishes even without understanding his reasoning, Stephen Michael referred to Francis as Frank Redmonds, although McNamara was on the mailbox in the lobby and everyone else in the home referred to themselves as a McNamara.

While Francis had been weak during other visits, Stephen Michael knew this time was different. Francis spent more time unconscious than he did awake. Stephen Michael would just sit and watch his father lie there. The younger man ran his fingers through his own hair to ease his nerves. A genetic tendency as Francis was known to do the same thing. Bridget smiled when she saw Stephen Michael do it.

"Are you afraid?" Stephen Michael asked when Francis returned to consciousness.

"Afraid of dying?" Francis responded weakly. "No."

Then after pausing for a second to think, Francis added, "Well, I should say I am no more afraid of dying than I was of living. It is all a mystery to me. I don't know where I was before I was born, maybe I am just going back there. Who knows?"

Fatigued from even trying to carry on a conversation, Francis drifted back to sleep midsentence. Stephen Michael started to leave but heard his father call out: "Can you hear her son? It is your mom!" Francis's eyes were open but he stared through his son—he was blind altogether, to this world at least. Those would be his last words. Francis's journey of forty-nine years ended that night. With mixed feelings, he assumed his story would die with him. Yet once last irony.

Epilogue

The city contracts that Francis and Roberto so desperately tried to acquire came through. Roberto, giving a partner's share to Bridget, accompanied her to her new home in Goshen, a stone's throw from her best friend Eileen. Bridget lived well into her golden years and had enough money to help her and Francis's children.

Bridget also provided in her will for a donation to St. John the Evangelist Catholic Church in Goshen, asking that prayers be said for the soul of her devoted husband, Francis. She specified that not one but two sets of prayers be said for him, fearing an extra dose was required due to his checkered life.

Francis's eldest son, Stephen Michael McNamara, became a highly respected member of the community in Canarsie, Brooklyn, and a renowned ship captain. He and his wife Lottie would have six children, although two would die in infancy. Stephen Michael, himself, died of a heart attack aboard his ship, a place he loved more than any other. He was his father's son.

Stephen Michael had one son, Ralph Martin McNamara, my grandfather. The middle name of Martin was in honor of Martin VanBuren Rowland, the man who, with his wife Lucinda, adopted Stephen Michael. Ralph was stricken by polio as a boy, impairing function in one of his legs. The paralysis coupled with downturns in the fishing industry, prevented Ralph from following in his father's seafaring footsteps. Instead, Ralph became an office worker.

Finding a position at the Brooklyn Edison Company, he met my grandmother, Margaret "Loretta" Dolan. Loretta had been raised by an older brother after her parents died when she was 12 years old. Ralph and Loretta would go on to have two sons, Robert and—my father—Donald Francis.

Whether my father's middle name was in honor of his great grandfather, Francis McNamara, is not known. My father, himself, did not know the origin of his middle name and assumed it was just a name his parents liked.

Both my father and his brother would be born with and only use the Rowland surname. Nor would they have any contact with their McNamara relatives. The ties to that family and its name would be cut altogether. The boys would not get an explanation for the separation from their McNamara past, and they would have more pressing problems to deal with.

Their mother, Loretta, died during an ectopic pregnancy. Their father, Ralph, normally a social and humorous man, did not deal well with the loss. He started to drink heavily and, like his grandfather Francis, would go on "toots" where he would be unaccounted for days and weeks on end. Ralph, like his own father, would die of a heart attack at work. He was 55 years old and would be buried with the last name of Rowland.

Brothers Robert and Donald were taken in and raised by Ed and Eva Schuster. Although the boys were raised in trying financial times with the Great Depression and World War II, Robert and Donald would describe their childhoods in endearing terms. Ironically, the two brothers would marry sisters, Nancy and Josephine Burke. They would settle and live out their lives in the same neighborhood in Queens, New York. Their children grew up living within blocks of each other.

The last time I saw my father alive, his brother, my Uncle Bob, was at his side.

The rest of the story is still being written.